The Manchild

BY

Kenneth J. M. MacLean

The Manchild

ISBN: 978-0-9882125-0-3

A Big Picture Press publication
Disclaimer:
This is a work of fiction. Any resemblance of persons in this book to actual
persons, living or dead, is purely coincidental.

Cover Image Credits:

Marcus: http://www.123rf.com/photo_4312611_professional-young-model-
s–studio-shoot-portraiture-fashion.html [dimafoto] 123RF Stock Photo

Darcy: http://www.123rf.com/photo_11760241_close-up-beauty-portrait-of-
a-young-and-cute-blond-girl-with-hair-style-over-white-her-face-is-turne.html
[carlodapino] 123RF Stock Photo

New York: http://www.123rf.com/photo_7324213_new-york-city-manhattan-
skyline-panorama-at-night-over-hudson-river-with-refelctions-viewed-from-
new.html [rabbit75123] 123RF Stock Photo

Mothership: http://macmave.blogspot.com/2011/02/alien-mothership-free-
d-model.html

Luca Carcelli: From Wikimedia Commons This image is a work of a United
States Department of Justice employee, taken or made during the course of an employee's official duties. As a work of the U.S. federal government, the image is in
the public domain (17 U.S.C., 101 and 105).

Contents

Part I – CHICAGO

CHAPTER 1

Joliet, Illinois

"Darcy, get in here and cook my dinner!"

Oh God, he's home already. She had hoped for a little peace and quiet after school.

"Yes dad."

She had learned to recognize even subtle differences in his mood, for it would affect how she behaved. If he was drunk and tired he would find the couch and sleep it off. That was the best, for he'd leave her alone. If he was just angry and not drunk she'd simply agree with anything he said and follow his orders explicitly. Usually after dinner he would go into the living room with a bottle of booze and turn on the TV. She would have to stay out of sight but respond instantly to any of his shouted demands. Sometimes she would get him a pack of cigarettes. If he ran out she would have to walk down to the corner store for more. Sometimes she would have to go for another bottle. If he didn't have the money she would pay for it herself. She learned to save some of the cash he gave her for food. The worst was when he came home drunk and sad, which usually meant a big fight with his current girlfriend. She would have to lock her door, push the heavy deadbolt, and not make a sound. That was their agreement after what had happened two years ago.

She was then only 14 but had already begun to blossom into womanhood. He had stumbled into her room that night, drunk. "You're looking very nice today," he had mumbled, reaching for her.

She didn't understand. "Dad?" Her voice rose in alarm. "What are you doing?" He reached for her shirt and was clumsily attempting to lift it over her head.

"Daaaad, *stop it!!*" But he hadn't stopped. He pushed her up against the wall and she felt her slacks falling to the floor. She struggled and screamed. In this seedy neighborhood east of the river nobody would care even if they heard. She managed to get her knee up by his groin and pushed up, hard. He collapsed to the floor, writhing in pain. She left him there to sleep it off.

Afterward she lay sobbing on the couch in the living room of their run-down two bedroom home. It had been horrible and ugly. His liquored breath was disgusting and his unwashed body reeked of stale sweat and cigarette smoke.

The next day her father had gotten on his knees, sobbing. He blubbered like a puppy and begged her to forgive him. Darcy knew he wasn't a bad man. Just stupid and weak and afraid of a lengthy jail sentence. In a drunken stupor he had mistakenly driven home instead of to his girlfriend. He wasn't aware that he had assaulted his own daughter. Sadly, she knew it for the truth. Darcy could only feel sadness for the object of his affection, if that's what it could be called. The poor woman!

Even at the tender age of 14, Darcy was strong. She had gotten a double dose of character to make up for the lack of it in her father. She came to pity her father. She felt about him a compassion one might feel toward a sick animal with an incurable disease. She had also been forced to develop a sense of humor. Without that she would have gone crazy. It helped her dissolve the constant state of tension she lived with.

And so she cooked for him, kept his ramshackle house as best she could, went to school year round – to avoid coming home, mostly – and waited for an opportunity to leave.

One day just after her 16th birthday a luxury car stopped at the curb just in front of her. She was walking down the street in front of her house in the industrial section of town. A scrawny but well dressed man walked out and introduced himself. "I'm looking for girls," he said.

"Girls?" She knew what that meant. Either prostitutes, dancers, or porn movies. It also meant money. "For what?"

Jake Holden saw the sharp intelligence in the girl's eyes and frowned. He also recognized that defeated look that said, 'what options do I have?' That was good. Despite her bedraggled clothing the girl was beautiful. She carried herself with a certain grace that would photograph well. He knew one thing: men would be attracted to her. He had spotted her two blocks away.

"Movies," Jake replied, staying back. There was something compelling about this girl but he couldn't put his finger on what it was.

Darcy thought for a moment, thinking that Jake Holden best resembled a starving rat looking for something to eat. And he had found her! "How much?" she asked.

Jake was pleased with the girl's bluntness. This one would cause no trouble as long as he didn't mistreat her. He had no intention of doing that; his small-time operation could afford no trouble with the law. Jake saw something special in this one. Something special called *money*. "What's your name?"

"Darcy," she replied to Jake the Rat.

"All right Darcy. Come into my car and we'll talk business."

The upshot of it was that Darcy made a porn film, which did very well for Jake. On an impulse he sent the video to a distributor he knew in Chicago.

Two weeks later he received a call from Royalty Services in Chicago. Jake almost swallowed his cigarette in his excitement.

"We understand you have a girl named Darcy Regier," said a woman's voice.

Regier? So that was her last name. "Uh, yeah. How the hell did you find out about her?"

"We saw your video." The woman spoke with thinly disguised contempt.

Royalty's reputation preceded it. Jake knew that the small but exclusive service had a reputation for providing sophisticated companionship. Royalty had a reputation for upholding traditional values, and for integrity. On the street it was well known that if you dealt with them honestly you got a fair shake. God help you if you didn't. If he was going to give up his best girl it was going to cost them.

After an hour of negotiation he agreed to give Darcy to Royalty (if she was willing) for a fat commission. Jake was damn sure she'd be willing. He didn't have the talent to get the most out of Darcy. He knew she was ready to split on him anyway. Just like all his best girls.

"She's underage," Jake advised. "Not quite 17."

"Yes, we know."

Jake knew he was speaking to Chantelle Hudson, private secretary to Holderness Parkinson, the big boss. The all-seeing-eye. Jake shivered a little.

"We'll send a car for her at noon on Saturday, with your payment." Jake heard a click at the other end. He did not miss the implications: Darcy had better be there.

Chantelle sat in her office in downtown Chicago. She knew that the old man himself had his eyes on this girl. Chantelle had shown him Darcy's video. Both of them recognized her potential immediately. She possessed an unconscious natural grace and astonishing beauty. It was clear that this one might even attain the elite status of courtesan. At Royalty, a courtesan was an accomplished and educated lady of exceptional beauty capable of easy association with high-profile clients. These women often spoke a foreign language and played an instrument, were familiar with fine art, conversed easily on a wide variety of subjects, and were masters of sexual technique. They also made fantastic sums of money for themselves and Royalty Services. These women came almost exclusively from wealthy and/or educated backgrounds. A few lucky ones of indifferent upbringing, like Darcy, could also make the grade.

Chantelle sighed. She picked up the latest edition of Upper Crust magazine from her desk, which had a feature on the party given by the Prince of Monaco. At least a dozen of these highly skilled women had been present at that gathering. She spotted them immediately, merely by an inspection of the photographs. It was the lifestyle she had always wanted but for which she would never qualify.

She got up from her desk, walked across the plush carpeting, and inspected herself in the full length mirror against the wall. Her angular reflection screamed long, bony, and awkward. Long and bony was OK but awkward was not. Raised in the exclusive North Chicago enclave of Kenilworth, she had attended the best schools and started her career as a successful investment banker. But that life paled. One evening after work she saw an impeccably dressed woman emerge from a black limo in front of a downtown hotel next to Askew Securities. The driver idled in front for a few minutes, and Chantelle spoke to him. The next day she called Royalty. Within a week she successfully interviewed for the recently vacated position of office manager. From there she had quickly made herself indispensable to Holderness Parkinson, ensuring that the business side of the agency ran like clockwork. She was always invited to Parkinson's exclusive private parties. Sometimes she gained entrance to gatherings given by Royalty's important clients.

Chantelle walked back to her desk, her thoughts returning to the Regier girl. Royalty never allowed anyone underage to work. But Holderness, as he was known to those few of his intimates, was not above starting training a little early for promising candidates. He knew that he would eventually recoup his investment many times over.

Chantelle thought contemptuously of Jake Holden's film, a poorly made video with no plot and cardboard characters. Jake was a loser, but even he had recognized a diamond in the rough. The young girl leaped out of the screen like a searchlight on a dark night. They had already run a thorough background check on Darcy Regier. Father on welfare, mother remarried and living in California, an only child, no known relatives. Royalty's policy was never to accept girls from the streets. In this case an exception would be made.

And so Darcy was given into the hands of Danielle Hunter, who trained her in the art of female escort. Darcy could hardly believe her luck. During the thirteen months before her 18th birthday she had exchanged the hovel and her drunken father for a small, but luxuriously appointed company apartment in the eight-story Royalty brownstone. She had a windowless bedroom, a private bath, and a small living room with a large sofa. There was a small desk in her bedroom and a TV in the living room, with windows that looked out onto the Chicago skyline. In return she was expected to work hard to learn her trade. She knew that society probably saw her as little more than a high-priced prostitute. Darcy didn't care. Her life now was a lot better than the mean streets of Joliet, Illinois. She quickly forgot about Jake Holden and her father.

Darcy learned to speak with proper diction and grammar. She attended informal gatherings at Royalty and at low-key society parties, learning how to behave in polite company and how to converse. She was taught how to shut up and listen when the conversation veered off to a subject she was not familiar with. She learned how to be a companion in any social situation. She was taught how to dress impeccably and learned to love the subtle, classic lines and colors of her enormously expensive clothing. She was required to keep herself meticulously clean and attractive at all times, even at home when no one was around. Regular exercise was demanded. Eventually all of these things became a pleasurable, lifelong habit.

Just before the end of her training Darcy questioned Danielle. "What am I supposed to do when a client wants sex?"

Danielle laughed. "You're on your own there, honey. Mainly, you just give them what they ask for." Danielle explained that every consort developed her own style, based on her likes and dislikes.

Fortunately Darcy had never used drugs or alcohol. Such things were expressly forbidden to Royalty employees unless the lady was a long-term companion. These special women, almost always over the age of 30, were knowledgeable of wines and champagne, and would drink in moderation with a client if requested. Consorts were never to take drugs and to report clients who did to Chantelle.

Darcy was also required to read many books on subjects relating to her clients' areas of interest. She enjoyed that too. It was demanding work. Twelve hour days spent in deportment, ballet lessons, art appreciation classes, instruction in sexual entertainment, reading, and regular exercise left her tired but happy at the end of the day.

Darcy began her work at the elite executive category, for which the service was paid $2000 per hour. Some of that money found its way into her bank account. Enough to buy Danielle Hunter's silver BMW and an astonishing assortment of designer clothing for every occasion, with several thousand dollars left over. Darcy's cynical friend Cindy often remarked that Parkinson made a lot more off them than he ever gave back. But Darcy knew that the agency's expenses were enormous. It had cost plenty for her training and some girls never made the grade. She knew she probably would never fulfill the promise Holderness had for her. She intended to leave after her five year contract was up.

She enjoyed her job except for the sex. Sex was something she did when required, not something she felt. It was like getting the oil changed in her BMW: necessary, but boring. It held no pleasure for her but no pain either. Inside she was numb to it and wondered whether she would ever find a man who could make her feel loved.

Darcy was gregarious. She loved the parties and the occasional travel. For the most part she also liked her clients. Even before her first assignment she had become one of Holderness's favorites.

Holderness Parkinson, now almost 75, should have been born two hundred years earlier. He was a very large, big-boned man with a full head of white hair. His penetrating blue eyes were set in a wide, not unhandsome face with a big nose, a wide mouth, and thick, heavy eyebrows. He was old school and operated on his own strict moral code. He was named after the estate of the Duke of Holderness in England. Parkinson loved women, esteemed them in his own way, and surrounded himself with them. He liked money and luxury even more and would accept nothing less than the best. Upon this idea he had based his company. That, and the maintenance of standards and values from a bygone age. In his own circles he was highly respected. He was completely unknown to the general run of what he considered to be an increasingly barbaric society. He had slowly and carefully built an impeccable reputation among the upper crust over the past 35 years. Royalty Services dealt only with clients of the utmost respectability. He would and did refuse service to anyone who abused their privileges with his ladies, no matter how wealthy or important they were. Holderness went to enormous efforts to ensure the confidentiality of his clients. In this way, Royalty Services became known as the most exclusive, safest, and most discreet service in North America. His client list read like a Who's Who and included movers and shakers in the entertainment industry, diplomats and political figures, corporate leaders, and royalty. Important but little-known figures in the shadowy world of the military and the intelligence services were also on Royalty's client list.

Immediately after she had reached 18 years of age Darcy was introduced to her first client. Thom Madigan was the corporate CEO of Pantheon, Inc., a leader in the plastics industry. "He asked for you personally," Chantelle told her. "You've started pretty much at the top of your classification and Holderness has a lot of confidence in you. Don't blow it."

But she did blow it.

In preparation for her first assignment Darcy had been required to carefully study the files on her client. She learned his areas of interest so that she could converse intelligently. She committed to memory such things as Madigan's favorite foods, his musical tastes, and his sexual preferences. Royalty always assigned rookies to easy clients. Darcy knew that tonight's encounter would involve a long dinner at an exclusive Chicago restaurant and afterward, perhaps, they would go to Madigan's room. He was known at Royalty as extremely easy to please and an extravagant tipper.

She was driven to the restaurant dressed in a smart-looking business suit and led to a private table in the back. The room had ten elegantly furnished tables and was occupied by other executives. Darcy had no idea whether the other women she saw were companions like her or merely wives, secretaries, or business associates. She loved the tastefully decorated room with its thick, dark blue carpeting, lit only by candle light. Crystal chandeliers hung from the ceiling, each holding several dozen candles. Above each table hung an elegant, silver filigreed fixture containing several more candles. Each threw a soft but unobtrusive glow onto the heavy white tablecloth. The place settings were fine china, real silverware, and an elegantly folded dark red napkin. Madigan rose to greet her as she approached his table. He seated her.

Darcy was thrilled. It was one thing to read and practice what might happen during an encounter, but quite another to actually experience it. The pudgy man before her was only an inch taller than her five feet six and in his mid 50s, she guessed. He exuded a calmness that soothed her.

The evening started off well. Surprisingly, he first asked about her. She flushed and nervously stammered out her responses, knowing she should relax. Madigan seemed interested and put her at her ease.

Fortunately he did not speak of plastics, for about that she knew nothing, nor did she care. It would be hard to keep up even a pretense of interest there. Fortunately Madigan led the conversation to his favorite subject, Renaissance painting. In particular, the Dutch masters of the 17th century. Darcy was delighted to speak on this topic, having devoted an entire week to the study of these paintings. In preparation for her assignment she had seen an exhibition of them at the Chicago Museum of Art. Like a good consort she let him lead. She remembered to speak clearly and with good diction. As he opened up she inserted her own comments, which were received enthusiastically.

At first Thom Madigan seemed surprised that Darcy knew so much. He was prepared for polite acknowledgment. It soon became clear that the girl had a genuine interest and knowledge of these paintings. His intention this night, as usual, was merely for feminine companionship. He preferred women between 18 and 25 because …because they made him feel young again. People thought that being an executive was a piece of cake; that you just went to meetings and played golf the rest of the time. They never heard about the 17-hour days, the endless round of struggle keeping the corporate train on the rails. And the travel. It was getting harder and harder for his body to adjust to the changing time zones. When he arrived at O'Hare three hours ago he could barely get his butt off the plane.

He would arrange for a cute young thing to sit with him at dinner, and try to capture some of her youthful energy. If she had a brain so much the better. That was why he utilized Royalty's services. Parkinson's attention to detail and his customer service were legendary. Thom made it a point to stop often in Chicago.

He had been married twice but it had never worked. He needed the softness, the receptiveness, and the beauty of a woman to balance out his testosterone-filled days. When he called the agency his intention was to eat, converse, then trundle up to his room and sleep. It had been a long flight from London and he had a full schedule tomorrow.

But Darcy had surprised him tonight. As they talked and ate he began to feel better and better. It had been a long time since he felt that way about a woman. She was just a chit of a girl but seemed so polished and sure of herself. Was it just an act? He gazed at her lovely face as she described her reaction to the Vase of Flowers with Watch, by van Aelst. It was one of his favorites. He tried to look behind this girl's social mask and discover the level of her sincerity. He concluded that she was completely guileless. It was incredibly refreshing.

He interrupted her. "Darcy, would you be willing to come up to my room?"

She started at the interruption but recovered smoothly. "Of course." Darcy knew he didn't have to ask. It was all part of the package, but she liked that he did so anyway.

"Then let's go." He called for the check and a car and she noticed how quickly the waiter responded. They rose from their chairs and walked outside. A driver was already waiting. She noticed that although Madigan was at least 40 pounds overweight his movements were sure and confident. Maybe it might not be so bad, she told herself. She remembered to walk gracefully and, as she had been taught, slightly behind and to his right.

When they reached the hotel room Madigan immediately went to the bed and began to remove his clothing. She did likewise. As she gazed down at his fat, unappealing body he suddenly transformed into her father. Her eyes widened. For a split second a look of loathing and revulsion marred her features. Just for an instant, but her client noticed. His reaction was immediate.

"I'm sorry," Madigan said, closing down to her. "I didn't realize how you felt about this."

Darcy was ashamed. She had been trained how to handle such situations but she was very young. The hurt on Madigan's face and in his eyes was uncomfortable. She knew she had committed the cardinal sin of any companion. She had humiliated her client and herself as well. Pale and shaking, she dressed quickly. She remembered enough of her training to walk gracefully across the room. As she reached the door she bowed to the man on the bed. "I can only offer my profoundest and most sincere apology." She left the room and closed the door quietly behind her.

It was standard practice to call for an agency car, which would pick her up from the hotel and take her back to her apartment. Tonight, however, she would take a cab. There would be no fee and no tip for her. This job, temporary as she hoped it would be, was her ticket out of poverty. This night she would go home empty-handed. Her past had finally caught up with her and she feared the worst. What would happen when Chantelle heard of her failure? She would be fired of course. She would find herself on the street, the hovel in Joliet her only destination.

Back at the hotel Thom Madigan kicked himself. He had been an ass, allowing his pride to overcome his better judgment. Something had happened to turn her from him. As he reviewed the incident he understood it probably had little to do with him. A memory, perhaps, of an unpleasant event in her past. Madigan cursed himself for a fool. He had ruined what should have been a wonderful night! Well, he would be in Chicago again soon, for the stockholder meeting. He'd ask again for Darcy. Next time they'd have dinner and leave it at that.

There was something about the girl, but what was it? It wasn't just physical beauty, it wasn't a feminine thing. She was ... unusual. He recalled the events of the evening and realized that in her company he felt a presence. Was he in love? No, that wasn't it. It was something he couldn't identify, but it was something good.

Just then he heard the phone ring.

"Thom!" a booming voice said. "It's Mike. How the hell are you?"

Thom sighed. "Michael, I am fine. I assume that you'd like to know what happened at Royalty tonight."

"That's right," the voice boomed. Michael Grossman, the CEO of Telluride Electronics, was one of the country's most successful manufacturers of computer accessories. As the dollar fell and labor became cheaper Grossman had found his niche and had led his firm into the top 50 blue chip companies in America. But Mike was about a subtle as a one-legged buttkicker. "I have to say that it was an amazing experience."

"Was it worth the money?"

Madigan almost choked. Grossman was a great CEO but his personality could be categorized by one word: tawdry. Should he tell him about Darcy? The man might eat her up. Madigan laughed.

"What are you laughing about?" Grossman demanded.

Madigan ignored him. No, that would never happen. Darcy would wrap him around her finger. Wouldn't it be great to trap the big fatso with something he couldn't have? It would drive him crazy. With Parkinson to protect her Grossman could do nothing.

"Ask for a girl named Darcy."

"Darcy? That's not even a girl's name. Is she ugly?"

Thom sighed like a man who was trying to explain quantum physics to a water buffalo. "Just ask for her, Grossman. I guarantee you won't be disappointed."

CHAPTER 2

W HEN Darcy arrived at her apartment Chantelle was already there, sitting on the sofa and drumming her polished fingernails on the end table. "Tell me what happened," she ordered.

Darcy explained without embellishment and waited for the axe to fall.

"It happens to everyone. Just make sure it doesn't happen again."

"But—"

"I interviewed Madigan right after you left. He said he liked you."

"He did?"

Chantelle smiled. "Don't worry honey, we gave you the easiest client available at your level." She plopped a manila envelope on the table in front of the sofa. "Here is the file on your next client. Make sure you study it thoroughly. Don't screw up next time or you'll find yourself right back where you came from."

Two days later, Michael Grossman called. Chantelle answered.

"I'd like to have a girl named Darcy tonight," Grossman boomed. "She's really a girl, isn't she?"

Chantelle moved the phone away from her ear in distaste. A screamer. A barbarian. Certainly not the right client for a newbie like Darcy Regier. "Darcy isn't available tonight sir."

"This is Michael Grossman sweetheart. One of your customers, Thom Madigan, told me to ask for her. What I want, I get."

"You can't have her." Grossman ... Michael Grossman. She brought him up on her computer. A fat slob, the very worst kind of client. Insensitive and loudmouthed, wouldn't appreciate the subtlety of Royalty Services. The kind who thought money could buy everything, including class. Why doesn't he just go to one of the cathouses downtown?

"Who the hell do you think you are? I pay good money, I expect good service."

Chantelle spoke sweetly, with just the correct note of hauteur. "Sir, we reserve the right to refuse service to any client."

"You refuse?" Grossman was incredulous. "Do you know who I am? Why, I'll—"

"Perhaps you would be better off with another service. Go to the Cats Meow downtown and ask for Jake Holden." She paused for a second. "Jake will set you up in the style to which you are accustomed."

Chantelle could hear the man frown over the phone.

"Oh hell," Grossman said, sighing. "I'm sorry. I get carried away sometimes."

Chantelle decided to be forgiving. Of course Holderness could and did refuse service to inappropriate clients, but Royalty only did so in egregious circumstances. Grossman was recommended by Thom Madigan, and his company was listed 48th in the country in sales. Not a man to offend lightly. Moreover, Royalty would not want to irritate one of their best customers. "All right, Mr. Grossman. If you want Darcy tonight you can have her, but only under these conditions."

Chantelle briefed Grossman about Royalty's rules and got his agreement to sign them when he arrived. She knew how to talk to men over the phone. She had a sexy, vibrant voice, but never allowed herself to appear on video. It was old-fashioned, and lent an air of mystery to the client. Would Darcy be able to handle this guy? The Regier girl would have to play it by ear for there was not much time to study the client. At Royalty, two strikes and you were out.

But Darcy did well. So well, in fact, that Grossman was enthralled with her, and recommended her to a number of highly placed CEOs and executives.

During the next five years Darcy had a very successful career. She was in constant demand and remained one of Holderness's favorites. She was even invited occasionally to one of his private parties. These old-fashioned gatherings were indistinguishable from a 19th century ball or dinner party, complete with servants.

On her free time she sampled the night life on Chicago's north side accompanied by Richard, one of Royalty's chauffeur's. She especially liked Chenier's, an upscale club (on the Royalty approved list) that featured music and dancing. One time Richard took her to one of the back rooms where some of the high rollers played games of chance for high stakes. It was exciting to watch the play. The sums wagered were sometimes fantastic. She couldn't believe people existed who had so much and yet were willing to throw it away on the roll of a dice or the fall of a card. Another time Richard took her to a Cubs game at Wrigley Field. Darcy didn't care much for sports but she found herself yelling and screaming with 30,000 other fans just the same. It was exciting to be with so many people in such a small place. It was an event! A happening.

Darcy discovered that she liked to drive fast. She got Richard to take her to a racetrack, where she was given instructions on handling the BMW at high speeds. She got the car over 150 mph on the straightaways, and found that she was a pretty good driver. From that time on Darcy drove her BMW at breakneck speed on the highways, and sometimes in and out of traffic in the city. She was stopped several times by the Chicago police. Eventually she became well known by all of the traffic control officers. When she turned on her charm none of them could resist her, even the women. She never got a ticket.

She remembered the first time it had happened, on a warm summer day in early July, right after the holiday. She had just returned from a shopping trip on N. Michigan downtown when she heard the siren behind her.

Darcy rolled down the window as the officer approached. He was a big burly man with a gun on his right hip and a silver badge pinned to his short-sleeved uniform shirt. She gave him her best smile. "Hello officer!" She spoke as if she was glad to see an old friend.

The man, used to abuse, started. The stern look in his eyes vanished. "You were going 60 in a 35 mile an hour zone." He looked at the impeccably dressed woman before him and something inside him relaxed. He smiled. Unconsciously he responded to the eternal power of the feminine to soothe and inspire the masculine. "You could kill yourself driving like that, young lady."

"I know officer, I'm sorry." She was still smiling. "This car is so fun to drive. It's really boring going the speed limit."

The officer laughed. "That's just what my daughter says." He realized he wasn't doing his duty and said, more sternly, "Let me see your driver's license." Darcy quickly pulled her billfold from her purse and handed it to him, as well as her Royalty Services card.

The officer noted that her purse was almost empty. It contained only the billfold and a small cosmetics case. When he saw the card his eyebrows rose a little. Royalty had very good relations with the Department and could always be counted on for a hefty donation to the police officers fund. Some of the high muckety-mucks, he knew, made use of their services. "I'll be right back." He went to check her license on the traffic computer. As he expected, her record was spotless.

He walked back to the BMW. "I'm required to give you a ticket, Darcy, but I won't this time. Please drive carefully."

Darcy grinned. "Yes officer, I will. Thank you."

Darcy waited until the police car pulled away from the curb and was out of sight. She stomped down hard on the accelerator, pulled quickly out into traffic, and made an illegal U-turn. She *loved* the sound of screeching tires!

Darcy always liked to say it was the gawkers and the slow drivers that caused traffic problems.

CHAPTER 3

J UST after her 20th birthday Darcy attended a very unusual gathering that would affect the entire course of her life.

Royalty limos drove her and twenty Royalty consorts to the Esquire Hotel building. Instead of going up they took an elevator several floors down, getting off in the middle of a large hallway with very high ceilings. Walls, floor, and ceiling were black and made of some plastic-like material she had never seen before. A windowless subway vehicle awaited them. The women piled in, chattering excitedly. Darcy's observant eyes noticed something funny about the single track upon which the car rested. There were no ties, like on the subway. She could see no wheels on the vehicle. Maybe it was some new high-tech thing. She soon forgot about the oddity as the car began to silently speed forward. Darcy couldn't see anything but received the impression of tremendous but controlled power. The vehicle accelerated quickly and seemed to be going very, very fast. She could feel no G-force however. After about twenty seconds they stopped before a huge door that slid out, opening to the most amazing space Darcy had ever seen.

The first thing she noticed was the floor. It was covered in a thin, multicolored carpet that looked alive. The colors constantly and subtly changed like a kaleido-scope. She thought it was the coolest thing she'd ever seen until she looked across the room and saw a curved, bluish green sculpture. It was an animal captured in mid-air, about ten feet high. The figure was connected to its platform by a thin wire that couldn't possibly support that much weight. The animal had a very smooth, dolphin-like torso, a head like a cat, a short stubby tail, and four legs that each ended in a foot with six toes. The other women oohed and aaahed. Darcy walked toward the creature, transfixed. Was it alive? She stepped forward and touched it. The figure felt smooth and hard, like marble. The thing was so lifelike it appeared to be something living, frozen in a force field. The person who made this was beyond a genius.

Darcy looked around the room. Several dozen more of the sculptures had been placed at various points in the room, each depicting a different animal. They were all astonishing. The little tables upon which the figurines rested were of glass or clear quartz, and equally remarkable in their design. A single spiraling leg grew into a hand, or a paw, or a bowl which held the sculpture. It appeared to Darcy that each table had been specifically designed for the piece it held. The room was well lit. The intensity of the light was the same everywhere but she could find no light fixtures. Where does the illumination come from? She looked up and saw a beautiful light blue ceiling, curving over the space, with a small, whitish-yellow sun painted on it. Below the ceiling was a rounded molding that emitted a soft glow. Perhaps that was the source of the light, but then how did it fill the room so uniformly? It was like being outside on a sunny day. The space was huge, at least 300 feet in diameter. She sat on one of the sofas, taking it all in. The sofa molded itself to her figure most agreeably.

The place couldn't have been more opposite to Holderness Parkinson's 19th century mansion, but she liked it a lot better. It had a comfortable and exotic feel to it. Even the air smelled …different.

Her job was to circulate and converse and she realized she had been neglecting her duties. Her companions had already engaged themselves. Darcy heard the soft buzz of conversation that she enjoyed so much. There were about 50 people in the room, equally divided between men and women.

She found an unattended man, approached him, and introduced herself. She quickly sized him up. He was about five inches shorter than her with very fine features and perfect skin. He looked like a child! But no, he was gazing at her with unusually large and round eyes that had gold irises. His gaze bespoke enormous intelligence. Those unusual golden eyes were probably from contact lenses.

The man motioned her to one of the sofas. When she was seated she turned politely, intending to start a conversation. She would have no trouble finding a topic, for she was bursting with curiosity to find out about this incredible room.

The man gestured peculiarly and turned his eyes upon her. Darcy suddenly felt a hypnotic and overpowering urge to move closer to him. She was held by that compelling gaze, unable to look away. Involuntarily her muscles tensed. With a great effort of will she broke eye contact.

As she looked up she saw a look of shock and surprise on the man's face. It was a very pleasant face that displayed perfect symmetry. As part of her training Darcy had studied facial analysis, for it sometimes indicated personality traits or tendencies. This curious man seemed almost emotionless. He reminded her of the elegant silk flower arrangement on the corner table in her apartment. Beautiful, but sterile.

She returned her attention to the man and he gestured again, gazing at her fixedly. Darcy felt an even more compelling urge to move toward him. This time she also heard a voice in her head: "Come here." Darcy fought off the compulsion and lowered her eyes. She was seriously going to freak if this guy repeated his performance a third time. Her training said that it was perfectly all right to ignore anyone who stepped over the line of propriety, and this qualified. She was about to get up and leave when the man rose in one effortless motion and walked away. Darcy was astonished at the grace and beauty of such a simple movement. It made her feel awkward as she regained her feet and approached an older man with white hair, hoping he wouldn't weird her out too.

Out of the corner of her eye she observed the strange man pull out something from his pocket and speak into it. The device glowed with a multicolored energy like the floor covering. Darcy received the impression that the man was talking about her.

That night was one of the best, and the strangest, of her life. Her personal radar was on full blast. She made it a point to converse with everyone in the room. She counted two more of the fine-featured men, each of them almost a carbon copy of each other. All three had come out of the same mold.

On the ride back to her Royalty apartment the women chattered excitedly about the incredible room, the food, and the people they had met and talked to. None of her companions had noticed anything unusual about their clients. Or maybe they did, but just didn't care.

The next day Darcy called Chantelle and began to ask questions. The older woman told her to forget about it.

"Those sculptures were amazing!"

"Yes they were. You are not to mention your visit to anyone outside this agency, do you understand?"

"Yes. But I noticed three men with gold eyes and—"

"Darcy!" Chantelle barked.

"Yes?"

"For your own safety you should never talk about those men with anyone." Chantelle's voice, normally steady and authoritative, trembled with fear. Darcy felt her stomach curl up in a knot.

"Why?"

"The question is not open for discussion. Just forget about them. In fact, forget you were ever there."

Darcy couldn't forget. She often returned her memory to that party, for it had been a very unique and unusual experience. Unearthly. It wasn't until several years later that she found out who the strange men were, and the reason for the Royalty presence that night.

Eight months after her 22nd birthday, at the end of her contract, Darcy left the agency. She loved the luxury and comfort of the lifestyle but found it increasingly difficult to cater to the needs and whims of men. She had finally outgrown her fear of poverty and wanted her own life. Darcy knew that Parkinson was reluctant to let her go. In a little over four years she had more than justified his investment, and held the promise to be a fine courtesan. He liked her a lot and she liked him too. But it wasn't enough.

He met her in his cherrywood paneled office with its huge desk, old-fashioned phone, and paintings on the walls. "You're one of the best Darcy. A lady in every sense of the word. I'm very sorry to lose you."

She kissed him and thanked him. "You've taken me out of the gutter and I'll never forget that."

"If you ever want to come back to us you have only to call."

Darcy threw her fate to the wind. She sold most of her clothes and carefully packed her belongings into the BMW. She left the big city, traveling south until she found Midland. It was a nice small town where she could start a new life. And maybe meet somebody she could love, and who would love her.

Darcy's idea of that person was vague. In her fantasies she thought of an older, well educated man. Someone successful and socially adept who could love a strong, impulsive, independent woman. Someone who wouldn't place a lot of demands on her. Someone for whom sex wasn't that important.

The face of her ideal man was blank, just as her future was blank. She had no idea what she wanted from life and had no skills other than as hostess and companion. She did know how to talk to people. Well, she knew how to talk to *men*. For women she had no thought or interest. Darcy had gotten on well with her companions at the service, but she could not relate to them. She loved fast cars, fine clothes and fine food (although she hated to cook). Darcy discovered that she had mechanical aptitude. When the dishwasher had broken in her apartment she looked up the part on the internet, bought herself a toolkit, read the schematic, and fixed the thing herself. It had made her enormously proud. She told Cindy, in the apartment next door.

"You fixed it yourself? All you have to do is call the guys in Facility Services. That's what men are for."

Darcy quickly discovered that Midland was a wealthy university town, but also sports crazy. That was good because her association with people in Chicago who liked sports had been minimal. Unfortunately there were a few retired corporate executives from Chicago who might know her or recognize her. That was bad, but the odds were against recognition.

Darcy moved into a nice furnished apartment in a residential section of town that rented reasonably. Compared to her quarters at Royalty it seemed shabby. She was used to stay in the finest hotels, eat in the most expensive restaurants, and travel the world in style. Now she found herself in a small town with no source of income. Fear stabbed at her guts. For the past five years she had not a care for the necessities of life, which were provided by others. She thought of her father (whom she had never called since the day she left for Chicago) and the squalid house in Joliet. She could be right back there again. In a panic she reached for the phone and almost dialed Chantelle.

Darcy took quick stock of her possessions. She still had enough designer clothes to fill the walk–in closet, a set of china, lots of expensive jewelry, and $15,000 in the bank. That wasn't much. She had left Royalty just before she could have made some real money. Holderness had told her that as a successful courtesan she could have been a wealthy woman, but she knew she could no longer lead that life. Oh well. After five years of hard work she wanted to explore this town and have a little fun!

Then, one summer day three weeks later, she met Marcus.

Chapter 4

THREE weeks after she arrived in Midland Darcy saw a very tall figure walking down the street across from her apartment building. He moved easily and gracefully. She stopped her BMW by the curb to take a look. To her surprise, it was a boy. Or was it?

She got out of the car with the engine idling, and approached him. She stopped on the sidewalk about twenty feet along the path of his direction. His head was down and he was lost in thought. She saw a man – a boy – well over six feet tall with big hands, thick black hair, and a black stubble of beard surrounding a swarthy but not unhandsome face. He was dressed in jeans and a black cotton shirt on this hot summer day. She stood there, amused, wondering whether he'd run her over. He was only two feet away when he became aware of her presence. Effortlessly he completely stopped his movement and looked into her eyes. It was a remarkable demonstration of physical control. She wondered what kind of a guy this manchild was. A jock, probably, without a mind.

Marcus Riley gazed calmly down at the most beautiful girl he had ever seen. About a foot shorter than his 6 1/2 feet, she had large brown eyes, full lips, a small button nose, and a head of blond hair attractively arranged in windblown curls. Marcus noticed a pair of small, exquisite sapphire earrings. She wore a silk blouse with short sleeves, designer shorts, and a pair of expensive shoes with low heels. To him she looked like a fashion model. She stood there, completely comfortable as if she owned the sidewalk, gazing up into his blue eyes with a mixture of curiosity and amusement.

"Uh, hi," Marcus said.

"You want to go for a ride?"

"A ride?" His brain had been contemplating the vagaries of market movement. He was completely unprepared for her, or her request.

"That's my car over there," Darcy said.

Marcus noticed her silver BMW idling at the curb. "Well, I was just about to go home and get something to eat—"

"Good!" she said, walking toward the car. "You can take me out to lunch."

"I don't have any money on me."

She turned quickly around to face him. "OK, I'll take *you* out to lunch."

He smiled. Darcy noticed how his face lit up. There was something intriguing and deep in that smile. She decided that she liked him.

Marcus followed her into the car. Before he could buckle his seatbelt she floored the BMW, screeching the tires and driving him back into his seat. She ran the stop sign and just missed a truck, which honked its horn angrily. Darcy smiled. She glanced over at Marcus, still trying to secure his seatbelt. Darcy weaved in and out of traffic twenty miles an hour over the speed limit. She watched her passenger out of the corner of her eye, trying to get a read on him. He seemed calm and composed so she slammed on the brakes and yanked the car over quickly in a right turn that sent his body leaning into hers. Darcy accelerated the BMW quickly down the busy downtown street.

Marcus righted himself. He felt like a cat on his way to the veterinarian but maintained his composure.

Darcy saw a nice restaurant and quickly pulled the BMW left into the driveway, rocking Marcus against the door. She pounded the brake pedal (sending Marcus forward this time) and came to a stop perfectly situated between two cars in the restaurant parking lot.

Darcy was cheerful. "What's the good of having a fast car if you can't take advantage of it?" She smiled across the seat into Marcus' face.

"Not much I guess," Marcus replied. This beautiful Madonna was slumming, he thought, and had apparently picked him up off the street on a whim. What was a sophisticated older woman doing in a small college town like Midland?

During the next three months Marcus discovered that Darcy lived down the street in the Midland Heights apartment complex. She'd occasionally knock on his door and invite him out. A couple times they went to the movies and dinner. Once they went to the Midland Museum of Natural History downtown, where she found unattended corners and kissed him several times. Marcus liked that. Once they went to the lake south of town. She caused a sensation in her thong bikini and Marcus liked that too. The last time she came to one of his martial arts competitions. A couple of the kids from school were there. The word spread that Marcus had a hot girlfriend. Darcy was more than four years older than he was and as far as Marcus could tell, didn't have a job or do anything. Maybe she was rich. Marcus liked her and liked to be seen with her.

One day at school Ike Lambert, the closest thing he had to a friend, slapped a disk down on his desk.

"Look at that tonight and tell me what you think tomorrow."

That night after he'd done his homework and planned the next day's trading, Marcus sat down with the disk. It was a porn movie called "Jason's Revenge." Five minutes into the film he saw a young Darcy appear on the screen, and ten minutes later in a sex scene. Marcus thought she couldn't have been much more than 16. The movie sucked but Marcus watched it anyway. Every time Darcy appeared his eyes became riveted to the screen.

The next day a lot of the girls were angry with him. They must have heard about Darcy from Ike. Marcus was very tall and good-looking but he had never shown the slightest interest in any of them. That was from necessity, not desire, but what could he do?

"What's the matter, we're not good enough for you?" they said to him. The girls knew that Darcy was out of their league.

The guys were all over him and wanted to meet Darcy. It looked like his cover was going to be blown. After his parents died last year he had held off the social workers and the school authorities by getting the landlord to pose as his uncle. At lunch the guys were standing around one of the tables against the side wall.

Ike spoke for them all. "All we want you to do is introduce us to her."

There was shouted agreement.

"Have you fucked her yet?" asked Gary Crosby, a powerfully built linebacker on the football team.

"No. She's not that kind of girl."

That generated hoots and hollers. "Oh yeah, she's not that kind of chick," said DeShawn Brown. "She's only a *porn star.*"

"Yeah, with some guy screwing her brains out," agreed Johnny Chang, who took karate with him at the Midland Academy of Martial Arts.

Marcus snorted. "A porn star? I doubt it. That flick was probably made in somebody's basement."

"Then what's it doing on the shelf at Adult Video's?" Ike asked.

"That place? *You* could probably make a video and get it stocked there."

Everybody laughed. Ike was only about 5'4" and always horny.

"So when do we meet her?" Gary demanded.

"You don't."

"Stop holding out on us Marcus," Gary said. "If you aren't going to introduce us then tell us where she lives. We'll make our own arrangements." Gary rolled his pelvis back and forth, grinning lewdly.

"Just leave it alone OK?"

"No!" Gary said, reaching up and flicking his finger against Marcus' skull. "Dickhead! What's she to you anyway?"

"A friend."

More hoots.

"I think he's gay," said Charlie Hicks, a skinny musician in a local band that sometimes played at school events and private parties.

"Fuck you Charlie," Marcus said.

"Fuck you Riley," Gary said. "Ever since your mom and dad died there's something fishy going on at your house. It's just you and your uncle over there, and he's never around …" Suddenly, comprehension dawned on Crosby's face. He sneered. "You don't even have an uncle. You live there all by yourself."

"I do not!" Marcus flared, giving himself away.

"The hell you don't."

"There's one way to find out," Charlie said. "We'll go to the principal and see what he says." He looked at Marcus challengingly.

Now Marcus was really scared. How had they found out? If they knew what he and his landlord had pulled off they'd both be screwed.

A dozen faces were staring at him, waiting for a response. "I'm not telling you."

Crosby exploded. "The hell you aren't." Crosby gripped Marcus' shirt and shoved him against a wall. Crosby was three inches shorter but had a grip of iron. Marcus felt his nerves calm and a feeling of power surged through him. He looked down at Crosby's angry face and said calmly, "Please take your hand off me."

Crosby felt his fist untighten and he found himself taking a step backward. The anger had gone out of him and he looked up at the taller boy.

"How did you do that?" he said, confusion written all over his face.

"Do what?"

"Make my hand let go."

"I didn't do anything."

Gary looked at his hand as if it had been remotely controlled.

The others had seen the same thing. Some force had taken control of Gary's hand and then his body. They regarded Marcus with a mixture of awe and fear.

"Did they teach you that in karate?" Ike asked. "I want some of that."

Johnny Chang laughed nervously. "Mental discipline is part of karate. The ability to project intention is something else entirely."

Charlie said, "C'mon guys, let's get outta here."

Everybody left Marcus except Johnny. "Can you teach me what you just did?"

"I don't know what I just did." Marcus suddenly understood that he had experienced an instant of total clarity. In that moment he had been able to marshal his thoughts around one idea, with absolutely no counter-intention. "I take that back. I do know what I did but I don't know how I did it."

Johnny gave him a strange look. "All right. I'll see you in class on Friday."

Marcus was hungry but lunch period was over. At least he hadn't told them where Darcy lived. He walked out of the cafeteria and down the hall to a really boring biology class.

The situation with Marcus' landlord was reaching a crisis point.

After his parents died he couldn't stand living in their house. There were just too many memories. So he took his settlement, which was only $10,000 after probate, and found another place in a neighborhood. It was within walking distance of Midland East high school.

The place at 1235 Traver Road was run down, one of those seedy old houses in a decent neighborhood two miles from the Carleton university campus. Marcus decided to rent it after seeing the "For Sale" sign on the property. It had been there for two months. He figured that the house was a rental property and Mr. Pelco was a negligent landlord. Marcus approached Pelco in his small, messy downtown office with a proposal. "I'd like to rent the place for a year and fix it up. In another year I'll have the money to buy it."

Pelco looked him up and down. "Get outta here, kid." Pelco was a stocky, swarthy man with thick lips, sunken eyes, and a stubble of beard. His hands, lying on the desk, were thick and hairy.

Marcus handed him a check for $2,000. "Here's first and last month's rent, plus the security deposit."

Pelco's eyes widened and he looked at the check. "How do I know it's good?"

Marcus raised his eyebrows as if to say, 'Don't be stupid.'

Pelco flushed. He copied down the account number and called the bank, verifying the funds.

"Why do you want that house?" He hated the damn place and so had everyone he'd shown it to. He had promoted it as a startup home but the place didn't take. He had been forced to rent it out to students for the past three years and didn't want to waste his money getting it in salable shape. Even if he did it would probably sell at a loss. Douglas Pelco didn't for a minute believe that the kid wanted to purchase the property, or that he could. But he wasn't about to turn down $2,000. "Suit yourself. You can move in on the first of next month."

"I want the place cleaned first," Marcus said. "And the windows washed."

"Making demands, are we?"

"All right." Marcus picked up his check from the disorganized desktop. "I'll see you later."

"Goddamn kid." Pelco swore to himself and saw Marcus reach the door. "OK. You're right, it's a bit dusty in there."

Pelco assured Marcus that all of the appliances were in working order, as well as the furnace. Marcus knew he should insist on an inspection but he didn't know any contractors. His father, a market analyst – a former market analyst, he mentally corrected himself – had taught him about real estate. Dad had taught him about a lot of things, as if he had a premonition of his own death.

"There's one more thing," Marcus said, handing over the check. "If this is going to work you have to be my temporary uncle for the coming year."

"You're out of your mind Marcus Riley. Go get your own relative."

"I don't have any." Well, that wasn't exactly true. He could have gone to live with his cousin's family in Los Angeles. But they hadn't spoken in years. He didn't like crowded and hectic southern California. Midland was just fine with him, for now at least.

"Too bad. I could lose my real estate license. I'm not going to do it for $2,000." He handed Marcus' check back to him.

Pelco had him over a barrel so Marcus explained his situation. "I need an adult to keep the social workers and the school administrators off my back until I become of legal age. My parent's house was sold in probate and I received $10,000 from the settlement. I also have some money in my market trading account that will cover the rest of the rent."

Market trading account? Maybe Marcus Riley was some kind of whiz-kid. Didn't look like it though. But he had the kid's account number and he could verify the entire year's rent. If it turned out OK he'd go along. There was quite a difference between $2,000 and $12,000. Things were really tight these days in real estate. At least for him.

Douglas Pelco's experience with renters had not been completely satisfying, but this kid was clean and didn't have any tattoos or lip rings. He looked trustworthy, if there was such a thing. "OK kid, I'll call you tonight."

Marcus handed back the check to Pelco. It must have burn marks on it by now, he thought. "Earnest money."

Pelco smiled. "All right Marcus. I wish I had more renters like you."

When Marcus was fourteen his father began to show him the intricacies of the stock market.

It did not seem odd to Marcus that his father would do so. Marcus' mind was wide ranging. He was one of the best baseball players on the Midland East team but his interests went well beyond those of a normal teenage boy. Marcus' parents and teachers could see that the fourteen-year-old had a remarkably mature understanding for one so young. Marcus' physical development ran alongside his mental development. At fourteen he was already two inches over six feet with broad shoulders and large hands and feet. His face had already begun to lose the boyish quality and become the face of a man. Tam and Louise often remarked that their son had, like the weather in the northern Minnesota town of their birth, skipped spring and gone right into summer.

Tam Riley was a securities analyst for the main branch in Midland of Real-Bank, a Chicago-based regional bank. Tam's job was to advise the bank on its own investments. His specialty was computer analysis. He would analyze financial data, spot trends, and develop forecasts. He made recommendations to buy or sell investments or securities. More often than not he was correct. Even though he made only a modest salary he stayed in his position because he wanted the experience. It was Tam's intention to leave the bank within the next five years and start his own company.

Marcus loved computers and mathematics, and was a quick learner. After several months of instruction he gained an intuitive feel for market trends. It got so that he could choose the stocks that would rise. His father saw that Marcus' predictions often coincided with those of his software program. As a game, and to keep his son interested, Tam had Marcus write down his predictions. After six months Tam performed a comparative analysis. To his astonishment, Marcus was right more than the computer. Tam found that Marcus' predictions were most accurate on a day-to-day basis. He had the peculiar ability to predict upticks and downticks in a stock's value.

"How do you make your determination, son?" Tam asked one day.

"I'm not sure, Dad. I need to see the monthly, weekly, and daily moving averages. I can just see patterns. There's a sort of web of light in my head, like a spider's web or something. Each little strand represents one stock. The whole thing seems to be alive. From the web I can usually tell whether the stock will go up or down the next day." Tam's eyebrows rose a little, but he was not worried. His son was clearly extraordinary but displayed no unnatural eccentricities of character.

Tam noticed that Marcus' accuracy decreased the further out timewise, but that was only natural. The market was a dynamic system that exhibited the properties of chaos. Like the weather it became harder and harder to predict on a weekly or monthly basis.

Tam realized that Marcus' predictions crossed markets. He was just as accurate with tech stocks as blue chips. "You know son, you might do well as a day trader."

That suggestion caught fire within Marcus' mind. After school and homework he pretended to trade the market, keeping a record of his transactions. He started with a theoretical $1,000. At the end of three quarters, or nine months, he showed a paper profit of $20,826.

Tam was amazed. Father and son sat down together in front of the computer one night in Tam's study, just after Marcus' 15th birthday. Father and son studied Marcus' files. "Look son," Tam said, "you lost almost everything when the market dipped 600 points last July."

Tam remembered that the sudden downturn had been caused by a series of failures in the tech sector, which had sent shockwaves throughout the investment community. Yet Marcus had recovered and had still realized a significant profit. "You should optimally trade your system when the market is quiet," Tam advised his son.

Marcus smiled. He was as tall as his father now and even more broad-shouldered. As he held his father at gaze a sudden feeling of dread overcame him. The web of light in his head, which heretofore had represented the ups and downs of market movement, suddenly transformed itself into the world lines of his parents. Marcus saw clearly that somewhere in the near future, both of these lines terminated abruptly.

"What's the matter son?" Tam asked, hearing Marcus' sudden intake of breath. His son's face had gone pale.

"Uh, nothing dad."

The eyes of father and son met and held for just an instant. In that instant was an eternity of comprehension. Tam felt the strands of his life assemble. In that timeless moment part of himself passed over into the consciousness of his son. Marcus knew that on a subconscious level his father had also felt the premonition of his own death.

Tam let out a sigh. A smile came over his face; a peaceful, serene smile, as when a dying soldier communicates important information that may change the course of the battle. Marcus sensed a terrible sadness within himself, coupled with an overwhelming feeling of love for his father. His eyes watered and he threw himself into his father's arms. "Don't go, dad!"

Tam laughed. "Of course not. I'm not going anywhere."

Deep within him Marcus knew that was not true.

CHAPTER **5**

Dᴀʀᴄʏ walked into his study without bothering to knock. Marcus sat at his computer reading today's stock quotes and entering the data into his market tables. From the three month moving averages, it looked like a slight uptick for Google, Pfizer, and Dell tomorrow. That's where he'd put his money. The market had been quiet for months, and that's when his investment program worked the best.

"I thought I should move in," Darcy said, interrupting his concentration. He hadn't even heard her enter.

He felt the chair rock. She had kicked it with her foot. "Did you hear me?"

He turned around in his chair. Darcy looked down at him with a mixture of amusement and irritation.

He stood and faced her. "Yes, I heard you."

"Well?" she said, placing her hands on her hips.

She's impulsive and beautiful, he thought.

Darcy craned her neck to meet his gaze. "I could help you pay the rent every month. I've still got some money left. I'm looking for a job ... and I absolutely *hate* my apartment."

She knew Marcus didn't need the money. He was only seventeen, but so damnably self sufficient! It intrigued her and annoyed her.

31

Marcus looked at the woman in front of him and felt a surge of electricity go through every cell in his body. She wasn't like any other girl in school, probably because she was older. He didn't have any patience with them even though he got along OK with them. He couldn't get too close or they might start asking questions. He needed just a few more months until he was legally an adult. He would buy this house, get the nervous landlord off his back, finish high school, and take control of his life. For that reason he had deliberately not made too many friends at Midland East. He held everyone at arms length. Thank God dad had left him the password to his personal trading account at Merrill Lynch before he died.

It was good Darcy that offered to help him with the expenses. He didn't like the idea of anyone mooching off him.

Marcus made his decision. "I've got two spare bedrooms. Take your pick."

Darcy stepped forward and threw her arms around his neck. *He's gorgeous. I could do a lot worse than this manchild.* "I thought I'd move into your room. Unless you're gay that is."

She thought to get a rise out of him and was disappointed.

"No," Marcus said, laughing into her brown eyes. "I'm definitely not gay." The thought of her in his bed made him shiver with anticipation.

She stepped away and smiled at him, an alluring feminine smile that challenged him and invited him at the same time. She seemed to be saying, 'Let's see if you can handle me.' Then she walked quickly out of the room. Marcus heard the front door close and a car engine start.

Now how did that happen? He had just gotten himself a roommate.

Two hours later Marcus was still at the computer, researching a new stock. He heard a car door slam and then the thud of something hitting the hardwood floor in the foyer. After several minutes Marcus heard the sound of hard, quick footsteps. His door opened violently. It crashed against the plaster wall, the handle making a little dent in the plaster. A flake of it fell onto the throw rug. Marcus noticed things like that.

Darcy was angry. "How about a little help? I'm your roommate now!"

"OK." Marcus brushed by her, not meeting her eyes. The last thing he wanted was an argument. He went out to the car and grabbed two heavy boxes from the big trunk, lifting them easily. He placed them next to one that had cracked open, spilling its contents onto the floor. Marcus said nothing. Darcy watched from the porch as he lifted the last of the boxes from the trunk, walking them into the house and setting them gently upon the floor. He was very tall yet moved fluidly. She noticed with approval how wide his shoulders were. Not even 18, he was physically already a man.

Darcy did not offer to help while Marcus worked quietly. She was tired after having to haul her stuff up a flight of stairs into the car from her basement apartment. She liked the fact that he didn't make a fuss. After two more trips he had unloaded the car. Marcus turned and walked back into his study.

Marcus heard a knock on the door. Darcy poked her head in. "What kind of a guy won't help his girl unpack her heavy stuff?"

Marcus was irritated. He noticed that one of the boxes had made a scratch on his newly finished hardwood floor. He'd sanded and refinished it himself with a little help from one of Pelco's contractors. Darcy was not at all the kind of roommate he had envisioned but he was pleased that she had referred to herself as his girl. It made him feel needed, and important.

Darcy kicked one of the offending boxes. "Take this one into the kitchen," she commanded, pointing to a box that had "Fragile, dishes" written on it in black magic marker.

"I already have dishes."

"Oh, you mean those plastic things you probably got at a garage sale? These are real china. I'll remind you to take good care of them."

He just looked at her. His eyes said, 'That's why you just kicked the crap out of them.'

"They're packed very well," she said, as if that explained everything perfectly.

Marcus shook his head and smiled wearily, like a father to a rambunctious child. He towered over her.

A flush of red infused Darcy's cheeks. *Ooooohh, Marcus Riley, don't ever do that again or I'll slap you silly!*

Marcus saw her reaction and laughed, infuriating her even more. She had spirit and spunk. Something in his heart melted just a little.

Darcy calmed herself and looked up at him. The manchild was gazing down at her, completely sure of himself.

"How did you get to be so self confident?" She was angry and curious.

Marcus shrugged. "I've always been that way. My parents didn't beat it out of me."

Darcy hung her head for a moment. *Yeah, not like mine.*

Marcus stepped forward, put his finger under her chin and gently raised her head. "Cheer up!"

Darcy smiled. Maybe it's going to be all right, she thought. Maybe she finally found a good guy. A voice in the back of her mind said, 'Is there such a thing?' She turned abruptly and left the room.

Marcus saw a tear running down her cheek. Did I say something? he wondered. He lifted the boxes and placed them in the appropriate rooms, each one having its destination written on the top. Then he went back to the computer and planned the next day's trading cycle.

Two hours later he walked out of his study and into his bedroom. It had been transformed. Darcy had taken the spare bureau, which had been his mother's, for her own. On it he saw perfume, lipstick, a large jewelry case, and a vase of flowers. A mirror hung over the dresser. Marcus unhooked it, expecting to see a bent nail hanging precariously from cracked plaster. Instead, she had carefully drilled two holes and installed anchors in each one. The mirror's wire was securely fastened to two screws protruding from the anchors. He had been immersed in his research, and only dimly aware of her movements about the house.

He replaced the mirror and saw three wall hangings, each one firmly secured. A nature scene, a photograph of da Vinci's pieta, and one of those Dutch masterpiece paintings hung above the bed. Marcus went over and examined the painting. He knelt on the bed and admired the incredible detail of every stroke. Just then he noticed that the old gray bedspread had been replaced by one in pastels. The flowers from the bureau filled the air with a pleasant fragrance.

Well, it sure didn't take her long to make her mark. He thought about the nick in the plaster in his study and chuckled to himself. His new roommate was beginning to grow on him a little.

Marcus looked around the bedroom and decided it was an improvement. A big improvement. She had not over-decorated. The space now had a feminine touch. He smiled and walked around the house, intending to complement her, but he could not find her. He looked out the big picture window in the living room to the driveway. The silver BMW was not there.

Marcus walked into the kitchen and read the time from the clock above the table. 7:15, and he hadn't had anything to eat since breakfast.

Where was she? Oh well, he'd order a pizza.

Just as he was about to pick up the phone he heard car wheels screeching in the driveway. Darcy appeared in the kitchen with a big paper bag that smelled really good. She got two plates from the cupboard and some silverware, and sat down.

Darcy opened one of the plastic containers and began spooning mahkmoor onto her plate. "I found this great little Syrian restaurant at the mall."

"What'd you get me?" Marcus was amazed that out of all the places in town, she'd found the Taste of Damascus. It was his favorite carryout food.

"I got you *kibbe, babbaganouj,* and *tebooleh,*" she said, pointing to his un-opened container. "And some rice pudding for desert."

Marcus sat across from her, watching her. She ate gracefully, out of habit. She was unaware that he was staring at her, his plate untouched. She had gotten him the only four things he had ever eaten from the Damascus, as if they'd lived together for years.

"How did you know what I liked?"

She looked up quickly. "I didn't." Darcy resumed eating.

After dinner Darcy put the dishes in the dishwasher and cleaned the table and the sink. Point for her, Marcus thought. He liked things neat. He went to the bathroom and when he came out she had left again. Well, she was unpredictable, and he didn't own her. He just would have liked to know where she went.

He did his homework and then sat on the couch, turning on the History Channel. Tonight was the conclusion to the series on the rise and fall of the Roman Empire, and he didn't want to miss it. Every 15 minutes he found himself looking out the window, expecting to see Darcy's car. He grew more and more worried.

He slapped himself mentally. She's 22 years old and can take care of herself. Maybe she decided to sleep at her furnished apartment tonight one last time. He was disappointed. He had felt a sense of excitement and anticipation all day. Normally that feeling came from the eagerness he always had about the next day's trading. Would his predictive model make him money, or would he lose? Would he be able to make even finer adjustments to his predictive algorithms? But that wasn't it. Darcy was the main source of his feelings. The thought of her next to him made him suddenly anxious. He'd never made love to a girl before, and she probably had a lot of experience. How would he stack up next to her other lovers?

At 11 the show was over and Marcus shoved the recordable disk back into its sleeve. He had hardly been able to pay attention to the last half hour of the program, thinking about Darcy. He went to bed; disappointed, worried, and angry that his new roommate hadn't bothered to include him in her plans. He tossed and turned until he fell into a restless sleep.

Sometime later that night he heard the bedroom door open softly. Marcus was instantly awake. In the dark he heard the fall of her clothing to the floor. The sheet was pulled back. He was lying on his side and couldn't see her in the dark.

"Hi," she said cheerfully.

"Are you all right?" The worry showed in his voice.

Darcy was thrilled. "Did you miss me?"

"Damn right I missed you! You didn't tell me where you were going or …"

Her fingers touched his lips and he quieted. Mission accomplished, she thought. Now let's see whether I'm actually going to enjoy this. Something told her that she would. She kissed him. It was a good kiss. He felt good and he smelled good too.

"You're not wearing any clothes."

"I always sleep naked." Marcus felt a little jealous, still miffed that he didn't know where she had been or what she had done. Had she been with another guy? These were emotions foreign to him but he could not deny that he felt them. "You're not wearing any either."

"That's right." She pressed herself against him.

Marcus' anger evaporated as her arms closed around him …

That night was the best of his life, by far. She showed him how to make love, how to touch her and where, and all the pleasure points on her body. What amazed him was how she responded to him. At the end of that amazing night he understood that a woman's body was a very sensitive instrument. If played properly he could evoke in his lover the most passionate responses.

They talked and explored each other all night. At 3 in the morning they ran down the stairs naked to raid the refrigerator. Then they ran back up the stairs to the bedroom and threw themselves into each other's arms again.

Marcus spoke to her as the first rays of the morning sun softly illuminated the room. "You know that old saying, 'it's better to give than receive?'"

She propped herself on an elbow and smiled down at him. "With a little more practice you're going to be really good." She was looking forward to the nights to come. He wasn't even eighteen yet but he had soft hands. The martial arts training had apparently given him a certain grace and confidence that had quickly overcome his teenage awkwardness. Oh, it felt so good to be cared for! All those years she had been the provider, had to cater to the tastes of her clients. She hadn't really enjoyed the sex but tonight was different. Now she had someone to look out for her needs.

Part II – MODIFICATION

CHAPTER **6**

14,000 years ago

"Look at these primitives," Ussht-Kzzr remarked with contempt as they flew over the planet's major land mass. Here in the Desert they had expected to find nothing. Unexpectedly their scout ship had come upon this blue jewel in an obscure solar system with but one smallish, yellow sun.

"Yes sire," replied Brzzt, the drone of Ussht-Kzzr. "I have cataloged 38 other stations so far, as per your instructions."

Ussht-Kzzr was surprised. "So we are not the first! I assure you that we will be the last."

"Yes sire. All of the stations I have noted are not weaponized."

"Good. It should be child's play to use this planet for our own purposes."

Brzzt was silent. These Qrrk-Kashar were genetically arrogant. It was best simply to answer questions and to offer nothing.

Ussht-Kzzr remained thoughtful for several hours as their small, two-man scout craft circled the planet. Brzzt knew that he was making plans.

Ussht-Kzzr spoke suddenly. "We will return to Draco Tau and immediately make preparations. Take two males and two females from the planet for the Qrrk-

Ytil. Prepare a detailed report for the Council and send it to me as soon as you have finished."

"Yes sire," Brzzt replied. He quickly plotted a course and retrieved two of the primitive hominids, storing them in the small cargo area. The creatures shrieked and moaned, clawing the walls and themselves. Brzzt was afraid they would come to harm so he placed them in stasis for the return journey. Then he went to work on his report. Ussht-Kzzr would spend his time rewriting that report to reflect his own cleverness. Even though Brzzt did all the work he didn't mind. He was but a drone. It was the way of the Xorg.

The scout craft arrived a six-day later on their hot, arid planet.

Brzzt transported the hominids to the central Qrrk-Ytil laboratory, and returned to his dwelling.

Ussht-Kzzr went to his chambers and applied ceremonial dyes to his thick, leathery skin. These dyes represented the colors and heraldry of his bloodline. Then he entered Council chambers, which were housed in a luxuriously outfitted cave sheltered from the planet's hot blue-white sun. He faced the Council's head and bowed low, indicating submission. The Council was permanently in session at all times during the six-day. He saw that Belial himself, the alpha, was present along with his personal drone, who acted as his secretary. It was a stroke of luck.

"Report," Belial commanded. This was Ussht-Kzzr's signal to give a brief summary of his mission.

"The planet is perfect, sire. The population is approximately two million, composed of primitive hominids ripe for genetic manipulation." Ussht-Kzzr worded his short brief in the most glowing terms, to reflect glory upon himself. He explained about the planet's atmosphere, its specific gravity, its rotation, orbit, length of year and day, and other important data. He also reported the presence of other unarmed research stations.

Belial's reptilian mouth widened in satisfaction. "You have done well, Ussht-Kzzr." Ussht-Kzzr appreciated the use of his proper name, a sign of respect which meant that he was in favor. Just as he was about to smile, Belial spoke again. "That is, if you have submitted a completely unembellished report."

Ussht-Kzzr stiffened slightly and Belial noticed. Belial saw Ussht-Kzzr's discomfort and was satisfied. This one would cause no trouble, but to maintain control fear must be sustained. "Bring in the Qrrk-Ytil," Belial commanded his secretary. This was Ussht-Kzzr's signal for dismissal. He bowed low before exiting the Council chamber. He hoped that his report contained no inaccuracies or it would be his head.

Ussht-Kzzr contemplated his report and the alpha's reaction to it on the way to his personal cave. The alpha was a monster, a foot taller and much broader and muscular than any male on Tau. Belial was the ceremonial name for the commander of the Xorg. His title was always earned in hand-to-hand combat among the Qrrk-Hazur, the planet's elite warriors. The Belial was a special bloodline among the Tau; one genetically bred for superiority. Whoever occupied this position was naturally looked upon with awe and obedience. The warrior bloodlines dominated the planet and made all decisions. The Qrrk-Ytil, the planet's educated elite, were vital to the race's success and included the bloodlines of the elite geneticists who were responsible for successful Harvests. Qrrk-Ytil were also used as advisors and so had a say in planetary decision-making. A small section of the Tau bloodlines were explorers, the Qrrk-Kashar. These were specialists like himself who discovered underdeveloped planets in this crowded galaxy and prepared them for Harvest. And then there were the drones, whose bloodlines were impure, and so beneath notice. Over seventy percent of the male population were drones, utterly subject to the orders of their superiors. To maintain genetic diversity it was necessary to infuse the bloodlines occasionally with new genetic material. Therefore the drone population must be large. It was a system that had worked well for them, Ussht-Kzzr thought, even before their Life Reading Index had reached the proper threshold to propel them into this dimension almost 100,000 rotations ago.

It was typical of the Tau that Ussht-Kzzr never thought about the females on Tau. They were breeding stock; partners for mating and sexual enjoyment.

After Ussht-Kzzr left Belial confronted his picked coterie of geneticists.

"We have discovered a new planet!" Belial said expansively. "You have already had a brief look at the samples. What say you, Ipqu-Ayt?"

The Qrrk-Ytil was nervous in the presence of the alpha. "Sire, the present period of severe cold could cause an interruption of the purity of the bloodlines if we establish them now. It would be better to wait."

Belial flared. "To wait for another Harvest? When we have such promising samples? How probable is it that the bloodlines, if we establish them now, will become damaged?"

Ipqu-Ayt quailed inside but showed no fear. "The probability, sire, is over sixty percent that too many will die during this period to properly maintain genetic purity. Without the proper genetic foundation, a successful Harvest is improbable."

Belial crashed his huge paw upon the stone table, causing it to shake. "You say this, knowing that there are already 38 stations from other systems already present upon the planet? Are they not already polluting the hominids? Are they not setting up their own modifications?"

Ipqu-Ayt bowed his head in submission. "This, sire, is unknown."

Belial stared down every one of the Ytils, and they all bowed their heads. "Proceed with the genetic program," he ordered. "Begin establishing the bloodlines immediately."

Ipqu-Ayt raised his head. "Yes sire. It shall be done immediately."

"Miscreants!" Belial bellowed. "Why are you still standing here?"

The Ytils all vanished, scurrying away, thankful not to have been punished.

CHAPTER 7

Ancient Babylonia, 1746 B.C.

Sᴇsʜᴛɪ walked along the riverbank, swollen now with rainwater from the summer storm. The path was narrow and filled with rocks. Beside the path loomed huge boulders, as if a giant had smashed his axe at the distant mountains and broken them to pieces. There were legends of such mountains far to the north, mountains made of ice. It was a thing unbelievable.

His hard leather sandals scraped the dirt as the hot sun baked the ground. Seshti thought of the coming Imperial Summit meeting in Kish. Abi-ramu himself would be there, he who had sat in the councils of the great King Hamurrappi, now four years gone. It was said that Abi-ramu had the ear of Samsu-iluna, the current king.

A great meeting was planned in Kish, and a great feast. All of the conquered city-states, and the local villages around the capital, must send their representatives. Seshti was eager to reach one of the fine hostels in Kish. These hotels were legendary for their hospitality and their food. It had been a long day on the road. His mount had strained a hock not three miles along and he had sent the poor beast back to its stable. He shouldered the pack that was strapped to the horse, which carried his clothing and toiletries. Seshti proceeded on foot for the ten mile walk to the city.

A weary Seshti arrived in Kish just before dark. The city was ablaze with light from thousands of oil lamps. Music and loud voices filled the air. He saw girls in long white tunics serving food and drink to men sitting outside, talking and debating. Suddenly a soft voice was in his ear. "Honored guest, please come and experience the hospitality of our hotel." Seshti turned; it was one of the girls. She was dressed in a light blue tunic and had long black hair. On her wrists were silver bracelets. "You are here for the gathering?" she asked, smiling.

"Yes," Seshti replied, pulling out the clay tablet that identified him as the representative from the outlying village of Kish-mubalit. The girl glanced at the tablet. "Come."

Seshti was impressed. As he followed behind the girl in the dusky light, her tunic rustling, he saw workmen sprinkling water on the roads and walking paths to keep down the dust. Soldiers guarded every entranceway and road. There was to be no trouble in Kish, he thought happily. I can do my business here and go home to my wife and family.

The air was scented with frankincense, sweet grass, cedarwood, and myrrh. Surely tomorrow's feast would be spectacular. He found himself trembling with excitement at the thought of the great gathering. Representatives from as far away as Ur would be in attendance. Delegates would come from the conquered states of Rapiqum and Eshnunna to the north. Important powers to the south like Larsa, Uruk, Lagash, and Eridu, would also send their envoys. Hundreds of men walked the streets but he could not see their costumes in the vague light. Tomorrow he would rise before dawn and observe. He would listen to the talk and understand the prevailing sentiment.

The purpose of the gathering was unknown to him. Seven days ago a soldier had pounded upon his door, handed him the tablet, and ordered him to appear in Kish at the appointed time. Apparently the meeting was so well organized that each representative had already been assigned to a hostel. This regulation was the work of the great King Hamurrappi. Hamurappi had organized Babylon and its outlying cities, instituted a census, and brought his code of laws to the people. Nothing was to be left to chance, he thought, as he followed the girl down a lighted path.

The girl turned off the path and into a small courtyard where she bowed before an impressive-looking madam dressed in a red tunic. The older woman glanced at his tablet and asked for his sword. He was surprised, for no man surrendered his weapon to another for any reason. The woman spoke firmly. "No weapons are allowed in Kish until the end of the feast. You must carry your identification with you at all times, openly visible. Delegates who do not have proper identification will be forcibly escorted from the city. By order of Abi-ramu, Imperial Counselor." She said the words quickly, as if she had already done so hundreds of times. He wanted no trouble and handed over his weapon. The woman directed him to a dining area where a flour cake of dates, apricots, and figs was being served on large wooden tables. There was beer and a spiced chicken dish containing garlic, onions, leeks, cumin, coriander, and mint. The savory smell of the food reminded him that he had spent eight hours on the road. Seshti ate and was directed to a small open room enclosed by three walls, with a wooden slab for a bed. He spread his blanket, thanked the gods for a safe journey, and retired for the night.

At dawn Seshti awoke to the sound of movement in the hallway. Men were moving toward the dining area. Seshti had a breakfast of apricots, figs, and another of the flour cakes. He was ready to walk the streets. Already the marketplaces were busy with local vendors. The talk was all of the meeting. Seshti learned that the gods themselves would speak to them!

He approached a group of delegates talking by one of the market stalls, but the members walked away. He wandered the streets for over two hours. Representatives from each of the powerful city states surrounding Babylon congregated together and shunned outsiders. The envoys were easily distinguished from the local population by their distinctive garb and their official seals.

Seshti himself was dressed like a common citizen of the time. He was Semitic, about six inches over five feet in height, with dark hair and features, and a beard. Both men and women had long hair and scented themselves with perfume. Seshti avoided this affectation because his wife did not care for it. Seshti wore a common white linen tunic reaching to his feet and a turban to shield his head from the baking sun. He carried a walking stick with a carved and decorative head. Many of the women he saw revealed a bare left shoulder. All of the foreign delegates wore mantals and decorative, red- and blue-colored robes in patterns that identified their wearer's city. All carried their personal seal, used to imprint their letters and other documents. Every delegate openly displayed their official Imperial Summit seal.

Seshti noticed that the representatives from Ur always wore red sashes over the left shoulder. Those from Uruk wore distinctive helmets that covered the forehead and sloped to a point in the back, with hand grips on both sides. In hand-to-hand combat these helmets could be removed very quickly, and were deadly weapons.

Every time he drew near a gathering of delegates they lowered their voices and avoided him. Seshti wondered whether their talk was conspiratorial. He was disappointed, for he had wanted to test the temper of the coming summit.

He turned his mind to the happier task of admiring the cheerfully decorated buildings and hostels of the city. All of the structures in Kish were made of brick. At this time, colored and decorative bricks were making their appearance. Seshti was amazed to see that many of the buildings were faced with enameled tiles of blue, yellow, or white. These tiles were often adorned with animal and other figures in glazed relief. Even more amazing were the number of gaily clothed and attractive women in public. He noticed that a beautiful young girl was trying to catch his eye. Seshti moved quickly away, not wanting to tempt fate. Prostitution was legendary in Kish but he was loyal to his family and his wife.

After several hours of walking he went back to the hostel. He ate and went to his room, instructing his hostess to wake him in time to walk the short distance to the temple at the heart of the city. The meeting was to begin an hour before sunset. The feast would begin directly after the end of the summit. According to the talk, the feast would continue all night and the following day.

Three hours later Seshti was groggy from his nap as he followed the multitude into the temple. Men were streaming toward the entrance from every direction. It was clear that he would be one of the last ones to enter. He had never seen so many people in one place. The temple in Kish was huge and could handle many hundreds of people.

The temple was open to the sky but the main altar at the front was shielded by a brick roof. Carved representations of the gods lined the back of the semi-circular altar. Foremost among the gods was an unusual Marduk, displayed as a winged giant with a serpent head. Seshti recognized Enlil, the god of weather and storms, and his half-brother Enki. Tiamat, the dragon goddess and her husband Quingu were familiar to him. Ashur, the god of war, was represented with a reptilian head. There was a four-legged creature with the head of a lizard, which he heard was Baal. This must be a new god, Seshti thought. Where is Ea, the god of wisdom? And Ishtar, goddess of love?

Seshti decided to hover at the very back of the crowd. He felt a nervous anxiety, as if one of the gods was displeased with him. No one was on the streets. All residents of Kish had been ordered to stay indoors until the beginning of the feast. The soldiers who had been patrolling the streets were all inside the temple for the time being. He heard ritual chanting behind the altar. The men finally settled in their seats and the talk died down. Seshti heard the rhythmic beating of a drum. Huge torches were lit and placed at the sides of the altar, illuminating it. A group of huddled children were brought forth in a cage and placed at the right side of the altar. A procession of priests in dark blue robes entered the altar from the left, holding aloft a banner of a fire-breathing dragon. A herald introduced Abi-ramu, imperial counselor. Seshti expected to see someone tall and impressive. Instead a small, wizened man with a great white beard walked to the front of the altar.

Abi-ramu spoke with a trembling voice. "Today all Babylon has the privilege to hear in person the great Belial, representative of the gods of our people. You have all been called to carry his message far and wide, to tell the people of your cities and villages that a new Order has begun." Abi-ramu paused and looked nervously around the room. The great man looked frightened. "Belial says that he comes from the sky, from the abode of the gods, with a special message for humanity ..."

Suddenly a gigantic figure appeared from behind the altar. It materialized out of one of the statues. A gasp went out from the multitude. A monster almost nine feet tall. It had dark green skin, short claws protruding from hands and feet, and the face of a reptile. Seshti shuddered.

"Humans!" it thundered. Seshti noticed that even as it spoke the thoughts of the creature vibrated inside his head. "I am Belial, representative of the gods who rule you! You have been created by us, your gods, thousands of years ago. Your world is controlled by us in ways that you do not understand and that are invisible to you. From this time forward we will see to it that the human race will expand to cover the entire face of the earth." When the creature said 'human race' Seshti understood the creature to mean 'vermin.'

"There will be conflict and war for thousands of years into your future. This struggle will prepare you for the dawning of a glorious new era! We will speak to you through your gods and your priests. When you see miracles, impossible things, we are there. Remember that we see you even though you can never see us. We are watching."

The monster paused and raised his arms into the air. "Humans! (again Seshti understood 'vermin'). Understand that we are as far above you as the insects that crawl in your dirt!" Belial lowered his arms. "Know that in four years a mountain tribe will come forth from the north to lay waste to your cities and to rule you for 600 years. They come with the blessing of your gods. You will fight and many will be killed, for that suits us. For centuries into the future the story of humanity will be the same. War, conflict, and also advancements in medicine and technology (here was a concept Seshti could not understand), to allow you to breed more efficiently. And to kill each other more efficiently!" Belial roared with laughter.

The monster then turned to Abi-ramu, who cowered behind the statue of Marduk immediately behind him. "Human! Come forth!"

Abi-ramu, hunched over, humbled himself before the great creature. Like magic, three clay tablets appeared in the monster's clawed hand. "Vermin, while the others feast and indulge themselves, you and your minions will distribute the tablets to all of the delegates."

Belial stared at Abi-ramu. "You have made the copies as I have instructed?"

Abi-ramu, shaking, nodded affirmatively.

The monster turned back to the assembly, still holding the three tablets. "These are your orders! They contain instructions on hygiene, the proper preparation of food, and most important, ritual sacrifice to the gods. You will obey them to the letter, especially the rituals for sacrifice. These ceremonies will allow your priests to communicate with us. Without these instructions your race will never breed properly. Pay attention to the construction of the statues that represent your gods, for these will help your priests and your initiates to communicate with us. Humans! None of you is to leave the city until you have signed for your tablets and carried them with you to your home villages."

Belial then raised his arms to the heavens. "Let the feast begin!" It then turned to the cage, unnoticed by everyone. A black liquid ran from the creature's mouth as it moved quickly to the cowering children. Suddenly, with one swipe of its left paw, it ripped open the door to the cage and impaled one of the children. The creature drank the child's blood and pointed its blood-soaked muzzle to the sky in ecstasy.

Seshti heard angry shouts from the front row of delegates. Several of them rushed the monster, but they were unarmed. Casually, with a careless sweep of its right paw, Belial struck the charging men and sent them, broken, into the crowd. Another charge, and the same result. The delegates stared in horror at the screaming children on the stage and their mutilated companions. Fear resonated to the back of the temple and touched each of the representatives, rooting them to the spot. Seshti, at the very back, was horrified and frightened out of his wits. He fled the temple.

Belial watched the scurrying little human and was pleased. The creature emanated stark raving fear. He fed upon it, as he was feeding upon the emotions of all present. That was what these pathetic rabble had been bred for: to provide the life energy that his people needed to survive. In the back of his mind Belial considered the hominid genetic alteration program. It was necessary to establish the select bloodlines and the priests to lead them. The twelve bloodlines would be susceptible to Tau archetypes and the psychic suggestibility that would enable communication with them. These bloodlines would have special knowledge, but only enough to generate a feeling of superiority over their fellows. The rest of this rabble would follow their leaders. It was glorious! Millennia of feeding and then, at precisely the right moment, the planet would be theirs to harvest. Belial saw thousands of years into the future, after the population had grown into the billions. It would be the greatest Harvest in recorded history. He knew that this program had worked before and would work again. Belial turned back to the gathering of humans.

Seshti, maddened with fear, turned his head in flight and saw the monster turn once more to the cage. He ran to his room in the hostel, grabbed his traveling bag, and fled the city. He would rush home and immediately move his family to the west and to the north. To Aram, to the great city of Damascus, in what is now modern day Syria. He would raise goats and chickens and teach his children compassion and love. He would try to forget that evil, unspeakable thing at Kish.

But Seshti knew he could never forget.

Part III – NEW YORK

Chapter 8

Thom Madigan was flying back to Chicago from a meeting in Shanghai on a hot Sunday in June. He suddenly thought of Darcy. He would call Royalty and arrange to have dinner with his favorite companion. After that first disastrous date he had been afraid the girl would shun him. Chantelle had assured him that the girl harbored no ill-feelings toward him. Her revulsion had stemmed from an incident in her past, when her father had raped her. Madigan shuddered, remembering what Chantelle had told him about her home life. What kind of a man would want to have sex with his own daughter?

He thought about Darcy and their second meeting four years ago. Parkinson would have sent her to him, willing or not. But it wouldn't have worked. That was the problem with women: they always got things on their own terms. He was not the kind of man who wanted to force his attentions on a woman. He wanted her to come to him willingly, even eagerly. How do you arrange something like that with a woman? He had never been able to make it work. As CEO he could issue orders, confident that they would be attended to. He had gotten used to his wishes being fulfilled. But you can't order women around. He had found that out for certain after the second of his two failed marriages.

He remembered that second meeting with Darcy because it had been an epiphany. He had to humble himself, get outside himself and just BE with her. That experience had helped him immensely at work. He was no longer as stressed and was able to think more clearly. Madigan shook his head, unbelieving. An 18-year-old girl had shown him that! After that they had a number of successful evenings. He had become infatuated with her. Not so much in a man-woman way (well yes, that for sure) but in a more person-to-person way.

At that time he wondered if she had the same effect on others. Was it just him? Later, Parkinson told him that she had been consort to some very powerful men in business during the past five years.

Madigan dialed Royalty from his cell phone. "Royalty Services, Chantelle speaking. How may I help you?"

"Hello Chantelle, this is Thom Madigan."

"Hello Thom!" Chantelle replied enthusiatically. Madigan was delighted to hear real pleasure in her voice.

"I'm going to be in town this evening. I'd like to see that delightful girl, Darcy Regier. Is she available?"

"I'm afraid that Darcy has left the agency." Chantelle spoke with real regret. "But we have a number of other girls who might be suitable."

Thom felt as if he had been kicked in the stomach. "Left? She's left you?" He shouldn't feel like this about a call girl, but he did.

"Yes, Mr. Madigan. As you know, we sign our courtesans to five year contracts. Very often the girls want to return for at least one more term. But Darcy felt restless. I don't even think she knew why she wanted to leave. Holderness was very upset. She was one of his favorites." Mine too, Chantelle thought.

There was no response. Chantelle waited for thirty seconds and said, "Mr. Madigan?"

"I'm sorry, I was trying to gather my thoughts." He paused again, startled at the intensity of his disappointment. He had learned, as a hard-ass CEO of one of America's most important corporations, to quickly move on. "Yes, I would like to see one of your girls tonight. Preferably a young one. Make it clear to her that no sex is involved. I just want to be with a beautiful woman and enjoy her company. You know the kind I like."

Whatever happened tonight, he was going to find Darcy. There was something special about that girl and he knew she had no family to speak of. Only a drunken father. He would find her and who knows ... something might happen. Meanwhile he would try to enjoy his evening; it would cost the company plenty.

"I think we have three girls that would be suitable," Chantelle was saying. "Call us from the airport. We'll send one of the Rolls' to pick you up."

Thom smiled, pleased despite his irritation about Darcy. "Do you still have that blue Rolls by any chance?"

"Yes sir, and it's available."

"Good! I'll be arriving at O'Hare in twenty five minutes."

When Madigan arrived at the airport a driver and a shiny blue Rolls Royce awaited him. "1957?" he asked the driver.

"Almost," the man smiled. He was about 25, medium height, and dressed formally in an expensive suit with gold cufflinks and real leather shoes that were shined to a high gloss. "1959. Isn't she a beaut?"

"Indeed she is. I'll be meeting another beauty shortly."

The driver grinned and put his hand to his heart. "Oh, if only."

Thom was sympathetic. "Don't despair kid. I can set you up."

The driver shook his head. "No sir, thanks for the offer. The rules are strict. No employee may fraternize with the women while on duty. Under any circumstances. I knew it when I took this job, but I'm having second thoughts now."

"I can imagine." The driver opened the side door and let Thom in the back seat. "All those beautiful women and you can't touch them."

Rick couldn't have agreed more. "We're not allowed to talk to them, even in the car." It was a good thing Parkinson never found out about his extracurricular activities with Darcy when she had first joined the agency. Back then he was just 19 and Darcy was the most beautiful woman he had ever laid eyes on. Fortunately not even Royalty cared to monitor the activities of its employees during their off time.

"How can they stop you from talking to the girls in the car?"

The driver pointed to a very small black object above Thom's head. "That's a video camera. There are five of them in each car."

Unusual, Thom thought. Was it thoroughness or paranoia? Madigan wondered about the personality of Holderness Parkinson. He had heard whispers that the man was dangerous and slightly off his rocker. Then he began to get excited about the evening and the woman he was about to meet.

"How do you keep these expensive toys from rusting in these brutal Chicago winters?"

The driver smiled. "Call me Rick if you'd like. Every six months the vehicle is detailed and rust-proofed. We have a special order line to the company and a service tech who has trained in Great Britain. Any parts we need are shipped air cargo. It's horribly expensive but Royalty charges enough for their services."

They chatted for the half hour drive from the airport to the old Royalty building near Grant Park.

Thom spent a pretty good evening with a young lady named Chantrice, a tall African American woman. He didn't care what color they were or how tall they were, as long as they were women, smart, and could make him feel like a man.

Afterward he signed the invoice for an extremely expensive evening. Chantelle interviewed him. Thom responded positively but there was still a vague dissatisfaction. Chantrice had been wonderful but there was something missing. He asked to see the man himself and was granted an interview with Holderness Parkinson in his spacious office.

Madigan looked around the room and felt like he had been transported two hundred years back in time. The room had dark cherry paneling and the walls were filled with oil paintings of famous men. An old-fashioned gold telephone sat atop Parkinson's solid oak desk, looking like it had been the first one ever made. Parkinson's desk did have a keyboard and a huge monitor. Thom turned to the wall behind him and saw several large monitors hung on the wall. It was a strange combination of modernity and old-fashionedness.

Thom decided to be blunt. "Why did you let Darcy Regier go?" He spoke more harshly than he intended.

Parkinson's eyebrows raised a millimeter and he smiled with that upper-crust coolness that instantly depresses pretension. "I don't run an agency based on indentured servitude," he replied politely. "My girls are free to go when they have fulfilled their contracts with my agency."

"Do you know where she is?" Madigan asked.

"I believe she is living downstate, in the university town of Midland," Parkinson replied. "Yes, I feel her loss just as deeply as you do. There is some quality to the girl that draws ones attention. She possesses a certain ... *elan.*"

"Yes, that's it." Madigan replied with excitement. "I don't know what it is, Parkinson, but I intend to find out."

Parkinson pulled out a desk drawer and retrieved a small, gold-leaf covered book. He flipped through the pages. "I know of a discreet and reputable detective agency with, ah, connections. If you call this number they will track the girl down." He sighed and met the eyes of his client. "I have wanted to talk to Darcy for over a year but I haven't. I felt it would be an intrusion on her privacy and the breaking of a promise I gave her. I am glad that you have decided to contact her. If you would keep me informed as to developments?"

Parkinson rose, signaling that he wished to end the interview.

"Of course," Madigan said. "Thank you for your time. I will be seeing you again."

Thom Madigan entered the car that would take him back to the Fairmont Hotel. He felt as if some of the strings of his life were being pulled in another direction, away from business. Toward what?

Chapter 9

On Monday night Jake Holden sat at the main bar of the Cats Meow, a downtown Chicago nightclub. It was crowded as usual with high-class drunks, beautiful women, executives from some of the downtown law offices, losers, pimps, off-duty cops, ward heelers, an Alderman, and a couple of made guys. Just a typical Chicago titty bar, Jake thought, and laughed. He was supposed to go on duty at midnight. His job was to keep an eye on the Black Fighters, a new south side gang that was starting to deal in Outfit territory.

An hour ago Holden had seen the Chief of Police go up the stairs to the back rooms for a little conference with Luca Carcelli. Hintzman was accompanied by a funny looking little guy with dark skin and big eyes.

His drink tasted awful and his cigarette even worse. He was chain smoking again. His lungs felt like the day he had sanded drywall for ten straight hours on one of his father's union jobs.

Jake shouted across the bar. "Hey Bobby! Why is my life so screwed up?"

The bartender grinned. He was one of three at the main bar; a large, thick, burly man with a bullet head, big hands, and a right hook that could fell an elephant. "You got it good Jake, you just don't know it."

"Fuck," Jake muttered. It had all started with that girl from Joliet, what was her name? Darcy. Darcy Regier. The girl that got raped by her old man. He'd made a video with her and then had to send her off to Royalty. He made a pile of money on it. Everybody said how bad it was, but everybody had a copy. Then he got noticed by Luca Carcelli, one of the Outfit's top bosses. Then it was "do this, do that" and what could he do? He was nothing, a skinny kid from the streets with no life and no future. He had to do what he was told. Jake was sick of it.

"Hey Bobby, you remember that porno film I made six years ago?"

"You never made no porno film," Bobby joked. "That was an exercise video!" A couple of the guys around the bar hooted and guffawed.

Jake ignored them. He was too far down the totem pole to object to anything. Just a lousy runner after all these years. "There was a girl on that video. The most beautiful girl I ever saw."

Bobby grunted something unintelligible and began to make drinks. In quick succession he made a martini, a daiquiri, and two PushUps. The PushUp was a new drink with orange juice, coconut milk, and gin. Jake timed him and it only took six seconds. The man's dexterity fascinated him. The big bartender's hands were blurs as he picked up bottles and measured by feel. When he was done he had four drinks on the bar and they looked perfect.

"I'm gonna go talk to Luca. I want him to see that video."

"He already seen it once. Aint that enough?"

Jake replied sullenly. "That chick is a money-maker, I can feel it. I made a pile off her before that fuckhead Parkinson grabbed her. Then he made a lot bigger pile. I think she'd make a good lay for Luca, and money for me. I'm gonna find her."

"Sure, go ahead. What will you do with her when you get her?" Bobby spoke derisively.

"I'll take her out of this crummy town and make some real porn videos. California, that's the place! It's the center of the porn industry."

Bobby snorted. "Don't be a dingus." He made more drinks and effortlessly slid them down the smooth, shiny wood surface. "Luca needs you to keep track of those gangs down the street. He aint never gonna let you go anywhere."

"We'll see about that." Jake stamped out his cigarette on the bar, leaving a brown stain on the lacquered surface.

Bobby spoke menacingly. "You better watch that kid. You ruin my bar like that and I'll leave a mark on you too, only a bigger one. Tomorrow morning you come early and fix it."

"Yeah, yeah, don't worry." Jake was afraid of what he'd done. Damn his temper! "I got mad that's all."

"I been telling you to get control of yourself for years. You never listen."

"I'm going upstairs. Gimme one of those gin and tonics. A big one."

"You gotta pay. Luca says no more credit."

"Fuck!" Jake was steaming now. He reached into his pocket, found a ten, and tossed it onto the bar. "Here's your blood money. Gimme the drink."

Bobby mixed the drink. Jake drained the glass. "Keep the change."

"There aint no change."

"Fuck! Did the prices go up again?"

"Watch your mouth in here Jake. The prices always go up. You better calm down if you're going up to see Luca. He don't like interruptions and he don't like his employees flying off the handle."

One of the guys at the bar, a small-time hustler, laughed. "Yeah, Jake's an employee!"

Jake sat sullenly on the bar stool. He fiddled with his glass and tried to get his temper under control. With what he knew he could create a lot of trouble. He knew a lot more than people thought he did. Everybody thought he was stupid but he studied history. He studied the Outfit. Back in the 1990s they'd redistricted the First Ward, Capone's old territory, out of existence. Operation Gambat had indicted Alderman Roti and D'Arco Jr., the Outfit's man in Springfield. The Outfit lost control of Chicago's judges. Then in 2005 the Family Secrets operation had cut off some important heads. Everybody said the Outfit was finished. But when the boys got out of jail they expanded the business into the drug trade. The Outfit became much less visible. That didn't mean they had lost influence. Far from it.

Jake knew that the Outfit traditionally stayed away from drug trafficking. The boys preferred to earn from loan-sharking, online gambling operations, and insinuating their crews into legitimate businesses, gradually taking them over. Now they were dealing too and were fighting the gangs for control of the drug trade. The Outfit had now expanded their influence across the country. They had mellowed somewhat. Killing people had put them under too much pressure from law enforcement, and was now discouraged. That was smart. But some of the street gangs didn't think that way. They offed people, including Outfit dealers and runners.

On one hand Jake was proud to be associated with the biggest crime organization in the country. The Outfit now had affiliations in twenty states. On the other hand he hated being low man on the totem pole. Nevertheless he made it his business to know names and places and operations. Jake would have been shocked if he knew that he was probably the world's leading authority on the Chicago crime organization.

Jake glanced gloomily down at his empty glass. The world was filthy. He raised his head and looked out from the bar through the large front windows. People were walking by with smiles on their faces, totally oblivious. These so-called citizens had no idea what was going on.

Jake shook his head and threw off his morbid mood. He had to do something about his life. It had to be now or he'd remain stuck here forever, like a butterfly pinned to an insect exhibit.

He slid off the bar stool and walked slowly upstairs, hoping that Carcelli would be free to give him a few seconds. As he walked up the wide, plushly carpeted stairs he saw the Chief of Police come out of a smoke filled room at the top of the stairs. Chief Hintzman was accompanied by a small, dark-skinned little man who looked like he could model for death threats. Hintzman's face was pale. The small man's face bore the expression of one who had just given unpleasant orders and who expected immediate compliance. As the two men passed Jake on the stairs, Holden threw a glance at the small man beside Hintzman. Jake received a severe shock. The man's eyes were yellow slits. When he gazed at Jake for a split-second his soul froze. The man's expression was utterly cold and completely without emotion. He'd been around two of Carcelli's stone-cold killers once, but this guy made them look like Donald Duck. The Chief was normally a gruff and blustery man. Today he was subdued and fearful. Jake noticed that Hintzman kept himself as far away from his companion as possible on the curved stairway. Jake wrenched his gaze away from the little man and rushed up the stairs.

Jake reached the top of the stairs, shaken. He tried to compose himself. He could see smoke coming from one of the rooms so he poked his head in. Luca Carcelli was seated at a table smoking a cigar. His profile was turned to Jake's left. It looked like Carcelli was in a bad mood.

Jake spoke deferentially. "Mr. Carcelli, can I have a word with you?"

Carcelli turned in his chair to face him. The capo was probably 65 or so, with grayish-white hair, a big head and big ears. Carcelli had slightly protruding eyes that made him look like a rageaholic lemur. Jake was shocked. He had seen Carcelli's expression just before the older man turned to him. It was the face of a man who was terrified. As soon as the capo saw him he became angry. "Whattaya doing, coming up here?"

"I had an idea how we could make some money," Jake replied.

"I already make a lot of money!" Jake had the distinct impression that he was angry at someone else and was taking it out on him. "What do you know about making money, ya little shit?"

Jake had to hold back his temper. Carcelli was known for being stupid. The only reason he wasn't a garbage man was because he got made. He was true 100% dark Italian, and that was his ticket. Something had clearly upset him though. Jake knew he had to tread very carefully. "Sir, do you remember the video with that amazing girl in it? The one that sold over 20,000 copies?"

Carcelli's eyes lit up. "You mean the girl we gave to old Holderness Parkinson?"

"Yes sir, that's the one." So the stupid jerk remembered. Darcy was his girl but as soon as the Outfit found out about his deal with Royalty they demanded a piece of the pie. A very large piece, Jake remembered sourly. He tried to keep the irritation off his face.

"God she was a sweet piece of ass, wasn't she?"

"I thought, boss, that we could pick her up and use her in a bunch of videos." Jake tried to keep his excitement down and his voice from squeaking. "They'd sell so fast we couldn't keep 'em on the shelves. We'd sell them all over the internet. At twenty bucks a pop, that's easy money."

Carcelli's eyes showed interest.

"I could make the videos, I've done it before," Jake suggested. "We could even make 'em in California."

Carcelli rose from his chair and looked at Jake with contempt. "You? Make videos? You'd fuck 'em up." The capo sat down again and rubbed his chin, his eyes staring past Jake into space. "But it's a good idea, kid. For once you actually turned out to be useful. I'll have Nitti find her and pick her up."

"But—"

"Get outta here asswipe!" Carcelli waved his hand angrily and Jake quickly scurried from the room. The capo held grudges and acted on them.

Jake was incensed that Carcelli was going to steal his idea and his girl again. He ran blindly down the stairs and collided with a girl bringing up drinks. "You stupid jerk!" she cried, watching the liquor stain the beautiful carpet.

Jake tried to act as if he had done nothing. If Carcelli saw that stain .... He walked as slowly as he could out of the building, hoping someone wouldn't stop him. Fortunately the place was too crowded for that. In half an hour it would be time for him to go on street duty. Fuck that. Jake ran to the parking garage three blocks over to get his car. He'd leave first thing tomorrow, after his shift. No, tonight. He'd blow town and put 500 miles between him and Carcelli. Jake drove back to his apartment to get his stuff, thankful for the first time in his life to be a nobody.

Nobody would miss him, nobody would care. He was going to get that girl before Nitti found her and ruined his plans.

Upstairs, Luca Carcelli sat thoughtfully. He had two calls to make; one good, and the other made him feel sick. He opened his cell and spoke. "Guido, get me Nitti. Yeah, right away."

Ten seconds later his phone rang. The sour face of Frank Nitti III appeared on his screen. Nitti claimed to be the grandson of Joseph Nitti, the adopted child of Frank "The Enforcer" Nitti. "Hey Frankie, I need you to do something."

"No problem boss, I aint busy. What is it?"

"I need you to pick up a girl. You remember that video I showed you back about six years ago? The one made by that little scumbag Jake Holden with the hot girl in it?"

"Oh yeah, that one. It's a piece of garbage but I still watch it sometimes."

"Yeah. I thought it might be a good idea to bring her here. We could make some more videos with her. Some good ones. They'd sell like crazy and I'd give you 30% of the action if you set everything up."

"Forty."

"Thirty five."

"C'mon boss, give me a break."

"Thirty seven fifty goddamit, and consider yourself lucky."

"All right. You got any idea where she is?"

"Aint got a clue. Somebody over there at Royalty might know."

"Good idea. I'll track her down and bring her to you as soon as I can."

Carcelli hung up. He reached into his pocket and brought out one of the disposable phones he always carried with him. These phones were good for only one call and they were almost untraceable. He dialed another number, a secure, encrypted private line to his contact. He didn't know where he was calling or the guy he spoke to, other than his name was "Joey." Whenever he needed product, or he had a problem, he had to call this guy.

"Joey, it's Luca."

The voice on the other end was curt. "This is a bad time Carcelli. Make it quick."

"Fuck off Joey, you make time. Now listen. Some fuckstick just came up here with the Chief of Police. He said he was from some four-letter outfit I never heard of. That's your department, so I'm calling you. He wants us to knock off an Alderman because he's been investigating some pedophile ring in the city. If I don't do it, he says, we don't get more product. I got no sympathy for child molesters. You tell that sonofabitch we won't do it, no way."

The voice on the other end paused a moment. "Is the Alderman Barry Courvall?"

"Yeah, that's the guy. I got no beef with him."

"I think I know what that's all about. You better leave it alone and do what he says."

"Why shouldn't we stop a pedophile ring? The filthy perverted bastards, we oughta kill them all and do a favor to the human race. I got nothin' against that Alderman anyway."

Joey was sympathetic. "I feel the same as you do. But you don't have any idea of the forces involved here, Luca, or how your product gets to you."

"I don't care how I get it as long as I get it."

"You better keep it that way Carcelli. The more you know the scarier it gets."

Luca suspected that Joey was some kind of intelligence agent, probably with a high security clearance. He seemed to know a lot about the world outside the United States, and how things worked. "Fuck that Joey, I aint hittin' that Alderman. You can tell that little shit where to stick it."

Joey sighed. This guy Carcelli was valuable but he was a stupid pain in the ass. "I'm merely pointing out that you are dealing with very powerful people. Let me look into it Luca. I'll get back to you. If this guy is who I think he is, it's very unusual for one of them to get involved in, ah, the field. This must be a ball-breaker emergency. My advice is to do what he says."

"Yeah, but you better give me a damn good reason why!"

Joey replied testily. "Let me give you a little lesson, and I'll make it quick because I'm busy. Number one, you know all about the Black Nobility, right? You are a bloodline descendant. Your line probably goes back at least to the oligarchic families of Venice and Genoa, Italy—"

"How do you know so much about my bloodline?"

"Let's just say it's a little hobby of mine. Your line, Carcelli, goes back to at least the 12th century when your ancestral families held privileged trading monopolies. It probably goes back to the Roman Empire. That's why you got made."

"Yeah."

"As far as I know there are about a dozen important bloodlines on the planet. You are in the powerful position you are in mainly because you are a member of one of these ancient lines. It's the same in the corridors of power all over the world. In business, in entertainment, in politics, in crime, you name it. You can be a nobody and get to a high position by sheer ability and hard work. But when you get high enough you always bump into one of these bloodlines. Just like a knockaround guy is never going to get made, because he doesn't have the right history. *Capisci*?"

"Yeah, but where is this going? Are you going to call off that fuckstick or not?"

"Just shut up and listen Luca. You might learn something. I'm trying to explain."

"OK, hurry up."

Carcelli heard fingers drumming on the desk. When Joey resumed, it was with a sharpness in his voice. "Behind the mob in Chicago there's your connection here, to ... never mind. You might think I'm hot shit Luca but I'm just a tool somewhere down the pyramid. I take orders and see that they are carried out because if I get out of line, something is going to happen to me and my family. That's how it goes, right? In Chicago and in DC and everywhere else where there's power."

"Jesus Joey, get to the point."

"The point is, dumbass, that in the matter of product you and I take our orders from someone else. Some of the guys giving those orders are really dark. That pedophile ring your Alderman Courvall is investigating, that's part of it. He's getting too close. That's why you have to get rid of him."

"I don't like it Joey."

"Neither do I Luca, but just see what happens if you don't. By the way, who was the guy who came in with Hintzman?"

"I don't know. I was about to clock him when he looked at me and squashed me like a bug."

"What did he look like?"

"He was a dark, scary little guy, with oily black hair. When he got pissed his eyes got really big and yellow and the pupils went vertical, not horizontal. Like the eyes of an animal. He was cold, Joey, really cold, and he scared the living shit out of me."

There was no response at the other end for several seconds. Joey felt that his contact had gone stone cold with fear. "Joey? You still there?"

"Yes. Listen Luca, here's some advice. Don't fuck with this guy. Whatever he told you do it. You understand?"

Joey's voice sounded frozen and numb. "Yeah. But who is he?"

"I don't know for sure. You definitely don't want to cross him."

Luca was getting the creeps. "For christsakes Joey. Do I get my product or not?"

"As soon as we read in the paper that Alderman Courvall is out of this world."

Carcelli closed his phone. Things were getting too complicated.

Speedway gas station on W. North, Chicago

Two days later Alderman Barry Courvall was on his way to deliver a speech at the Puerto Rican Arts Alliance on Humbolt. He stopped to gas up at the Speedway on W. North. He pulled back out into traffic and made a left onto N. Central Park. At that moment a truck marked "Costigan Construction" came barreling down Central Park at over 60 miles an hour, running a red light.

Courvall looked in his side mirror. He saw the truck and slammed on his brakes. It was too late. The truck smashed into Courvall's driver's side door, crushing it. The alderman was killed instantly.

CHAPTER **10**

DARCY was happy. She had been living with Marcus for over a year now. Marcus graduated last year and took title to the house. They had worked out the financial arrangements. Marcus would pay the mortgage because it was his house. Darcy would pay the utilities. Her $15,000 in savings had dwindled down to $4,000. She knew she would have to find a new direction for her life, and a job. But for now it was OK.

The day after Nitti's talk with Carcelli, Darcy was in Marcus' office, gazing at his big monitor screen. "What are you doing now?"

Marcus was researching the markets. It was a hot summer day in July. He had the air conditioning on as low as it would go. Marcus glanced up and saw Darcy's beautiful face above his. She smelled wonderful. He leaned up and kissed her cheek, then went back to his computer.

"You didn't answer my question."

Marcus explained for the dozenth time. "This is what I do to make money. My father was a securities analyst at one of the Chicago banks. He taught me how to day trade. He taught me all about banking and investing and finance. I practiced for over a year without investing any real money and did well. I developed my own trading formula, but it requires a lot of work and study."

"How much do you make?"

"This past year, about $50,000 profit."

"Wow. That's great!" She studied the screen for several minutes. It was filled with mathematical formulas. "I don't understand any of it. What are those equations for? How did you learn all that stuff? They don't teach it in high school."

Marcus chuckled. "They sure don't. My dad taught me after school."

"But how did you learn it? "You're only 18."

Marcus shrugged. "Almost 19. I don't know Darcy, my mind just naturally gets it. I read these symbols like you read words."

Darcy placed her foot on the chair and swiveled it so that Marcus was facing her. "Who are you, Marcus Riley? Are you some kind of genius? There's something about you that is ... I don't know ... different."

"And you aren't different?"

"Me?" Darcy was astonished. "I'm just a girl from the gutter who learned how to be an expensive whore."

Marcus ignored her self-deprecating comment. It was an attitude he would have to deal with, but not now. "You genuinely don't think you are unusual at all, do you?"

"Of course not."

"Then why have you never found any guy you could be interested in? Other than me, the weirdo?"

Darcy was speechless for a full minute. "I don't know. I never thought about it I guess."

"You are the most beautiful girl I've ever seen. Men look at you all the time. They come up to you even when I'm with you. You have had your pick ever since you left Joliet. Somehow it never seems to work out, does it?"

"That's right. But there's a simple explanation: we were meant for each other." Darcy spoke matter-of-factly. "It's normal, it happens all the time."

Marcus drew her into his lap and turned her face toward him. "Believe me, you are unusual, Darcy. I can feel it and so can everybody else. I have this ... ability, to see information. It's like a web of light in my head that connects things together. It's one of the reasons I am so good at trading the market. I also see people in my web. I see you standing outside the normal run of life. You are special somehow. It's one of the reasons I like you, it's not just your physical beauty."

"Really?" Darcy jumped up from the wheeled chair and kicked it, sending Marcus across the floor to the other side of the room. "Come catch me!" Darcy turned and raced toward the front door.

"Stay inside!" Marcus shouted.

Darcy had already reached the door and was through it, letting hot, humid air (and a bunch of bugs) into the cool, air conditioned living room. Marcus wrenched himself out of the chair. He rushed out of the house like an Australian sheepdog chasing an errant sheep. He saw that Darcy was racing down the street, running as fast as she could along the sidewalk. Marcus had to stop to close the door. That pissed him off because Darcy was a fast runner and he didn't know what kind of mischief she was likely to get into. As he ran down the street after her he felt like a parent chasing a wayward child. *She's* supposed to be the adult. She's four years older.

"Darcy, where are you going?" he shouted behind her.

"Follow me and find out! If you can catch me!"

Marcus groaned and continued his pursuit. Darcy had reached the corner. He saw an oncoming car not ten feet from where she was.

"Darcy!" He was scared out of his mind. If she took two more steps she'd be right in its path. "Darcy!" he screamed, louder than before.

Darcy abruptly turned on her right foot, shoved open the door to Stacy's, the local market, and vanished into the building.

It took Marcus another twenty seconds to reach the corner. When he entered the store he saw Darcy standing by a rack of magazines, looking full of mischief.

"Darcy what are you doing?"

"You never would have caught me if I didn't want you to." Her eyes shined with devilry.

"You almost got yourself killed!" People started to turn their heads.

"I did not. You're talking too loud, silly, and upsetting the customers."

"Tell me you saw that car about to run the stop sign."

"What car?" Darcy's expression was innocent.

"I knew it. You didn't even see it."

Darcy drew herself up to her full five and one half feet. "Of course I did Marcus."

Marcus couldn't tell whether she was lying or telling the truth. It was one of the things he liked about Darcy: he couldn't read her like he could other people. She was deliberately trying to provoke him, he knew that much. He stepped toward her at the magazine rack. He was just about to sweep her off her feet and carry her home when she stepped suddenly into his arms and kissed him. By this time the entire store was observing their little tableau. The store manager came out of the back office. "Hey you kids. This isn't a brothel, get out of here!"

Marcus felt embarrassed and tried to break the kiss but Darcy wouldn't let him. She was determined to get full satisfaction. One of the store patrons laughed, and then another, and a woman clapped. Soon the whole store was laughing. Darcy finally broke the kiss, arranged her hair, and bowed. "I apologize for our boisterous and unseemly conduct. But I had to teach my boyfriend a lesson." She spoke in her most cultured Royalty voice.

The woman who began the clapping nodded approvingly. "That's the girl. Get him in harness now and you won't have any trouble later on."

"A lesson?" Marcus cried. "What lesson?"

Darcy flounced away and walked to the door. She turned her head and gave him a come-hither look, then raced out of the store.

"Darcy!" He turned to the assembled shoppers and shrugged. "She's like a little girl." He raced off after her.

When they got home, panting, Marcus was concerned. "Tell me what that was all about."

Darcy swayed her hips and walked toward the bedroom. "I was just trying to get you in the mood. You spend hours in front of that computer and you never notice me."

Marcus followed and closed the bedroom door. "I always notice you. That wasn't why you staged that little performance."

"You're not very bright," she said, lying on the bed and opening her arms. "But I'll take you anyway."

The next day Darcy received a text message. It said, "DARCY, JAKE REMEMBER ME? I GOT A BUSINESS PROPOSAL FOR YOU. COMING SOON. JAKE HOLDEN."

God no, she thought. Not that rat! A wave of nausea swept over her as she recalled her Joliet past. How did he find me? How did he get my number? What does he want? More porno flicks, that had to be it. Was she never to live down that stupid video? In a panic she got into her BMW and drove around the city for hours until she felt drained and apathetic.

When she got home Marcus met her in the foyer. "I was just about to go out to the Damascus. You want anything?"

"I'm not hungry, no." She went into her room. There were three bedrooms in the house. Marcus had his office and she had her private space where she kept all of her expensive clothing, her books, and some valuable things Holderness had given her.

She heard a knock on the door. "Darcy, are you OK?"

"I don't know Marcus. I need some private time."

"OK. I'll be back in half an hour with some food."

When Marcus came back Darcy was still in her room. "Hey, I've got some babbaghanouz. Come out and let's eat."

"No thanks, I'm not feeling well."

Marcus could tell she was close to tears. "Can I do anything?"

"No! Please just leave me alone."

Marcus sighed. He decided to eat and then watch a little of the White Sox game.

The next day Darcy's phone rang. Nervously, she checked the caller. It was Thom Madigan, her former client! As the phone continued to ring she considered ignoring it but decided that postponing the inevitable would just make things worse.

"Hello?"

"Hello, is this Darcy Regier?"

"Yes, who is this?"

"Now Darcy, you wouldn't put off an old friend would you?"

Darcy sighed. She knew he'd recognize her voice. She had over twenty evenings with him over her five year tenure with Royalty. "Hello Thom how are you?"

"A lot better since I found you." Thom was cheerful.

Darcy cut right to the chase. "Thom, why did you call? You know that you and I can mean nothing to each other."

"I beg to differ sweetheart. I'm not calling for a date or anything like that. I just want to talk to you, person to person."

Darcy was relieved. She really didn't want to hurt the man's feelings but she wanted no part of her former life. She did not want to meet anyone she had known while at Royalty. "But Thom, why? I retired from Royalty because I wanted a life I could control."

"I've asked myself that very question a number of times Darcy. I don't have an answer. I just know that somehow you are important to me. I feel as if our life paths are going somewhere together. Whatever it is it's important. Both of us are mixed up in it."

Ever since Jake texted yesterday she had felt a strange feeling, as if her life *was* about to go in a radically different direction. She was looking forward to change. Living with Marcus was fun but her life with him was going nowhere. Just like at Royalty, somebody else had control of her wellbeing. Marcus made the money and owned the house. She was basically just a call girl again with only one client. Should she confide in Thom? Of all her clients he knew her best. He was older, not like Marcus, and experienced. "It's funny you should say that Thom. I have been feeling something like that too."

"I knew it." Thom was excited. "It will be an adventure."

Despite herself, she giggled. The old man sounded just like a little boy. "Will it?"

"When can we talk?"

She knew that if she went out with Thom, Marcus would be offended. In many ways he was so mature but in reality he was just a kid. "All right Thom. I can meet you at the French Café on Friday at noon." Marcus was great but he didn't have any buddies. He was a loner and stayed in his office most of the time, researching his stupid stocks and securities. The hours from 12 to 2 on weekdays were safe. He never stirred out of his office during that time.

"Where is that?"

"It's in downtown Midland on the corner of Fifth and Liberty."

"OK. Today is Tuesday. I should be able to get away for an afternoon to talk. I'll see you Friday at noon."

Frank Nitti the Third called the Royalty number.

"Royalty Services, Chantelle speaking."

"Let me speak to Richard Botsford."

"Who is calling please?"

Fuck. He forgot about that straight-laced bitch receptionist. "This is Franklin Nittsfield." Nitti spoke in his best polite society voice with his polite society alias. "I'm looking for a driver for a freelance job. Richard has worked for me before."

This was the standard line he always used to contact Rick. Royalty drivers often did freelance work on their off-time. His request shouldn't cause the nosy bitch to be suspicious.

"One moment please, I'll route your call to the garage."

"Royalty Services, Rick speaking."

"Ricky boy, guess who?"

"Nitti! What do you want?"

"That's no way to talk to your buddy Franklin Ricky boy. I need some information."

"What kind of information?"

"There was a doll used to work for you guys, named Darcy Regier. The Boss wants to know where she is."

Shit! He wasn't going to betray Darcy, no way. Especially not to that criminal Carcelli. "Sorry Nitti. I don't know where she is. She blew town last year and nobody knows where she went off to."

Nitti modulated his voice to a more threatening tone. "Don't fuck with me Botsford. We happen to know from our informants that you know where the bitch is."

Rick cursed himself for ever getting involved with these crooks. When he was 18, just before he got the Royalty job, he'd done a few driving jobs for a local hustler. Small-time robberies, stuff like that. Later he learned that the guy was run by Luca Carcelli, the mobster. He was just a stupid kid at the time but ever since then he'd been forced to cooperate. He was Nitti's boy; their unwilling informant at Royalty Services. He said nothing. Maybe a meteor would fall out of the sky on Nitti's ugly head.

"I aint got all day Botsford! Let me have it or you won't have that cushy job you got much longer."

"Dammit Nitti! She's in Midland, downstate. Lives in some house on the east side of town, two miles from the university. Some kid bought it from a realtor guy named Pelco. She lives with him. You can check the address with Pelco. Now go fuck yourself." He hung up, an act of impotent defiance. He felt like a coward for ratting on Darcy.

One night he asked her to marry him after handing her out of the car. He felt like a trailer park boy asking a famous movie star for an autograph. She refused, of course, but made him feel that his proposal was flattering to her. He was pretty sure that Nitti already knew where Darcy was. It was just Carcelli's way of keeping his minions groveling in the dirt.

Midland, Illinois

Two days later Marcus and Darcy got into a fight.

They were dressing to go out to dinner when Darcy's cell rang. "Oh shit," she said, and put it back in her purse. It was another one of her former clients. That big fat idiot Michael Grossman.

"Who was that?" Marcus asked.

"Nobody. Somebody from my past I don't want to talk to."

Marcus said nothing, but met her eyes skeptically.

"Don't do that Marcus. I don't like it."

"Do what?"

"Try to pry into my past. You know how much I hate it."

Marcus leaned forward. "I don't know anything about you. I want to. You can't hide from me and pretend that we have a relationship."

"Why not? I told you I was a high-priced whore. I met a lot of men and had sex with some of them. I lived in luxury. Then I had enough. End of story."

"Sorry. You can't palm me off like that. It's insulting. I'm not one of your clients you don't have to get personal with. You're not working on commission here. Who called?"

"It's none of your business! Just because you sleep with me doesn't mean I have to answer to you."

"All I asked you was a simple question. It's something even strangers ask and get answers to every day." Marcus spoke calmly. "So who called you?"

"I don't want to talk about it."

Marcus stared at Darcy but she wouldn't meet his eyes. "Was it one of your former clients?"

"Yes! It was one of my fucking former clients! Are you satisfied now?"

"No I'm not satisfied." Marcus felt something hot coming from his *tan tien*, an energy that was rising to fill his entire being.

Darcy felt like she was standing next to a geyser that was about to explode. She'd never seen Marcus like this before. Half afraid and half curious what would happen, she was silent.

"Are you going to answer my question or not?"

The energy from Marcus was getting stronger now, she could feel it.

"Who called you?"

"Fuck you Marcus. I'm not telling you."

For the first time in his life Marcus felt a welling, uncontrollable anger. He wanted to strike out. Usually in a crisis his pulse slowed and he felt a mental clarity and a heightened sense of physical strength and coordination. But the feeling was growing stronger. Through a fog of anger he remembered that his dad sometimes had these fits. Maybe it was hereditary.

Darcy took a step back, fearful. She saw Marcus' right hand open and begin to rise. Marcus, with a strong effort, calmed himself and felt the energy inside him slowly dissipate. "I really like you Darcy, but I need something more personal than just a roommate. You need to be honest with me and open up a little."

"I don't know *how* to be personal," Darcy hoped she wouldn't set him off again. "I know how to act in social situations, I know how to converse intelligently, I know a little something about fine art, and I know how to make love. That's it. That's what you get."

"I want more. I want to know about *you*."

"I just told you! Don't you get it? My father raped me when I was 14. I can't open up to people, not to anyone." Tears began to roll down her face. "I should have stayed with Holderness. He knew me and accepted me for what I am."

"I accept you for the greater person you can be." Marcus was coldly calm now. He couldn't stand it when she cried.

"Oh shut up Marcus. I have no idea what that means."

Marcus flared up again. "It means that I want you for more than just a piece of ass. Every time I try to lift you up you bring yourself back down."

"So what if I do?" Darcy was shouting now.

"One last time," Marcus demanded. "Who called you?"

Darcy silently folded her arms in front of her and looked defiant.

Marcus lost it again. "Take your stuff out of my bedroom. If you want to stay here you can sleep in your office. Apparently all you want is a roommate. That's exactly what you have now." He stormed out of the bedroom, walked into his office, and slammed the door.

Darcy felt her legs shaking. This was a side of Marcus she had never seen before. It frightened her. She went cold inside and knew she had to get out of here, out of Midland. It had to be right now.

Darcy walked back to her room and quickly packed her clothes. She went to the bedroom and collected her jewelry, grabbed her bags, and lugged them out to the car. Then she jumped into the BMW and drove out of town. After two hours on the road she realized she was traveling east on I-70. To New York.

Chapter 11

Jake Holden arrived in Midland early Friday morning. He had discovered Darcy's whereabouts through one of the Outfit's many informants. It was the way the Boss kept track of who was being naughty and who was being nice. Some of these guys were small-time just like him. One night last week he got one of them drunk at the Meow. A pickpocket who called himself Fingers.

Jake walked up to Darcy's house and looked in through the front door, which had a little piece of circular glass at the top. He had to reach up on tiptoes. He couldn't see anybody. Jake rang the bell a couple of times. After the third ring a tall guy came striding down the hall and ripped open the door. "What the fuck do you want?"

Jake was surprised. He knew that Darcy was living with some kid, but this guy was a giant with a black stubble of beard and a nasty temper.

"I'm Jake Holden, an old friend of Darcy Regier's, from Joliet." Jake moved back a step. This manchild was intimidating; he'd probably make a good bar bouncer. "I'd like to talk to her for a minute."

Marcus studied the figure on the doorstep and didn't like what he saw. A scrawny little punk dressed in worn jeans and a black leather jacket. "An old friend, huh? If you're such an old friend how come I never heard of you?" As soon as he asked the question he knew how stupid it was. Darcy never told him anything about her past.

"How should I know? Sorry to bother you. I just want to see her for five minutes."

"Well, you're out of luck. She left here two days ago and I haven't seen her or heard from her since."

"Fuck!" It was the story of his life. Just when he thought he had a break it all fell apart.

Marcus was bitter. "I've called her 25 times in the past two days. I've left voice and text messages but she hasn't responded. So much for friendship, and that bullshit about 'we were made for each other.' What a load of crap."

Jake couldn't care less about the kid's feelings. "Where did she go?"

"How the hell should I know?" Marcus was ready to take this guy's head off.

Jake felt like a chicken about to be attacked by a pit bull but he held his ground. "She's supposed to be your girlfriend! You gotta know something—"

"Get lost, Jake Holden." Marcus slammed the door in Jake's face.

Jake stood there on the front porch, unbelieving. He hadn't even thought what might happen if he didn't see Darcy. It looked like that big kid pissed her off and the stupid chick must have skipped town. So what was he going to do now? He couldn't go back to Chicago. He'd missed two shifts already. You just didn't do that with Luca Carcelli. If he showed up now he'd be meat.

Wait a second. Fingers told him about one of the Royalty chauffeurs. This guy said that after Darcy left Royalty she might go to New York and model. Was it worth the trip? Hell, he didn't have any place to go and he'd always wanted to see the Big Apple. A city almost as corrupt as Chicago, and with more people. If Darcy was there he'd hear about it. There was something magnetic about that chick, something that attracted people. If Darcy didn't pan out there were lots of other hot women, lots of action, and a big market for good porn. Why not? He was through in Chicago anyway.

Jake got into his beat up Ford Taurus, filled up his tank, and headed for New York City.

Two hours after Jake Holden left Midland Marcus heard the doorbell ring again. The sound incensed him. He went striding toward the front door, intending to tell whoever it was to fuck off. He jerked open the door and saw three men standing on the porch. At first glance they looked like the Three Stooges in suits. Moe faced the door and two bigger guys stood behind him. Moe was a man of medium height, slightly built, wearing a perfectly tailored suit. He had a pockmarked face that looked like it had been shot at by a bunch of kids with BB-guns. Behind him stood two guys dressed in white turtlenecks and suit coats, staring off into space. "Who the fuck are you?" he asked Moe belligerently.

Frank Nitti III smiled cynically. "Whoa, kid, watch yourself there. You thinking about poppin' me?"

Marcus' mind cleared. He saw that these guys weren't comedians. They looked like well-dressed collection agents or mobsters. Mobsters were the last thing he expected and he almost laughed. "I'm so angry right now I feel like wasting all three of you." He studied the guys standing in back of Moe. Both of them were muscular beefeaters. "Now it doesn't seem like such a good idea."

Nitti laughed. "Hey that's pretty good, kid." He looked Marcus up and down and nodded his approval. "You want to come work for me? You got a good pair of shoulders and I like your attitude."

"I don't know what I want right now. My girlfriend left me and I'm torn between killing myself and killing her. If I ever find her."

"Well kid, better to kill her—what's your name anyway?"

"Marcus."

Nitti turned toward his left. "Hey Benny did you hear that? Marcus! That's a good Italian name." He turned back to face Marcus. "You Italian, kid?"

"Mostly Irish, but I've got some Italian blood, yes."

"All the better. You wanta work for me?"

"Not right now." Marcus faced Nitti and his muscle squarely and felt a welcome calmness and mental clarity. His pulse slowed. Every muscle in his body was ready to respond to danger. He didn't know what was going to happen but he was ready.

"I like your style, Marcus. Maybe we'll talk about that later." I like this kid, Nitti said to himself. He shows no fear. "I hear you're living with a girl named Darcy Regier. My boss has a business proposal for her."

Marcus ignored this. "Who are you and who are those guys?"

"I'm Franklin Nittsfield. These boys back here are Benvenuto and Guido."

"You guys are right out of Goodfellas. What could you possibly want with Darcy?"

"Never mind son, it's best you don't know. You got any idea where she went?"

Marcus' face assumed hard lines. "I have no idea, Franklin Nittsfield. I told her to move out of my bedroom because she was being stupid. I went into my office to sulk for a while. When I came out she had packed all her stuff and was gone."

Nitti laughed again. "Ya went to your room to sulk! That's a new one."

Marcus made no reply. He didn't know what to make of these guys. They looked like people you see in movies, not in real life.

"Did Darcy ever say anything about going to New York?"

"She never told me anything about herself." Marcus spoke bitterly. "That's why I got mad at her."

"Good fuck though, eh?"

Marcus glared, but was silent.

"Ho, ho! Look Guido, our big cock is scratching in the dirt. Get set." Despite himself Nitti was impressed. This man-sized kid had some kind of power; he could feel it. They said Capone possessed that kind of power. The power to sway men and get them to do what he wanted.

"All right kid we'll be goin'. I gotta ask the boss whether he wants me to keep chasin' her down."

The three men left the porch and got into a black limo that was sitting in front of the house. Marcus hadn't even noticed it. He cursed himself for being so unobservant. After the vehicle left Marcus grabbed his phone and sent Darcy a text. "WATCH IT DARCY SOME MOB GUY CAME HERE THIS MORNING LOOKING FOR YOU. BE CAREFUL MARCUS."

At 1:30 PM the doorbell rang again. "Go away!" Marcus shouted at the front door through his open office, which was at the far end of the living room. The bell kept ringing. Sighing, Marcus opened the door and saw a rotund man of medium height, about 50 or so. He had a round face that probably looked at life cheerfully during normal times. Now he was frowning. Marcus saw another black limo parked at the curb. The man spoke without introducing himself. "Where is Darcy?"

"Do you work for the Three Stooges that were just here?" Marcus was profoundly irritated.

"The Three Stooges?"

Marcus decided that this guy, whoever he was, wasn't connected with those mobsters. "You're the third person today who has asked me that question. Who the hell are you?"

"Oh, sorry. I forgot my manners. It's just that – well, all right I suppose I should introduce myself. I'm Thom Madigan, CEO of Pantheon Plastics."

"What is a corporate CEO doing here in Midland, asking about an obscure girl half his age?"

Madigan flushed. "Ah, I guess it might seem a little strange to you. I'm one of Darcy's former clients at Royalty Services."

"Are you the guy who keeps bothering Darcy, calling her all the time?" Marcus took a half-step toward Thom on the porch.

Madigan backed off. "You must be Marcus, right?"

Marcus spoke harshly. "Yeah I'm Marcus. You've got thirty seconds to explain yourself or I'm going to knock you off this porch and call the cops. You're the third jerk today who has come here looking for Darcy."

This tall young man must be Darcy's boyfriend, Thom thought. He recognized the signs of a lover's quarrel and decided to be polite.

"I'm sorry Marcus. Darcy agreed to meet me at noon this afternoon at a restaurant called the French Café but she never showed up. I just came over to see if something had happened to her."

Madigan's calmness defused his anger. Marcus sighed wearily and stepped aside, opening the front door to allow the older man to walk through. "You'd better come in. You might know more about what's going on than I do."

Madigan entered the house and followed Marcus into the kitchen. "Do you want some coffee?" Marcus offered. "I usually don't drink the stuff but Darcy loved it. I could use a cup right now."

"Sure." He'd had nothing since he got off the plane two hours ago in Chicago. He felt too anxious to eat anything at the restaurant.

Madigan sat down with Marcus and they talked for two hours. Marcus told Thom about their big fight and learned all about Darcy's upbringing. He was able to identify Jake Holden as the punk in the leather jacket. Madigan revealed a lot about Darcy's life at Royalty. He also found out a little about Darcy's boss, Holderness Parkinson.

"She's actually a very famous consort," Madigan told Marcus. "You see, at the CEO level there are a lot of workaholics and we usually don't get along well with women. Our marriages either fail or are miserable. So we seek our entertainment elsewhere. Royalty is known worldwide for its superb service and beautiful women. More important than that, its absolute discretion. Darcy has been a companion to a lot of very successful and powerful men."

Marcus sat back, astonished. "Why would she tell you all this stuff and not me?"

"Don't sweat it Marcus. You didn't do anything wrong." Madigan was sympathetic. "She had to tell me. Royalty charges fantastic fees for their services. The girls have to do whatever we ask them."

Marcus looked up sharply at that. Madigan replied quickly. "Within reason of course."

"You still haven't answered my first question. Why do you want to see Darcy again?"

Madigan shrugged his shoulders. "I don't know. I just wanted to talk, I guess, like old times."

The man and the manchild sat together silently for a while, drinking coffee. Finally Madigan broke the silence. "Do you have any idea where she might have gone?"

"No, I don't have a clue."

Madigan drummed his fingers on the table nervously. He had drunk too much coffee and he was on edge now. "She always talked about going to New York to model. Maybe that's where she went."

Suddenly Marcus saw the web of light in his head and he knew that Madigan was right. People and their world lines appeared before him in a 3D light matrix. As time moved forward the strands in the web moved and reattached themselves into new nodes. He saw himself, Darcy, Madigan, Jake Holden, and that mob guy at one potential vortex: New York City. There were other possibilities but that one node had the highest probability outcome. It was just like the Schrödinger equation in quantum mechanics except this was about people, not subatomic particles.

Madigan saw Marcus straighten in his chair. His demeanor, which had been apathetic and lifeless, became energized.

Marcus leaned back in his chair and laughed. He was out of his funk now and back in control. "You're right Madigan. She's in New York." He said it with complete certainty.

"How do you know that?" Madigan was curious. "What were you doing just now?" He had seen Marcus looking at something over his head and out into space, as if it was completely real. When Thom turned his head toward the kitchen wall he saw nothing.

Marcus debated with himself. Should I tell him about the web of light? The only living person who knew of it was Darcy. He had tried to tell Johnny Chang once, in one of their martial arts classes. But Chang didn't get it. Marcus looked across at the older man. Thom Madigan was successful, a CEO, a man of the world. He had come all the way from Chicago just to see Darcy. Marcus didn't think it was coincidence that Madigan was now talking to him. He didn't believe in coincidence but he did understand pattern recognition. His market trading and stock analyses taught him that there were coherent, recognizable patterns in every system that had organization. The web of light showed him Madigan was here as a variable in some ongoing pattern of human relations. Besides, he needed some guidance. He was just spinning his wheels in Midland, going nowhere.

It took Marcus an hour to explain it, along with his personal history. When he was done Madigan nodded. "OK I believe you. I have always thought there was something special about Darcy. You have that too."

"So what should I do with my life?" Marcus asked. "Besides going to New York to find Darcy?"

"That's easy Marcus. Your path is laid out right in front of you."

"It is?"

"Sure. You have a head for math, finance, stock and securities trading, and analysis. If you made $50,000 last year on your own you might do very well in New York. Here." Madigan took out a card and wrote on the back of it. "When you get to New York take this card to the NYCBankCorp offices at 299 Park Avenue. Give it to the receptionist. I'll call Carl tonight and fix up an interview for you with NYC's Global Transaction Services department. If you're any good you'll have yourself a job in the heart of the money center capital of the country."

Marcus was amazed but skeptical. "You mean I'm just going to waltz into NYCBank headquarters, give somebody a card, and get my shot?"

"That's right Marcus. That's how it works. Almost everybody I know in business – and I only know successful people – got their start by knowing somebody in the right place."

Marcus still looked skeptical. "Don't worry kid. If you're not good enough you'll fail quickly. All I'm doing is giving you a chance to prove yourself. You'll be competing against some really smart and really tough people. You'd better be on your toes."

Marcus felt better. He didn't want any handouts. He felt a wave of excitement course through his body at the thought of going to New York and getting it on with the best of the best. Then he remembered that NYC, like all the New York banks, was in trouble.

"Didn't the government have to bail out NYCBank? I heard the government has a 25% stake in the company."

Madigan shrugged. "After the banking crisis of 2008 the big money center banks were essentially nationalized, whether the banks and the Fed want to put it that way or not.[1] But banking and finance are constants. As long as there are businesses there will be the need to finance them. My friend Carl Waverley says they are always looking for brilliant analysts. You might fit the bill."

Marcus still looked skeptical. "The last time I talked to Carl Waverley he was bemoaning the lack of quality in his department. They have a lot of brilliant kids who are social misfits and older guys past their prime." Thom gestured at the polished wood floors in the hallway and living room. The house itself was clean and in good order. "You did all this yourself, including the purchase of the house, without any help. That shows initiative, a good work ethic, and a practical nature to go along with a good analytical mind."

For Marcus, it was all starting to fit together now. New York was the place! "How did you meet Carl Waverley?" Marcus asked.

Madigan looked sheepish and Marcus groaned. "Don't tell me. Royalty Services."

"That's right Marcus."

"Who is this guy Holderness Parkinson? He doesn't seem like your typical owner of a brothel."

Madigan laughed. "What is a typical brothel, Marcus? How would you know what a brothel is like?"

Marcus flushed.

"I only met Holderness Parkinson once. I don't know anything about him. But the man has a certain …presence."

The men were silent for about a minute, each with his own thoughts. Marcus was thinking that he'd have to plug Parkinson into his web and see where the connections went. Thom was thinking that he had missed Darcy this time, but he had to be in New York in a couple of months.

"When are you going to make that call?" Marcus said suddenly.

"I'll call Carl on the way back to Chicago. I'll tell him to expect you on Monday morning."

Marcus smiled. The eyes of man and manchild met. Thom laughed. "Pack your bags and book a flight this weekend. Leave your car here. You'll have no use for it in the city."

"Are you going back to Chicago?"

"Yes. I have to fly into Philadelphia tomorrow morning."

"Then tell your driver to wait a few more minutes. I'll book my flight and you can drive me up."

At 4 p.m. Frank Nitti called Chicago from a downtown Midland restaurant.

"Yeah Frank, what is it?" Carcelli said.

"Boss, the Regier girl took off and nobody knows where she went. I nosed around but she don't have many friends in town. My guess is New York. You want to see if I can track her down?" Nitti was hopeful. Thirty-five percent of that action would be some good money.

"Nah, come back to town. I got a little job for you. We got some business in New York in a few weeks. You can try to find her then."

"OK boss, I'm comin' back up right now. This little pisshole town is full of eggheads and citizens."

CHAPTER **12**

DARCY arrived in New York on a hot Saturday afternoon. She had spent a restless night on the road at a bad motel in Reading, Pennsylvania. During the long drive she kept thinking about Marcus and what a dolt he was. Why couldn't he understand that she didn't want to talk about her past? What was so important about things that already happened? She couldn't forget the look of savagery on his face when he told her to move out of their bedroom. She had gone cold with fear and realized that she could no longer stay in that house. His anger reminded her of her father on one of his drinking binges. Dad was often a mean drunk. He sometimes hit her and he tried to rape her. Was that Marcus' fault? "He's just a kid," her inner voice said. "You can do a lot better." "Oh yeah?" she said out loud. "Who then?" "Go to New York and meet some nice man. Somebody rich who will take care of you," the voice said. "You should have done that as soon as you left Royalty."

She remembered the exit interview she'd had with Holderness Parkinson. He handed her a list of New York modeling agencies. "These agencies are the best of the best. They cater only to the upper crust at exclusive private showings, usually by invitation only." Then he wrote her a glowing introduction on his personal gold-leaf stationery, with the distinctive Royalty seal at the upper left. "Of course you may try your luck at the other agencies. But I suggest that a woman of your accomplishments not lower herself to the gauche and the noveau riche." Parkinson's manner was lofty. "Let the popular agencies display tawdry, gaudy, and ostentatious clothing for those unable to appreciate classic designs." Darcy had to hold back a smile. In many ways her benefactor *was* 200 years behind the times.

At the motel in Reading Darcy had called Audrey's, the first number on the list. "Hello, my name is Darcy Regier. I am a former employee of Holderness Parkinson. I—" She felt stupid calling herself a former employee but she didn't know how to describe what she'd been doing.

A feminine voice responded pleasantly. "Darcy Regier! Well, well, well. We were wondering when you'd call."

Darcy was astonished. "You have been expecting me to call?"

"Holderness has been calling once a month to check up on you. My name is Kathleen, Kathleen Barr. I am Audrey Quenioux's personal assistant. We have been hoping to see you. When can you get here?"

Darcy laughed as the tension of the past 24 hours suddenly lifted. "Oh, you don't know how delightful you have made me feel, Kathleen. I would love to meet you whenever it is convenient."

"Are you still in Midland, Illinois?"

Darcy was about to ask how she knew she had been living in Midland, but of course it was Holderness. "I'm on the road in Reading Pennsylvania."

Darcy could almost hear Kathleen wriggling her nose in distaste. "Oh dear, that won't do at all."

There was a pause as someone put a hand over the phone. Darcy could hear muffled voices. "Darcy, why don't you stop by my apartment this evening in New York?" Kathleen said. "We'll have a cozy talk and discuss what we should do."

"I'd love that Kathleen, thank you."

Darcy received directions to Kathleen's Manhattan apartment. Kathleen told her to store her BMW and take a taxi to her destination. Kathleen gave her a good place to put her BMW and said she'd call ahead for her. After she hung up the phone Darcy felt better than she had in several days. Holderness was obviously looking out for her. But she was already beginning to miss Marcus.

Marcus flew in to New York and took a harrowing taxi ride from JFK to 299 Park Avenue and the NYCBank building. His taxi driver looked like Chris Rock with a turban and he drove like a coke addict who was late for his fix. After surviving that journey his interview was going to be a piece of cake. Marcus was dressed in his only suit. It was a bit wrinkled from the flight but he didn't have time to do anything except pay the cabby and hurry up to the massive receptionist's desk. A beautiful woman was seated at the desk. She had short-cropped black hair and was impeccably dressed in a gray business suit and white blouse. Marcus gazed at her appreciatively without trying to be too obvious. The woman met his eyes coolly and appraisingly, with just the hint of a smile. Next to her sat an armed security guard.

Marcus presented his card and the woman nodded approvingly. "Mr. Waverley is expecting you."

"You mean I get an interview with Carl Waverley himself?" Marcus gawked and felt as stupid as the small town kid coming to the big city for the first time.

"I'm Carla," the woman said. She smiled and handed him her business card. "Yes, you do get to see the man himself. Go to the 19th floor. He's in suite 101, just to your left as you come off the elevator."

Marcus walked to a bank of elevators. As he waited he glanced at the card Carla had given him. It had the NYCBank logo and underneath it said 'Carla Waverley Securities Analyst.' The card had her business and her home phone number. Wow, is this an invitation to call her? Is she Carl Waverley's daughter? Maybe things moved a lot faster in New York! Carla was impressive, smoothly professional, and confident. And gorgeous. The kind of woman that could make a guy forget about Darcy Regier.

Marcus walked the plushly carpeted hallway on floor 19. He saw an L-shaped corner office with wide windows in front, enabling anyone who came near to see inside. He presented himself at the receptionist's desk and saw that the entire suite had large windows looking out over the New York skyline. It was an impressive view. "Marcus Riley to see Mr. Waverley," he said to a middle-aged woman with streaks of gray in her hair.

The woman barely glanced at him. "Go right in Mr. Riley."

Marcus walked into Carl Waverley's private office and saw a clean cut, good looking man, probably in his mid-forties. Waverley was a little above medium height with intelligent blue eyes that quickly looked him over and took Marcus' measure. Waverley had the lean but not skinny build of the athlete. He was totally bald. Marcus noticed that the office was sparsely furnished. Waverley's desktop was clean, with only a computer terminal and a crystal sculpture upon it.

Thom Madigan told Carl Waverley what to expect, but at first glance the kid exceeded his expectations. He was very tall, with broad shoulders and a permanent black stubble around his chin. Marcus exuded an aura of …something. He would take this manchild's measure and see where it went.

Waverley held out his hand. "Welcome Marcus, please have a seat." The older man had a strong grip but Marcus did not try to make the handshake competitive.

Waverley noted that the young man seemed at ease in this strange environment. He was pleased. Thom Madigan knew people and he said this one might be a gem. "Let me get right down to business, Marcus," he said after they both sat down. "You are here because my good friend Thom Madigan recommended you. I know that you are just out of high school and you might be wondering why you have been suddenly given an opportunity at this level."

Marcus nodded. That was precisely what he had intended to ask this important executive.

"Thom Madigan is the best judge of people I have ever seen, Marcus." Waverley spoke in a quiet but powerful bass voice. "He built his company, Pantheon Plastics, out of nothing. He hired young men just like yourself, trained them, and let them build his business for him. He says you're a genius. A recommendation from him is almost a guarantee of success."

A genius! Marcus had no idea Thom Madigan thought that highly of him. That made him even more determined to succeed. He didn't let his excitement show. He sat calmly across from the older man and nodded his head.

Waverley was impressed. Normally a youngster like Marcus would either be fawning with gratitude or odiously arrogant. This kid seemed quietly confident.

"I have a busy schedule and I can't spend a lot of time with you. I'm going to hand you off to Beatrice. She'll get you started. The first thing is the standard aptitude test we give to all our prospective securities analysts and traders. I'll be frank with you Marcus. We are desperate for top-notch analysts and traders right now. Especially in the CDO unit within the Issue Services division, and in the Equities Services division. Normally we require a college degree before we would even consider you. I'm making a reach with you but I'll trust to Thom. You'll quickly find out what we're about if you can pass muster and absorb the training. I'm putting you on the fast track. Are you ready?"

Marcus replied emphatically. "Yes sir, I'm ready!" And he was. He felt that he was in the exact right spot. The web of light in his head was pulsing as if it were getting ready for some heavy use. A thought occurred to Marcus. "Sir, if you don't mind me asking, is Carla Waverley your daughter?"

The man behind the desk smiled and met the eyes of the manchild across from him frankly, a man-to-man look. "Yes she is, as a matter of fact."

"Sir, if she's a securities analyst, what was she doing down at the reception desk?"

Carl Waverley's smile broadened. This kid had balls, and lots of curiosity, to challenge him on his very first day. Great securities analysts were inveterately curious and traders had to have cohunes of steel.

"Carla insisted on meeting you herself, don't ask me why. She was with me last Friday when I talked to Madigan about you."

"Thank you sir. I just wondered because she gave me her business card."

The older man's eyes flashed. "Did she give you the one with her home phone number on it?"

"Yes sir. I kind of wondered about that."

Waverley laughed. "Watch yourself around her, kid. She's brilliant, one of the best around here. She scored 48 out of 50 on the test you are about to take." He wanted to add, 'and she'll eat you up,' but he didn't.

Wow, Marcus thought. He had only been in New York for an hour and already his life was racing along at light speed.

Waverley rose from his desk and Marcus shook his hand. "Go out and see my personal secretary."

Marcus noticed how quickly Waverley dismissed him. As he walked out of the office he glanced back. Waverley's attention was completely off of him and on to something on his computer screen.

That first day was a whirlwind of activity. Beatrice took him to a small office that was set up like a classroom, with long tables of computer terminals and several dozen chairs. "Pat, this is Marcus. Give him the standard aptitude test and let me know how he does."

Pat used a remote to turn on one of the terminals and activated one of the desktop apps. "OK Marcus, this is NYC's proprietary test for securities analysts. It tells us whether you have the potential to invest a lot of time and money in you. If you fail you walk out the front door and never come back. Got it?"

Marcus nodded.

"You have exactly one hour to complete the test from the time you click the start button. *Comprende*?"

"Understood." Marcus immediately got started. His breathing slowed and he felt a calmness wash through him that brought with it a heightened sense of mental acuity. He could see the web of light in his mind, pulsing.

Pages of symbols appeared with instructions. Marcus smiled. Pattern recognition, his strong suit. He looked over the exam; it was like a sophisticated IQ test. The first question presented two 4-by-4 grids of symbols and asked him to determine which one in the second grid shouldn't be there. There were 50 questions and each of them grew more sophisticated. His pattern recognition skills did not fail him for the first forty questions. After that he consulted the web of light. He placed all of the symbols he saw mentally into the web, and watched how the patterns formed. In 35 minutes he was finished. He clicked the "done" button. A message box appeared. "Are you sure? Once you click OK you cannot change your answers." Marcus clicked OK.

"What is this, a joke?" Pat asked.

Marcus replied calmly. "If it is the joke is on you." Always after utilizing the web of light he felt a sense of well being and certainty.

Pat snorted. "It's your funeral son."

Marcus heard a printer start up.

"I have to print out and grade the test by hand. It's company policy. We don't want anyone rigging the tests."

Marcus waited around for twenty minutes while Pat checked his answers. He wanted to tell Pat that all of them were right but he didn't say anything. Nobody likes a smart-ass.

"What the fuck!"

"Are you surprised I got a perfect score?"

"How did you know you got them all right?"

Marcus shrugged and gave his standard answer. "Pattern recognition is my strong suit."

"What's your last name Marcus?" Pat was belligerent. This jerk-off kid had come in here and aced one of the hardest tests in the industry.

"Riley. Marcus Riley."

"Marcus Riley, you're either a psycho freak or the next head of the securities division. Nobody has ever gotten a perfect score on this test before."

Marcus leaned back in his chair, feeling very pleased with himself.

Pat spoke disdainfully. "Don't get cocky, hot-shot. This is just a test to determine if you have aptitude. We'll see how well you do when you are about to sign off on a billion dollar deal with the company's money. Hot-shots like you flame out very quickly."

Marcus made a guess. "Like you, Pat?"

Pat's face twisted in anger. "Fuck off Riley!"

Marcus didn't want to get off on the wrong foot, so he became conciliatory. "No offense, it was just a hunch. I've always been good at tests."

Pat felt a little better. He hated arrogant assholes who thought they were better than everyone else. "I scored a 47, in the 98th percentile. I just didn't have the personality for trading. When it came time to execute I just couldn't do it. Too nervous I guess. So now I'm here."

Marcus tried not to display too much of the confidence he felt. "I'm hoping to do well."

Pat shuffled the papers. "Unless you jump off a bridge first. We're playing for high stakes here, Riley."

Carla heard about Marcus' score that evening as she was pulling up her sheer black nylons, about to go out for the evening. She was intrigued and a little envious. A 50! She had tied for the highest score on record and a 19-year-old kid had just blown everyone else away. Marcus didn't look like a kid. Was he just a boy in a man's body? How mature and confident was he really? Carla knew how to challenge him. New York provided a lot of places to test a person's mettle.

She found herself wondering how good he was in bed. She didn't anticipate any problems there either. She remembered the way he looked at her this morning. Supposedly he had a girlfriend already, but they had broken up. She'd found that out from dad. Not that it mattered. She was waiting for him to call her, but would he? She'd deliberately given him the card with her private phone number. If he didn't call her tonight she would call him tomorrow. He's in the accelerated training program now, spending 14 hours a day in the classroom. The kid would be ready for some action.

Carla Waverley stretched out her 6' 3" frame and admired her legs. Men told her they were the best pair of legs in New York. She could have been a hugely successful model but the securities game excited her and thrilled her. At heart she was a gambler, and she was about to do a little gambling with the manchild Marcus Riley.

Marcus didn't finish his first day of training at NYC until after 9 p.m. He walked back to his trainee apartment on 51st street and plopped down on the bed. He was tired. His third floor apartment had a small bath, a living room with a TV and a desk, and a small kitchen with a microwave and fridge. The dark green carpets were thick and the lighting came from filigreed glass sconces on the walls. Although small, the place had the tantalizing smell and feel of luxury. Marcus liked it.

He called Darcy's cell phone again. As the phone rang over and over he was thinking more about Carla. This morning he was waiting for the elevator to open and turned toward the lobby. He saw Carla smoothly rise from the receptionist's desk and slowly walk out of the building. She was dressed in a hip-hugging black skirt that ended just above the knee and wore three inch heels. Wow. She towered over everyone in the lobby. Wherever she went people moved aside. The eyes of men glanced her way. Were those hips swaying for him or was that how she walked naturally?

He felt guilty about his carnal interest for the boss' daughter. He had better be careful. Carl Waverley struck him as a man inordinately proud of his daughter.

"Hi this is Darcy," the phone droned, breaking his reverie. "Please leave a message." Marcus was about to do so when he heard Darcy's anxious voice. "Marcus? Is that you?"

Marcus heard Darcy's voice and felt great relief but he still couldn't get Carla out of his mind. "Yes it's me Darcy, are you OK? What are you doing and why did you leave so suddenly?"

They talked for half an hour and got caught up. Darcy told him that she was modeling for one of New York's most respected modistes and was making money again. Marcus filled Darcy in on his long day. He told her of the convention on his front porch on Friday. "First Jake Holden, then some mob guy named Franklin Nittsfield, then Thom Madigan. I was so mad at you, especially when you wouldn't return my calls and texts. After you left I just sat around and moped. I guess it's good that I'm here."

"What did that Nitti guy want?" Darcy was fearful of that name, which she knew from Holderness Parkinson.

"Is that his real name? I think he wanted you to come back to Chicago."

Thank God she was in New York then.

Marcus spoke proudly. "I got the highest score ever on the aptitude test."

"I kinda miss you," she blurted, hoping he'd feel the same.

"Yeah, I kinda miss you too."

"What are we doing in New York?" Marcus asked.

"I liked living with you Marcus but we were going nowhere. Isn't it exciting being here? I actually think it's better for both of us."

Marcus had to admit that it was. "I'm tired and it's only Day One of my program. I've got weeks and weeks to go yet." Should he tell her about Carla? "And ..."

"Yes?"

"I met this girl today."

"What girl? Is she pretty?"

"Ohmygod Darcy, you should see her. She's over six feet tall and she wears three inch heels. She's the daughter of a VIP here at the bank."

"Do you like her?"

"Uh, sort of, but not the way I like you. She's ... I don't know ... tempting."

Darcy sighed. "What do you mean, you don't like her the way you like me?"

"I don't know ... you and I, we *fit*. But this woman, wow, she's ... overwhelmingly beautiful."

Darcy knew the type. She had seen dozens of women like that in her travels all over the world, at some of the most exclusive locations and venues. Predators. She had to remember that Marcus had only ever been to Chicago and Midland. He was a hick, basically. Although she was only 23 she was a woman of the world, with broad experience in social situations. She had had lots of flings with some very powerful and important men. And lots of sex, even though she didn't care that much about it. Marcus was just getting his feet wet. She understood with a woman's wisdom that if she wanted Marcus she would have to let him go for a while. She sighed again.

"I'm sorry Darcy. Did I upset you?"

Darcy could feel the concern in his voice.

"I feel like I can tell you anything, so I did."

Darcy smiled even though she felt like crying. As long as she had that trust she had him. She steadied her voice. "Yes Marcus, I'm really glad you told me. I want to hear all about your experiences. Don't hold back anything."

"Hey that's great Darcy!"

Marcus sounded almost like a little boy, she thought.

"I'm going to need someone to talk to if my days are going to be like this. Six days a week, fourteen hours a day, only Sundays off. The only good thing is that I have an expense account, so I have a little money to live on."

"Maybe you could come see me at one of my shows. You can't get in unless you have a printed invitation, but I can get you one."

"I'd like that. When is it?"

Marcus heard some rustling of paper. "I'm looking in my appointment book ... oh! My first show is a few weeks from now, a Sunday evening at 8. On Lexington Avenue in the Upper East side. In one of those elegant places for the filthy rich."

"I'm beginning to think that rich is good and that luxury is good. They've set me up in one of their trainee apartments. It's really nice here."

"It *is* good, Marcus, as long as you have your head on straight." Darcy never forgot her humble and difficult upbringing. She was gently nudging him about Carla even though she knew he wouldn't get it.

"Yeah." Marcus stifled a yawn. "I've had a big day and I'm tired. I think I'll go to sleep."

Darcy felt herself tearing up again. She missed him beside her. "OK Marcus. Will I see you on the Sunday?" She asked a little more anxiously than she intended.

"Yes, I'll be there. I've never seen you at work. It will be fun."

"Good. Call me after work every day if you want to."

"It's a deal."

Marcus managed to see Carla every day. She worked in Securities and Fund Services in the Equity Services department, executing transactions. Every day she wore something different that accented another aspect of her body. On Wednesday she approached Marcus as he was eating a sandwich in the cafeteria. Heads turned as she walked into the room. The trainees were silent as they recognized Carla Waverley. Today she wore a low cut designer blouse with a sapphire on a gold chain that nestled between her breasts. She was sexy and exciting.

"I'm going to the 23 tonight with a bunch of friends. Do you want to come?"

"What's the 23?"

"It's a nightclub, silly. We can dance, drink a little, and have a good time."

The thought of dancing with this woman excited him. He wondered what she would wear tonight. "Are you going to wear those heels?"

She threw her head back and laughed. "Marcus, you are so deliciously refreshing."

"What time?"

"I'll be there at 10. You have to tell the doorman the password or you can't get in. Bring money. There's a $100 cover." She bent over and whispered in his ear. "Dionysus."

Marcus frowned. "That's a bit late for me. I have to be back here by 7 a.m."

Carla straightened abruptly. "Then don't come." She was irritated. Who does this kid think he is? She knew successful men who would die to go out with her. "Stay home and drink your milk."

Marcus met her eyes and Carla felt his anger like a laser blast. Her eyes widened. Even though she was standing and he was sitting, she felt him to be in the superior position. That was an unusual feeling for her. "How did you do that?"

Marcus replied crossly. "How did I do what?"

Carla studied him thoughtfully. She was in no way disconcerted by his emotional outburst; it excited her. I wonder if he reacts to men the same way? Is he a barker or a fighter? It made her want to find out. "Project your anger. I felt it like a blast of hot air from an oven."

Marcus shrugged. The question bored him. "I may or may not come. Thanks for the invite. Maybe by 10 tonight I'll be in a better mood."

Everyone in the lunchroom was now watching the play. Somebody dropped a plastic cup and the sharp sound was loud in the silent room.

Carla's eyes flashed. She wasn't used to being brushed off by young men. The analytical part of her brain told her that she had badly misread Marcus' character. She took his last statement for a semi-apology and was mollified. "Don't miss out on the fun." She spoke cheerfully and walked slowly out of the room, letting everyone see that she was in control.

When she got back to her trading desk she couldn't concentrate. The oaf had had the audacity to be bored in her presence! Even so, she could tell she excited him. Was he a good dancer? She could wear her heels and not look down on him. She liked that.

Tonight. If he came to the club she would take him down a peg.

Marcus finished his day at 9 p.m. and walked the three blocks back to his apartment on 51st street. He was fried but couldn't stand the thought of just going to bed. What the hell, why not take Carla up on her offer? God she was exciting, and those legs! Was she good in bed? Was she one of those dominating types? He wanted to find out. Marcus washed his face, combed his hair, and straightened his clothing. There might be a dress code at the 23 but he decided to go as-is.

He walked over four blocks on Park to a large commercial building. About 50 feet before the main entrance there was a door set back in a little alcove off the street. Marcus heard music coming from somewhere inside. A couple of limos stood outside, and three taxis. A chauffeur was opening a door and a smart looking woman got out of one of the limos. She opened the door to 23, whispered something to a man standing in the dark, and disappeared down a flight of stairs. A man got out of one of the taxis and did the same thing.

Marcus opened the door and was confronted by a truly large man wearing a skin-tight, short-sleeved black shirt, black pants, and black leather shoes. The man's eyes were almost level with his. He was at least 30 pounds thicker than Marcus' 225.

"Dionysus," Marcus said softly.

The man backed off a step. "I don't know you."

"Carla Waverley invited me." The man relaxed. "Yeah, she said some smart-ass kid might come tonight, and to let him in. Are you 18?"

"Yes. 19."

"Break out some ID." Marcus decided not to argue. He took out his wallet and gave the man his driver's license along with the $100 cover.

"Midland Illinois, huh? You don't happen to know a bouncer at Densinger's do you? He calls himself Big Tony. Friend of mine from north Jersey."

Marcus grinned. "Never been in the place. Only college kids go there, and some drunken academics."

"Yeah, Tony told me about some professor named Martins who knocked him down one night over there."

"I heard about that. It made the news last year. He was trying to accost one of the students and they kicked him out. Caused a big stink at the university."

"All right kid, I guess you're OK. But I gotta frisk you before I can let you in. No weapons allowed in the joint."

Marcus submitted. The man did his job quickly and thoroughly.

"OK, you're clean. Watch yourself down there. Some pretty unscrupulous types come here that wouldn't think twice about taking advantage of a rookie." He held out a meaty hand and Marcus took it. "If you get into trouble, ask for Frank."

"Thanks, I'm not staying long. Just long enough to dance with Carla."

Frank rolled his eyes at the innocence of youth. He stepped aside to let Marcus descend the stairs.

Marcus saw a band playing on a small stage in back. The 23 had a bar off to the right against the wall, a dance floor in front of a stage, and a hallway on the left. A bony, disheveled man came out of one of the rooms, holding a drink.

"Marcus!" He heard a shout and looked to his right. Two dozen small tables were scattered in front of the bar. Seated there were people of every description. "Marcus, I'm over here!" He saw Carla's hand in the air. He walked over to a set of three tables that had been drawn together. At one of the tables a white line about four inches long was on the table. A guy in a suit was taking powder up into his left nostril.

Carla introduced him to the group. "Marcus, on my right is Denise. She's a manager at the Clarion not far from here." Denise was a small woman with bleached blond hair, large earrings, and a slightly pinched face. She raised her glass. "Prosit."

"Next to her is Martin." Carla waved her hand at the disheveled man Marcus had seen a few minutes earlier. He was wearing a crumpled suit with a crooked tie. "Hello Marcus, how the hell are you." His words were slurred.

"Martin is a broker at Morgan Stanley," Carla explained.

"Over here is my friend Stacy." Carla pointed out a woman with enormous breasts dressed in a black, tight-fitting shirt with a bared shoulder, jet-black hair, too much red lipstick, and a tattoo on her neck. She had a dissipated look. The cynical expression she wore looked habitual, as if it were etched on. "Stacy designs clothes for Harrold-Sturgis." Judging by her attire, Marcus thought, she could use a good designer herself.

Carla pointing out the man who had just snorted cocaine. "That guy over there is Freddy Mercury." Freddy was a very thin man with a hawk nose and deep-set eyes whose pupils were almost black. Marcus raised his eyebrows and she laughed. "Just kidding of course. His name is Freddy Colangelo. He's a DJ."

Freddy was staring hard at Marcus, and he acknowledged the man with a nod. "Do I know you?" Freddy asked in a high-pitched voice. The man's gaze was intense, as if the mind behind it was going 100 mph down a road that was too bumpy for comfort. He was nervously tapping his finger on the table.

"I don't think so."

"I thought I saw you in Chicago once. You were talking with some mob guy."

Marcus laughed. "I've been to Chicago but I don't know any mob guys." Except maybe for the Three Stooges, and Franklin Nittsfield.

Carla spoke sharply. "Shut up Freddy, you talk too much." Carla said sharply. She indicated a burly, heavy-set older man with curly brown hair and ears that stuck out from his head. "And last but not least, my friend Brian." When Marcus looked into Brian's eyes they were icy cold.

"Brian is a hot-shot trader at Wells Fargo. One of the best in the business."

Brian raised one eyebrow and turned his level gaze on Carla. "*One* of the best?"

Carla replied coldly. "That's right. Next to me."

Brian smiled slightly, a sneer. Marcus didn't like this guy. He was hard, like a piece of polished steel.

Freddy came over to the table and laid down a line. He handed Marcus a small straw. "C'mon kid, try it. You might like it."

Marcus stared at the white powder. He knew Freddy was trying to get a new customer. Some people said you could get a great high from cocaine and he was willing to try it once. He took the straw, snorted the line, and coughed. The stuff irritated his nasal passages. Freddy looked at him expectantly. After a short time Marcus felt better than he ever had in his life. A rush of well-being and sexual desire infused his body. He was full of energy. His heart was beating rapidly.

"Good, eh?" Freddy said.

"Unbelievable. What happens when you come down?"

Brain smiled cynically. Stacy looked at Freddy with distaste. Carla was watching both of them intently.

Stacy stood abruptly. Marcus watched, fascinated, as her breasts rolled and swayed under her shirt. He felt a surge of pure lust. "I'm going for another drink," she said. "Come with me Marcus?"

"OK, lead the way."

As they walked to the bar Stacy deliberately nudged him with her hip toward the hallway. "I don't want the drink." She threw her arms around his neck and pressed herself against him. "God you're beautiful," she whispered drunkenly, with her head on his shoulder. "Let's go back to one of the rooms and fuck."

Her breasts felt amazingly good against his chest. Stacy rubbed her body against his, exciting him. He wanted to take her top off.

"C'mon kid I want to suck your cock. You can put your hands on my boobs. I can see you want to." She grabbed his hand and quickly led him to one of the small rooms at the back of the hall. She slammed the door, turned toward him, and slowly took off her top. Marcus stared, fascinated, at two beautiful mounds of rounded flesh. He slowly reached out and put his hand on one breast. They were a lot bigger than Darcy's. He loved the feel of it. He took the other one, slowly massaging it. She groaned, took two steps back, and lay back on the bed.

"C'mon Marcus I'm all yours." Marcus was so horny he couldn't believe it. He was totally fucked up and it felt fantastic. He removed Stacy's slacks and her panties. Slowly he moved his mouth upward, kissing the soft skin of her thighs, and then taking her in his mouth. He massaged her expertly until she climaxed. Then she got on top of him and returned the favor. Wow! So that's why people do drugs and have sex. It was amazing.

"Marcus, you're fantastic," Stacy said afterward, lighting a cigarette. "Where did a kid like you learn how to make love like that?"

Marcus' face turned red. "I had a good teacher." He thought of Darcy and felt guilty as hell. He had come here thinking about Carla and had wound up in bed with a perfect stranger. It was the probably the coke, which was beginning to wear off a little now.

"What's the matter?" Stacy asked.

"Nothing. I just thought of my girlfriend. We broke up a couple weeks ago."

"Do you love her?" Stacy began to put on her clothes.

"I don't know. Maybe. I guess so. I don't know."

Stacy smiled. Marcus noticed that her face transformed. The cynical expression had completely vanished. It was amazing. "You have a great smile."

"Do I?" Stacy spoke self-deprecatingly.

"Yes you do. When you smile like that your face lights up. You should do it more often."

Stacy stared at Marcus. Slowly, the smile crept around her face again.

"Yeah, like that. You look beautiful."

Again Stacy stared at Marcus, astonished. She had received two genuine compliments from a man in less than two minutes. She was half-drunk; maybe she was dreaming. It was unprecedented though. Men just wanted to grab her boobs.

"You don't believe me? Go look in the mirror."

Stacy slowly walked into the small bathroom and looked at herself. She was inwardly excited, as if she were about to get a present at Christmas, but afraid of what she would see. "For fuck's sake," she said, unbelieving. "I am beautiful. At least right now."

"Damn right you are."

Stacy walked back into the room and threw herself into Marcus' arms. "Thanks Marcus. Whatever you did worked."

Marcus smiled. "When you smile like that it makes me want to smile too."

"Amazing." Stacy glanced back into the mirror. "I don't know what's going to happen next, but I think it's going to be better than what's happened so far." She nodded to Marcus, opened the door, and walked confidently down the hall. Marcus followed silently behind. Stacy approached Carla and said something. She turned right and walk up the stairs and out of the club. Carla bent down and snorted something on the table top.

Marcus approached the table. "What did you do to that girl?" Carla asked. "She usually gets wasted and we have to call a taxi to take her home."

Marcus shrugged. "I didn't do anything. She had ... an epiphany, I guess."

Carla's laugh was brittle. "An epiphany? What's that? A good fuck?"

"Something better than that I think."

"The only thing better than sex is a good trade."

Freddy interrupted. "Want another line? This shit is really good."

"No thanks. I'll pay you for the line though."

Freddy waved his hand carelessly. "If you want any more you come see me, you hear?"

"Sure. I think I'll go home. I'm starting to come down."

Carla leaned in closer. "You just had sex. Naughty boy!" Inside she was seething. Marcus was hers but Stacy had marked him for her own. She'd walked off with him before she could do anything. Fortunately there was still time tonight to test him.

"Let's get out of here," Brian said. "I'm bored. Let's go find some action."

Carla smiled. "I'm up for that." Here was her chance to test Marcus. "Let's head across the river."

"Good idea. We'll see how the other side lives."

Carla looked at Marcus. "Don't quit on me now. I'm going to show you a part of New York that not many people get to see."

"Why?" They paid their tab and began walking up the stairs.

"Because I want to." Carla shook her hips as she walked in front of him.

They never made it across the river that night.

Marcus waved a hand at Frank the doorman as they came out onto the street. It struck him suddenly that women in New York were attracted to him. He could have as much sex as he wanted. Or was that just a feeling brought on by the drug? He had enjoyed making love to Stacy. And Carla, he wouldn't mind having her in his bed either. But when he compared them both to Darcy they didn't measure up somehow.

As they were looking around for a taxi a group of jumpy young men suddenly surrounded the party.

"What is this?" Martin said. "This is Park Avenue not Bed Stuy."

One of the men shouted nervously. "Shut the fuck up. We're looking for Brian Anderson. We know he went in here. You!" The man pointed a switchblade at Brian, who was standing next to Carla. "You're Anderson."

Denise screamed. "Tell the bitch to shut up," the guy with the switchblade said. He was a edgy, thin kid with a bony face.

Brian said something but Marcus didn't hear. He had already taken a step back mentally and looked at their attackers. There were five men. Four of them were about his age. A fifth man stood back. He was the alpha, and might be armed. The other guys were dressed in loose, dark clothing.

Brian was looking at the fifth man with contempt. "You send this pack of dogs to do your dirty work, Jordan?"

"It takes a pack of dogs to deal with a snake like you. You aren't going to slither away this time."

"What's this about?" Carla stepped away from the action. She was excited, Marcus noticed, and not afraid.

"This asshole," Jordan said, indicating Brian Anderson, "is privately and illegally selling unregistered securities. He took me for thirty grand."

"Prove it," Anderson said.

"This isn't a court of law. You fucked me, now I'm going to extract my pound of flesh."

Marcus knew that something was going to go down less than a second before it happened. Jordan gestured, and the toughs all went for Anderson. Martin, the disheveled broker, stepped back. Freddy, who had trailed the group coming up the stairs, had somehow slipped off. Nobody noticed that Denise was still in the circle. She panicked and began to move. He saw a knife flash toward Brian. Brian sidestepped and the blade was going right for Denise.

Marcus stepped in, deflected the blade, and twisted the tough's arm. The knife clattered to the cement. The other three men attacked Brian Anderson. Martin ran out of the circle and down the street. Marcus held on to the tough he had disarmed. Carla stood there with an expression of eagerness on her face.

Well, well, well, Carla thought. The manchild came through with flying colors. The drug was kicking in and she wanted him now, really badly.

Anderson drew a gun and pulled the trigger. One of the toughs staggered, a hole in his shoulder. "You shot me!" he screamed. Marcus let go of the man he held. This wasn't his fight. He didn't like Anderson.

The two remaining toughs launched themselves at Anderson's feet, knocking him down. The gun flew out of his hand. Marcus' tough picked up the gun. They heard a police siren in the distance. Jordan spoke. "Thanks boys, get going. I'll take it from here." Anderson got up and Jordan slugged him. The three thugs ran off, taking their injured comrade. Marcus took Denise's arm and led her away. He looked over his shoulder and saw that Anderson and Jordan were slugging it out on the street in front of the club. The door to 23 had darkened and the music stopped. Carla came up to Marcus as he turned the corner.

Marcus saw a taxi and hailed it. He put Denise in the cab.

"C'mon," Carla said. "Let's go to my place."

Marcus excused himself. "I'm exhausted. I'm going home."

Carla grabbed his arm, roughly. "You fucked Stacy but you won't fuck me?"

Marcus could tell that Carla was really high. She must have snorted a lot more of that stuff than he had. If she reacted to the drug like him she was probably in heat right now. He was still high enough to want her.

"OK, let's go."

She opened her cell phone to call a cab.

"Let's walk. It will clear my head."

Carla spoke urgently and began to walk quickly. "It's on 5th Avenue by the Park. Hurry up or I'll take you right here."

Wow, this drug was powerful! He was about to have sex with a beautiful woman for the second time in an hour.

Marcus woke up the next morning, groggy. He hardly remembered what had transpired last night. Carla was already gone. He looked at the clock and groaned. It was already 7:30 and he was late for his training. As he hurriedly left Carla's apartment, he realized that he hadn't called Darcy.

At lunch Marcus texted a message to Darcy. 'SORRY I FORGOT TO CALL LAST NIGHT. HAD A WILD NIGHT. STAYING HOME WILL CALL YOU AT 9:30.' He'd tell Darcy all about his crazy night after work, and maybe she'd be able to help him sort it out.

"Did you have a good time last night?"

Marcus looked up quickly. He was off in a corner of the cafeteria, in a little alcove. It was Carla.

Marcus looked her over, astonished. She was impeccably dressed as usual. Her face was fresh and clean and she showed no signs whatsoever of their violent, drug and sex-filled night. "How do you contrive to look so good today? I'm a mess."

Carla laughed, pleased with the compliment. "I go out almost every night."

"You have a lot more energy than I do."

"I've got a little help with that." Marcus found out later that she took amphetamines in the morning after a late night out. He could tell she was hanging around because she wanted to ask him something. "OK, spill it."

She raised her eyebrows. "Am I that obvious?"

"I can read people pretty well."

"I wanted to know whether you thought Stacy was any good in bed. You had sex with her didn't you?"

"Yeah. That was cocaine I sniffed last night, right?"

"Yes, the best stuff you can get. Freddy knows a supplier who gets it from a private airport upstate, right off the plane."

"Does it make you feel horny?"

She laughed. "God you're such an innocent Marcus. Yes, it makes me horny. Didn't you notice?"

"I don't remember anything after we got back to your place."

Carla was angry. "You remember having sex with Stacy but not with me?"

Marcus grinned sheepishly. "It must have been the drugs."

"What did you think of Stacy?"

"Uh, I like Stacy. I think she's going to turn her life around."

Carla laughed. "Do you mean you like her boobs?"

Marcus wondered whether someone as intelligent as Carla could be so deliberately obtuse. "No. We talked for a little while after we did it. I think she had some sort of life understanding." Marcus spoke a little sharply.

"Why, because you had sex with her?"

Marcus locked his eyes to hers. He had never tried activating the web of light to read another person but he was going to do it now. Carla wasn't stupid but she was acting like an idiot. He suspected there was something dark inside her. Associating with her might not be a good thing for him even though she was Carl Waverley's daughter. He relaxed and sent the light over to her.

Suddenly he *was* Carla Waverley. He was looking at himself through her eyes. She was waiting for him to answer. He was both Marcus and Carla, but Carla didn't seem to know that he was inside her head. Wow!

"No," he heard himself saying. "It wasn't just about sex. I don't know what happened, I can't remember. It was something about her smile." Then he did remember. And when he remembered, Carla knew it too.

"Oh, so that's how it was," Carla/Marcus said. Marcus now understood that dark place within Carla. She was intensely competitive and had to be the best at everything. That made her jealous in matters of sex and love, and unobservant (or uncaring) about the way others felt. She had a big blind spot, that was all. He learned that Carla played tennis, like her father, and was very good at it.

"Yeah. I really don't remember anything after we got home Carla," Marcus/Carla said. "I think I was half asleep."

Carla/Marcus agreed. "You weren't very good. I practically raped you and you never noticed."

When Carla spoke he could see himself and when he spoke he could see Carla. It was kind of like playing chess with yourself. You just turned the board and saw the pieces from the other person's perspective, except you understood the next move she was going to make. Carla seemed a lot calmer, and they had achieved a good understanding.

"Do you want to come out again tonight?" Carla/Marcus asked. "I want to take you across the river." Marcus could see that she wanted him to see how beautiful she was, how tough she was, and how competent she was to handle anything. She wanted him to admire her. In the back of her mind was the idea to take him away from Darcy Regier, and to get back at Stacy for taking him away from her last night. For some reason Darcy occupied a good deal of her thoughts regarding him.

"Thanks Carla. I'm staying home tonight," Marcus/Carla said. "I have to call Darcy."

As soon as he said it he knew he shouldn't have. Carla got really angry and the web of light exploded and deactivated. "Oh, so it's Darcy is it?"

"Sure. She's my girlfriend."

"Some girlfriend." Carla was mocking. "You just had sex with two other women last night. When was the last time you saw her?"

Marcus squirmed in his seat. "Well, she lives in East Manhattan, somewhere in the low 80's." It sounded lame even to his ears.

"Yeah, all the way over in East Manhattan." Carla was sarcastic. "All right, you talk to your little girlfriend Marcus. I'm going to have a good time tonight."

As soon as Marcus got home he phoned Darcy. She answered right away. They could see each other clearly.

"Did something happen last night?"

"Yeah. I really don't want to tell you but I'm going to. I realized a couple of things last night."

Darcy was prepared for the worst. When Marcus told her about the cocaine and the sex, she wanted to scream. "You were so worried about my former clients calling me. Then you went out and screwed two other women."

Marcus was unapologetic. "How many men did you screw in your career? I'm just a novice compared to you."

"That was different!" It was totally unfair for him to bring that up. "That was just business. You did it for pleasure. I was living in Joliet with a father who raped me. I had to find something else to do or my life was over."

"So you decided to do a porn film and then hire yourself out as a sexual consort. You could have done a lot of other things." This conversation was not going how he wanted it to, Marcus thought.

"I could not! What could I have done? I had no skills, no training. I still don't."

He wanted to change the subject but what she said bothered him. "You could have found a real job like real people do. A job that didn't require you to have sex, the very thing you are objecting to about me."

"Fuck you Marcus. You're an idiot." The screen went blank.

Darcy felt terrible after she signed off. She hoped Marcus would call her back. He didn't.

Thursday afternoon Carla visited him at lunch, looking spectacular as usual.

"How did it go with Darcy?"

"She hung up on me." Marcus felt depressed.

"I've got the cure for that." She said this with an air of excitement and mystery. "Come with me."

Marcus followed her down the hall about 200 feet to the elevator. They went down into the sub-basement. When the doors opened Marcus was in the coolest room he had ever seen. An octagon of eight trading stations, each with a double deck keyboard and ten big-screen monitors, surrounded a bunch of servers. A huge cable led from the servers and went into the wall. Five men and one woman were at their stations.

"Oh my God." Marcus' jaw dropped.

Carla saw a look of sheer ecstasy on his face. She could feel his excitement. She had been a fool to attempt to take him across the river. This guy had trader's fever. She knew she could hook him right here.

Carla took her seat at a station that was slightly raised in relation to the others. She was still wearing her heels, Marcus noticed. When she sat down everybody in the place greeted her like an old buddy. She blew everybody away with her sheer presence.

Carla gestured with her hand. "Come! I'll give you an overview of what we do here."

Marcus stepped over to the huge desk and saw himself sitting there one day.

"This is the equity trading section. We do automated trades using prepro-grammed algorithms."[2]

Marcus nodded.

"We have two main fund groups. One is medium-speed and the other is high-speed. The first trades in and out of shares in about a second and holds them for an average of two or three days. Those are the medium-speed funds. The high-speed funds usually make thousands of trades a second and hold them for a few minutes."[3]

Marcus looked around the trading room, still dazzled.

"By the end of the day we will usually have bought and sold about 10 million shares. The profits go to the company with the fastest hardware and the best algorithms, which enable us to spot and exploit subtle market patterns ahead of everyone else. Now pay attention, Marcus. The idea is that at the end of a typical day we hold no shares at all. Got that?"

Marcus nodded. "We're traders, not investors."

Carla was pleased. "Correct! We make money for our clients via our trading algorithms and a few spot trades. The market is driven daily by algorithms that notice a tick, drive into it, stir up the other algos and draw in a few retail traders, calculate the asymptotic peak, sell early into the peak, dump on the down side as any humans jump in with late bids. Then we tie up the lose ends, update a database table with another row of winnings, reset, and resume the search."[4] Carla was excited and intense. "That's part of what you are learning right now in your training."

Marcus nodded.

"The entire process probably typically takes about 120 seconds. With multiple threads running across the cloud you could get a hundred of these events running concurrently, each generating around $100 to $1000 profit on exchanges per event. It all depends on who jumps on and how stupid they are. That gets us, if we do it right, at least $10,000 of cleared profit every two minutes across the entire cloud. On a good day with plenty of random volatility we could double that. It's just like printing money."[5]

"What happens if you do it wrong?" Marcus asked.

"A lot of it depends on the algorithms and the latency factors, which you'll learn about. You can also lose a lot of money."

Marcus was seeing Carla in a new way. He had seen her degenerate side, on the streets and at the 23. Here in her element she was a sparkling diamond. Today she was wearing a short gray skirt that hiked up when she sat. When she turned to face him in a three-quarters view, she leaned back and let him take a good look at her long legs. Wow.

Marcus thought of the guy who had administered his aptitude test. "Did a guy named Pat used to work here?"

Carla scoffed. "That guy? Balls made of water." She looked directly at him. "He scored really high but he couldn't cut it." Her eyes said, "Can you?"

Marcus didn't respond. He didn't like to play games and ignored her attempt to goad him.

Carla noticed. *Point for you, Marcus Riley.*

"The reason we have this setup is so we can reduce the time it takes to execute a trade. An order can only be fulfilled by one trader. Whoever gets the order and can execute it first wins. We want to eliminate precious microseconds by reducing the physical distance between our servers and the exchanges as much as possible. Understood?"

"Yes." Marcus was taking it all in.

"Electronic signals travel close to the speed of light in a copper cable. One foot of cabling equals one nanosecond of latency."

"Couldn't you reduce the time by using fiber-optic cable?"

Carla smiled. "Good question, but the answer is no. When optical fiber is used instead of electrical cable, the signal moves more slowly. The speed is reduced by about one-third. So information in fiber will travel only about eight inches in one nanosecond."[6]

"How important is the latency time for us?" Marcus asked.

Carla noticed the 'us' and was pleased. "Another good question. Some HFT traders co-locate their facilities next to market exchanges. We use a service that offers market data feeds, connectivity to trading venues, co-location, and risk monitoring. All we have to do is drop our trading apps into their trading platform.[7] We do High Frequency Trading but we design our algorithms for only certain kinds of trades."

"OK. I'll understand that better when I see the algorithms."

Carla smiled. "Those algos are designed by PhDs in Mathematics and Quantitative Finance. We trade, not program. You couldn't possibly understand them."

"Of course I could." He wasn't bragging. The web of light was a responsive information system that he could program to solve any kind of problem. It worked best with dynamic problems that involved pattern recognition.

"Who do you think you are, hot shot?" Carla spoke deprecatingly. She turned ninety degrees to face him. He was looking down at her swivel chair.

"Stop looking at my legs."

Marcus slowly raised an eyebrow (something he learned from Darcy) and tried to put on an expression of offended dignity.

Carla laughed. "That's a good trick. How do you get just one to go up?"

"I don't know. But if trading is as exciting as your legs I'm going to have a lot of fun here."

"It's not fun and games," she said sharply, even though for her trading *was* fun and games. All good traders have that attitude. "We're dealing with billions of dollars in client money."

"Sure. When do I get to start trading and when do I get to see those algorithms?"

"You don't. Not until you complete your training. And then," she said, looking directly into his eyes, "you do an apprenticeship. Under me. Then, *if* you're good enough, we might let you trade some of the clients' money."

"Sounds like fun," Marcus said, and he meant it.

"What I've told you is just the surface; it's a lot more complicated than that. Now I'll take you back upstairs. I want to ask you something." She got off the chair and headed for the elevator. When they got in she pushed her pelvis against him and put her mouth on his ear. "Tonight, Marcus Riley," she whispered, "come over to my place at 10. I've got some more of that coke."

Marcus got back to his apartment at 9:15. He had barely enough time to take a shower and make himself presentable before walking a mile to Carla's at 5th and 60th. As he stepped into the shower he told himself to stay home tonight and go to bed early. He should call Darcy and apologize and figure out a way to get back together. Marcus saw a mental image of the trading room and Carla with her skirt hiked up to mid-thigh. He knew he couldn't resist. He knew he shouldn't do any more drugs but the high from it was incredible. Coming back down wasn't that bad. Once more, he told himself. He would enjoy Carla tonight, then call it off.

A little voice in the back of his mind asked him how he was going to break it off when Carla would be his superior at NYC. Marcus ignored it.

Darcy left a message when Marcus didn't call that night. She was missing him terribly and was sorry that she had blown up at him. She walked into the living room with her shoulders slumped.

"Darcy, snap out of it!" Kathleen said. "Don't tell me you are thinking about Marcus again."

Darcy sighed. "I am. I know it's stupid. I think I love him."

"Darcy, now really. You're in New York. There are lots of intelligent, rich, and able men out there who are dying to meet you."

"You forget that I've gone out with dozens and dozens of men like that when I was at Royalty. Cultured men, rich men, boozy men, obnoxious men, corporate men, intellectuals, artists, rock stars, politicians ... I've met all types. Compared to Marcus they're all boring."

"Boring!" Kathleen practically screamed the word. "I'll tell you who's boring: a nineteen-year-old kid who would rather sit in front of a computer than go out and have fun."

"He's almost twenty," Darcy lamely pointed out.

"You got it bad girl. You need to get out tonight. Some of the girls and I are going to Belinos over on East 83rd, at 10. Great food, expensive, but they have dancing. Lots of men go there. After that we'll walk the streets and see what happens."

Darcy checked her phone. Still no messages from Marcus. "You're right, screw Marcus. Let me freshen up and I'll be ready to go."

And so it went for several weeks. Marcus was getting his brain fried in the accelerated training program fourteen hours a day. He was getting fried even more at night with Carla and her friends, going out till the late hours, having sex, and doing coke. The high from the stuff was incredible. The sex, mostly with Carla, was amazing. He never saw Stacy again. Maybe something good really did happen that night with him and her. Carla remarked on it one night at the 23 when Brian Anderson asked about her.

"Where is that chick with the big boobs?" Brian had a black eye and a bandage on his left wrist as a result of his fight with Jordan. Marcus wanted to know what happened but the rule here was that you never asked anyone about their private life.

Carla spoke sharply. "You mean Stacy. We've only been going out together for a year."

"Yeah whatever, Stacy, big boobs. She used to get drunk with us all the time."

"I don't have a clue what happened to Stacy," Carla said.

Marcus stared at Carla through a drug induced haze. She was beautiful, alluring, and exciting. He would have her again tonight and he couldn't wait. He felt his personality changing and that scared him. Somehow he and Darcy never connected; maybe she was as busy as he was. He barely had time to eat, much less talk on the phone. Darcy's first show was coming up this Sunday. He hadn't forgotten that. He planned to be there even if he was fucked up.

Marcus rolled over in bed and groaned, looking at the clock on Carla's bedside table. Carla was out cold. They had snorted several lines each, and had wild sex for four hours straight. He felt like total crap. He still hadn't called Darcy because he was too tired and didn't have the energy to get his phone. Marcus turned over and went back to sleep.

The next night at the bar, Brian and Carla insisted he go across the river with them. Marcus felt energetic after a line so he said yes. "Let's go to that heroin house," Brian said. "I'm tired of coke."

Carla agreed and they drove off to East Brooklyn, into a really bad neighborhood. Marcus had no idea where they were. The street was filled with trash. The three traders approached a broken down house. Two guys with guns stood out front on the sidewalk.

One of the men brandished his gun. "Get back over on your side. We don't need no white trash over here."

"Fuck off," Brian said. "My piece is aimed right at your cock."

The man looked down and saw something sticking out of Brian's right pocket. It looked like a gun. His partner pointed his gun at Brian. "I got you covered, man. You three get the fuck out of here."

Brian grinned. Marcus was amazed; the man seemed right in his element. "We want to get high and we've got money. We're not looking for any trouble."

The two guards looked at each other and shrugged. "You pay now mother-fuckers. Then you get your juice."

Brian reached into his pocket with his left hand and pulled out a wad of bills. "This will cover it with some left over."

The other guy came over and took the money. After he counted it, he nodded to Brian. "OK, go on up."

Marcus didn't remember much about what happened after that. Brian showed him how find a vein in his arm and shoot up. After a couple of minutes he felt really mellow. He rested against a wall with peeling paint. He was spaced out and he felt good. This high was totally different from coke. Marcus liked it. There were five others in the house. A woman got up and walked over to a man lying on the floor. She pulled down his zipper but the man waved her off. "Go away." Marcus was really getting sleepy. Another man came shuffling into the room. He saw Brian get to his feet and grab Carla. "Get up."

Carla was like putty. Brian reached under her skirt and pulled down her panties. Carla began to struggle. Marcus wanted to help but he was seeing the world in a sort of hazy, feel-good stupor. It's all right, he told himself, and he believed it.

Carla felt Brian lift her skirt. She tried to stop him but the man was incredibly strong. He held her pinned against the wall with his right arm while he got himself out with his left. Carla knew that Brian was going to rape her. She realized that he hadn't shot up and was still high from the coke they'd done before they left the bar. He had set her up! She had been a fool but she knew what to do. Her knee came forward and up and caught him in the groin. Brian gasped and fell to the floor, writhing in pain. His gun fell out and Carla grabbed it. She waited for him to recover. Brian had tried to bed her before and she had always refused. Now she knew why: the guy was a total scumbag. She had totally misjudged him.

After a couple of minutes Brian rose from the floor. He stood hunched over in pain. "You goddam bitch. Give me my gun."

Carla said nothing. She looked down at him with utter contempt. "If I ever see you again after tonight I'll have a couple of my friends castrate you, you little prick. If I were you I'd get out of town."

She knew that Brian knew she was well-connected. Carla handed him the gun, satisfied that Anderson knew she meant it.

Brian started walking gingerly to the door. "Let's get out of here." Carla rearranged herself. She walked over and kicked Marcus. "We're going, get up."

Marcus arose unsteadily, still in a daze. This was kinda cool, but he liked coke better. As they walked down the steps onto the sidewalk one of the guards spoke.

"Don't come back down here no more motherfuckers." The three walked down the block to where Brian had parked his car. They went back to Manhattan. Brian dumped Marcus and Carla off on 51st street.

"Hey Carla," Marcus mumbled, "you got another line?"

"Take it easy Marcus!"

"I need some energy. Just a little snort."

Carla laid it out on the back of her long right hand. Marcus took a sniff. Almost immediately he felt better. "Thanks."

Marcus and Carla heard a screech of tires and saw Brian drive off. "What a jerk," Carla said.

"Are you OK?" Marcus asked.

"Yeah. I'm never going out with that guy again."

"Good. He's evil. Do you want me to walk you home?" Marcus hoped she'd say no because he didn't know if he could make it that far.

"No, the fresh air will do me good." Marcus saw her stride off and was amazed. The woman had unlimited energy and strength. He felt lightheaded but was on-edge from the coke. He realized he forgot to call Darcy. Again. What time was it? A little after one, maybe it's not too late.

Where did she live anyway? Somewhere in the low 80's by 2nd Avenue. He was about to call a cab when he saw one and hailed it. "Second and 80th street," he said. The cabbie was a small brown-skinned man who looked like a Pakistani or someone from India. Marcus had never seen so many people from so many different countries until he came to the City. That is how he referred to New York now, as if it were the capital of the world.

Neither Marcus nor the driver had anything to say. Marcus got out on the corner of 80th street and paid his fare. He had no idea what he was doing here. Hoping to see Darcy? Why didn't he just call? He opened his phone and saw that she had texted him at 9:35. He mentally kicked himself. For fuck's sake, what am I doing with my life? He didn't even like the tenor of his own thoughts now. He was swearing too much in his head. Every day he sounded more and more like that coke dealer, Freddy. Fuck! Was he a cokehead now? A drug addict? He tried to bring up the web of light in his head, maybe it would tell him somehow where Darcy was. It was dead. He couldn't think straight anymore.

He saw a party of women walking toward him along 2nd street. Four women. One of them looked like ..."Darcy!" Marcus shouted, running madly toward them. "Darcy!"

One of the women saw him a block away and screamed. Marcus stopped and tried to get himself together. He approached the women slowly. "Marcus!" Darcy cried. She looked him over with wide eyes. "What's happened to you?"

"What's happened to me?" Marcus was astonished. "Nothing."

"Is this that Marcus guy you keep talking about?" Kathleen said, contempt dripping from her voice. "Look at him."

Darcy was shocked by Marcus' appearance. He was thinner, his hair was out of place and he had a dark stubble of beard. The front of his suit coat was stained with white splotches. His pants were wrinkled and had a rip by the right knee. His eyes were crazy and wild.

"Darcy I have to talk to you. Something's wrong. I think ... I don't know ... but I think I'm falling apart."

"A cokehead," one of the women said. "I recognize the look."

"Run Darcy run," Kathleen said. "This guy is trouble."

Darcy wasn't feeling too well herself. She had much too much to drink tonight. After their last conversation she didn't want to criticize Marcus for doing what she herself had done. But coke! That wasn't like Marcus at all.

"Why haven't you called me or returned my messages?" Darcy asked.

Marcus thought of Carla and the drugs. What could he say? "I—"

"It's that bitch Carla Waverley isn't it?" Darcu was really angry. "You've been having sex with her again?"

"I—"

Kathleen approached him and got in his face. "If I were a man I'd punch your lights out you scumbag."

Marcus felt the woman's suppressed hostility. In a daze, he understood it was directed at him. He didn't know why and he couldn't seem to get his thoughts together. Suddenly he felt faint. His knees buckled. He was going down. Vaguely Marcus felt his body hit the cement.

Darcy stared down at Marcus, unbelieving.

Kathleen opened her phone and called a cab. "Where does this asshole live?"

"I don't know, he never told me," Darcy was about ready to cry.

"What a creep."

Darcy knew she should be angry. Instead she felt her heart ready to burst. This wasn't how their lives were supposed to go. A few months ago they were both happy in Midland. Maybe they should have stayed there.

One of the women was talking. "... look in his pockets and get his wallet."

"I don't even want to touch this guy," one of the women said. "He's filthy."

Darcy noticed that a little spittle had run down Marcus' cheek. Impulsively, she reached into her purse and brought out a handkerchief. She tenderly wiped his face even though the cloth scratched on his heavy stubble. The mid-September night was getting cold and she began to shiver.

"God Darcy, don't," Kathleen said. A cab appeared around the corner of 81st street. Darcy helped the cabbie drag Marcus into the back seat of the cab. Marcus was mumbling unintelligibly.

"Please take this ... man ... to Park Avenue and West 51st," Kathleen instructed. "He lives in the NYCBank trainee building." She handed the cabbie $25.

"I've seen this before," the cabbie said in a lilting south Asian accent. "The young ones, they go too fast too soon." The driver got back in his vehicle and pulled away.

"Garbage removal," Kathleen said.

Darcy reached into her purse and reimbursed her friend. "No, he's my responsibility. For better or for worse." Till death do us part? Darcy burst into tears.

Marcus didn't wake up until noon. He didn't care that he had missed the morning's training. He wasn't going in. He was wasted but he knew how to remedy that. Just a little snort ... his body was demanding more of the stuff. But that was impossible. He wasn't a drug addict. Or was he? He sat up in bed and knew that he sure as hell didn't want to see Carla today. She'd probably look as fresh as a daisy. Where the fuck did that phrase come from anyway? Was a daisy fresher than other flowers? Were flowers fresh? God, his mind was wandering. He had to get himself together or he'd flame out just like Pat said. Maybe he already had.

Marcus stumbled out of bed and went into the little apartment refrigerator. It was empty. How was he eating? He didn't remember eating anything for the past three days except at the cafeteria.

He needed an angel, like that guy in the old movie who wanted to kill himself. His father called it "It's A Horrible Life." The angel would tell him just what to do and he would get his life back on track.

His cell rang. Marcus mindlessly answered. "Hey kid, you want to buy some fuckin' coke?" It was Freddy on voice/vid. "You can't live off Carla forever."

Marcus winced. What was the difference between coke and fuckin' coke? "You look just like the kind of angel I'd get."

"What?" Freddy gaped. The kid was losing it for sure.

Marcus realized he had to get his thoughts together. Normally that would be easy but this morning his mind was out of control. "I'm done with coke Freddy. I never want to see the stuff again."

"Ah c'mon Marcus. You're just overdoing it that's all. You do it in moderation, you get a great buzz, you have fun, it's no big deal."

Marcus laughed cynically. "You probably tell that to all your customers before they get hooked."

Freddy explained patiently. "You don't get it kid. A lot of the traders in town use it, and amphetamines too, to keep them going. It's part of the culture. Nothing bad or wrong with it."

That was Carla, Marcus thought. He'd seen amphetamines in her medicine cabinet. If he kept going he'd wind up just like her. Was that so bad? She was beautiful and successful and really smart. She looked good all the time. He could talk to Carla about stuff that interested him. If he tried to talk trading and securities with Darcy she'd just stare at him like an idiot. Carla's life seemed to suit her. But does it suit me?

Marcus felt he was at a crossroads in life. He tried to activate the web of light but it wouldn't come up. Fuck!

"Marcus? Are you still there?"

"Yeah Freddy. I'm too fucked up to think straight. I don't know what to do anymore."

"You've been going too hard, kid."

"Yeah Freddy. How do I get off this stuff?"

Freddy paused for thought. He liked Marcus. The kid was the only person who had ever treated him with some kind of respect. He decided to cut the boy some slack. "Go see the doctor at NYCBank. His name is June I think. He knows about addiction. The word is he's discreet." NYCBank had some experience dealing with drug addiction, Freddy knew. Some of his best customers were traders. The dirty little secret was that for decades, cocaine had been a prevailing vice among day traders, bankers, and brokers on Wall Street.[8] He was only too willing to supply it. Freddy could see that Marcus was unusually susceptible to the drug. Fortunately, NYCBank's policy was to try to salvage their people before they went down the tubes.

"Thanks Freddy." Suddenly Marcus felt a wave of well-being surge through his body. He felt an overwhelming love for Freddy, for Carla, for Brian and Stacy, and Denise and Pat, and all the people he had ever met in his life. Where the fuck did that come from?

"I'll go see him today." Marcus spoke with great warmth.

Freddy felt the love come right through the connection. He usually got pissed when he lost a potential customer. Not this time. "Marcus, man, I'm glad I know you."

"I'm glad I know you too Freddy." And he meant it. Marcus closed the connection and walked into his bedroom. He felt much better but he didn't know how or why. The feeling of love and warmth was still with him and it felt really really good. It somehow canceled out stuff like Freddy just being a scumbag and a drug dealer who ruined people's lives. Or Brian being a fraudulent securities dealer who took money from innocent people, and who had tried to rape Carla because he couldn't get her any other way. Was that what they meant when they said that love was blind? Was it bad to love someone when what they really needed was to get their asses kicked? He would have to ask Darcy about that. Carla wouldn't even understand the question. That difference highlighted the choice he had just made.

Marcus grabbed a sheet of notepad paper and a pencil from the bedside table and made a list: (1) see the doctor and get off coke (2) call Darcy and make up (3) get some healthy food (4) get clothes dry cleaned and pressed (5) get out of NYCBank and interview for another job.

Marcus looked at what he had written. He knew he'd have to stay away from Carla and the nightlife or he'd wind up in the gutter.

He felt like shit but he got dressed and went in to the bank to see Dr. June. June was a funny looking guy of indeterminate age, barely over five feet tall, with big eyes and no facial hair. He was wearing a toupee.

"Doc, I need to get off cocaine. I think I'm addicted."

If the doctor was surprised he didn't show it. "Yes, I know you. You're that brilliant trainee, Marcus Riley."

"How do you know that?"

Dr. June looked him up and down as if to say, "Kid, you're six and a half feet tall and you go out with the boss' daughter."

Marcus felt as stupid as an English Lit student in physics class. "Uh yeah. I have a problem and if I don't get it fixed I'm going to lose my job."

"All right son, wait here." Dr. June went back to his private office and examined his collection of medicinal vials. Each vial was approximately three inches high, in startling, rich colors, with different geometric patterns worked into the design. He selected a dark purple flask, poured in an herbal mixture, and capped the bottle. He wrote out a list of Chinese herbs and returned to the front.

The little doctor handed Marcus the flask and the list.

"Wow this is beautiful. What's in it?"

Dr. June decided to be cautious. It really didn't matter what he put in the bottle; even water would work. "It's a new pharmaceutical, Marcus. Take one drop when you get up in the morning and another before you go to bed at night. It will help to reduce your body's craving for the drug."

June handed Marcus the list of Chinese herbs. "Go to the SHL Clinic in East Manhattan right now and tell them I sent you. Bring this list. Dr. Shen will know what to do."

Marcus squeezed the little glass dropper and drew off some of the liquid. "All I need is one drop?"

"Yes. Just place it on your tongue and wait sixty seconds before you swallow."

Marcus shrugged and squeezed out a drop. The liquid had a very pleasant and soothing aroma in the bottle. After a minute he swallowed. "Hey doc I feel better." Already he felt a slight lessening of the craving. Maybe he'd be able to make it through the night without another fix. One thing was for sure. He wasn't going out with Carla again.

Marcus left the building and called a cab. On the way to the herbalist he called in sick and told the bank he'd be in first thing in the morning.

Darcy had just gotten out of bed and eaten breakfast. She felt like crying. There was still no message from Marcus on her phone. The image of him sprawled on the cement last week was almost too much for her to bear. It was shocking. She had told Kathleen that she loved Marcus. Did she? Should she let him go?

She searched her heart and understood that she did love him. Although he was physically a man, emotionally he was still a boy. He needed time to mature. For the first time she understood that Marcus was in way over his head in his job, competing with much older men and women. As she thought of Carla and NY-CBank she began to get angry. How could they let this happen to a young trainee? Was there no supervision over there? She was seething now, but it felt a lot better than being depressed. What could she do?

Her first show was this Sunday evening, in two days. She had to get out of her funk. She decided to make one more phone call. If Marcus really wanted her he would have to make the next move. She grabbed her phone and left a voice/video message.

"Marcus this is Darcy. I love you, but if you want me you have to come get me. I'm done crying and worrying about you. My show is on Sunday at 8 p.m. I've sent the invitation as an attachment to this message. If I don't see you Sunday" –

she had to pause and stop her voice from trembling – "I will assume that you have decided to be a cokehead and fuck Carla for the rest of your life ... and ... and that you don't want me anymore."

She tried to find a good way of signing off but she couldn't. She put the phone back in her purse and sat at the breakfast table with her arms crossed and her hands on her shoulders.

God, Marcus. Be there on Sunday.

Chapter **13**

Marcus grabbed his phone and called Darcy. She didn't answer so he left a message. "Hi Darcy I figured out some stuff and I'm going to leave NY-CBank and get a job somewhere else. I'm not going to do coke anymore because it destroys your mind. I saw a doctor today and he's got me on some drug that's really helping me. Don't worry. I'll be there on Sunday and I'll expect you to be beautiful as always. I gotta go now and confront Carla and Pat and tell them I'm leaving. I'm kind of scared to do it. I have to play a man's part; I'm done being an asshole. This weekend I'm going to look for another place to live, hopefully closer to you. I'll try to see you on Sunday."

Number two on his list was to get some healthy food but he didn't feel like eating. His stomach was in a knot. He needed to talk to Pat and Carla right now or he'd never do it.

It was a cool late September day but Marcus was sweating profusely after he walked the four blocks to NYCBank. When he showed up in the training room, Pat instantly realized his intent. "Flame out!" he said, sneering. "You didn't even last six weeks!" All the other trainees looked up and recognized the famous kid who had scored perfect on the aptitude test.

"Too much coke, it fried my brain," Marcus said.

"Coke?" one of the trainees said, his eyes popping.

Marcus grinned. "It's a long story."

Pat hooted. "You'd better go see Carla. She was looking for you at lunch."

"Is she down in equities trading?"

"Yeah. Too bad you'll never make it there, hotshot. At least I tried."

Marcus shrugged and walked out. Carla spotted him immediately when he got off the elevator. "Did we wear you out last night?" Today her feet were in flattops. She had to look up three inches to see him.

Marcus spoke abruptly. "I'm done here. I'm going to interview someplace else."

Carla's face silently went through astonishment, anger, and then contempt. "I'm surprised and disappointed Marcus."

Suddenly Marcus had an idea. He turned on the web of light in his head and it came up, thank God. He sent it over to Carla. "Do you *want* me to stay?"

Now he was Carla and he could fully understand her response. Her first reaction was, "I'm not going to lose him, he's *mine*." Next she thought about Darcy, and whether Darcy had gotten to him. Third was the idea that Marcus might turn out to be one of the best traders ever and if so, she wanted him in her department where she'd get all the credit. Marcus almost had to laugh. Carla's competitive nature made her personality one-dimensional. He realized he would have no trouble at all with her if he made his position absolutely clear. Carla appreciated firmness and decisiveness because she was so committed to one thing. In that sense she was a natural leader.

"Yes," Carla said. "But no more of this flip-flopping around."

"I'll stay under three conditions."

"You dare to give me *conditions*?" Marcus could see that she wanted to get her way always because she would feel like a loser if she didn't.

"Yes. Number one: I'm getting back together with Darcy. Two: I'm not doing any more drugs. Three: From now on our relationship is strictly business. I'm an employee of NYCBank and so are you. No fraternizing outside of work. And four: Stay out of my personal life, it's none of your business."

"That's four conditions not three." Carla spoke without thinking, needing to be right. The nerve of this guy! No man she was interested in had ever talked to her in that tone. Certainly not a 20-year-old kid. None of them had ever dictated conditions on her relationship with them. *She* dictated and they complied or they got dumped. She was Carla Waverley! The hottest woman in New York, and the smartest too. The daughter of one of NYCBank's most important executives. Carla had another shocking thought. "Do you actually have the temerity to dump *me*?"

Marcus' lips trembled. Thank God she couldn't see into him or she'd probably kick him in the balls. He could read her like a text message now. It was kind of funny observing her reactions. He liked the word 'temerity,' he'd never heard it before.

"Yes, I'm dumping you. As of right now."

Carla's mouth moved up and down but nothing came out. Anger, disbelief, hatred, astonishment, and incredulity rapidly sketched their emotions on her face. Finally she stamped her foot on the painted cement floor. The *crack!* startled the other traders. She finally concluded that Marcus was delusional. A genius, perhaps, but a deluded genius. To dump her for that little shrimp Darcy Regier? Why, it was absurd. Then the thought crept into her head that maybe Marcus *was* a genius and that his actions were somehow beyond her understanding. She dismissed that as ridiculous. Then she thought: he might eventually be better than me. It galled her and fascinated her. She thought about her work and her position. Her department had the best trading record in the City. She wanted that to continue.

Carla made her decision, the winning decision. She would accept his defection from her sexually but she would have him as her subordinate. He would shine his light on her and she would benefit. This would also be for the greater good, for everyone in the department and the company would gain monetarily and in reputation. Here Marcus was surprised. He didn't think that Carla had thoughts for anyone but herself. He could see now that that side of her personality was evident, just undeveloped. Marcus felt that same feeling of well-being that he had when he talked to Freddy.

Carla smiled and Marcus shut down his web of light.

"Why didn't you say so before, kid?" Carla said.

"You're rather difficult to say no to."

Carla threw back her head and laughed. "All right Marcus Riley, have it your own way." Carla took her seat at her trading station, watching her monitors. She liked this assertive Marcus much better.

Marcus saw that she had completely switched him off, just as her father had done during his interview. He got on the elevator and walked down the hall to the training area. Pat was belligerent. "What are you doing here?" All the trainees looked up.

"I'm back." Marcus felt like a Tyrannosaurus Rex confronting a bunch of house cats. "I'm not going anywhere."

When Darcy got back to her apartment after a long day at work and a stopover at Belinos for drinks, she was feeling a little tipsy. She'd drunk too much again, worrying about Marcus. Just as she picked up her phone, it rang.

"Hi Darcy, it's me." Darcy looked him over. It was hard to tell on the small phone screen but he had cleaned himself up and looked fairly normal but a lot thinner. "I've decided to stay after all."

She'd gotten his message on her lunch break. Now he was reneging. "That goddam Carla!" she shouted. "That fucking *bitch!*"

"No! Wait!" The screen went blank. He quickly called her back but she didn't answer, so he left a long text message explaining what happened with Carla today.

Darcy was nervous. Although she had traveled the world with some very rich men, she had never modeled. She had been in New York for only a few months. Almost every waking moment had been spent in learning her new trade. Of course she had a huge head start. At Royalty she studied deportment and learned to be comfortable in the presence of rich and cultured gentlemen. But modeling was much different. Most of the audience would be women, and buyers. She had to learn the correct moves to show off Audrey's classic clothing to it's very best advantage.

Three months ago Kathleen had walked her in to meet Audrey Quenioux at her private studios. "*Vraiment,*" the modiste remarked. "This one is of an elegance." Audrey walked around her, looking closely at her lines and her figure. The modiste told her to walk across the room. "Yes, she has *raffinement.*" Audrey clapped her hands. "It is good. Well done Kathleen. We will use her at the Frick showing."

Kathleen gasped. "Do you think so madame? So soon?"

"But of course," Audrey replied. "She is everything Holderness said she would be."

That is how her new career began. And the clothes! Oh, to wear one of Audrey's dresses to a party would be to cause a sensation. The most expensive fabrics, the most elegant and classic lines. For each dress the hair must be worn a certain way, the shoes must be so, the jewelry must be this and only this and worn here, you must move in this manner and stop so, and turn the body this way and the face that way. Each of Audrey's creations were hand-stitched and enormously expensive. Darcy tried on and modeled dozens of items from classic theater dresses, cocktail dresses, party dresses, summer and winter wear, hats, blouses, sweaters, brassieres, shoes of every description, and on and on. Her days began at 7 a.m. and did not end sometimes until past 10 at night, after going out with the girls. When she got back to her apartment she was exhausted, but it was so exciting! To look her very best at all times, to look the lady of quality at every hour of the day, had reminded her of her time with Royalty. Her opinion of herself soared. Then she thought of her upbringing on the mean streets of Joliet. Audrey Quenioux must never know of that or her modeling career would be over. The modiste was almost as old-fashioned as Holderness. Audrey would never accept a vulgar and tawdry *canaille* representing her brand.

The Frick showing was the highlight of the fall season for those with impeccable taste, Audrey said. Everyone who was anyone would be there. On the day Darcy was so busy she hardly had time to think of Marcus. Now it was almost 7:30 and some early arrivals had already come. A special stage and runway had been set up in the stately mansion on 81st street and Lexington, in an immense wood-paneled ballroom lighted by crystal chandeliers. Would Marcus appear? If he did not it was over and she would close her heart to him forever. It would be too painful otherwise.

Four women would model for Audrey this evening. They were all backstage fluttering nervously, chatting, and getting into their costumes. Two assistants hovered around the women, ensuring that all was perfectly as the modiste required. A greeter was present. She announced the names of all who entered just like the old movies she had seen. The showing was to last for 60 minutes. Each model would present four times. Darcy, being the newest, would go last. She would be able to peek from backstage at the more experienced women as they "walked the plank" down the runway.

Darcy looked around the room and spotted Marcus. He was here! Marcus looked fine tonight, wearing a dark blue double-breasted suit and black shoes. His thick black hair was combed neatly. His persistent black stubble of beard made him look ruggedly handsome. Her heart leaped with pride. The eyes of many of the women were drawn to him. He was thinner now and wilder with a ragged edginess that made him even more dashing and attractive. She opened the theater curtain and waved to him. His eyes lit up. "Hi Darcy!" Marcus took a seat in the front row.

At that moment a magnificent woman entered the room. Darcy heard the greeter call "Carla Waverley." She couldn't believe it. Had Marcus been lying to her all along? Darcy's heart jumped in her chest and her face reddened with anger.

"Oh dear!" Christine, one of Audrey's assistants, was very upset. "Darcy! You must be calm tonight."

Darcy took a few deep breaths. Christine was correct of course. It would not do for Audrey Quenioux to have any inkling of trouble tonight. Fortunately the modiste was in another room, putting the final touches on an evening dress.

Darcy gazed at the woman as she walked slowly down the space that separated the seating, which was arranged in an arc. A giant! The hussy wore three inch black heels and a skirt that was much too short for this venue. Blatantly showing off those legs. Darcy had to admit that she looked beautiful in a cold, brittle sort of way. Carla was dressed in a business suit, in stark contrast to the other women who wore more elegant clothing. Carla entered the front row and brazenly sat down next to Marcus.

Marcus was angry. "Carla! Didn't I tell you that we were not to socialize outside of business hours?"

Darcy saw the woman turn her head, barely acknowledging Marcus' presence. "I'm not here to see you, child. I'm here to see this Darcy Regier."

Darcy could tell that Marcus wanted to hit her and she felt a little better. But how would she do on her first opportunity, when that woman sat staring at her? The bitch probably came to disconcert her. Darcy decided not to allow Carla Waverley to disturb her performance. She had learned at Royalty how to command herself and push down her nervousness. She would do it tonight. She would make Audrey Quenioux and her designs look magnificent and show this barbarian banker how a true lady handled herself.

When it came time for her to walk the plank Darcy had composed herself. There were no empty chairs. Darcy estimated that at least 75 women were in attendance. Her first costume was a classic silk evening dress, dark blue, with short sleeves and a square bodice. Her blond hair was piled high on top of her head in a coiffure Audrey called the Waterfall. Darcy wore elegant teardrop earrings with diamonds in them. Around her neck was a string of natural pearls. She walked out slowly, just as Audrey had instructed. She had the pleasure of hearing Marcus gasp. She did not look directly at Carla, of course. Her performance tonight was for Marcus and the other women in attendance. Darcy could see the scowl on Carla's face as she examined Darcy and glanced disapprovingly at Marcus' infatuated stare. Good, you cokehead bitch. See how your betters handle themselves.

Darcy turned just so, and back again, showing the elegant lines of the dress. Her movements were as smooth as the silk she was wearing. She saw approval in the faces of the women in the audience. When she turned to walk slowly back up the runway the audience broke into spontaneous applause. Darcy was so thrilled she went too fast and felt one of her heels hit against the other, throwing her slightly off-balance. The curtain had already opened slightly and she saw Audrey Quenioux wince backstage. Darcy knew she had erred. But she slowed down in time and recovered as the curtain opened fully. As she turned toward the dressing room the modiste hissed at her. "*Pour l'amour de dieu,* girl, watch your step!"

The show went by in a blur for Darcy. Her fourteen hour days in training had proven out. The next three performances went off smoothly, even though she had to rush out of and into the next costume, have her hair redone, and change jewelry. Each time she walked out onto the runway she saw Marcus' jaw drop further and further, and the scowl on the barbarian bitch's face grow deeper. Each time the audience applauded her enthusiastically. By the end of the evening Audrey Quenioux was all smiles. Two buyers came quickly backstage and accosted the modiste. The other girls were happy that the new girl hadn't fallen on her face. The women in the audience were filling out order forms. Three expensively dressed men came into the dressing room and ogled two of the models. In the old days, Darcy had learned at Royalty Services, men from the upper crust would offer girls *carte blanches* and ruin them in society. Today such conduct was accepted as part of the business.

Darcy didn't want to take off her costume. She left the stage by the back and walked up to the first row, where Marcus sat with Carla Waverley. The crowd was buzzing with talk of the show. Darcy didn't acknowledge Carla's presence. "Well, Marcus, what do you think?" She saw that Marcus' eyes had followed her all the way to the seats. Darcy was pleased that Marcus' gaze was frankly admiring. She could tell he lusted after her and that made her feel even better. Best of all, his eyes were on *her* and not the giantess sitting next to him.

Carla rose from her seat and ascended to her full height, towering over her. My God, Darcy thought, she's almost as tall as Marcus! And those legs! She had to admit that the woman was overwhelmingly beautiful, just as Marcus had said. She didn't wonder how her manchild could have fallen for Carla Waverley.

Carla gazed down at Darcy and sneered. "So this is little Darcy Regier."

Heads turned as some of the elegantly dressed women in the audience sensed a social confrontation. The room quieted. Marcus remained seated, not wanting to stick his nose in a cat fight. He felt that Darcy could handle herself.

Darcy held her position and nodded slightly, as a social superior might do to an inferior. "Yes, I'm Darcy Regier."

Marcus, in his chair, had to stifle a laugh. Darcy, with that one gesture, had dismissed Carla and reduced her stature. Carla didn't notice.

Carla looked her contempt. "A pretty, fluttering little thing, aren't you?"

Darcy raised one eyebrow just so. On her face was the correct look of hauteur. She said nothing, waiting for the other woman. All eyes in the room were now turned toward the magnificent intruder and the girl who had modeled Audrey Quenioux's clothing so superbly, and who had made them feel as elegant and beautiful as she.

Darcy slowly looked Carla up and down, as if to say, 'observe this vulgar intruder in her business suit.'

She met the eyes of the women observing the scene. "I detect a lack of breeding in this one." It was incredible what a gesture, a look, could do, Marcus thought. Somehow Darcy had contrived to make Carla look small.

Many of the women laughed but Marcus did not want to offend his future boss and kept silent. Darcy's entire demeanor and her responses were perfect. She was totally in control.

Carla's eyes blazed. "Why you stupid little mannequin. What are you good for but as a statue for pretty little dresses?"

Instantly the gazes of the other women turned hostile.

Carla had erred badly, Marcus saw. She had let her resentment of Darcy overcome her better judgment. But Carla had no social sense. She just dominated wherever she went and that usually worked for her. But here, Carla had rudely violated the subtleties of social intercourse. She was out of her element.

"*On peut toujours compter sur elle pour raconter des blagues*," Darcy murmured. Two of the women, who apparently understood French, laughed loudly.

Marcus saw that Carla was about to burst with frustration and anger. For a moment he thought she might strike Darcy. After a moment Carla stifled her rage, turned on the balls of her feet, and strode out of the room. When the door closed, Darcy received another round of applause. She bowed and smiled.

The crowd began to buzz again. "Oh how entertaining!" one of the women remarked. "We came to see clothing and we got a play as well."

Audrey Quenioux had seen the whole thing and was astonished. She rushed up to Darcy. "But do you speak French my girl?"

"No madame. I learned a few phrases at Royalty and was taught how to pronounce them correctly."

"You were magnificent. Who is this young gentleman, and who was the *canaille* who just left?"

Darcy introduced Marcus. "This is Marcus, my boyfriend. The woman who just left is his boss."

The modiste's eyes widened. Audrey gazed at Marcus. "That woman, she is your superior?"

Marcus almost laughed. Audrey's expression conveyed the impression that Carla was about as valuable as a pile of lint blocking a dirty dryer vent. "Well, not yet. I'm still in training. One day she might be."

"Now you know how to handle such a one," the older woman said. "You must be firm with them."

Marcus grinned. "Yes ma'am." He agreed entirely.

When Carla Waverley got back to her apartment she was seething. That little tramp! Masquerading as a woman of high fashion and culture. She probably came from the mean streets. As soon as she thought it she knew it was true. She would investigate this Darcy Regier. She had seen the little woman who was her boss, and noticed her superior attitude. When the woman found out about Darcy she would never again allow that little bitch to work in her boutique.

Part IV – INTERVENTION

CHAPTER **14**

The Palace of the Alephs, Draco sector, Draco Epsilon (Mutawa) 12,000 years ago

Aleph One spoke to Aleph 102, senior geneticist within the panel of genetic biologists. "Please report on the latest genetic modification experiment." Aleph's One's large, liquid eyes with their golden irises expressed fear and forlorn hope.

The semi-annual gathering of Alephs included all disciplines and was chaired by the Prime Aleph. The first day of the meeting covered the most pressing issues for all beings in the Epsilon system. The Prime Aleph sat at the center of a large circular room, illuminated by soft golden light. The other Alephs sat on floats in a tiered arrangement like a stadium. As Aleph One gazed about the conference room, he observed with dismay that all present seemed to look even more identical than at last year's meeting. Or was that just his imagination? His race had light gold, perfectly smooth skin with no body or facial hair. The clones all had very small noses, thin lips, and very large, round eyes with gold irises in the shape of a vesica piscis. Their limbs were long and ended in dexterous, six-digit hands and feet. Their genitalia were shrunken.

Aleph 102 spoke gloomily. "Unfortunately the recent attempt at genetic diversification has not resulted in significant change. The last 500 clones from the Mutawa line have shown a 0.09% deterioration in the coefficient of vitality, and a mere 0.07% increase in the compatible reproductive function."

"What you are saying is that our race is continuing to devolve toward a genetic dead end," Aleph One declared.

"That is correct sir. I am very sorry. Unless we are able to infuse our genetic material with new life our race will gradually diminish in vitality, intelligence, and sustainability. Our clones will eventually be born retarded and dysfunctional."

Aleph One's smooth, refined face showed anguish.

"If present trends continue," Aleph 102 concluded, "we estimate race termination in approximately 5,000 years."

"Aleph 101, please report on your galactic compatibility survey," Aleph One commanded.

"A rigorous biological survey was taken of planets within a radius of 100 light years. Aleph One could see Aleph 101's six-fingered hand nervously tapping on the surface of the conference table. This was not a good sign. "We have identified only five suitable candidates, and four of them are marginal. However, the fifth candidate planet is composed of primitive hominids who have the most exciting collection of genetic material we have ever seen in the galaxy."

Aleph One straightened in his float and his expression immediately became animated. "Do you mean there is hope?"

"Yes, there is hope. These hominids exist on a planet within an obscure system with a single G-type star. We are certain their DNA has already been modified. The Seeders have implanted their Light Codes within the species, which happens with every sub-prime species awaiting genetic evolution to galactic standards. However, we have also observed significant activity from the entities in the Tau system. This race, as you all know, is degraded. The Tau have deliberately altered the genetics of the hominids to prevent their natural evolution."

"Then we must act quickly," Aleph One decided. "Has the planet been claimed by another system?"

Aleph 105 responded. "The planet of the hominids exists within the Desert. There are no formal claims to it. However, we found at least 78 permanent or temporary stations from 37 different sectors. Analysis of the hominid's biological material shows 23 distinct genetic codes have been grafted onto their Biological Information System."

"That is remarkable!" Aleph One felt excitement. Excitement was a wonderful emotion that occurred less and less frequently in his life experience. It was a sign of genetic health. "Why is there so much activity on this obscure planet?"

"Unknown," replied Aleph 109, from the Intelligence Service. "We discovered these hominids only 47 rotations ago ..."

Aleph 101 interrupted. "If our team has access to biological material from these hominids we may be able to match their codes with ours and enhance the viability of our own genetics. We may even be able to save our race."

Aleph One spoke quickly. "Do you mean that there is hope for sexual reproduction?"

"Hope, yes. But there is no certainty. Our researchers have reported that the best we can expect is an infusion of fresh genetic material that will make our clones stronger and more energetic."

"This information is extremely satisfactory," replied Aleph One. "Have you liaised with the Intelligence Services? Is there a problem with obtaining genetic material from these hominids?"

"The planet is wild, Aleph One," Aleph 109 offered. "The variety of environments and species is astonishing. Most of the bases, except of course for the Draco Tau barbarians and two other factions from the Orion sector, are research facilities. If we avoid the Tau we should be able to easily capture a few of the hominids and transport them back to our system."

"That is welcome data, Aleph 109, thank you," said Aleph One. "Proceed immediately to procure this much-needed genetic material."

Aleph 109 nodded affirmatively and exited the conference.

"The next order of business is Aleph 204's report on the Tau. Aleph 204?"

Aleph 204 was unusually tall for an Epsilon, reaching almost six feet in height. His birth was hoped to have presaged a great leap in diversity for the race. This clone, unfortunately, had turned out to be an irregularity.

"The Tau have successfully established a foothold on Epsilon-Gamma." The audience gasped. "Yes, a star within our own system. It is reprehensible but there is nothing we can do."

Aleph 204 continued. "The Tau are only interested in primitive species, arresting their development, and creating slave races which they can eventually harvest. Therefore our race, which is close to termination, is not currently attractive to them."

A wave of relief echoed through the assembly.

"The Tau trap their subjects through the use of barbaric and repetitive rituals that involve blood sacrifice and other degraded practices. These invocations are designed to invoke specific vibrations that resonate to the Tau. The goal of the Tau, or Xorg as they call themselves, is to alter the consciousness of those who participate in these rituals. These dark ceremonies sensitize the hominids to the awareness of the decadent intelligences of the Tau. They are used to establish means of communication with the Tau. Of course these practices stultify the growth of new, developing races." Aleph 204 shuddered. "The Tau feed off the lower emotions that emanate from the biology of their slave races. Without these lower energies the Tau would die."

Aleph One, and the others in the conference room, collectively thanked their gods. Although the Epsilon had taken a wrong evolutionary path they had not utterly degraded themselves. Their race was weak and deprecated but still honorable.

Aleph 204 continued. "That is why the Futures Committee is concerned. Once the Xorg establish a vibrational foothold in a system they can eventually bring down the resonance of the entire system. This creates more opportunities for their control paradigm. We must avoid this at all costs."

"Yes," one of the Alephs commented. "A descending resonance gradually makes us more susceptible to races like the Tau, who embrace violence for its own sake."

Aleph 102, the senior biologist, spoke. "It is both ironic and abominable that such a cruel and atavistic race are vital and able to freely reproduce, while we struggle from generation to generation just to survive."

Aleph One spoke to Aleph 313, the Council's race vitality expert. "What is the current Life Reading Index for the Epsilon?" The Life Reading Index was the Epsilon measure of their race's viability. Plotted against the Resonance Index, which measured their current dimensional position in the multiverse, it determined the health and survivability of their race.

"3.0873," Aleph 313 stated. "During the last rotation we lost another 0.0002 basis points."

"Does the presence of the Xorg indicate that we are already falling dangerously close to the dimensional boundary?"

"That is undetermined. We can say, certainly, that the Tau presence in our own system is an indication that our Life Reading Index is much too low."

After hours of discussion Aleph One made his determination. "Our race is not energetic enough to deal with the Tau contamination in our own sector, much less the planet of the hominids." Aleph One spoke desperately. "We *must* procure new genetic material and make it possible once again for sexual reproduction. Then perhaps we can avoid the mistakes we have made in the past ..."

Draco Sector, Draco Tau (Xorg) 3,000 years ago

"Get over here fool!"

The drone, a look of hatred on his broad reptilian face, muttered imprecations under his breath. He stood insolently before his superior.

"Imbecile, why have you not monitored the viewport?" Ubar pointed to a cube about three feet by three feet by three feet. The monitoring device was a transportal, and it wasn't a device at all. It was simply a section of space-time that had been programmed to resonate to a specific galactic coordinate. That coordinate was on the planet of the earthian hominids. The transportal allowed the user to observe everything at the coordinate site. The video could be zoomed in or out at any magnification. If the user at the site had a receiver, communication was possible. The transportal operated on the subtle scalar bandwidth beyond the electromagnetic spectrum. They were an accepted part of an ancient galactic technology that had been around for billions of years. One simply carried a transportal in one's pocket, unfolded it to the required size, and activated it via a targeted thought impulse.

The drone replied impudently. "There was nothing in it."

Ubar swiped his paw at the insolent inferior, knocking him down. "Miscreant, there is activity in sector six of the earthian planet. The prime sector!"

The drone got up and faced his master. His tongue flicked in an out of a mouth filled with sharp incisors. "If I were not your drone I would kill you where you stand."

Ubar threw his head back and fed on the sweet, sharp energy of hatred. He felt energized. "Good! That is the proper attitude. But you have abandoned your post. Return to your quarters, I shall monitor the device myself. You are reduced a half-step in rank."

The drone, seething, strode quickly out of the observation chamber to a small cave in back that served as his personal space. Ubar fed again off of the delicious energy. 'That one,' he said to himself, 'needs watching. He will soon organize other drones against me.' This thought excited him. It meant intrigue, and the opportunity to completely defeat his enemies. Once he did that there would be more enemies to destroy. It was glorious.

Ubar gazed in the tank, which showed a pastoral scene on the earthian planet. The little vermin were performing one of their 'black magic' rituals, complete with the sacrifice of animals and a virgin hominid. They were invoking the Belial, as per the instructions laid down by that entity 700 of their earthian years ago in Babylon. Ubar watched as the little animals slit the throat of the screaming child. The hominid's blood dripped onto the stone altar. Ubar fed from the life force of the female hominid as its life force departed the body. He knew that the great Belial himself was also feeding, as was the entire Council.

A voice intruded. "Scum! Your job is to observe and take notes, not to feed!" Ubar laughed. The voice was from the worm Tattannu, a messenger drone from the Council. "Do not overstep your bounds, insect, or I shall personally slit your throat." Ubar felt the castrated reptile's fear before it cut off the connection.

Ubar observed the scene from the transportal. The priests were secluded within one of their temples. The little hominids recited the incantation repetitively, setting up a powerful resonance. This resonance opened the communication lines within the ethers to the Xorg, and to Belial specifically. Each ritual called for a slightly different incantation, which would call forth a different 'god.' The earthian hominids were not intelligent enough to activate a transportal, so communication must be established in a less efficient manner. But it was still very effective, if clumsy. The little fools! The hominids intended to call upon Belial to give them power. In fact they were setting up a vibration that would trap their souls within Belial's personal resonance. After several of these rituals the 'priests' would in effect be the psychic slaves of Belial.

"Sabete Latepo," the little hominids chanted, kneeling upon the stone altar. Ubar recognized the control spell. Each priest lit one of thirteen candles and dripped its wax into the blood of the sacrificed virgin. "We call upon the great Belial to give us power and domination over our subjects. The vermin will do as we tell them, always to obey. Obey or die. Belial, we call upon you to give us your power!" The priests then drank the virgin's blood, chanting "Sabetto Lepati." Ubar saw Belial appear before the priests. Their hominid faces and clothing were stained with blood, the life-giving blood. Ubar knew that the Belial had sent his essence through the channel established by the incantation. The priests, awed, shrank back in fear. Belial fed, growing stronger.

"Vermin!" he shouted, towering almost nine feet tall above the humanoids. "Your wish is granted. You now have the power of life and death over those whom you rule. Remember: the first born child from each household is to be sacrificed to the gods. Failure to obey this injunction will result in your slow death. Ensure that the symbols of your gods are placed upon the holy places, informing the people of their subjugation." Ubar saw the demon snarl and growl menacingly. Belial took a step forward into the gathering. The priests, maddened with fear, began running around the chamber. Belial laughed, threw his head back, and fed again on their energy. Then the demon disappeared.

Ubar was trembling with excitement. Oh, to be in control of the Council and to have first feed from hundreds of rituals upon the earthian planet! In the back of his mind was the intention to kill Belial and his minions, usurping his title and his power.

Another of his underlings arrived to take the place of the drone who was demoted. "Ekurzakir, reporting for duty sir." This drone was broad shouldered and well muscled, with a thick head. Ubar sized him up as stupid but useful. One who would follow orders unquestioningly.

"Monitor the device and take meticulous notes," Ubar commanded. "The scum who had your post has been demoted."

The big reptile nodded. Ubar felt no hatred, ambition, or any other appropriate emotion. This one might be trusted, but his scope would be limited. No matter, he would use this one in his plan to overthrow Belial and take over the Council.

Ekurzakir spoke suddenly. "How goes the Plan?"

Ubar's head jerked quickly around to confront him. So this one was curious, was he? "What business is it of yours, menial?"

"It is the business of every Tau to implement the Plan to the best of his ability," Ekurzakir replied.

A spy! Ubar thought. Was Belial already on to him? Oh, this was delicious. Belial must already fear me. He would test this drone's knowledge. Too much knowledge would indicate that he was indeed a spy, for drones received only enough information to do their jobs properly.

"What do *you* know of our great Plan, you scoundrel?" Ubar saw a flash from the reptile's eyes. Good! This one has given himself away. He would keep this scum close to him and feed him disinformation.

"What everyone knows. Slowly increase the humanoid population, eventually controlling the billions with a select group of trained vermin. We keep the elite bloodlines safe by giving them snippets of the ancient galactic technology. This keeps our control group well ahead of the masses. Then we harvest, and begin again. This has been our way since the beginning."

"This is not knowledge a drone should have. You are a spy. I will kill you now."

Ekurzakir smiled thinly, in no way cowed. "Do not reach too far, Ubar. Your ambition is known at the highest levels."

Ubar was pleased. This scum was openly acknowledging himself as a plant. Ekurzakir's message was that he could not be harmed, having the protection of Belial. "Monitor the device, reprobate. While you are here you are my slave. Fail to execute even the most trivial of my commands and you shall die."

The drone nodded. This was as it should be. Their relationship was established. Master and slave, superior and subordinate.

Ubar walked out of the observation chamber to his plush quarters inside the cave, elated. If Belial was monitoring him, it indicated his increased status and power. Dare he challenge the Great One himself? Surely it was now something to think about seriously.

CHAPTER **15**

New York City, three months after Darcy's first show

"Darcy, guess what?" Kathleen said. They were in Audrey's little boutique eating sandwiches on a small dining table. "We're going to a party tomorrow evening!" Kathleen was practically breathless with excitement.

"We go to lots of parties," Darcy said.

"Yes, but this one is special. We've been invited to the big fundraising bash for Senator Fazio, the favorite for the Democratic presidential nomination. Of course there will be a big party afterward and a very private one for the VIPs. That's the one we're going to. Isn't it exciting?"

Darcy nodded to Kathleen. She had been to a few of those.

"There will be CEOs, movie stars, society lights, important pols, it's absolutely exclusive."

"You are a social butterfly Kathleen. You always keep up with the latest celebrity and fashion news."

"Of course. We cater to the unreachable and private world of the upper crust. These are our clients."

Kathleen was thin and excitable with short-cropped red hair, and always wore large circular gold earrings and red lipstick. Fortunately she was also very competent as the boutique's manager because sometimes Kathleen's nervous excitement was irritating. Darcy was careful to hide those feelings. She would forever be grateful to Kathleen for bringing her to New York and Audrey Quenioux.

"You helped us to get there."

Darcy was astonished. "Me? All I do is put clothes on my body."

Kathleen snorted. "Silly girl. Since the Frick show we have positively been all the rage. You have become the face of our little boutique. That's what Audrey has always been looking for – a girl who could take us over the top and into the most exclusive circles."

Darcy was now Audrey Quenioux's primary show model. She had worked a number of very small but remunerative private showings uptown. These private parties only required one or two girls and opened the doors of the boutique to those who did not wish to appear in public.

Darcy replied modestly. "I'm happy. I really enjoy what I do and I like working with you and Audrey."

"That's another thing. You don't draw attention to yourself, you're not a diva. One of the old society dragons said to me the other day that you don't put yourself forward. She said your company manners are perfect."

"If they are I learned them from Holderness."

"You have a good pedigree."

Darcy winced but said nothing. A good pedigree? Deep down she knew herself to be a fraud.

Kathleen stopped to chew a big bite of sandwich, and put her hand over her mouth. "You have noticed that you've been featured in the last two monthly mailings?"

Darcy smiled but inside she was nervous. It made her feel good to see her pictures adorning the mailings to the boutique's clientele. She wondered what would happen if Audrey, or any of their exclusive clients, ever found out about her background in Joliet. It was her constant fear. Her past would always travel with her. Fortunately Holderness had not told Audrey anything about her past.

"You know how all of this started," Kathleen said.

"Not really." Darcy replied as cheerfully as she could.

Kathleen laughed. She studied Darcy intently for a few moments. "You really don't, do you? It was your very first show and the way you handled that Waverley woman. She's famous around town for her brains, her ambition, her beauty, and her vulgarity. I can still remember every word that was said."

"Oh?" Darcy had managed to forget that incident quickly. Carla Waverley had frightened her. She knew the woman hated her.

Kathleen laughed. "Oh yes. I circulate at all of our shows, it's part of my job. A lot of society women were at that show. They still talk about your handling of her."

Darcy knew she had outward refinement but Carla Waverley was the true blood. She was just a mongrel. She tried to change the subject. "Where is the party?"

"At the Palace mid-town. The Fazio campaign has booked the entire Villard Ballroom for the night for the movers and shakers. Afterward the crème-de-la-crème gather together and party. We'll model a few select outfits up in one of the Tower penthouse suites. Afterward ... the night is ours."

Kathleen was positively giddy with anticipation. Darcy knew the drill and what was likely to happen. A lot of horny men would be there looking to get laid, and lots of drugs and alcohol. Somewhere hidden away, in a back room, other kinky stuff would go down. She didn't want to think about that.

That night she called Marcus and told him about the party. "Would you do me a favor and wait down in the Palace lobby at midnight? I should be out of there by then and you can take me home. You can eat in the restaurant if you're hungry."

"If I take you home I'm staying the night Darcy. I have to be up at 6 tomorrow morning and I'm horny as hell."

Darcy paused. They were both so busy there hadn't been time to see much of each other since the Frick showing three months ago. "Are you still seeing Carla?"

"Screw Carla. She's my boss, that's it."

"That's just what I'm afraid of." Darcy felt a harder edge to Marcus. New York had sharpened him. He used to be a sweet and tender nerd who adored her. She didn't know what he was now. Did she want to find out? Her heart needed reassurance.

Marcus felt her hesitation. "I haven't had time to breathe since I lost it that night. I graduate from the program in two weeks and I gotta stay focused. Carla is the opposite of focus."

"All right. I kinda miss you."

"I miss you too."

The New York Palace was built around the old Villard mansion, with a 55-story tower rising above it. Kathleen, Aubrey Quenioux, and Darcy entered the two story marble lobby from the courtyard at 9:00 p.m. The three women sat down to have something to eat in the bistro-style lobby restaurant. It was late December, just after

Christmas. Darcy shook the snow off her elegant boots. Apparently the fundraiser itself was already underway in the famous Gilt restaurant. Their part would come after the event at a private showing in one of the penthouse suites on the 54th floor. The ladies ate and wandered around the mansion, taking in the elegance. They had been told to sit in the lobby restaurant from 10:00 p.m. and wait for the signal to ascend to the penthouse.

At 10:30 a man from the hotel staff took them to the Towers private reception area. A concierge took them to a high-speed elevator where they were whisked up to the 54th floor. A dressing room was set up in a small bedroom. Darcy modeled for an hour to a small but very appreciative audience of men and women. Kathleen took a few orders. Two of the men had no interest in the show and were watching her carefully. Were these guys from the Fazio campaign? One of them approached Darcy as she walked out of the dressing area. "Would you and your friends like to join the party in the Villard ballroom?" He was about medium height with curly brown hair on top of a fine-chiseled face that indicated refinement.

Behind her, Kathleen gasped. "Oh yes, please, we would so much!"

Darcy smiled. "I'm with the Audrey boutique sir, and not on my own tonight." She turned to the little modiste. "Madam, is it *convenable*?"

"Certainly my dear," Aubrey acknowledged. "We will all three attend."

"Excellent." Darcy thought the man's response was too enthusiastic, as if he had been sent upstairs on an errand for someone else. "Take these passes and show them to the doorman."

They were whisked down to the second floor of the mansion on one of the private Tower elevators. The concierge gave them directions. "The party is in the Villard Ballroom, just follow the music."

The three women checked in with the doorman. When they walked in Kathleen was delighted. "Look at those beautiful chandeliers!" The tables were moved back and a small band was playing. A lot of people stood around with drinks, chatting. A few were dancing. The room was very crowded. Darcy saw that food had been piled on the tables around the back and the sides of the room. The three women slowly moved their way through the crowd to one of the tables, which had little sandwiches on china trays.

Darcy picked up a little sandwich and took a bite. "There must be at least 350 people here. Senator Fazio must have had quite a successful fundraiser."

"Oh yes," a man behind them said. The three women turned and saw a younger man about Darcy's age in a slightly rumpled suit. He was eyeing Kathleen appreciatively. Darcy thought he was one of the Fazio campaign staff. "At $10,000 a plate, very successful. But the heavy action is in there." He pointed to an elevator door at the back of the ballroom.

"Oh really?" Kathleen said. "What's so special about it?"

The young man eyed Kathleen. "My name is Alfred."

Kathleen laughed. "I'm Kathleen. This is Darcy. Our boss is Audrey Quenioux, of Audrey's boutique." Audrey was standing beside Darcy.

Darcy knew that Alfred would try to get some action tonight and from the looks of it Kathleen would be happy to oblige. It was Standard Operating Procedure for such parties.

"Who is that man standing in front of the door?" Kathleen asked. Ahe pointed to an elevator door at the back of the ballroom. Darcy noticed that a waiter was standing inconspicuously in front of the door. The man didn't look like a real waiter. He was very thick, almost rotund, but muscular. He had on a flowing white robe and carried a staff with a dragon's head carved on it. The bulky man wore a strange looking headpiece shaped like a fish. Like a churchman, or the pope. His costume was totally out of place and he should have looked ridiculous. But the man fit right into the scenery as if he was supposed to be there. She noticed that the door had a purple gargoyle symbol painted on it.

"Hush-hush," Alfred replied, answering Kathleen's question. "A select gathering of big-wigs. Top security."

Before Darcy could reply a tall figure appeared before them. It was Carla Waverley! Behind her Darcy recognized the figure of that weasel, Jake Holden. She felt her knees buckling but managed to stay upright.

"What's the matter Darcy Regier? You look a little pale."

Darcy didn't know what to say so she said nothing. She tried to keep her composure. Heads began to turn, as usual, when Carla Waverley was present in company.

Jake Holden stepped quickly to Carla's right and spoke loudly. "There is my beautiful little whore!" Both antagonists were now confronting her. Darcy remained silent and ignored the taller woman. She looked at Jake Holden with what she hoped was an expression of complete neutrality, as if she had never met the man before.

Audrey Quenioux looked up at the towering figure before her, impressed despite herself. It was the same woman who had appeared at the Frick show, wearing those three inch heels again. Once, to make an impression, perhaps. But twice? The wiry man beside her was clearly a street person, and of a vulgarity.

Carla was sarcastic. "How is your drunken father in Joliet? I hear that the porn video you made with Jake here is still selling well, especially in Chicago."

"*Cette femme est une carnassière*," Darcy said softly. Audrey laughed.

"What did you say?"

Darcy remained silent. Jake said nothing. He was just window dressing. Where had she dug up that worm? Why did Carla despise her so?

Carla moved a half-step closer, getting in Darcy's face. "Do you deny that you were a whore in Joliet, and that you starred in a disgusting pornographic movie? It wasn't even a good one." Carla was practically shouting now. The conversation in the room had died down, all heads turning toward them. It was a repeat performance from her first showing over three months ago.

Darcy had heard rumors about Carla's nightlife and took a shot in the dark. "What about your nightlife, Carla Waverley?" Someone in the crowd snickered. Darcy saw smiles on the faces of several of the men.

Jake Holden didn't care what game this Amazon was playing. He intended to make his business proposal to Darcy after the party even though it seemed more and more ridiculous now. At least he would have the $500 Carla had offered him to accompany her tonight. He was broke as usual. Jake looked longingly at Darcy. God, what a porn star she would make in those expensive clothes. The money they could make! But Regier had obviously grown up and was no longer the desperate street girl. She was clearly a polished and sophisticated society woman and probably had more money than he would ever see in his life.

Carla turned to face Audrey. She had rehearsed the punchline with Jake and she delivered it flawlessly. "Your employee is a slut. For this ... pussy ... to model your superb clothing in the houses of your genteel customers is an outrage."

Darcy saw several nods of agreement. The sentiment of the crowd was turning against her. Carla perceived this and smiled. Jake leered at her.

Audrey Quenioux stepped back and looked closely at Darcy. What Carla had said had the ring of truth. Yet the girl before her was perfect and had been vouched for by Holderness Parkinson. More important, Darcy was now the face of her boutique. This affair must be handled delicately. Audrey smiled, perceiving that Darcy was barely holding herself together. The modiste was well aware of Carla's nightlife and her sexual exploits. "Miss Waverley, you are famous in New York." She stepped back and waited.

It was a risk, Audrey knew. Many of the Fazio supporters here were businessmen and businesswomen. They would probably identify with Carla, who was dressed smartly in a form-fitting gray suit. But Carla's companion was conspicuous and looked like a small-time hustler. Audrey hoped that the presence of this *voyou* would remind the gathering of Carla Waverley's own vulgar exploits and that her accusations were hypocritical. She placed a look of uncaring calm on her face. Inside she was deathly afraid. If the sentiment of the crowd went against Darcy the boutique could be ruined. The incident would be the talk of the town. But the girl's very demeanor exuded refinement. Could anyone looking at Darcy conceive for a moment that she was not a cultured gentlewoman? It was Carla's word against the reality of Darcy.

Audrey realized that Darcy was about to panic. Somehow, what this woman said must be true! She could see that Darcy was about ready to collapse. Audrey placed her hand on Darcy's shoulder, squeezing lightly, steadying her. Carla and the other man continued to leer at her. The little modiste felt Darcy steady and saw her raise her head to smile at the giantess. Ah, Audrey thought, smiling. This is breeding and courage!

Audrey Quenioux held her breath as the outcome hung in the balance. After several moments of silence someone laughed and a voice was heard. "Carla, you have just officially stuck your foot in your mouth." Someone else chuckled and a woman asked her companion to get her a drink. A woman commented on Senator Fazio's speech. And just like that it was over. The hum of general conversation grew louder and Carla walked away.

"Hey, where's my money?" Jake followed Carla through the crowd to the ball-room entrance like a little dog at his master's heels.

Carla hissed. "Silence you fool! You'll be paid outside."

A few in the crowd laughed at the scene and shook their heads. The disreputable little man behind Carla didn't even reach her shoulders. Audrey was amused. The Waverley woman was truly *magnifique*, but much too abrasive. She breathed a sigh of relief. Darcy wanted to hug her.

Alfred, who had remained next to Kathleen during the confrontation, asked her if she wanted something.

"Oh yes, I'm dying for a drink."

Alfred pointed to the front of the room. "There's a small bar over there." The pair moved off.

Aubrey Quenioux spoke to Darcy. "I have had enough excitement for one night. I am going home and to bed."

Darcy was about to go with Audrey when she noticed that the waiter/guard at the elevator door had stepped aside to let an unusual looking man walk through. This man also wore a purple robe but it had two dark purple stripes. He also wore one of the funny hats and carried a staff. At that moment the man in the white robe glanced up and met her eyes. Darcy understood that she would also be welcome to enter the elevator. Her curiosity got the better of her. Darcy began to inch her way toward the door in the over-crowded ballroom. A few eyes were upon her but she was used to that. As she approached within ten feet of the door she could see that the guard was completely motionless, almost like a statue. His eyes were focused on a spot in the distance, over her head.

Darcy found herself directly in front of the door. The guard bent down and whispered to her. "Darcy Regier?"

Startled, she could only nod her head affirmatively. The guard stepped aside and pressed a button at the side of the elevator door, which opened silently. The elevator began to move down quickly as soon as the door had closed. She felt trapped. Oh God, what have I got myself into this time? Darcy noticed that the walls of the elevator were covered in strange symbols. The elevator had only been moving for a few seconds when it stopped and the door opened. Darcy walked forward. A man in a black cloak with thick brown hair appeared immediately, smiling thinly.

"Come this way, Darcy." Darcy began to walk down a darkened hallway when she noticed, on her left, a small room with no door. The room had concrete walls painted black. Three men in robes were performing a macabre ritual on a stone altar. She felt cold, musty air coming from the room. The only lighting was from candles. A woman in a revealing robe lay upon the altar. The three men were chanting something in a strange language. Latin? Each man held a smoking torch in his right hand and a knife in his left. One of the men took the knife and moved it over the woman's belly, drawing blood.

"What are those men doing?" she demanded.

Her guide spoke harshly. "That is not for your eyes." He moved to stand in front of her, shielding her view. "Your presence is required elsewhere. Follow me."

Darcy was led down the dimly-lit hallway and they stopped before a door painted in gold. Inscribed on the door was a star chart in black and white with the Greek symbol epsilon at the center. Once more Darcy asked her question. "What were those men doing in there? Who are you?"

"I am Mr. Dalyrimple," the man said, opening the door. "Please enter. Someone is waiting to see you."

Mr. Dalyrimple? This was not the man's real name. Darcy received a severe shock when she turned to survey the room and its occupants. On the floor was a multi-colored rug and a sculpture of a dolphin that rose six feet into the air. The animal was suspended from an impossibly thin wire. On a couch at the center of the room two strange men with the unusually large eyes and gold irises sat together. She had seen such men at that strange Royalty party six years ago.

Dalyrimple exited. A tall blond man with long hair tied in a pony tail, casually dressed, approached her. "Ah, Darcy Regier. Welcome." The man gazed at her intently. "You may remember my friends Mr. Gemmi and Mr. Nye."

Gemmi and Nye? Was this some kind of a joke? From her studies at Royalty, she knew that Gemini is represented by the twins, Castor and Pollux. Gemini was also associated with the planet Mercury, a planet god known for its intelligence and high education. Maybe these guys were from NASA?

The tall blond man stepped back. The two men on the couch arose suddenly and very fluidly, taking a step toward her. They were completely hairless. Darcy realized that the two at the Royalty party must have been wearing headpieces. Suddenly she felt a strong hypnotic command to walk with them. The vision of a door to a room that looked like a laboratory appeared in her head. She felt her leg moving forward ... somehow she knew that the invitation was not sexual ... these guys weren't even human. As soon as she thought it she knew it was true. She stopped abruptly. The big round eyes of the two creatures widened in surprise. "If you want me to go to that room I will, but on my own terms." Darcy spoke as calmly as she could, even though she was becoming frightened.

One of the creatures, who stood slightly over five feet, looked to the other. Except for a few trivial differences the two men were identical. They were both dressed in skintight, sleeveless gold suits. Both had very smooth golden skin and were hairless, and seemed to have very small packages. Their heads were large compared to their thin bodies. At that moment she knew why she was here.

The creature on her right stiffened. "I see that you have already divined our purpose," he intoned. The voice was liquid and the accent was Indian or south Asian.

"Not entirely." Darcy noticed that the blond man with the pony tail was standing unobtrusively at the back of the small room. His arms were crossed in front of his body. "Before we begin I have two questions. Well, one statement and one question. You guys are not from earth. But what are those men outside this room doing?"

The man beside him spoke. "Call me Mr. Gemmi," he said, waving his hand slowly in the air. It was a fascinating gesture to Darcy who was trained in deportment. The gesture had been performed unconsciously with amazing grace and elegance. "Those fools out there are contacting the Tau."

"The Tau?" Darcy said.

Mr. Nye spoke. "The Tau are a degraded race that has recently entered our dimension. They have insinuated themselves within our sector. Reptilian. They have been interfering with your genetics and your spiritual development for over 12,000 years."

Mr. Gemmi spoke bitterly. "It's what they do."

"Why do they wear those silly clothes and engage in such strange rituals?" Darcy asked. "I've heard about necromancy and black magic and Harry Potter and spells, calling up demons and things like that. Isn't that just for children to have fun with, or for wierdos?"

"These rituals are designed to establish communication with individual Xorg entities," Mr. Nye said. "The fools who engage in them conceive that they are somehow gaining power and influence in your society."

"Xorg?" Darcy asked.

Mr. Gemmi performed his hand gesture again. "Xorg is what they call themselves. The specific gravity and the atmosphere of many of our planets in Draco is close to yours. They, and we, can spend some time here without harm. The Xorg are humanoid reptiles who stand on two feet. Their average height is approximately eight of your feet. Their primary symbols are the dragon and the serpent and their derivatives. The gargoyles you see on many of your churches and other buildings show the true origin of these religions, and of your corporate and governmental organizations. Your race, your planet, has been controlled by cabals and secret societies who communicate with those degraded entities via the rituals you observed before entering this room."

Darcy dismissed this. "That's just a lot of conspiracy stuff. I'm not interested. As far as I'm concerned those guys are just nutty and whatever they are doing can't succeed because it's so stupid."

Mr. Gemmi raised his shoulders up and down in a shrug. "It is not our concern what happens to your race. Just so long as enough of you are left after the Tau have done with you. Your race's astonishing genetic diversity is what keeps our race from dying."

Darcy raised her eyebrows at this but the other Aleph spoke before she could open her mouth.

"Thank you Mr. Gemmi. The reason you have been called here is twofold. Firstly, you are already known to us as one who is resistant to our psychic suggestions. You should know that the Tau have arranged things in your biology so that each of you is subject to a psychic 'trigger.' By trigger we simply mean that all of you are extremely suggestible to hypnosis and mild trance states. These trance states can be brought about through language and certain patterns of sound and movement. These methods reach directly into your subconscious, overriding your conscious volition in the targeted area."

"Yes, I've heard of that stuff. Hypnotherapy, Neuro Linguistic Programming."

"Suffice it to say that the conscious minds of all of you are manipulated to some degree," Mr. Nye said. "Over the millennia it has been built into the fabric of your biological information systems, primarily through religion. Modernly through advertising, entertainment, news, and other mass media. Your internet has allowed these psychic 'trigger' patterns to spread around the globe."

"I don't know what you are talking about."

"Certainly you do." Mr. Gemmi moved his hands and his body in a pattern that Darcy did not recognize. "I have already placed you in a mild trance state. Now, I will pull the psychic trigger." Darcy felt the compulsion to move toward the laboratory door.

"How did you do that?"

"Remarkable," Mr. Nye commented to his partner. Then to Darcy: "There are not one in 100,000 of you who could have resisted that trigger. We discovered this at that party over six of your rotations ago. We tested you and discovered that you were resistant. Somehow, your genetic codes are mutating in the direction of greater self-consciousness. We find this to be a hopeful sign."

"Yes," Mr. Gemmi said quickly. "Any occurrence that has the possibility of hindering the Tau is a positive development for our race."

"You see Darcy," Mr. Nye said, "the only reason we are here on your planet is to retrieve samples of your earthian biology. We use these samples to diversify our clones. For over 12,000 years we have been gradually improving the vitality of our race, and soon hope to achieve sexual reproduction."

"I don't understand. Your race cannot reproduce itself naturally?"

"Yes," Mr. Gemmi said. "We are not here to harm you. All we require are biological samples. We would like a tissue sample from you. We are very excited to be able to use your evolving genetics to help our race reach stability and viability."

Darcy was nonplussed. "Are you the guys who abduct people and scare them to death?"

Mr. Nye glanced quickly at Mr. Gemmi. "We do not do such things. We ... "

Darcy was feeling impatient now. "Let's get this over with. I want to go home."

"You agree to allow us to take a sample from you?" Mr. Gemmi asked.

"Yes, as long as it doesn't hurt."

A look of disgust came over the faces of both the Alephs. "That is another argument we have with the Tau and their satellite races. Your medicine is ... a barbarism. Your so-called terminal diseases like cancer and heart disease and all the rest are trivially simple to cure."

"Alcoholism too?" Darcy was thinking of her father.

"All of them," Mr. Nye said. "Without exception."

The two Alephs both stepped aside, inviting Darcy to enter the laboratory. Darcy expected to see medical devices, test tubes, and a lot of other medical machinery. The room contained only a padded table and a desk with two small pencil-shaped devices and a small white cube that glowed softly.

"This won't take but a few seconds," Mr. Gemmi said, grasping one of the instruments. "Please lie down and be comfortable."

Darcy lay down on the table and felt her body melt into its surface. "Wow, this is great. You guys could make a lot of money selling mattresses."

Darcy saw the two Alephs glance at each other. Their large round eyes brightened. "I made a joke!" Darcy cried.

"Yes you did Darcy," Mr. Gemmi said to her as a parent to a child. "Just relax." Mr. Gemmi moved the device about three feet above her body in concentric circles. "We are sampling your biological information system. Every life form has one. It consists of subtle energy that surrounds the body and programs it."

"That's not what my doctor tells me."

The two Alephs looked at each other. "Xorg," they chanted in unison.

"Very good Darcy, thank you," Mr. Gemmi said, completing his scan. "Now let Mr. Nye take a few biological samples."

Mr. Nye moved his little pencil gently over her arm, and the tip of it turned blue. Then he moved it over her stomach and the device turned yellow. "Now," he said with great excitement, "do not be concerned Darcy. We need to get samples from your reproductive organs." The two creatures could barely contain themselves. Were these guys extraterrestrial perverts? The device moved down her abdomen and then gently between her legs. In one second it was over.

"Is that it?"

The two Alephs looked at each other and smiled. "Yes Darcy. We thank you profoundly, from our entire race. Tissue from females, especially a female of your relatively high development, is especially valuable."

Mr. Nye caressed his device like it was a newborn baby. "Quickly," Mr. Gemmi said. "Place the probe into the support chamber." Mr. Nye carefully placed the device within the glowing white cube.

Just as Darcy was about to ask a question the two Alephs opened a small door at the rear and were gone.

"That was interesting," she said to herself. "How do I get out of here?" She exited the laboratory and the blond man with the pony tail was there. "Are you human?"

The man laughed. "Yes, I'm human just like you. I'm an operative within an agency that deals specifically with the Epsilon. I'll take you to the elevator." The man gave her an appreciative man-to-pretty-woman look.

Just as they were about to enter the hallway a terrifying scream came from the front room, and loud shouting. Darcy raced down the hallway. A huge alien form appeared like a holographic projection above the table where a bloody woman was writhing. Darcy screamed and ran toward the elevator door. One of the robed men turned and she saw the face of Senator Fazio! Mr. Dalyrimple shouted an obscenity at the three men and hustled Darcy into the elevator.

"Oh God, get me out of here."

The blond man spoke bitterly as the elevator doors closed. "The bastards. The scum."

"What—"

The elevator doors opened and the blond man grabbed her elbow. "Get out of here as fast as you can." Darcy needed no prodding and pushed her way through the crowd. She made the hallway, grabbed her coat from the lobby, and went running toward the front door. Marcus saw her panicking form from the lobby restaurant and hurriedly followed her out. Darcy heard a familiar voice behind her that wasn't Marcus, calling her. She was so afraid she pushed open the front door and fled into the open air.

"Darcy!"

Darcy made it into the courtyard. She heard huffing and puffing behind her and turned.

"Darcy!" It was Thom Madigan! His breathing was labored and puffs of steam bellowed into the crisp night air.

"Oh Thom," she cried. "I can't—" Out of the corner of her eye she spotted Marcus jogging toward her. She was very frightened. A cab on the street stopped in front of the hotel and Darcy ran for it through lightly-falling snow. She hoped that Marcus would follow her home. Just as she made the sidewalk she saw Jake Holden run out from behind a shrub about twenty feet to her left.

"Darcy!" he cried, grabbing her. "Come with me to California. We'll make some great films together and a ton of money." Before she had time to reply a hairy arm wrapped itself around her and a hand went over her mouth. "Gotcha."

"Let me go!" Darcy screamed.

Thom Madigan, completely out of breath, finally arrived on the scene to find Darcy in the arms of a man with hairy arms and a pock-marked face. He was surrounded by two muscle-bound hoods.

Jake Holden stared at Frank Nitti with his two goons. "What the fuck are you doing here Nitti?"

"You little traitor!" Nitti swore, turning to face Holden with Darcy trapped in his arms. "You better get back to Chicago before Luca sends somebody out here to rub you out."

"Traitor? I'm no traitor," Holden objected.

"Release that woman!" Thom Madigan commanded weakly, bending over. He barely had breath enough for voice.

"Would ya look at that Benny." Nitti turned back to the chubby Madigan. "Real touching. We got a regular convention here, and all for this little piece of ass."

Benny was standing to Nitti's left. He pointed to a laboring Thom Madigan. "Who is this guy, boss?" Guido was facing Holden and raised a ham-handed fist. Jake shrank back.

"Good question Benny. Who the hell are you pumpkin?" Thom was now able to stand straight and breathe normally.

"I'm Thom Madigan, CEO of Pantheon Plastics. I'm a friend of Senator Fazio's. If you don't release that girl I'm calling the cops."

Nitti chuckled. "I don't know a Senator Fazio. Don't you worry about no cops. I got that covered."

Darcy was about to lose her mind. She was cold, and struggling in Nitti's grasp. She managed to bite him on one of his hairy arms. "Ouch! Guido, don't let her get away."

Darcy began to run toward the cab but Jake suddenly sprang quickly and caught up with her after she had taken two steps. These damn heels! "Come with me," Jake said, holding her firmly and signaling for the taxi driver to pull around. "We're going to California."

Guido was as quick as a cat. Swiftly he pounced on Jake and shoved him to the ground. Jake hit his head on the cement and felt woozy. He lay there watching the action in a daze.

Darcy tried to get into the taxi but Guido carried her effortlessly back to the limo and put her inside. He locked all the doors and disabled the release mechanism. That little trick was ordered special by Nitti after a Black Fighters drug dealer stole some money and got away from him one night.

Guido saw the cabbie, a man with a big white turban, reach for his remote dispatch mike. Guido reached in through the open passenger-side door, ripped the device out of the vehicle, and threw it under the wheels of a passing car. "Don't reach for a cell phone buddy or I'll punch your lights out." The man's eyes widened and he closed the door. The cabbie stomped his foot on the accelerator and sent his taxi out in front of oncoming traffic. Tires squealed and cars moved frantically out of the way on the slushy street. Guido heard a scrape of metal on metal but the taxi made it into traffic and sped away.

Guido laughed. Benny nodded approvingly. "That was funny," Guido said. "I think I'll try that again when I'm back in the city."

Thom Madigan had already dialed 911 and told them to get some squad cars down to the Palace. "A kidnapping is in progress," he told the dispatcher.

Marcus approached and calmly surveyed the scene. He had seen everything. Nitti, Guido, and Benny saw him and turned to face him. "Hey, it's that kid from …"

"Midland," Guido said, completing the sentence.

"Marcus, right?" Nitti said. "Hey kid, the offer still stands."

"What offer?" Marcus was trying to figure a way to rescue Darcy.

"What, you forgot? You come to Chicago and work with me kid. I can use a good man who aint afraid of a little action and who can keep his head."

Marcus saw Darcy inside the limo. She was pounding her hands on the window and screaming for help. Suddenly Marcus had an idea. He activated the web of light and sent it towards the mobster. He placed the web of light around the mobster's head. Now he was Frank Nitti III. In a microsecond he knew that this guy had killed three men, beaten up a couple of women, and threatened numerous persons. He knew that Nitti was in New York on business for Luca Carcelli. If he found Darcy he was to bring her back to Chicago. Marcus gently put the thought into Nitti's head that the Regier girl was more trouble than she was worth. She'd fight and argue all the way to Chicago. She was known to Holderness Parkinson.

Marcus knew it was a winner as soon as he put that thought into Nitti's mind. He could see the mobster's mind take up the idea and begin to imagine all the bad stuff that could happen. Carcelli hated Parkinson but knew he had powerful connections. Nitti knew that if the girl made trouble or if the videos turned out wrong, Carcelli would pin the blame on him. Fuck that, Nitti decided. He'd let the girl go and tell the Boss he didn't know where she was. Business had turned out good and his trip was already a success. Why complicate things?

"Hey Guido, I changed my mind," Marcus heard Nitti say. "Turn the bitch loose."

Guido was only too happy to oblige. Benny was silently thankful. They would have had to ride with a complaining woman all the way back to Chicago while Nitti sat up front drinking tequila and snorting coke and joking with the driver.

Guido opened the door and let Darcy out. She ran into Marcus' arms and sagged. "Take me home," she said, completely exhausted.

Nitti, Guido, and Benny walked back to the limo and got in. As it pulled away, Nitti waved to Marcus. "See ya kid!"

Thom Madigan was amazed. "What happened there Marcus? I saw it but I don't believe it. That was some kind of mind trick wasn't it?"

Marcus smiled wearily. "Yeah Thom. I'll tell you about it sometime when I'm awake. I gotta get some sleep; early morning tomorrow."

"All right Marcus. I'll call you next weekend and we'll catch up."

Marcus saw another cab approach the hotel and he signaled it. He carried Darcy into the taxi. "81st street and 2nd." When they got to Darcy's walkup Marcus was sleepy and really horny. Darcy was already asleep. Marcus laid her on the bed, took off her heels, and put the covers over her. He grabbed a pillow and bunked down on the couch. He wondered about her roommate Kathleen, but she didn't seem to be home. Then he was asleep.

From a second floor window in the Villard, a small man with oily black hair watched the entire episode. The man who held the girl had suddenly released his strongly held intention. It was the boy, he was certain of that. He did not know how it was done, and this disturbed him greatly. It was his job to observe these hominids for any sign of unusual abilities. His instructions were explicit: observe and report anything unusual in any of the earthians. Tonight he would make contact with his Master, the great Belial, and inform him of developments. He knew that the Great One would want to extract from the boy the secret of his power.

CHAPTER **16**

LUCA Carcelli's phone rang. "Yeah, whaddaya want?"

"It's Captain Kangaroo, Carcelli. Are you alone?"

"Oh it's you Joey. Yeah I'm alone."

"Good job on the Alderman Luca. You liked what you got in the last shipment?"

"Hell yeah. We been diluting it two to one and the customers don't know the difference."

"All right, the pleasantries are over. Did you send one of your guys to pick up a girl by the name of Darcy Regier?"

"Yeah I did, so what?"

"Because, Luca, she's strictly off-limits. Do you hear?"

"Can't a guy even get a piece of ass anymore?" Luca complained.

"This piece is special. Top top secret, absolutely hands off. I'm doing you a favor, *capisci*?"

"Yeah, yeah. What's so special about the *pucchiacha?*"

Joey chuckled. "If I told you I would literally have to kill you."

"All right. I'll tell Nitti to lay off."

"Good. Or you won't live much longer."

Luca could tell Joey wanted to talk. Joey always said he was his 'handler' and always used an encrypted, secure connection whenever they talked. Luca didn't know what organization the guy belonged to. Joey never said anything about himself, other than he had a family.

"Do you remember that funny little guy who came to see you, along with the Chief of Police?"

"Yeah."

"Was there something unusual about the guy?"

Luca thought about the little man who had, with one look, frozen him in fear. "Yeah."

"Did he look like the devil himself?"

"Yeah."

"OK, because you can't understand it unless you've seen it."

Luca was silent for a couple of seconds. That little guy made him feel like a *gavone*. It was something he would never forget. That night Chief Hintzman and the little oily guy waltzed into his private office without knocking. "Who are you?"

"I represent the powers that be." The little man gave his orders for the hit on Alderman Courvall.

"You little prick, this is my town. Nobody orders me around." Luca got angrily out of his chair to slug the guy, and then something happened. The little guy's eyes turned yellow. He glared at Luca so balefully that Luca had to shrink back into his seat. He felt like a pile of dogshit that had just been run over by an 18-wheeler. With one look the guy ? he didn't even know his name ? deflated him like a kid who just discovered that Santa Claus was a fat idiot in a suit. Luca had never felt so helpless in all his life.

"Does it make you shrivel up inside?" Luca asked Joey. "And make you feel like a bug about to be squashed?"

"So you did see it. I thought so by the way you described that guy."

"Yeah."

"It's enough to scare you half to death."

Luca exploded. "Who the fuck is this guy?"

"I did some digging around. Your oily little man is direct from MJ-12."

"That doesn't mean anything to me."

"It sure as hell does to me. Just be glad you took out Courvall, Luca, that's all I can say."

"All right. Tell me about this MJ-12." Luca was curious.

Joey sighed. "I'm tired of it Luca, so what the hell. These people—"

Luca heard the sounds of struggle in the background. Then the connection closed.

That evening, after dining at Alinea, Holderness Parkinson was approached on his way out by a blond man with a pony tail.

"Mr. Parkinson," the man said. "I have a special request."

Parkinson's attention narrowed. He carefully studied the man before him. 'Special request' was his personal code, and known to only a few of his trusted friends. Parkinson read the man and noticed that this fellow had the indefinable air of an intelligence operative. He had met several of these men during their exit interviews after using Royalty's services. Parkinson nodded his head.

"Please follow me."

The man directed him down a corridor past the kitchens to a room with a door at the back. "Please enter. One of our guests wishes to speak with you."

Parkinson shrugged and walked in. The room contained only a black leather couch with an end table next to it, upon which sat a black metal lamp with a tan lampshade. On the couch sat a petite man with thin features, almost golden skin, and no facial hair.

The man rose fluidly to his feet. "Hello, I am Aleph 229. You met me at one of your gatherings several years ago."

"Ah!" Parkinson was excited, his eyes widening in surprise. The man's pleasant sing-song voice was almost liquid. The man was only five feet tall but his presence was imposing. "You are the one who calls himself Mr. Nye?"

The Aleph smiled thinly. "No, that is my partner. I am called Mr. Gemmi."

"Yes Mr. Gemmi. You have information?" Holderness knew that these golden-skinned fellows were not human. He had learned a lot in his 30 years as director of Royalty Services and his ten years as a field operative. Certain intelligence operatives who were associated with the country's hidden, off the books programs were often involved in "ET" issues. Exotic technology, the black programs, above top-secret security classifications, and off-worlders were all connected somehow. Apparently he was about to find out more.

The Aleph bowed. "We want you to be aware of two things, Mr. Parkinson. As you may suspect, your planet is being influenced by certain visitors. The most influential of these off-worlders are the Tau, our mortal enemies. From your talks with those who use your service you are probably aware of the private networks on your planet outside normal channels. The most important of these calls themselves the Committee. The Committee …" The Aleph hesitated. No, this man did not need to know that. "The Committee's executive branch call themselves the Twelve. This group is the coordinating organization of the twelve most important human bloodlines."

Parkinson nodded but remained silent. This strange being had withheld information but he knew nothing of bloodlines. He would listen carefully and confirm the validity of the information later.

"Within this coordinating group there are two powerful factions," Mr. Gemmi continued. "One is allied with the Tau, a reptilian humanoid race that has been interfering with your racial development. Your human bloodlines were genetically established by the Tau just before and after the last dramatic climate change event on your planet. I believe you call it the Ice Age."

Parkinson wondered why he had been singled out for this information.

"You should be aware that the Tau and their human agents are planning a catastrophic event for your species. We have been unable to determine the precise nature of this event or its particulars. This faction is enormously secretive and dangerous. I will mention one name: Pietro Adolfone."

Parkinson thought rapidly. He had heard of Adolfone but knew almost nothing about him.

"The second powerful faction is a violent one that has been shooting down visiting spacecraft from other star systems. This faction has been secretly reverse-engineering what you call non-terrestrial craft, and is using the advanced technology for their own nefarious ends. This faction is also planning a culminating event. Again, we are unable to determine the precise nature of this plan, or whether the two factions are aligned or competing. A name to remember is Admiral Frank Conte. We believe that the plans of these two private factions are nearing fruition."

"Thank you Mr. Gemmi." Parkinson knew who Conte was. The man had used Royalty's services several years ago under an assumed name. He had not been welcomed back. "Why you are telling me this information? I merely operate an exclusive VIP service here in Chicago. There are more powerful and influential people who are better equipped to handle these problems."

The corners of Mr. Gemmi's thin lips raised slightly. "I think not, Mr. Parkinson. Our socio-event matrix for your planet indicates that you are the most appropriate person to contact."

Parkinson noticed the change of inflection and he smiled inwardly. So they are on to me are they? He kept his voice bland. "Why are you getting involved? We have no dispute with the Tau, or whatever you call them. Although Conte is probably a sociopath I have no reason to be aware of his activities."

Mr. Gemmi's lips curled more noticeably upward. "There is a saying on your planet, Mr. Parkinson: 'A word to the wise should be sufficient.'" The little golden-skinned man smiled. "We have been observing you almost as long as the Tau, for at least 10,000 years. I assure you that our interests are your interests. I am merely suggesting that you investigate. When you do you will see the necessity for immediate action. To put it bluntly, Mr. Parkinson, if your planet is subsumed we will be next. Your survival means our racial survival."

"Thank you Mr. Gemmi. I will look into this."

The golden-skinned man nodded. He walked to a small door at the back of the room, entered, and disappeared.

"Startled, Mr. Parkinson?" Holderness turned to see the blond man with the pony tail enter the room.

"Yes, but I have seen some unusual things in my day."

The man smiled. "If you have any questions, sir, you may contact Colonel Rodgers at Fort Meyer, or his assistant, Lieutenant Mutumbe." He stepped aside and waved his arm toward the door. "Thank you for your time."

Lost in thought, Holderness Parkinson walked slowly out into the corridor to the exit and got into a waiting Royalty limousine.

CHAPTER 17

Five months later

On a late May morning at 7 a.m. Marcus walked slowly up the steps of the NY-CBank building on Park Avenue and West 51st street, to the 19th floor. Today was his first day as an apprentice equities trader under Carla Waverley. He was excited and a bit nervous.

Marcus had passed his training with flying colors. He was now a registered General Securities Representative, a Corporate Securities Representative, and a Securities Trader. He would also complete the requirements to become a Chartered Financial Analyst, and would do it all from NYCBank's training room.

He had deliberately marked down one answer wrong on every exam so people wouldn't talk. He had still recorded the highest score ever on the Equity Trader qualifying test for NYCBank employees. Marcus was proud to think that he had advanced more quickly than anyone in the history of NYCBank's training program. All eyes in the department were on him. Some of them, like Pat, were waiting for him to crash and burn.

As Marcus reached the 6th floor his legs began to ache.

Why was he doing this again? Because he was a softie. He was sitting on his butt for fourteen hours every day with no exercise. A week ago he felt like a pregnant hippopotamus trying to get up the four flights of stairs to Darcy's walk-up apartment. By the time he reached her door he had been as out of breath as old Thom Madigan trying to chase Darcy down last winter at the Palace. His first goal would be to walk up 19 flights without stopping. Then, to be able to jog up those 19 flights without stopping.

Every morning he arrived at the building thirty minutes early in his workout togs. He carried a war bag that contained a fresh pair of underwear, socks, two clean shirts, two energy drinks, and his hairbrush. His three suits were in his personal locker in the NYCBank building, along with two pair of dress shoes and some ties. After his workout he showered and changed in the building before assuming his post. After work, and sometimes on lunch hour, he threw on his workout clothes, took the elevator down to the first floor, and made the trip back up the stairs. He was getting in shape the hard way.

Marcus finally reached the 19th floor after stopping several times to catch his breath. His legs were wobbly and felt leaden. Carla saw him coming out of the stairwell and asked him what he was doing.

"Trying to keep in shape." He was bent over and out of breath.

"Good. You better be in good physical condition to do this job." Carla spoke smugly. "I work out five days a week."

Marcus replied with a hint of sarcasm. "Do you still take amphetamines?"

"I do when I have to." Marcus knew it irked her to have to look up to him. She always wore her three inch heels to work just in case she met him in the cafeteria or in the hall. She was standing as straight as she could and their eyes were level, but Marcus was still slouched a bit from his trudge. He straightened to his full height. Now he was a quarter-inch taller than she, even in her heels. The corners of his lips inched upward and his eyes lit up. He looked right at her as if to say, "See, I beat ya!"

Carla's eyes narrowed and her lips thinned. "Marcus Riley, I'm going to be on you all day every day."

"Good. That's just the way I like it."

Carla's eyes softened a bit. "That's the right attitude."

"I know you're the best and I want to learn from the best." She was really a cinch to handle. Compliment her at regular intervals and don't fuck up. He never had to use the web of light anymore with her.

"OK bozo. Get cleaned up and meet me downstairs in Equity Services."

Marcus grinned. He knew she still had a soft spot for him. Their relationship over the past four months had evolved into a big sister – little brother sibling rivalry.

She was 26 and he was almost 21 now. Carla had five years on him and all the work experience. Marcus knew Carla was concerned that he'd eventually do better than she on the job. She was still sore that he had rejected her for Darcy even though she knew he wasn't really her type unless he was on coke.

Now he had to prove himself as a member of her team.

Darcy had the day off and was going to meet Marcus for lunch. She decided to surprise him and wait outside the NYCBank building to watch him come out. Secretly she wanted to know if he would be with Carla. Darcy knew he liked her best. But when they were together and discussed their work Marcus kept making admiring comments about the bitch. "She's so smart!" and "She knows ten times as much as I do!" Irritating stuff like that.

Marcus always entered and exited the building by the main entrance. Darcy dressed with particular care this morning in case Carla or any of his co-workers were with him. Today she wore a very flattering light-beige print dress with flowers, very spring-y on this warm May afternoon. Her hair was up in one of Audrey's particularly fetching coiffures. She wore the gold tear-drop earrings he liked so much.

As she stood waiting near the marble entrance Darcy noticed a little gypsy-looking fellow loitering across the street. He had oily jet-black hair, a small mustache, and wore earrings. There was something definitely not right about him. Several times his eyes had moved toward her. It was still ten minutes before noon and she decided to surreptitiously keep an eye on him. The man glanced upward occasionally as if he was communicating with someone in the building. A glass-enclosed staircase ran down the side of the building. Darcy squinted into the noon sun, trying to discover if she could see someone lingering there. There was no one.

After about fifteen minutes she spotted Marcus in the heavy glass turnstile by the front doors, and waved. Marcus strode up to her. "You look great Darcy."

Darcy was pleased that her efforts had been noticed and that he was alone. "Are you hungry?"

"I could eat a camel. My stomach has been growling for the past hour."

"Are camels tasty?"

Marcus laughed. "You're cute. That's what Carla says. I admit it's a pretty stupid saying."

Darcy thought the reference to Carla was inappropriate but she liked it that he thought she was stupid.

Darcy kept an eye out for the little guy as the pair began to walk toward 51st street. They had just crossed 53rd when Marcus stopped suddenly. "It's the El Guayaquileno truck! I heard about that food, it's supposed to be really good."

Darcy bumped into the back of Marcus. She saw the oily man following them. He was now on the other side of the street.

"Marcus, do you have someone following you?" Marcus grabbed her hand and walked to the food stand.

"Huh?" Marcus grabbed a menu from the man in the truck.

"Never mind. Let me know if you see a short man with black hair, dark skin, and earrings."

"Why, you want to go out with him?" Marcus spoke absently, choosing his item.

"Marcus!" He was completely ignoring her.

Marcus turned back to her and put his arm around her. "Sorry Darcy, I'm so damn hungry I can't think of anything except food."

"All right. What kind of food is this? It smells good."

"Ecuadorian, I think. Let's eat here instead of the bistro, OK?"

Darcy was a little disappointed. She wanted to sit and have Marcus' full attention, but she agreed.

"What's this about a short gypsy guy?" he said, ordering a chorizo Locro dish that smelled wonderful.

"There's someone following us." She explained what she had seen while waiting at NYCBank.

"I don't know. I've passed my qualifying exams but I'm nobody – yet – just another trainee. Why would anyone want to follow me?"

"Watch yourself, OK?"

Marcus saw the tender look in her eyes, and her concern. He put his Locro down on the counter and hugged her. "What will you have?"

They stood around for fifteen minutes chatting and eating. Afterward they decided to go for a short walk. Darcy saw an interesting little boutique as they passed 50th street. "Can we stop in here for a minute?" she asked Marcus. "They have some nice stuff."

Just as Marcus was about to reply a black car with no plates pulled up from around the corner to the sidewalk. The vehicle almost hit a parked car on the crowded street and came within inches of Marcus as he stood behind Darcy in front of the little store window. Two very large men began advancing purposefully toward them.

"What the fuck?" Marcus exclaimed. One of the men grabbed him and the other got hold of Darcy. Suddenly Marcus' mind cleared and he felt the steady calmness that always came over him in a crisis. In a split second he had the web of light out. He planted a suggestion in the mind of the man who held Darcy to release her and go back to the car. The man let go of Darcy. Marcus did the same with his guy, who had already dragged him to the back passenger side door and was opening it. The man released him and was about to enter the car when the little gypsy guy appeared. He pulled a gun. "Get in the car or I'll bloody the street with both of you."

Marcus turned on the man with his web of light still activated and got the shock of his life. Standing behind him was the projection of a gigantic reptile.

"Marcus!" Darcy screamed. "Do you see that thing?"

Belial was loosing control of this human contact. The target hominid before him was blocking the resonance channel with a blue field of mental energy. Belial, enraged, sent a burst of energy at the blue light surrounding his human. It had no effect. At that moment a powerful resonance from the boy tore the channel completely. Disaster! Belial's essence transferred to the human and the body took his reptilian form. Foaming at the mouth, Belial rose unsteadily in the now reptilian body. He chanted imprecations in his Xorg language. People were stopping in the street, staring. Darcy was terrified. Strange noises were coming from around the reptile. His voice deepened. Belial desperately attempted to find the correct incantation to break the grip of the hominid's field of force. Darcy didn't understand the chanting but she felt its malevolence. Bystanders who were close to the action stepped back, repulsed by the vile force of Belial's presence. People began running toward the macabre scene, taking pictures with their phones, and talking excitedly. Belial felt the human body losing consciousness. He made one last effort to repair the connection but the life force of the human was fading. He fed on its death throes but knew that he must now withdraw or die himself. Enraged, and with the last of his energy, he struck out at the boy in front of him. One of his clawed paws caught Marcus lightly across the face, leaving bloody scratches. With his last breaths he cursed the hominid violently and promised him a slow, agonizing death.

Marcus, although buoyed by the web of light, was barely able to hold on in the face of the creature's malignant tirade. It had called itself Belial. He knew he was in the presence of something demonic. Belial's energy almost turned him inside out. His face hurt like hell but he didn't have time to think about it. He had to protect Darcy. The creature before him was shaking, foam was coming out of its mouth, and a black bile oozed from its nose. Finally its knees buckled and it fell heavily to the sidewalk.

Stunned, the crowd was completely silent. Vehicles on the street stopped. All that could be heard on the busy New York street was the sound of idling automobile engines. After a few moments sirens could be heard in the distance. A helicopter slowly entered the scene from above. The door to the boutique opened and a woman stepped out, completely unaware of what had happened in the street. She saw the reptile lying dead in the street and screamed. The crowd woke up. People began jabbering, screaming, crying, and shouting all at once. A news crew shoved a path to the reptile and began taking images. The helicopter now hovered only 100 feet above the crowd. "Leave the streets immediately!" a voice from the copter commanded. "This is a national security emergency! All citizens are to vacate this area at once!" Three SWAT teams arrived on the scene and began shoving people out of the way, knocking some of them down, and clearing the area. A dozen men dressed in black suits stood in a circle around the creature, preventing anyone from observing the scene.

Marcus went to Darcy and held her. "What is that horrible thing? Are you all right?"

"Yeah, he just grazed me." Marcus felt his cheek. "I think I know what it is but I'm not telling anyone. "

"Why not?"

"Because it's so strange no one would believe me." Marcus was analyzing the information he had received from the creature, whose body was now beginning to morph.

"Look Marcus! The body is beginning to lose its reptilian form."

"You're right Darcy." The reptile was slowly turning back into a human.

The web of light made it possible to *be* another person. Marcus had been Belial for almost thirty excruciating seconds. What he was learning from the creature's thoughts was freaking him out.

Darcy was glad Marcus had his arms around her.

Marcus saw two official-looking vehicles approaching. The SWAT teams had completely cleared 49th, 50th, and 51st streets. A big-wig military guy got out of one of the cars and was ordering people around. He came up to Marcus and Darcy. "You're coming with me."

"No we're not," Marcus replied. "I'm taking my girl home."

"You're not gong anywhere except where I tell you son. This is a national security matter now." He gestured to two men who had followed him to the scene.

"Get these two into the car and take them to SECOR-Tau. Have what's left of that body transported to the lab stat! Get it off the street." He pointed to the first vehicle sitting on the sidewalk, with the two abductors still inside. "Interrogate these two clowns. I want a full report by 1800."

One of the men grabbed Darcy and the other reached for him. "Wait!" He had gotten something from the reptile and he used it. This military guy seemed not to be shocked by the body in the street and might understand this strange incantation. He said it. The man's eyes widened in shock. "How the hell do you know that?"

"I know a lot of things you don't know." Marcus spoke with complete certainty. "If you don't release us right now I'm going to tell it all."

The man got right up into Marcus' face. "I'm Colonel Rodgers, son, Air Force intelligence. Don't play cute with me."

Marcus put out the web of light and knew the man was telling the truth. Suddenly he was really, really pissed, even more angry than he had been with Darcy that time. Marcus felt the web of light evaporate. From somewhere within him he felt a malignant, violent, cold-blooded rage. He looked down at the colonel. Marcus' face was contorted into a twisted mask. "Vermin! Even if you wanted to kill me you couldn't, you fucking little hominid. If you don't let us go I'll rip the hearts out of all of you and drink your blood."

Colonel Rodgers stepped back, appalled. He had only seen the look in the eyes of this boy one time in his life, when he had met one of those Tau. It had completely turned his guts to water. He glanced down at the body in the street, which still had a recognizable reptilian form. Colonel Rodgers shuddered.

Marcus was amazed. Where had that repugnant emotion come from? He realized it had come from Belial. Somehow, its personality had leaked into his. Oh God, what have I done? Darcy was looking at him in horror. From somewhere a long way away he heard rancorous laughter.

Marcus was more afraid than he had ever been, but he could still think clearly. He calmed himself, took a deep breath, and tried to activate the web of light. When it came forth he smiled. When he had the light activated he always felt serene and always made the right decision. He knew what he had to do now. "All right Colonel, I'll come with you. But you leave Darcy here. She has nothing to do with this."

Colonel Rodgers quickly recovered himself. He was a hardened veteran of many battles in Iraq and Afghanistan. Before joining SECOR-Tau he was considered the toughest man around, which is why he was assigned to deal with these reptiles. Rodgers was certain that the creature on the street was a remnant of a Draco-Tau, an alien race hostile to humanity. Even the most psychotic human being was a pimple on a pickle compared to one of those creatures. He gazed intently into the boy's eyes and saw no evidence now of demonic possession. But it had been there earlier. You couldn't explain it to anyone unless they'd seen it themselves.

Marcus Riley had been touched by these monsters and so had he. Colonel Rodgers felt a kinship with the boy now, a shared sense of danger. Just like those who had been in combat developed the strongest possible bonds of camaraderie; and yes, love. He knew that Marcus Riley was barely 21 years old, just a child. A manchild, he decided, looking up at the broad shoulders and a face mature beyond his years. The colonel decided to go beyond the strict ET protocols. "I understand, Marcus. But your girlfriend Darcy has been under observation for six years. Both you and her know about the alien presence on earth, and have had physical contact with ETs. That means you must be thoroughly debriefed. It's now a matter of national security. I am asking you as a personal favor to come with me to Washington. We promise that we will get this done as quickly as possible."

Marcus was still shaking from his encounter with the evil creature. He thought the colonel said that Darcy had met an ET. Cute little Darcy? He turned to her with an expression of shocked amazement. "Have you really seen an ET?"

"Oh God, Marcus, don't remind me." Darcy was thinking about that horrible party last Christmas. She noticed Colonel Rodgers staring at them impatiently. Marcus was bleeding and the sounds of the helicopter overhead pounded in her ears. The SWAT cordon with their weapons raised made her feel faint. "Please Marcus, take me out of here."

Marcus turned to the colonel. "All right, we'll come with you." He wanted to find out why Darcy had never told him about something so monumental. He wanted to pick the colonel's brain about that ugly thing who had attacked him.

Darcy smiled weakly. "Can I inform Audrey of my absence so she doesn't worry? Marcus will have to inform Carla Waverley."

"Yes," Rodgers said. "You can do that in the car. Marcus will have to have his cuts examined as well. We'll leave right now and be in Washington in two hours."

Kathleen was in the boutique answering phones when she got a call from her friend Heather. "Oh my God, Kathleen. Turn on the TV quick. Quick."

"Heather, what's going on?"

"Kathleen, shut up and turn on the TV. NOW!!!"

Kathleen went over to the wall-mounted unit and turned it on. The camera showed the body of a reptile lying on 50th street. A helicopter was hovering overhead, blasting orders to vacate the area. Just within the camera's view Darcy stood with that cokehead Marcus Riley.

"Audrey!" she shrieked. "Come in here!"

A voice on the TV was speaking. "No need to worry ladies and gentlemen. A new science fiction thriller is being filmed on the streets of New York today." The announcer chuckled nervously. "Things are a bit out of hand but the police are restoring order." The soap opera that was being shown resumed.

"A science fiction film?" Audrey asked. "*Ca me paraît suffisamment.*" Aubrey shook her head.

Kathleen texted all of her friends and they texted all of their friends. The video was on the Web and around the world in less than one hour.

Holderness Parkinson saw the incident live while checking the financial channels. He instantly recognized Darcy Regier. The boy next to him was probably Marcus Riley. He recorded the feed. Using his imaging software he made several images of the creature in the street. Parkinson studied them carefully. He saw something alarming.

Parkinson leaned back in his thick leather chair. So the warning from Aleph 229, the one who called himself "Mr. Gemmi," was accurate. He focused on the reptile's lower body, zooming in on the feet. He zoomed back out and looked the image again. This creature was clearly not a man in a reptile suit as the news reporter was proclaiming. The thick leathery skin of this creature had the patina of living flesh. The rest of the body was equally genuine. No matter how clever, special-effects designers could not completely mimic the quality of a living body. An examination of the feet convinced him. This creature certainly did not come from earth.

Parkinson knew of the special Air Force units devoted to the investigation of all ETV crashes, and the even more secret organizations dedicated to ET contact. He understood the protocol. When the colonel appeared on the scene he knew what would happen next. Darcy and the boy would be rushed to Fort Meyer and debriefed.

Quickly, Parkinson went into his private office and punched a button on the floor with his foot. A small desk with a gray terminal and an old-fashioned red plastic phone rose out of the floor. He moved his chair over to send an encrypted message to Elder Li Qiang in Beijing, China. Along with the images of the amazing event in New York he texted only five words:

"THE DRAGON KINGS HAVE ARRIVED."

CHAPTER **18**

BELIAL, after his near-death on the planet of the hominids, was still enraged when he returned to his body on Draco Tau. He had lost his humanoid contact! The humiliation of it still rankled. He was in an ugly humor. Now he would have to find another and that would take time.

The Draco Tau planet was the fourth out from its star. It was hot, arid, and rocky. The atmosphere was thinner than earth's. The sky was a deep purple dominated by the huge blue-white sun, classified as a B7III giant. The night sky contained a spectacular collection of stellar classifications, dominated by blue and white A and B stars and also cooler yellow and orange F, K, and G stars. The planet's rotation and its orbit determined a day of about 28 earth hours and a calendar divided into 70 six-day periods. The atmosphere of the planet contained significant amounts of methane, and much less oxygen than on earth. Even so the Xorg, a hardy race, could survive in the atmosphere of earth for significant periods of time. Their biology was very adaptable.

The landscape of the planet was mostly flat and the soil thin and rocky. The surface had excellent heat retention because the crust was pockmarked with tiny holes that trapped the warmth of the burning sun during the day and radiated it back during the night. The planet's atmosphere yielded an almost uniform air temperature of approximately 110 degrees Fahrenheit. Many natural caves dotted the surface and underground. Only the most hardy vegetation grew, except in areas where there were underground aquifers. Water collected into these *tinajas*, or natural rock formations, and in waterholes. Here, sub-species drank and ate, always watchful for predator reptiles or desperate *Shiga*, the planet's only flying species. Shiga resembled vultures on earth and fed on necrotic tissue. Sometimes they would attack other species in packs of three or four. Around water numerous *Argul* would   gather, standing on watch. Argul, a small reptile whose meat was favored by the Tau, was the most numerous sub-species. Unlike earth, environmental and biological diversity on Draco Tau was very limited. Therefore the planet's biomass was small. The dominant reptilian species lived in specially outfitted caves shielded from the blazing sun. Individual dwellings were widely separated. The Tau had no families except for breeding periods when males and females came together for sexual intercourse. Xorg society was organized in a top-down hierarchical control structure, exactly suiting the Tau temperament.

Unlike reptiles on earth the Tau had no scales on their skin, which was thick and leathery and shielded them from the fierce ultraviolet and gamma radiation of their sun. Tau did not tolerate cold well, nor could their bodies remain exposed to their sun for more than a few hours at a time without suffering what they called "boiling blood." The Tau were predators. Their diet consisted strictly of meat. Their liquid intake, like human cats, was absorbed from the tissues they consumed. Tau liked their meat fresh-killed. They drank blood as earthian humans drink water, for blood contains the life-giving essence. All male Tau were trained as warriors. No exceptions were permitted. Those who were born defective were killed. Females were subservient and existed to give birth to male offspring. As a result of this policy, and the low biomass of the planet, the entire Tau population numbered only ten million, of which 75% were male.

Belial wasn't thinking about any of this. His one and only thought was for revenge. He had been humiliated in combat by one of the earthian hominids! Now every malignant who had designs on his position would attempt to subvert him. Therefore he would call a *Hangul*, to demonstrate to the entire planet that he was still fit for leadership. His primary challenger, he knew, would be the reprobate who called himself Ubar.[9]

Belial called his minions to him. They entered his personal chamber, a palatial cave with 50 foot ceilings and a rock floor that had been painstakingly smoothed for comfort. Normally subservient, Belial now detected a predatory eagerness in his subjects. They smelled weakness. The scum!

"A Hangul must be held in three days time at the Central Hojo!" he commanded.

He looked balefully around at the two dozen of his personal minions, pinning each set of eyes. "Any scum present who would like to try their luck, step forward now!" He waited for a full minute and no one came forth. "It is decided then. I am your master. The slightest deviation from my commands will be punished by instant death."

Everyone nodded. A quick death was itself a humiliation, an insult. A warrior dies slowly, inflicting the maximum amount of damage on his enemy. The ultimate humiliation was death by execution, a swift strike of the *Mughal* and the head sliced off. The *Zorghal,* in which the warrior's hands and feet were cut off first before the head was removed, was unthinkable. The Zhorghal was reserved only for the greatest acts of cowardice or sedition. It required the elimination of the offender's entire bloodline: males, females, and children. Even more egregious, the permanent striking of the bloodline name from Tau genealogy. The Zhorghal was required to erase all taint from the malefactor's biological information system, which would infect the race genetics. It had only happened six times in the long history of the Xorg.

Belial pointed to his first lieutenant.

"Miscreant, you will arrange for the Hangul."

This one jumped quickly to obey. He then pointed to his second lieutenant.

"You will gather three warriors and come to my personal communication chamber. You will monitor the hominid 'Mar-cus Ri-ley' on the earthian planet for every second of his existence. I have placed the entity's complete Identification Resonance in a report in my chamber. You will prepare special incantations that resonate specifically to this hominid. At the proper time I will use it to possess him."

The second lieutenant jumped to obey, but more slowly than the first. This reprobate called himself Rihat. He was clever and ambitious. Rihat would never challenge him openly but would plot some subtle intrigue, which was why he wanted him close.

Belial looked around the silent gathering.

"Am I understood, delinquents?"

Heads nodded forward respectfully.

"Return to your duties immediately!"

After his minions left Belial seethed, wallowing in his favorite life-giving emotion, and plotted revenge. He would have a rematch with this Mar-cus Ri-ley. When he defeated the hominid he would drink his blood and feed his body to the Shiga.

Beijing, China, Meeting of the Party Elders

Zhou Wei, Li Qiang, and Xiang Ri sat around a beautiful bamboo table, drinking tea. The three Elders were seated in a private conference room at Tsinghua University, not far from the Yuan Ming Yuan, the old summer palace. They were the senior members of the Elders Council, an advisory group to the country's political leaders. This group often exercised great influence on China's national and international policy.

"Examine these images," Li Qiang said, spreading along the tabletop hardcopy images that had been relayed to them by their friend, Holderness Parkinson, in New York. "What do you see?"

Zhou Wei, the youngest, was the first to understand. He gasped. "The six-toed dragon!"

Xiang Ri grimaced while he made sure, removing his glasses and counting the digits of the great beast. "Yes, the number of toes of the dragon is six, signifying the lineage of the ancient Dragon Kings from the sky."

There could be no doubt. Spontaneously, the eyes of the three Elders met in a moment of frozen silence.

All understood the ancient legends of the dragon and their possible return at the end of the world. Dragons had always been the symbol of the Chinese Emperor. Hsi, the first Emperor, was said to have had a dragon's tail. His successor, Shen Nung, was said to have been fathered by a dragon.[10]

"The Chinese Imperial Dragon has five claws," Zhou Wei remarked.

"And the other dragons four," Xiang Ri said.

"We must verify the existence of this creature and whether it is genuine," Li Qiang said. "I will consult with Colonel Chen Yi-Chun of the Exobiology Department of the Ministry of State Security. I will also inform the Unification Board."

"Please report back to us as soon as possible," Zhou Wei requested.

Elder Li Qiang nodded. All three were shocked by the images. Ancient history, long ignored as superstitious nonsense, had suddenly become terrifyingly real. "Our time may now be short. I wonder what can be done?"

The others had no answer.

Darcy and Marcus rode in the back seat of a luxury sedan headed south and west on I-95. When they walked around the car to get in, Marcus tried to identify its make and model. All insignia had been taken off the vehicle. They were taken to a secure military facility in Fort Meyer, Virginia, and locked in a small room with no windows. Colonel Rodgers escorted them into the building and through security. "I'm afraid I'll have to leave you now," he said, opening the door and motioning the two inside. "You may have to stay here longer than you were anticipating."

Darcy was upset. "But you said—" The door shut.

Marcus thought quickly but there was nothing he could do. His first thought was to call Thom Madigan. The two had been searched just after entering the building and their mobile devices had been taken. There was nothing in the room, which was lit by fluorescent lights, except a long table with built-in cabinets and drawers. The table was covered by a black slate top. Two metal chairs stood against the wall. The room had a small bathroom in back.

"Marcus, I'm scared," Darcy said. "This place looks like an interrogation room."

"It probably is."

They sat silent for about five minutes. The door suddenly opened and a blocky man in a military uniform entered. He had short-cropped black curly hair, a flat nose, and very full lips. "I am Lieutenant Mutumbe, your debriefer. If you cooperate you may be out of here in a couple of days. If you want to get intransigent we'll give you truth drugs and get it out of you that way. Either way we're going to find out."

Darcy was angry. "A couple of days! We can tell you everything in five minutes."

"I'm afraid not, Darcy Regier," the man replied. "You're going to discover what an ETV debrief is."

Marcus activated the web of light and got inside the man's head. Mutumbe was a combat trained Marine who had seen action in Iraq, where he had served with Colonel Rodgers. He had worked in the ETV unit for five years. A flag-waving patriot, but a man with a wealth of experience and a lot of knowledge about international affairs. Marcus was amazed to discover that this unit was devoted entirely to ETV crashes and extraterrestrials. So there really are ETs then! Mutumbe was a hard man and would stop at nothing to do what he thought was right. Marcus decided that it would be best to cooperate and not ask a lot of questions. He met Darcy's eyes silently and she nodded. Darcy may not be as smart as Carla, Marcus thought, but she was far more subtle. Darcy just got things.

"All right lieutenant," Marcus said. "Let's get this over with. We're ready to cooperate."

"That's the smart way," Mutumbe said.

Over the next three days Marcus and Darcy were taken literally over every second of any incident that could have remotely have had anything to do with UFOs or aliens. Question after question was asked until the full timeline of the events in New York was established. Sometimes they were separated and sometimes they were questioned together. Marcus found out about Darcy's conversations with the golden-eyed guys. Marcus was grilled rigorously about his web of light. Mutumbe was particularly interested in how Marcus had defeated the alien reptile. "You see, Marcus, as far as we know you are the only human who has ever come close to doing that." Mutumbe spoke in an awed voice.

"You mean there are more of these guys?" Marcus was incredulous.

Mutumbe grimaced. "I shouldn't have said that, but you've probably already guessed why we brought you here."

"Fuck."

"That's right kid. Now you might understand why it's important that you keep quiet."

They were silent for a few moments. "Tell me what you did to that alien."

"I've been thinking about that. When I entered the alien's head I was just trying to find out about him, a weakness, that I could use to defend myself. Then I realized that the web itself was a problem for him. He didn't like it at all. I also discovered something about our genetics being changed. Some of us are mutating and have to be destroyed."

Mutumbe asked a lot of questions about the web of light. Marcus couldn't tell the lieutenant how it worked or how he generated it. "I don't know, it just ... happens when I want it to."

"That's not good enough Marcus. If you don't make some more sense I'm going to send you in to the lab boys. That can get pretty uncomfortable."

What Marcus really wanted to know more about was ETs. Whenever he tried to ask Mutumbe about them he was quickly shot down. "I ask the questions, you answer," Mutumbe said.

The next day Marcus was probed and analyzed in a medical lab to determine the source of what Mutumbe called his "force field." The lieutenant was present at all times. Marcus tried to explain that it wasn't a force field, more like a viewport that allowed him to see perfectly inside another's mind. The scientists had all kinds of theories but no explanations.

After the end of the third day they were finally done. Lieutenant Mutumbe warned them not to discuss their experiences at the base. He told them to say they had been sightseeing in DC. "That reptile you saw was just part of a science fiction movie being filmed in New York." Mutumbe pinned them both with his eyes. "Correct?"

"Do you think people are going to believe that?" Marcus asked.

Mutumbe laughed. "Of course they will. What's the alternative? To believe that an evil alien suddenly materialized out of nowhere on 50th street?"

Darcy sighed, meeting Marcus' eyes. "All right lieutenant, have it your way."

"I'm not really worried," Mutumbe said. "People have been conditioned to think that the earth is alone in the universe. Even if both of you told the truth, most of the lemmings out there would think you were kooks. Your lives would go in a direction you wouldn't care to experience."

Marcus had to agree. Mutumbe gave them both a plausible story for their nosy friends and prying media types (cleared at the highest levels, of course). He told them that when they re-emerged into their lives they would be glad to have something to deflect vulgar curiosity. "If you stick to the story and not deviate the talk will gradually die down. Don't get ideas of becoming famous with this." The lieutenant was stern. "We'll shoot you down fast. Your lives will be a lot more miserable than if you just stick to the program."

Marcus could see the wisdom of this. Darcy also agreed and the lieutenant was satisfied. He was like a mini-dictator, Darcy thought. As long as you did things his way everything was happy, happy. If you deviated you felt his wrath.

They had a little time before they were cleared to leave the facility. Lieutenant Mutumbe lightened up a little, and told them a story. "This is a true story, no bullshit," he said.[11] "My boss, Colonel Rodgers, lives here on base. He has a daughter, we'll call her Dorothy. Whenever there is a report of a crash of an unidentified object anywhere in the world, the colonel is sent out to investigate. He is on call 24 hours a day, 7 days a week. When he gets the call, even if it is in the middle of the night, he has five minutes to get out of bed, pack, and dress. A car meets him in front of the house and he is flown directly to the site. This is a secure military compound. The colonel's daughter is 16 now. Since the time she was born until last year she had never been left alone in the house. Never. When the colonel goes out on business at least one guard is sent over to the house. I never understood why until last year.

"Dorothy had never been alone in her life and she didn't like it. After several years of asking she finally persuaded her father to let her alone in the house during one of his trips. Five minutes after the colonel left one afternoon she was in her bedroom. She heard a noise coming from her closet, a scratching sound. She was combing her hair at her desk on the other side of the room. In the mirror she saw something walk out of the closet. It was one of those reptiles. She began to scream as the thing came for her. She opened the bedroom door and ran down the hall into the bathroom. She opened the window and shouted as loudly as she could. Meanwhile she heard footsteps down the hall. A team of guys arrived and ran into the living room. We heard something bumping down the hallway and we ran in. We saw one of those reptiles, a huge thing, go back into the closet. We raised our guns to fire but the thing literally disappeared. Explain that."

Marcus sighed. "I should have stayed in Midland." If any of this was true the world was a really strange place and everything he knew about it was wrong.

Mutumbe laughed. "Welcome to the real world son. Funny isn't it: the real world is something you can't talk about. Only the bullshit that passes for reality is acceptable."

"Why don't you guys just come clean?" Marcus asked. "Tell the whole story and get people behind you."

Mutumbe grimaced. "It will probably come to that in the end. The problem is that the truth would scare the living shit out of ninety percent of the population."

Mutumbe had a little insert in his ear and it must have beeped or something. He straightened. "OK, party's over. You've been cleared. You only have five minutes to exit the base so snap it up."

"How are we supposed to get home?" Darcy asked.

"That's your problem." Mutumbe hustled them into the corridor. "This unit doesn't advertise itself. Driving you back to New York would pose certain ... ah, problems."

"Well, of all the rude things!" Darcy was indignant. "After all we've done for you."

In short order Marcus and Darcy found themselves at the Days Inn across Arlington Blvd. Darcy asked the woman at the desk how to get a rental car. It was a blazing hot day, sultry and humid. Darcy was still upset at the way they had been treated. Marcus realized that no one had bothered to treat his cuts, which were still oozing, although the medics had taken samples. That was very odd. What if he had gotten infected by that thing? Oh well, he'd just have to see Dr. June at the bank.

Situation Room, the White House

Representatives from the National Security Council, Navy intelligence, and Air Force intelligence met in an emergency session. Everyone at the inter-agency meeting had seen the video of the reptile. President Foley had asked CIA Director Felix Pantera to sound out the intelligence community and give him a briefing.

Felix Pantera chaired the meeting. He sat at the head of the table and asked for the opinions of all the men regarding the incident. The stoutly built Admiral Randall James, Vice Chairman of the Joint Chiefs, sat to his right. "That was clearly no science fiction movie. The JCS is aware of the Air Force units devoted to so-called non-terrestrial contact and craft. But we are told nothing." James looked accusingly over at Bobo Jacoby from Air Force intelligence, who smirked.

NSC Advisor General June Jones sat to Felix's left. Jones was a big muscular man and began by banging a meaty fist on the table. "Nobody's telling me anything. The NSC is in the dark." Jones looked over at Admiral James. "Air Force intelligence and the ONI refuse to divulge information about this. It's totally unacceptable." Jones stared at Draco Smith, the representative from the Office of Naval Intelligence. Smith met the eyes of Jacoby and they both grinned.

Felix didn't like this. The CIA director knew about Draco Smith and Bobo Jacoby. Both men were known for their participation in highly secretive clandestine operations, or black ops.

General Blair Dennis, the Director of National Intelligence, sat next to Jones. Dennis was an All-American type, blond with a handsome face and a square jaw. Before he spoke he looked over at Jacoby, who nodded slightly. "There isn't much I can tell you gentlemen. At the ODNI we aren't concerned with threats from outside the atmosphere of this planet." Dennis smiled ironically. "If there is such a thing."

Felix was observing closely now. He saw Dennis raise an eyebrow a half-millimeter toward Draco Smith. Felix's's radar twigged on Smith and Jacoby. They were dark and shadowy and seemed to exude a disagreeable psychic odor. The military intelligence boys were withholding information, but why? "Black ops bastards," Pantera muttered.

"What was that Mr. Pantera?" Smith said. "I didn't hear you."

"Nothing. I was just thinking that I don't know half the time what my agency is doing."

Smith chuckled but his eyes were cold. "We'll tell you everything you need to know about this one." Jacoby glanced over at Smith.

Felix was shocked. Clearly Jacoby and Smith were in control here. The NSC and the Joint Chiefs and the rest of the intelligence community were being played. Felix took a deep breath and calmed himself. "So what do I tell the president at the next NSC meeting? I'm supposed to brief him about this incident in New York."

"Tell him whatever you want," Smith said. "He only gets information on a need-to-know basis anyway."

Felix was angry now. He was about to reply when Smith spoke again. "And so do you." Jacoby's eyes met Smith's again and Pantera shuddered. Bobo Jacoby from Air Force intelligence seemed to be running Smith. Felix longed for the good old days when the military and the intelligence people sometimes actually cooperated. All he knew was that hundreds of billions of dollars were diverted every year out of the budget to a massive but shadowy organization that seemed to bypass the Agency and the other major intelligence services.

Admiral James saw Pantera's discomfiture and was sympathetic. He glanced at the CIA director with what he hoped was a look of confidence. He didn't really know anything but he wasn't going to admit it. He was here on a fishing expedition for the JCS. It was like that old book he'd read as a kid, *Seven Days in May*, about an attempted military coup. Something fishy was going on outside the chain of command and the JCS was out of the loop.

Pantera rose abruptly. "Who is in charge here?"

Draco Smith made a negligent gesture with his hand. He was very bored. Dealing with these civilians was a pain in the ass. When Senator Fazio became president things would be a lot easier. "Sit down, Director Pantera." The words were barely audible. Pantera felt a sucking energy around him, as if his angry emotions were being drained off.

Felix remained standing and spoke to Bobo Jacoby, a smallish man with a barrel chest and long arms with huge hands. Skilled in hand-to-hand combat, he was known as an elusive operative entrusted to lead the most sensitive and secretive missions behind enemy lines. "Tell us about what happened in New York."

"That's not on your need-to-know list," Draco Smith said.

"I'm not talking to you Smith. Jacoby, I want a briefing on that goddam reptile. And while you're at it I want to know what's going on in the restricted programs." Felix saw James, Jones, and Dennis both snap to attention.

"Why do you think we know anything more than you?" Jacoby answered.

Pantera didn't say anything. He tried to meet Jacoby's eyes but he had to break contact. It's been too long since I've seen combat, he thought. I'm getting soft. "I know you do and you know it too," Pantera replied. "So tell us."

Jacoby looked over at Smith and shrugged. "All you have to know is that there are other planets out there with life. Some of these guys are pretty fucked up. Certain, ah, elements within the national security establishment are dealing with the problem. The human race is nothing, Pantera, unless we wise up and get with the program."

"And what's the program?"

"Wouldn't you like to know," Jacoby said. The man's face was ugly and twisted. Pantera had to drop eye contact again. General Dennis shifted uncomfortably in his chair. Admiral James' face showed disgust. General Jones just stared at the two men with a grimace. Pantera could tell that Jacoby and Smith were very unpopular but they obviously had influence over everyone else.

"In a little while there's going to be a big surprise for the human race," Draco Smith said.

Pantera's eyes blazed.

"Don't worry DCI Pantera." Smith spoke with mock compassion. "Do your job and when it comes you'll be 'saved.'"

Jacoby laughed. "The Rapture is coming Pantera. Make sure you're on the right side."

Pantera rose abruptly, glared at the two men, and left the room. He wondered what President Foley would say when he told him about this meeting.

CHAPTER **19**

WHEN Darcy and Marcus got back to New York they discovered that they had become minor celebrities. Kathleen was agog when Darcy walked into the little boutique on 81st street. She asked so many questions Darcy understood what Lieutenant Mutumbe meant about the vulgarly curious.

"C'mon, Darcy, get real," Kathleen demanded. "This story you're telling sounds good but that's not all there is to it."

"You're probably right about that but honestly, I don't know what the truth is either." And she didn't, so she could say it with complete conviction.

Kathleen met her eyes for a few seconds and shrugged. "OK, if that's the way you want it. I thought I was your friend, but I guess not."

"Oh Kathy of course you are! Please don't make it any harder than it is for me. We did go sightseeing." (That was true. She and Marcus had seen the inside of the Days Inn. On the way to DC they saw the Monument out of the window of their car.) "Before we left we saw a guy on the street who made us tell him everything we saw. It was really boring and all they did was ask questions, and we had to answer them."

"What kind of guy?" Kathleen asked. "Was he cute?"

"Oh my God, no. Some military guy. He was very rude and unhelpful."

"My my. What did you tell them?"

"We told them the truth. We were looking in a shop window at some clothes ? well I was anyway, Marcus was looking at my legs I think – " Kathleen giggled ? "and then all of a sudden we saw a bunch of cameras and that helicopter, and that ugly body in the street. I never saw anything so lifelike. Then somebody told us we needed to get out of there, they were shooting a movie and they wanted it to look as real as possible. They asked us a bunch of questions, and then Marcus and I looked at each other. We decided we needed a vacation so we took off for DC. A spur of the moment thing."

"Movie companies use extras and they have to pay them," Kathleen said. "Those people on the street weren't extras."

Darcy shrugged. The lieutenant told them not to go into details. "Anyway it's over. I don't want to talk about it anymore."

Kathleen giggled. "You might have to. There were reporters around here for three days. They might come back."

"Don't we have a show next week?" Darcy asked, changing the subject.

"Yes." A voice spoke from behind an open door. Audrey walked out with a cloth tape measure around her shoulder and a pencil in her ear. "And some very exclusive clients too. Two new evening dresses and the 'sportswear' line for some clients who will be going to the US Open tennis championship in September. They need to look their very best."

"I suppose I'd better get back to work early tomorrow," Darcy said.

"*Vraiment!*" Audrey said. She pointed her pencil at her star model. "The next time you wish to take time off, young lady, s'*il vous plaît me consulter en premier!*"

Marcus had a much tougher time with Carla. He had now been an apprentice trader for a month, mostly watching and learning. He was legally able to trade but Carla had been watching him like a boil on a baby's rear end. When he showed up for work after missing three days Carla laid into him before the entire team. "If you don't want to be fired right now you'd better have a good explanation for missing all that time. We don't just take days off around here, Riley."

Lieutenant Mutumbe had advised him to stick to the story and not elaborate. "I got konked in the head when those stupid movie guys showed up. The dumbass in the lizard suit was supposed to attack one of the guys who drove up in the black car, but he missed and got me. Then they drove me back to my apartment and I basically lay in bed for three days. I think I had a concussion."

"Did you get checked out by a doctor?" Carla asked. "What happened to your face?"

"I was going to last night but I started feeling better." He felt his right cheek where he had gotten scratched. "The guy in the lizard suit did it. It was hot that day and he almost got heat stroke. He messed up."

Carla looked at him skeptically. The kid was trying to mess with her. "Next time you pull a stunt like that without checking in first you're done here. Do you understand?"

"Yes boss." Marcus spoke meekly. "I hear that the algorithm boys are going to show up again today."

"That doesn't concern you. It's way over your head." Carla was irritated.

"I don't think so."

Carla put a hand on her hip. "Oh yeah?" She looked around the room and addressed the other traders. "Listen to this arrogant kid. He takes off like he owns the company, then comes up with this." She turned back to Marcus. "You only have the equivalent of a couple of years of college. These guys are PhDs in math and quantitative finance."

Marcus shrugged. He would deliberately irritate her and she'd forget about his absence and it would all blow over. Besides, he wanted to study those trading algos. "So? That doesn't mean anything."

Carla was flabbergasted. "I knew you were arrogant but I didn't think you were delusional."

"Oh yeah? How much do you want to bet I can figure out whatever they're doing?"

Carla looked around the room. Everybody wanted in and she did too. "OK kid, but it's going to cost you a week's salary. Straight up, even odds, we each put in one seventh of the kid's weekly paycheck. Right guys?"

Everybody shouted an affirmative. "We'll split the kid's salary seven ways when we win." Everybody hooted at Marcus.

"You only win the bet if Sarah says so Marcus," Carla insisted.

"Who's Sarah?"

"She's the head of the quant team."

"OK by me. When are they supposed to show up?"

"Right after your lunch, hotshot," Carla said. "You don't get to study before then. You work right up until your lunch break." Despite her irritation Carla was impressed by Marcus' certainty. There was no chance he could succeed though. When he was like this, on edge, she liked him a lot better. It made her want him again.

"Deal!" Marcus said.

After lunch two men and a woman arrived in the training room. Their job was to tweak the complicated trading algorithms that had been designed specifically for Carla's trading engine. Carla explained that a hotshot trainee of theirs bet that he could understand their work. "He might pester you with a few questions," she told Sarah.

"How much did you bet?" Sarah asked Marcus. She was a petite but very well built brunette in her early thirties wearing round glasses with gold rims. Sarah was really impressive. Like Carla, she exuded an aura of self-confidence and competence.

"A week's salary," he replied.

Her eyes widened. "Well then, have a look."

After an hour it became clear to the team of experts that Carla's trainee was an amazingly fast learner. After two hours they pronounced Marcus a member of their team.

"Do you want to join us Marcus?" Sarah asked him. He was probably one of those savants who read code and math like English. She'd seen a few of those. Men usually, with no training, socially inept, who could simply pick up on the symbology after it was explained once. Marcus seemed to be pretty well-adjusted. He was a handsome devil as well. She stepped closer and noticed that the top of her head was well below his chin. A tasty morsel for sure.

Marcus was sorely tempted. This quant stuff would give him an opportunity to engage in some rarefied financial research. With his web of light he knew he could do it. The more he used it the more it expanded its scope and sophistication.

Carla saw him thinking and intervened. "Sorry, but he's contracted to us for a year with a no-compete for another year." She had lost her bet and $300, but she wasn't going to allow these geeks to steal her best trainee.

Sarah held out her hand to Marcus and he took it. She gazed up at the man-child before her. In her eyes was an invitation. "Come see me in two years, Marcus. We're at Orpheus Analytics. Ask for Sarah Blaisdell. We'll have a job for you I promise."

Marcus smiled. He felt flattered. Were all women in New York brilliant and flirtatious? "I just might do that."

Carla was irritated at the vignette being performed in her workspace, and with her employee. She could see the other traders grinning. Sarah was much too close to Marcus; her breasts were almost touching the kid. She was losing face. "OK enough of that. Are you guys done?"

"Yes." Sarah spoke with just the hint of a grin on her face that said, "Watch it Carla, I might just snabble him up." Carla rose to her full height and thanked Sarah and the team for their work. Her look said, "Don't let the door hit you on the way out."

Marcus saw the interplay of emotions between the two women and almost laughed. It was fun seeing two gorgeous older women fighting over him. The two men in the quant group could barely contain their amusement and that made him feel even better. Carla caught his smile and glared at him before escorting the quants to the elevator.

Carla walked back into the trading room. "Better watch that, kid. Sarah eats little boys like you for breakfast."

Marcus grinned and knew that he had really gotten to her. "Umm, sounds delicious." Carla flounced back to her station and didn't speak to him for the rest of the day.

Draco Tau

"Activity on the hominid planet, quadrant 6, sector [23.9009]," the communicator announced. Belial growled and switched on. Rihat was standing at the observation tank. Belial did not like the insolent tone of his voice. "Where is the hit?"

"The hominid who defeated you. Sire." Rihat spoke with suppressed glee.

Belial was furious. He would personally gut this scum when the time was ripe. But he was also curious. Communication between the stars was feasible using the transportal devices but both parties either had to carried one or there had to be a natural transportal on the other side. Belial could not understand how this vermin Mar-cus Ri-ley was able to access the ethers without assistance. It made him doubly anxious to defeat him.

"This is the seventh time the earthian hominid has been visible since your ... return," Rihat reported. "Each time the connection breaks after a short interval."

Belial understood. "Very well, reprobate. Gather five drones and continue monitoring the device. The next time that scum is available we will overwhelm and destroy him. Continue to monitor the activity of the principals." Belial signed off, not wanting to invite another veiled insult.

Tomorrow was the Hangul, where he would destroy Ubar and the other challengers. Then he would deal with Rihat. After that he would skewer the hominid Mar-cus Ri-ley.

That evening Darcy and Marcus went to St. Luke's Theater on 46th to see "Channeling Kevin Holbrook." Marcus and Darcy had divergent artistic tastes but Holbrook was one actor they both liked. On the way back to Darcy's apartment after the show they got into a whispered argument about the nationality of their taxi driver. Darcy said he was Pakistani. Marcus said he was a Sikh. Marcus activated his web of light and got into the driver's mind. He was right! The man's name was Darwat Singh and he was born in the Punjab. He was just about to shut down the web and tell Darcy she was wrong. A malevolent presence entered his mind and heard heard an angry voice. "Mar-cus Ri-ley, I will kill you and the female!" Marcus shut down the web and nervously looked out of the windows of the cab. Were they being attacked?

"What's wrong Marcus?" Darcy asked.

"For fuck's sake shut up!" Marcus shouted. The driver looked around at him and frowned.

"Marcus!" Darcy looked into his eyes and didn't recognize him. This was different from the cokehead Marcus. It was more like when that horrible creature had attacked him. Darcy shuddered at the memory and noticed that the three scratches on his face had still not healed.

Marcus shook his head to clear it. "I'll tell you when we get home Darcy." Marcus tried to regain his equilibrium. "I can't talk about it here."

Darcy noticed that his eyes had cleared and he was back to normal. "OK Marcus."

When they got home Marcus explained. "I think ... that whenever I use my web of light that reptilian creature can see me somehow."

"That's impossible Marcus. It's dead. We saw it in the street."

"I don't think so Darcy. I'm not sure how, but that thing is still alive."

Three weeks later

Marcus awoke shivering.

It had been months since he had touched cocaine or any drugs. It had been a battle. Despite Dr. June's little bottle and the Chinese herbs his cells still demanded more of the stuff. The mornings were the worst part of the day.

He hadn't dared to utilize the web of light since his last experience in the cab. But today he might have to. Today was his first day at his trading station without someone looking over his shoulder. He had advanced so rapidly that even Carla was astonished. He had done it without utilizing the pattern recognition abilities of his web. Perhaps his brain was being rewired; maybe he didn't need it anymore.

When he arrived in Equities Services, five minutes early, Carla was already there.

"Are you ready?"

"I was born ready." Marcus felt confident.

"Don't get cocky Marcus. You're just a rookie."

"I already passed almost all of the FINRA exams." FINRA was the licensing agency for all securities traders.

Carla put her hand on her hip and Marcus suppressed a smile. When she did that he knew he had stung her. It was his policy to "get" her at three times a day. Lately she had been treating him too casually.

Carla was dismissive. "We'll see how you do today kid."

Marcus grinned. A clean hit! "We're even so far." He saw her try to look forbidding. The hint of a smile peeped out and he knew she understood that their game was on again today.

"The market opens in fifteen minutes," she said, all business now. Carla walked to her station at the head of the octagon-shaped room. "Get your face fixed Marcus!" she fired across the room. "I'm tired of looking at those scratches."

At 2:15 p.m. Marcus saw a pattern in the market and executed a trade. "Marcus!" Carla shouted across the room. "What are you doing?"

"Relax, sweetheart. You'll see in about five minutes how brilliant it was."

Carla rose quickly from her station and strode over to his. "Listen hotshot, we don't need any drugstore cowboys executing hunch trades." Carla was very angry. The other traders were in full agreement. She had stung him good with her drugstore cowboy remark. Marcus looked calmly up at the tall woman standing beside hm. That's two for her and one for me.

"Why do you think we build those algorithms?"

Marcus spoke quietly. "You shouldn't robotically follow a system when a better pattern appears."

"This isn't a race track or a casino. You might have guessed right but that doesn't make it OK." All of these rookies were the same, she thought. Arrogant egomaniacs.

"I don't guess."

Despite her righteous anger (and she *was* right) Carla was impressed. The manchild sat there with complete and quiet confidence. His certainty calmed her down.

"No more of that crap," she ordered.

Six minutes later Marcus was proved right. The market ticked upward. Marcus' trade had made the company almost $80,000. Marcus looked up from his bank of monitors across the room to Carla's station and saw her staring at him. "You got lucky kid," she said.

Marcus grinned and saw her hot flash of anger. "Hah! Tied up!"

The other traders looked around, wondering what was going on. Carla shoved her head down to her keyboards.

At 3:49, just before the market closed, Marcus got into trouble. He saw another pattern developing but was not certain if there was enough time before close for it to mature. He had about 60 seconds to decide, and he needed his web! Oh hell, here goes. The web of light came up around his head. He saw clearly that there wouldn't be enough time. Before he could shut it down he felt a murderous rage inside his mind, and a powerful voice. "Hominid scum! You dare to defy me!" The voice ranted on, something about Argul, a prey species ... Marcus felt himself losing control.

"NO!" Marcus bellowed, fighting off the invasion. He was under psychic assault by at least five entities. He dimly recognized, in his mind, the creature he had fought in the street. He was totally freaking out and couldn't understand how something invisible could make him feel so horrible. Bethany, the trader who sat next to him, looked into his eyes and recoiled. Marcus was able to calm himself a little. When he did he felt the force of the assault diminish. That was the key. These demented beings thrived on anger and hatred so he would give them peace and calm. Gradually he felt the web of light shut down, and with it, the attack was over. Just before the end he felt one last psychic burst: "Mar-cus Ri-ley I will kill you."

Marcus began to laugh nervously as he regained command of his psyche and his body. Everyone in the trading room was staring at him.

"What was that all about?" Carla asked. Just for a second she had seen something completely alien and crazy in Marcus' eyes. She cocked her head at him. "You're not mentally ill are you? A former mental patient?"

Marcus could tell that the others were wondering the same thing. He knew he couldn't tell the truth. "Sorry, I was thinking about what would happen if I made a really big trade and it went wrong."

Carla snorted. Rookie! She was unsatisfied with this explanation, and so were the others, especially Bethany. But all of them had felt the same thing at one time or another, and they accepted it.

The buzzer went off signaling the market close.

When Marcus got home at 7:15 he took off his clothes and showered, trying to wash off the ugly emotions he had experienced that afternoon.

After the buzzer rang in Equities Services Carla called the usual post-market trade meeting. They went over the day's trading and analyzed their performance. Marcus came under intense criticism for his unprofessional outburst. Carla rode him hard about hunch trades. Bethany looked at him like he was a grease spot on the floor. The final summary showed that Marcus had made the trading desk look good that day, which would reflect well on them all. Sometimes the traders would hang out and go for drinks afterward. Marcus could tell that no one wanted him there so he walked out and took the elevator to his company locker. He changed out of his suit and into his exercise clothes, went down to the ground floor, and walked up the stairs. He could make it up 20 floors now without stopping even though he felt as tired as a sphincter muscle at a garlic eating contest.

Marcus gingerly walked down to the lobby, holding onto the railing. It was a hot and humid August evening. He was hungry. He stopped at a stand on 45th and devoured two fully loaded chili dogs, then walked slowly up the stairs to his apartment. He looked around the place with distaste. There were too many bad memories here, of drug-filled nights and insomnia and craziness. Now that he was employed at more reasonable hours he didn't have to stay here anymore. He should move in with Darcy.

Marcus stepped out of the shower and dried off, picking up his phone. He noticed that those damn scratches were still oozing. Tomorrow he would have to see Dr. June. One of the other company doctors had given him some kind of lotion but it didn't do anything.

His mobile rang. "Hi Marcus!" It was Darcy. "You don't have any clothes on."

Marcus could see Kathleen behind her, stretching her neck for a look at him, and then a hand covering the screen. "Kathleen, stop it!" he heard.

"I want a peek too. I want to see why you like this jerk so much."

Marcus put on a pair of shorts. "You can uncover the screen now."

"Oooh, he's cute," Kathleen said, leaning in to examine his bare chest. "Nice shoulders. Those scratches on his face are pretty sexy."

"Enough of that, Kathy," Darcy said. Then to Marcus: "I was thinking you should move in with me."

Marcus remembered his latest episode. "Uh, maybe that's not such a good idea."

"Why not?" He could tell Darcy was irritated. "Did you find another whore to fuck?"

Marcus ignored her insult. "No, but I had another episode at work today."

"Episode?"

"Yeah, you know, like what happened in the cab the other night."

Darcy put her hand to her mouth in a silent 'Oh!' "I don't understand, Marcus. We lived together fine in Midland."

"That was before that thing scratched me."

"You still haven't gone to the doctor," she accused.

"I did but the guy was a moron. I'll see Dr. June tomorrow. I'm just worried that if I blow up again I might hurt you."

Darcy sobered. She remembered his anger that night and how evil he looked. "What happened today?"

"You're going to think I'm nuts. Everybody in the trading room thinks so and I don't blame them."

"What happened?"

"I felt like I was being attacked by five ... entities. They wanted to kill me. It was fucked up."

Darcy didn't like it when he swore. The drugs had subtly altered his personality, and now this. Maybe it was better if he stayed away.

Marcus was secretly hoping that she'd take him in. He saw her hesitation and understood. "OK, we'll let it rest for a while. But now you know I want you. I want to live with you."

Darcy smiled weakly. "I want you too. Go see the doctor tomorrow OK? Maybe you got infected by that thing."

"I was thinking the same thing. I'll make an appointment tomorrow after work. Then I'll call you."

Darcy smiled. "OK."

When Marcus went in to work the next morning he was nervous. Everyone arrived at 8 a.m. even though the market didn't open until 9:30. A meeting was held to plan the day's trading. As he entered the room Carla noticed his scratches. Bethany looked at him and shuddered.

"You were possessed yesterday," Bethany said. "I saw it."

Marcus didn't deny it. He said nothing.

"What happened on the street that day?" Tom asked, making connections. Tom Shapiro sat next to him, to his right. Bethany Morgan, Carla's friend, was at his left in the octagonal trading room. "There was that lizard guy and he scratched you. I saw what Bethany saw in your eyes. I don't believe anymore that it was a movie."

Should he tell the truth? Mutumbe had threatened that if they did they'd be hauled back to Fort Meyer. He couldn't put Darcy that again. "Maybe it wasn't."

"But how?" Carla asked, fascinated despite her revulsion. She should call a psychiatric hospital and have this guy committed, but his value as a trader was too great.

Marcus didn't like the trend of their conversation. He could tell them about the web of light without angering Mutumbe, and it might distract them. "I have this ability, I guess you'd call it, to see patterns in my head. I call it the web of light. When I activate it I can understand complex systems and accurately predict the resolution of complicated, shifting sequences." He shrugged. "It's why I scored so high on the test and why I was able to understand those algos, and why I was able to make that trade yesterday. But there's a downside to it."

Carla scoffed. "A web of light? What does that mean? Are you on some kind of drug?"

"No. It's something I've always had. I saw my parents' death in a car accident a year before it happened."

The room quieted suddenly. He had said it quietly and with such certainty that everyone knew it was true. "I didn't know about that," Carla said.

"Yeah, it really sucked."

Nobody said anything for a moment.

"What about those scratches?" Bethany asked.

"I'm going to see Doctor June after work today."

"Put a band-aid on it or something. You look like a freak."

"OK."

"Go see the doctor now," Carla ordered. "We'll cover for you if you're late."

"OK."

Marcus walked toward the elevator and everybody sat down. Doctor June was on the fifth floor so he took the stairs.

He got through reception with no problem. It was really cool that the bank had their own doctors. There were three licensed physicians at NYCBank, serving over 400 employees at the main office.

"Marcus! Good to see you," June said, rising. They shook hands. Marcus again wondered about June. He saw a slight man, almost ascetic, with brown hair and piercing blue eyes in a very intelligent, minimalist face with thin lips, a small nose, and no eyebrows. His hair looked like it had been sewn on to the top of his head, or maybe it was a toupee. "Those are some nasty scratches you have there. Did you get them on the movie set?" June winked at him.

"Uh, yes." Marcus didn't know what to say. Did June understand about Belial?

"Relax. I can see you don't want to talk about it." June frowned and moved his face closer to Marcus, inspecting the scratches.

"I want to take a sample of that oozing and analyze it in the lab." June took a small, sterilized glass plate and carefully transferred the sample. "Wait here a minute. I want to put this under a microscope."

While Marcus waited he went over what happened that day. The funny little dark-skinned man had followed them down Park after he and Darcy left the NYCBank building. They had gotten to 50th when the guy went crazy. No, wait a minute. Darcy stopped at the little clothing store and two guys drove up in a black car and tried to take them. Yeah, then he activated the web of light and told them to let go of Darcy and him ... Then that little guy pulled a gun and told them to get in. He saw a holographic projection behind the guy. Yes, and then the little guy morphed into a huge reptile. How did that happen? Now Marcus had full recall of the incident. First he turned the web of light onto the dark-skinned guy and *then* he morphed. Marcus jumped up from his chair. Of course! It was the web of light that first activated the connection to this ... demon. Activating it must have created some kind of access for that entity. But what was it and where did it come from? Was it really a demon? Did demons exist? Was it an ET? An ET probably. He remembered the story Lieutenant Mutumbe told them.

June was back in the office and was scowling. "Marcus, have you been sick at all since you got these scratches?"

"No, not at all. I've been feeling pretty good." Except for when those entities take me over.

June held up the sample. "There is something in this sample that doesn't resemble anything I'm familiar with. It's not a virus, a bacteria, a spirochete, nothing I've been trained to recognize. I'm going to send this to Serven Biolabs. I'm going to drive it over myself right now."

"For fuck's sake doctor! Excuse me, that's a bad habit I'm trying to break – am I infected with some kind of alien virus?"

June cocked his head. "Why would you say that?"

"Uh, no reason I guess. It seems strange that you can't recognize it."

"Has anyone around you gotten sick?"

"Not that I know of."

"It's probably not a bio-hazard but I'm not taking any chances. Please wait in my office until I get back."

"But I'll miss the opening of trading!"

"This is more important."

June muttered something. Marcus thought he heard "the Alephs will want to know about this," but it didn't make sense.

"What was that?"

"Nothing." June smiled, his thin lips upturning slightly. "I hope to be back in three hours or less. You aren't to leave this room, do you understand? There's a bathroom in back."

Marcus nodded. "I'll tell Carla."

Just before lunch June came back. "As far as Serven can determine, whatever it is isn't harmful. But the sample's DNA is different than anything we have in our genome databases."

"What?" Marcus was alarmed. "You mean I've got some alien garbage inside of me?"

"That's the second time you've mentioned aliens," June said. He looked directly at Marcus. Suddenly, the pupils in his blue eyes grew larger and became yellow around the edges. Marcus saw clearly that June was wearing blue-colored contact lenses.

Marcus began to freak out. He remembered Darcy telling Mutumbe that her aliens had yellow cat's eyes just like the reptile!

Are ... are you an alien too?"

"What if I said I was, Marcus? What would you do?"

Marcus could see that the man was genuinely curious. After thinking for a few seconds, he shrugged. "Probably nothing. I mean, if I said anything at this point I'd probably get fired. Nobody would believe me anyway."

"That's right, no one would believe you. It's our best defense."

"*Our* best defense?"

"All I can tell you, Marcus, is that we are here working against the Tau."

"The Tau?"

"The reptiles. They are just as much a threat to us as they are to you."

Marcus was insanely curious. Just as he was about to question June somebody walked in to the office. "Doc, I need something for this sinus infection."

June winked at Marcus as if to say, "back to the John and Mary of life."

Marcus grinned. "I'd like to talk to you outside the office, Doctor June, if I may."

"Sorry Marcus. The time is not right."

"What does that mean?"

June ignored him, reached over to his desk, and grabbed a paper bag with a prescription written on it. "Here, take this. One capsule daily with a meal, and a topical cream applied three times per day. It will help to close those cuts."

Darcy was watching TV on Friday after work three days later. Kathleen left the apartment the day before to see her parents in Albany for a week. She left instructions.

"While I'm gone, no having sex with Marcus."

"Why?"

"You have to ask why? Just remember him in the street. That's the real Marcus."

"No it isn't. You've only seen him at his absolute worst. He's a great guy inside."

Kathleen groaned. "God Darcy, that's what every abused woman says about her guy. Open your eyes."

Darcy smiled. "Thanks Kathleen, I know you mean well. I don't have plans to see anyone this week."

But it didn't work out that way.

On the CBS Evening News, Kelley Scott ended the broadcast with this story:

"Do you remember that incident on 53rd Street in New York a few weeks ago, when filming for a new science-fiction movie got out of hand? Apparently there was a young couple in the middle of it all. The young man, Marcus Riley (picture), a securities trader at NYCBank, was scratched by the "evil ET" (ha-ha), a character right out of Star Wars. Riley went to his doctor to treat the three scratches on his face, which have not healed. Analysis of the tissue turned up a curious anomaly: a new form of DNA that has never been seen before. Scientists are excited about the discovery but baffled about the origins of the new genetic material.

(Chuckling) Don't worry folks it's not dangerous. But Riley's Scratches, as the new tissue is being called by researchers, is causing quite a stir. (Smiling serenely) Just goes to show, doesn't it, that sometimes truth can be stranger than fiction.

And that's our program tonight. Stay tuned for "Bastards," the new CBS hit comedy starring Martin Drucker and Wesley Carpenter ..."

Darcy called Marcus immediately but he didn't answer. She remembered that he didn't usually get home until after 7 p.m. She decided to surprise him. It was 6:29 now, maybe she could catch him coming out of the NYCBank building. If she didn't she knew a nice little cafeteria on 53rd. She was hungry. Darcy took a cab to 299 Park.

At 7:20 Marcus walked into the front lobby of the NYCBank building after his workout and an exciting day of trading. Darcy arrived a few minutes later. A bunch of media types were hanging around the front door. She hung back and saw Marcus step through one of the big revolving doors.

"There he is!" a voice shouted. Marcus looked around on the streets for a celebrity. He saw nobody he recognized. Out of the corner of his eye he saw a striking blond girl, about 17 years old, standing behind the media people on the sidewalk. She was looking at him intently. Marcus felt compelled to approach her. Just then a short, well-dressed woman in a business suit walked up to him and shoved a microphone in his face. He recognized Jessica Noory from WABC. Darcy referred to her as "that little nosy parker." Behind her stood three cameramen. "Are you Marcus Riley?" Noory asked. The reporter scrutinized his face, which had just begun to heal. Marcus looked over the heads of the crowd that had begun to gather. He saw the blond girl. She stood slightly to the right of the crowd.

Marcus caught the girl's eye and she ... shimmered. That's what it looked like to him. He wanted very much to talk to her but was blocked by the reporters. Someone was impatiently asking him a question. He didn't hear it; he needed to ask that girl how she did the shimmering trick. It reminded him of his web of light. Marcus was going to activate it and get in her head before she could leave the scene. He realized if he did he might go nutsoid again. Crap! The girl leaned her body slightly to the right and walked off. He got the idea that she wanted to meet him in a little cafeteria on 53rd.

Darcy saw the interplay and frowned. Was Marcus seeing another woman again? If so, she was going to let him have it right here.

The reporters were clamoring for answers. Like a switch turning on, Marcus suddenly heard the babbling voices of the crowd and the street noises blasting in his ears. A car honked right in front of the building and he winced. Someone rapped a question that sounded as loud as a jackhammer. "Are you Marcus Riley?"

Marcus felt mischievous. "No, I'm the Easter Bunny. Who are you?"

Noory was stern. "Don't joke with me Marcus Riley." Marcus sighed, knowing that he was playing with fire. This woman was known to be feisty and demanding and she always got her questions answered. A real diva. Marcus was at least a foot taller than Noory. He looked down at the top of her head. It was hard to take her seriously as she held the microphone up to his face with an outstretched arm. Noory felt this as well, making her even more impatient. Marcus wondered how long she had been standing there with her arm in the air. She had short, jet-black hair parted in the middle of her head, and was wearing perfume that smelled like ginger. "We know who you are!"

Marcus smiled. "Well then, why did you ask who I was?"

The woman's eyes turned to slits. "That was no filming for a science fiction movie last month and you know it. We checked with the city. Come clean, Riley. Where did you get those scratches?"

Marcus grinned. "My dog did it."

Noory's facial features flattened. Marcus could tell she was really angry. "Stop joking around."

"OK I will." Marcus changed the subject. "As long as I'm the center of attention I'd like to put in a plug for my girlfriend Darcy Regier and her boutique, Audrey's Creations, on the upper east side."

Darcy was standing well off to the left, out of Marcus' view. She was thrilled about the free publicity but didn't like the way Marcus had looked at that girl. She had seen the girl's gesture. Darcy felt that Marcus was going to meet her somewhere. At least it wasn't Carla again. Darcy saw more microphones being shoved in Marcus' face.

A tall, burly man with a square jaw shoved himself forward. Noory had to fall back. Marcus almost laughed at the play of emotions on her face, dominated by 'how dare you!'

"Riley," the man said, "you may not know it but a CBS report a few minutes ago stated that biomaterial from those scratches on your face is something completely unidentified. That's why we're here. What can you tell us?"

Another man elbowed himself forward. "Some people are saying that those scratches came from a real ET. What about that?"

Marcus was flabbergasted. "What? How did ..." He had to stop himself because he almost told them about Dr. June. June must have told the media. But why? Or maybe it was somebody at Serven Biolabs. Lieutenant Mutumbe warned him that even hinting at the existence of ETs in public would get him and Darcy locked up in Fort Meyer again.

"How did what?" Noory said, squeezing her way back to the front.

Marcus tried to smile nonchalantly. "How did you guys come up with that kooky ET stuff?" he asked the reporter.

"My sources have it on good authority that sample tissue was transported to a biolab this afternoon – Serven Biolabs – and that an analysis showed some sort of bacteria that is unknown to science."

Marcus was getting his composure back. "Then why are you asking me? I'm just a securities trader. Go talk to a reputable scientist and stop bothering me with nutty conspiracy theories."

It worked like a charm, just as Lieutenant Mutumbe said it would. The reporters were caught off guard and backed off half a step. Marcus moved quickly. He was a big man and his stair walking had put him into good physical condition. He straightened, assumed an air of offended dignity, and strode off down the street. He quickly made the turn on 51st and headed to 2nd.

Noory shrugged and completed her report. She knew there was a story here and she was going to get it. The crowd slowly dispersed. Marcus turned the corner on 2nd onto 53rd.

Walking down 53rd he saw a little bar on the corner with some tables behind a plate glass window. The girl was sitting there, drinking something. Marcus walked in.

Darcy had trouble getting through the crowd of reporters and bystanders. She didn't see Marcus turn the corner on 51st. She hurried up Park toward 53rd street.

Marcus sat down in front of the girl at the little table-for-two and looked in her eyes. He received a shock. Although she looked like a teenager her eyes radiated wisdom and experience.

The girl saw his discomfort and smiled. The warmth of it blew him away. Marcus desperately wanted to use the web of light and get inside her mind but he couldn't.

The girl spoke in a lilting voice. "Hello Marcus Riley." It was like music, he thought. He was mesmerized. Marcus looked stupidly at her, completely at a loss for words. A waiter came over and Marcus ordered a ham sandwich. He was always hungry after trading and walking the stairs.

The girl spoke softly to him. "Marcus, I want to tell you something and then I have to leave. We know about your ability, what you call your web of light."

"We?" Was this chick another ET?

"The Tau are monitoring you," she continued.

Omigawd she is. He observed her closely. She was absolutely beautiful in a sort of etheric, untouchable way. "That's the second time I've heard about the Tau today. Who are they?"

"The entities who psychically assaulted you four days ago. There are at least five of them present around you at all times. If you attempt to activate your web they will bring in a dozen more and overwhelm you. It is absolutely vital that you don't use it. Do you understand?"

Marcus nodded. "I already figured that out. I almost got creamed a few days ago when I tried to make a trade. But how would you know about that?"

The girl smiled and shook her head. All of her movements were smooth and graceful. "Marcus, there are ways of direct communication through space and time, through what you might call the ethers. The Tau have identified you as their enemy and are watching you carefully. Your web of light, as you call it, is like a unique signal that identifies you on a network. Every time you use it, it activates a particular resonance within the fabric of spacetime. Spacetime is actually a field of subtle energy. The galaxy is like a gigantic unsecured wide area network, do you understand?"

"Not really. I'll take your word for it." He had a startling thought. "Do you mean that ETs can hear our thoughts? That doesn't seem possible."

The girl smiled. Marcus thought he saw a soft golden light radiate out from her face. She was amazingly beautiful.

"No, only when you know how to project your mind in a certain way. Think of each star as a server and each planet as a node, and the galaxy as a big World Wide Web. You don't know it yet but when you use your web of light it's like activating your particular computer on the spacetime network. People who know can then see you and identify you."

"Wow!"

"Everyone has their own particular resonance. Once it has been identified it's like having a phone number to your mind. With proper training you can use it to send and receive energy and thoughts. That is how the Tau were almost able to trap you last time. The next time they will not fail. They just underestimated your strength, which is considerable."

The girl looked at him with admiration and Marcus' heart skipped several beats. He gulped, and she smiled. "These ideas seem strange to you, Marcus, but I am here to tell you to be careful. At this point in time you are a very important …actor …in a play that has a very, very large audience. I can't say anything more because my actions may inadvertently and adversely influence your future behavior. Do you understand?"

"Yes," Marcus replied automatically, even though he didn't. He was convinced that this girl was only 15 or 16 years old, but she was enhanced in some way. She was cleaner and brighter than a normal human being. She exuded an aura of quiet power, intellectual force, and feminine beauty. Marcus thought she was deliberately holding her light under a lampshade.

"Good." The girl brightened for just a second and he saw the light come out of her again.

"Wow." A couple of people looked over at them from adjoining tables.

"I'm sorry Marcus I shouldn't have done that. But all of you on earth are like this."

"No we're not. We're primitive." He was chewing his sandwich and wondered how he appeared to this amazing, delicate creature. A caveman eating the flesh of an animal and loving it, as Spock said in Star Trek.

The girl smiled again. "No Marcus. You just believe you're primitive. That's the only difference between us and you."

"Where are you from?"

"I am from the constellation of stars you call Orion. There are a lot of us on your side, far more than you can possibly imagine." She spoke mysteriously, hinting at some benign ET brotherhood or something. "Truly advanced races don't interfere with your development. Advanced technology is not the sign of evolutionary advancement."

"Uh, OK." Marcus was confused. "You seem friendly but what about those reptiles? Lietenant Mutumbe said aliens are hostile to us."

"It's a long story, Marcus. All I can tell you is that you meet up with visitors who are at your level of consciousness."

Marcus didn't know or care much about that stuff.

The girl brightened again and smiled. Heads turned toward her. "I have to leave before I make myself conspicuous." She stood to go. Marcus rose with her. "There is so much more I'd like to tell you Marcus," she said hesitantly. Marcus was the recipient of another admiring smile and it blew him away. She stood before him like a young freshman, looking up at a senior she wanted to go out with. Marcus knew this girl was on a wavelength way above his.

She turned suddenly and walked out of the cafeteria.

Marcus' brain was totally fogged and his thoughts were whirling around in his head. He was so excited he wanted to go back to the NYCBank building and run up twenty more flights of stairs. He had met three ETs in a month, and two today! It must be a dream.

Marcus seated himself and quickly finished his sandwich. He looked up through the big window to the street and saw Darcy standing there, a hand on her hip. Uh-oh! He was in trouble now. Marcus gestured for her to come in but Darcy didn't move. He went out and got her and heard a shout behind him as he exited.

"C'mon in, let's eat."

"Who was that beautiful girl, Marcus?" Marcus' waiter barreled out of the bar and pointed a finger in his face. "Hey scumbag, are you trying to dine and dash?"

Marcus looked him over contemptuously. "No I'm not. I was going to get my girlfriend to come in and have something with me. But you're being a prick so I won't." Marcus handed him $10 and put his arm in Darcy's, leading her away.

Despite her irritation she giggled. "That was great Marcus."

"Do you know that guy?"

"I've been here before. They have great food but that waiter is known to be belligerent."

Marcus looked back and saw the guy standing with his $10, looking like Idi Amin with nobody to push around. He laughed. "All right then, let's go somewhere else. I had a sandwich in there but I'm still hungry."

"So am I." Darcy stopped. "Wait a minute boy, you don't get off so easily. What were you doing in there with that gorgeous woman?"

"What if I told you she was an ET?"

Darcy's jaw dropped. "Are you serious?"

"Yes, I'm serious. She's the second ET I've met today. The city is practically crawling with them."

"Marcus!" Darcy said, pouting. "Don't you try to get out of it. You were going out on me again weren't you?"

"No! I swear, Darcy—"

"Marcus, I've already told you that if you hook up again it's all over between us."

"I swear, Darcy, that girl is an ET and she comes from Orion."

"Orion?"

"Yeah, you know, the belt of Orion. You can see the three stars right next to each other in the night sky."

Darcy wondered why she just couldn't get a normal guy. Marcus was a nut; really, he was. But then she remembered her experience with the Alephs and knew she was a nutter as well. The only thing that mattered was that he told her the truth.

Marcus saw Darcy searching his face. She must have been satisfied, for she relaxed. It was a good thing because they were standing in the street and people were beginning to look. Nobody recognized him much if he just walked with his head down. But when he drew attention to himself the curious always approached him. "Hey look Bob, there's that Marcus Riley!" a woman's voice said.

"C'mon Marcus. I know a quirky little bistro on Lexington." Darcy began dragging him down 53rd. It was only a block away. When they arrived Marcus saw that it was a French restaurant, Le Relais de Venise L'Entrecote. "I hope it's not too expensive," Marcus said.

"No, not bad at all, steak and fries with a really great sauce, stuff like that. But you can't get butter with your bread."

"Huh?"

"The French don't believe in having butter with bread."

"Oh really?"

"Yes Marcus. We were in here several months ago and that's what the waiter told me."

"And you thought I was crazy. These New York waiters are as tightly wrapped as an uncracked pistachio."

Darcy giggled. She was ready to forgive Marcus yet again. He was a pain but at least he could make her laugh. And he was wicked handsome, she thought, looking up at him.

"All right, bring it on," Marcus said as they walked up to the bistro. "A nice piece of meat sounds good." I wonder what that ET would think, he wondered.

After they were seated, Darcy spoke. "What did she say to you Marcus?"

Marcus related the entire conversation.

"It's hard to believe."

Marcus shook his head. "Not if you sat across from this girl. She was …more evolved than us."

Darcy shook her head in amazement. "Reptiles, Alephs, gorgeous girls from Orion. It's too weird."

"Yeah."

"So there are, apparently, lots of these extraterrestrials around."

"Yeah. She said just look around, in a big city like New York you might see some."

Darcy laughed. "All right. Let's play a game of Spot the ET." Darcy pointed to an impeccably groomed and manicured man who had just entered. "Look, there's one right there." Darcy leaned over and spoke in a whisper. "He's from Betelgeuse and he has superpowers."

Marcus laughed. He indicated a very fat lady who had just gotten up from her table. "There's another one. She comes from a heavy planet with a higher gravity than earth."

Darcy giggled. The waiter came over and they ordered. Darcy grabbed Marcus' hand. "After we eat let's go back to my place." She wouldn't allow him to have other women but he could certainly have her. Then she remembered Kathleen's warning. Should she? Oh why not.

Marcus brightened. "You mean it? I'm horny as hell."

Darcy smirked. "You're out of practice boy. You'd better remember your lessons."

"I am not!" Marcus objected. "I've had plenty of—"

Marcus had the grace to blush. "Yes that's right, plenty of sex with skanks like Carla Waverley. I'm holding you to a lot higher standard."

"Just you wait. I'll carry you into the bedroom and make love to you all night."

Darcy suddenly sobered. "Marcus, where are we going? Are we together now?"

"Uh, I guess, are we? I don't know."

"Do you want to be?" Please say yes, she thought.

"Yeah, I think so."

"You think so?"

"Let's put it this way. I'm not going with anyone, I'm not seeing anyone, and you are the best girl I've ever had."

"Is that a yes?"

"Yes, it's a yes."

Darcy was disappointed at his lack of enthusiasm but her social training didn't let it show.

CHAPTER **20**

"Marcus, come here for a second."

It was Carla. The market was closing in 32 minutes. "What's up?" Marcus asked, walking over to her station.

Carla pointed at the main screen, which showed all trades that had been made within the past 30 minutes. "Look at this. There's a pattern developing that our algos can't handle."

Marcus saw it immediately. "Are you thinking of making a hunch trade?" Marcus teased.

"I'm thinking that we need to tweak our trading algorithms. Do you see it? And where we need to go?"

Marcus was excited. "Yes. Give me the day tomorrow and I can reprogram."

"Good boy!" Marcus jerked his head around to stare at her.

"Sorry Marcus, I think of you as just an overgrown boy. But a very brilliant and handsome one," she added hastily.

Carla regarded him now as her little brother. He was OK with that because in emergencies like this she always deferred to him.

"Are you thinking what I'm thinking?"

She scrutinized him carefully. "Can you do it?" This was a volatile pattern that required perfect timing. Their algos were worthless here.

Marcus replied instantly. "Yes."

"All right then, go ahead."

Marcus was practically jumping out of his shoes. Could he analyze this pattern and execute the trade without activating the web of light? He was going to try, and the consequences be dammed. Everyone in the room had forgotten that little incident two weeks ago. He had performed flawlessly since then, regaining the respect of his fellow traders and fitting in socially with the group.

Marcus walked quickly back to his station. There it was, a complex pattern of ebb and flow. The market was very busy today. The pattern was changing constantly but it cycled in a similar fashion each time. He'd give it until 3:55 and execute just before the market closed. Today they were engaged in index arbitrage, exploiting the price discrepancies between indexes of stocks and futures contracts. Their algos basically hedged positions and executed (theoretically) only after a clear pattern emerged. But it was possible to manually trade at any time. If he had analyzed the pattern right the index should go down at around 3:55 and then back up just before the close. Two trades were involved, a sell and a buy. He had to hit it exactly right. If the market trended down at the close they stood to lose several million. But if he was right they would gain at least $800,000 and he would be a hero.

At 3:55 he made the buy. By 3:58 he would know if he was right. Marcus was sweating it. At NYCBank, Equities Services was supposed to follow the algos and not rock the boat. But Carla was counting on him now. She trusted him and he couldn't let her down. And besides, he had a rep to support. Marcus didn't know it because he was so excited, but he had already made his decision. At 3:57 the market was trending downward and he absolutely had to know now whether the pattern would change. He activated the web of light and saw it. He turned to Carla. "We have to buy between 3:59:50 and 3:59:52. The market is going to tick upward, I can see it."

Carla nodded.

Marcus would never make that trade.

On Draco Tau, ten of Belial's drones jumped in and overwhelmed him.

At 3:58 Marcus dropped silently from his chair to the floor. Bethany sat next to Marcus and thought, 'the kid can't handle the pressure. Just like Pat.' She gestured to Carla and pointed to Marcus. Carla nodded, waiting. The tension in the room was palpable and Marcus was secondary for the next 120 seconds. At 3:59:50 Carla gulped and pulled the trigger. Her ass was on the line now and if it went wrong she would be in deep trouble.

But Marcus was right. During the last few seconds the market moved up rapidly and the trade successfully executed. Cheers went around the room. The traders leaped from their chairs, congratulating Carla. Marcus was forgotten. Carla was flushed and excited. This was the most dangerous trade she had ever executed. It was an outrageous gamble, but she had trusted Marcus and he came through for her. She was just about to throw herself into the manchild's arms when she saw that Marcus was sprawled out on the floor.

Bethany went over to check on Marcus. "Oh my God!" she cried, stepping back. The other traders crowded around. Marcus was on his stomach and his body was spasming. "For God's sake, call a doctor," Bethany said. "He's having a heart attack."

Frightened, Carla reached for her phone to call Dr. June. Maybe Marcus was back on coke. She knew that cocaine could cause rapid heartbeat and that people had died from it, although she'd never had any problem with it.

When Marcus dropped to the floor he felt his entire consciousness melting down like the Twin Towers. Somebody, or some-bodies, were trying to kill him. He struck back but they, whoever they were, were too strong. If he could only fight harder! No they weren't trying to kill him, they were holding him for somebody else. He was really getting angry now and felt like a cat in a straightjacket …he couldn't move, the bastards! … Wait a minute, what ever happened to the composure he used to feel in a crisis? Again he realized that the drugs he had taken had subtly altered his neural pathways. But he could go back to the old Marcus Riley. He liked that guy better anyway. Trying to ignore his psychic captors, he rolled over on his back and tried to calm himself. As he did he felt the psychic control loosen.

"Looks like he's more relaxed now," Bethany said. "He's stopped spasming."

"Should we call 911?" somebody asked.

"No, he looks better now," Carla replied. "We'll trust to June."

Marcus, lying three feet from his work station, was in another world. It was a world of pain and heat and dry rocks and sand. He was lying on the floor of a cave. There were ten of those humanoid reptiles staring into a cube about six feet on each side. They were concentrating and didn't see him. Should he get up and walk over there? He saw a huge reptile come over and bark something at them. The others left. Then he felt the presence of one who called himself Belial. "Mar-cus Ri-ley," it said.

The psychic presence was terrifying; overwhelming. This Belial was truly a demon and something totally alien. He fought down his nausea and knew that Belial was planning a fight to the death. The alien was waiting for him to be ready. Whatever happened, one of them was going to die.

Belial attacked.

"God, look at him," Bethany said. A bluish glow began to emanate from Marcus' body. "I always knew he was a freak." Bethany noticed that the light was soft, and a beautiful dark blue. Who *was* this guy?

At that moment Dr. June walked in. His large eyes widened in surprise and shock. "Get back everyone."

"Do you know what's happening?" Carla asked.

"Yes." He could see, with his psychic vision, some activity on the mental plane.

There wasn't much he could do now except make contact with the human and try to give him some psychic support. He knelt beside the body and placed his left hand on Marcus' head. As he did so, he saw Marcus and a huge humanoid reptile standing opposite each other on the floor of a cave. It was Belial, the most dominant of the Tau! Surely, this human will die quickly. June was a trained Aleph but he knew he was no match for the leader of the Tau. He settled in, making contact with Marcus' mind. Fortunately their earlier conversation had established some affinity. June was able to observe and even offer advice. The Aleph's consciousness gradually left the room and transferred to the psychic confrontation on Draco Tau. Just before he was fully present in the cave he heard a voice. "Why aren't you doing anything?"

"It's the Tau," he murmured. Then he was on the floor of the cave, watching the two combatants.

"The Tau?" Bethany said. "What's that?"

Tom Shapiro, who sat next to Bethany, put his hand on Dr. June. He became very excited. Tom had picked up on something. "It's a battle between that alien we saw in the street, and Marcus."

Carla was shocked. "What? An alien? Where? What are you talking about?"

Shapiro kept his hand on June. "That was no science fiction movie. That was real. That alien is *real!*"

"You've got to be kidding," Carla said. "I'm calling 911." She wanted to put her hand on June like Tom had but was afraid for the first time in her life. All of the other traders had backed up a few feet from Marcus.

Tom replied sharply. "No! If you do, Marcus will die."

Carla was bewildered. "I don't understand any of this."

"Just keep quiet and let it play out," Shapiro said. "I'm getting some images. God, I can see it!" Tom saw in his mind an image of Marcus standing in front of a huge man who looked like a demon, or a gargoyle. Dr. June was at his side but a little back, and clearly was not part of the action. Dr. June was like a trainer at a boxing match, Tom thought excitedly. But how could this be happening? June was clearly here, in Equities Services. Where was this psychic play occurring?

"OK," Carla said, "we did well today, and the markets have closed. Everybody can go home."

No one did.

Marcus faced the gigantic reptile and tried to orient himself to his surroundings. Dr. June was behind him, steadying him, and giving him advice. He knew that this was no physical combat. If it was he would end up like an extra in a Terminator movie. This would be a war of wills. Whoever won would live and the loser would die, for the consciousness of the loser would be so bruised and battered that the body connected to it could not maintain its integrity. All this he knew without effort. He and Belial were connected now for the upcoming battle. Now that he was here, apparently on Belial's ground, he knew he could fully activate his web of light. As he did he saw Belial step back, as if blinded. Even supported by the web, however, Marcus was trembling. Belial represented demonic evil; baleful and terrifying in its intensity. He saw that human beings, across the millennia, had been conditioned to fear demons, serpents, and dragons. Things that looked like Belial. He saw, connected to Belial's mind, the motivation behind the Tau. He saw what the Harvest was and what it meant for the Tau, and why. All this he knew in the few seconds it took to adjust to his surroundings.

Marcus saw Belial prepare for the attack and he called upon his web of light to defend. He now held a beautiful dark-blue light sword, four feet long and light as a feather. The blade shimmered. At the blade edges a multi-colored light pattern shifted and moved. He knew he was prepared and that the sword would make all the right moves.

The Aleph stepped back, astonished. Where had this untrained human gained such powerful psychic abilities? It was well that he had, for Belial leaped quickly with his great paws outstretched to break Marcus' neck. The blue sword went toward the reptile's stomach. Belial swerved out of the way at the last moment. The Aleph stepped back into the corner of the cave, giving the two combatants plenty of room.

"Mar-cus Ri-ley," Belial hissed. "You choose to fight with swords?" In the reptile's clawed hands a huge broadsword appeared; a blade a foot wide. They fought. Belial like a demon and Marcus, helped and supported by Dr. June, as calmly as he could. Marcus felt the reptile's hatred and knew that it was what drove him and his entire race. As they fought he understood that as long as he kept his web of light on full, Belial could not harm him. He knew that he could not possibly win a physical battle against Belial; he was simply too powerful. Marcus remembered his martial arts training in high school: be like the Aikido master and provide as little opposition as possible. A fight requires two opponents. When a fighter repeatedly strikes the air, there is no fight.

Belial was becoming angrier and angrier. He threw images at the human, archetypes that had been designed to instill fear and terror in their race. But this hominid was immune! He had trouble seeing through a golden-yellow light that blinded his vision and dissolved the archetypes before they could reach his opponent's mind. The sword of this scum seemed to have an intelligence of its own, anticipating his every move. Belial realized, incredibly, that the vermin was only defending and not attacking. This was almost as humiliating as the Zorghal. A warrior fights to the death; he had sworn it! Enraged, Belial stepped up his attack but the light surrounding the humanoid intensified and he could not see his way.

"Look!" Tom said. "He's ... glowing."

It was true. Bethany could see that the subtle blue light emanating from Marcus' body had intensified. Dr. June was still kneeling next to Marcus with his left hand on Marcus' head. Tom was lightly touching the doctor with an outstretched arm. Bethany thought she saw something ...an image of Marcus holding a sword. God, was she going crazy too?

Carla became more and more impatient. Her trading room had turned into some kooky off-Broadway play. It wasn't right. She was about to walk over and kick Marcus awake when she saw the blue light. The other traders saw it too.

"It's a standoff," Marcus said to Belial. "You can't kill me and I can't kill you."

"Vermin! Scum!" Belial thundered. "You will die, Mar-cus Ri-ley, I promise you that!" The Harvest cannot come too soon, Belial thought, as he strode out of the observation chamber and back to his quarters.

Marcus stood, amazed, as Belial walked out of the cave. He turned to Dr. June. "How do I get back?"

June smiled. "Only your consciousness is here Marcus. We can return whenever you'd like."

Marcus spread his arms wide. "But how? This is so real!"

"Of course it's real. You understand now that reality is a product of consciousness, do you not? Your physical body is just a construct. Return to it simply by directing your thoughts toward it."

"But I don't know where it is. *This* is what's real now."

"Yes, that's the way it works. Where were you before you came here?"

"I was lying on the floor of the trading room." Suddenly he was back in his body.

Dr. June straightened and Tom stepped back, his eyes wide. The other traders stared at Marcus as he rose unsteadily to his feet.

"Did that just happen?" Tom asked. "I saw you holding a sword and there was a big demon and you fought. There was some kind of light coming out of you."

"It was just your imagination," Marcus said, thinking of Lieutenant Mutumbe. He wasn't going to acknowledge anything out of the ordinary, even if it was true.

"You were glowing," Bethany said. Carla nodded affirmatively.

Marcus laughed unconvincingly. "I was glowing? Yeah, right."

Carla stepped forward and spoke in a voice that was not to be contradicted. "I saw the blue light. I don't imagine things. I'm eminently practical, and I don't doubt the evidence of my senses. You were glowing."

"OK. I was glowing. So what? We made the trade, right?"

"You were in a cave," Tom said, ignoring the question. "You were holding a sword. The other guy had a big broadsword. You fought him off and you had a dark blue light around you, and some kind of yellowish light around your head. I saw it. The other guy looked just like that reptile in the street. He walked out and said some kind of guttural gibberish. What did he say?"

"You will die, Marcus Riley, I promise you that," Dr. June said softly.

"Aha!" Tom exclaimed, turning to June. "You saw it too."

Dr. June realized that the cat, as these earthians would say, was now out of the bag. Actually the cat had escaped when he had taken Marcus' tissue sample over to Serven Labs. That had been fortuitous indeed, even if it was sheer coincidence. The Alephs had agreed that the earthians would have to be accelerated in their knowledge of the extraterrestrial presence on earth. Otherwise, the Tau's plans for their Harvest would succeed. The Harvest must be prevented at all costs. June shuddered involuntarily at the thought of it and the bestial consciousness capable of carrying it out. If the Tau succeeded their Life Reading Index would jump dramatically and the Epsilon might be overrun. It was a matter of racial survival. And so he said, "Yes, I saw it. I was there with Marcus on Draco Tau."

"Draco Tau?" Carla asked.

"In the constellation Draco. The star, Draco Tau, is a type B blue-white star. Has four planets, one with intelligent life. We call them the Tau."

"We?" Tom asked. Everyone else was hanging back, not knowing what to make of this conversation.

"I am an Aleph, from Draco Epsilon. The Tau are our enemies, and the bane of all civilized planets."

Bethany was shaking her head. Her lips thinned. "I'm sorry, all three of you are crazy. The earth is alone in the universe, that's what my astronomy class said. That's what the news says, and who cares anyway?"

Despite himself, June threw back his head and laughed. "Oh, that is rich. When your very genes have been manipulated by the Tau, and your religions created by them. Adam and Eve and the serpent!" June was giggling. "The caduceus, your symbol of commerce and negotiation, with the two coiled serpents. Your medical staff, with the serpent coiled around the rod of Asclepius."

Bethany looked her disgust. "If you keep talking like that, doctor, I'll call the AMA and they'll pull your license."

"Go to it sweetheart," June said with a smile. These earthians thought much like the Tau but their sayings were sometimes very appropriate and fun to use.

"You mean you're an alien?" Tom asked. He had never looked closely at the doctor. He noticed the thin lips, the very pale skin, the thin nose, the overlarge eyes, and the complete lack of facial hair. Was he wearing a wig? "But where—"

Carla had had enough. "Cut the science-fiction crap. We have a post-trade meeting to attend to."

Dr. June nodded and walked to the elevator. Everybody went over to the big table at the front of the room where their meetings were held. Marcus was overwhelmed by questions from Tom. Bethany looked at Marcus in disgust. Carla gave him a look that said, "What are you up to now?"

"We're just going to forget what happened during the past fifteen minutes," Carla announced. The other traders were excited, not only with the trade, but with the events that had followed. Even Bethany's eyes were bright with excitement despite her professed disgust of Marcus. Carla liked anything that kept her guys on edge but she had to come down on Marcus' erratic behavior.

"Marcus, you're on thin ice again. If it wasn't for that trade you'd be out of here right now." The kid really was getting out of hand. Something told her that behind the wild events she had just witnessed was an underlying reality. Tom seemed to think so. And anyway, Marcus was exciting. Weird, crazy even, but she craved that excitement; it was almost better than trading. As long as Marcus didn't go postal and her department kept its trading status, Marcus would stay.

Bethany exploded. "What are you waiting for? He's a fruitcake and so is that doctor. Fire him now and let's get back to normal."

"You're possibly forgetting that Marcus was responsible for one of the most brilliant trades ever. He made us almost a mil. And Bethany—"

"Yes?"

"Keep your personal likes and dislikes out of this room. Nobody here is indispensable."

Bethany flared at the implied threat but she knew her friend well enough to understand her meaning. Bethany turned and faced Marcus. "All right. But as long as we're clearing the air I just want to tell Marcus that I think he's a nut and I don't want him speaking to me, ever, unless it's in here and it's business."

Marcus shrugged disdainfully. "Suits me. Commonplace."

"What's that?" Bethany was incensed.

"I said you're commonplace." Marcus' voice was thick with contempt. "No scope, no vision; you're just a lemming." He was surprised by his antagonism but it felt good.

"Why you crazy lunatic! You belong in a mental institution."

"Enough!" Carla barked. Her eyes met both Marcus' and her friend's. "I can replace both of you a lot easier than you think. Even you, Marcus."

Marcus snorted.

"Don't get cocky little brother. Before you came we did quite well and it was a lot easier to work." Well, it was easier, she thought, but a lot less fun.

"I'll say," Bethany agreed. Marcus ignored her for Carla's sake. He felt like slapping the bitch.

"Anybody else want to get something off their chest?" Carla looked around the room. The traders were amused at the argument and she relaxed. "Good. Sit down everyone. We have a post-trading meeting and I want to get it over with. I'm going out tonight."

That night Darcy called Marcus. "Want to go out tonight?"

"Yeah, I want to celebrate."

He told her all about his fight with the reptile. "He calls himself Belial. The guy is totally demonic, Darcy. Totally whacked."

Darcy shuddered. "Marcus, this is crazy. How can someone attack you out of thin air?"

Marcus frowned. "I don't know babe. This is the third time it's happened in a month. Remember what that girl told me in the cafeteria, about the mental network in space."

Darcy was really worried. She wanted no part of freaky evil aliens but she didn't want to lose Marcus. "What happens now?"

"I think it's over now between me and him. We had our fight. He knows he can't kill me and I can't kill him."

Darcy sighed with relief.

"Unless I have to use my web of light to make trades."

"It only happens when you use that …thing …of yours?"

"I think so. It's not fair. I need it sometimes to do my work."

"Marcus, I don't want you to ever use it again." Darcy was afraid for him.

"All right." He hoped she wouldn't make him promise.

"Can we get back to normal?"

"I guess." Whatever normal is.

The Vatican

At midnight, Archbishop George Rugglio of New Jersey walked from his Vatican apartment down a marbled hall. He got into an elevator that carried him to a sub-basement. He entered a large room with strange symbols and runes inscribed on the walls. At the back of the room was a stone altar and statues of pagan gods. Upon the back wall, high up, was the crest of the Vatican: the serpent-dragon Marduk. Beneath the serpent-dragon these words were inscribed: "*and the dragon gave him his power, and his seat, and great authority.*" *(Revelations, 13:2).* Below Marduk was a painting of Semiramis with a great crowned Sun head with its rays outspread. Above the sun, in Latin, were the words "The dawning of a new day."

Archbishop Rugglio was excited and nervous as he gazed around the room, lit only by candles. These clandestine ceremonies, attended by members of the secretive Sabbatean bloodline, were always kept hidden from the mainstream church and its officials. Pietro Adolfone, the *eminence grise*, was in front. Adolfone was clad in black robes and greeted all who entered. All present were robed, with the serpent-dragon Marduk prominently displayed on the chest. Each carried staffs with an ornamental head carved in the shape of the sun, in honor of the god Semiramis. Upon their heads were the fish-shaped miter in honor of the Babylonian god Dagon (Oannes). Cardinal Vencio the pope-apparent was there, as well as certain officials from the Curia and other Vatican departments. Twenty others attended, including wealthy corporate executives, a few important politicos, and a couple of financiers. All were rehearsing their incantations. The number of participants was 33. A large group of young boys dressed in revealing silk togas strolled languidly through the room.

After everyone had mingled for several minutes, Pietro Adolfone cleared his throat and the buzz of conversation slowly died into silence. "In the name of Marduk, Dagon, and Semiramis, I welcome you. The Biblical prophecies, which are our sacred duty to fulfill, are about to be realized."

[thunderous applause]

"Tonight, in the most important ceremony we have ever conducted, we are to receive our final instructions from the gods. It is vital that everyone present carry out their roles to perfection. No mistakes will be tolerated!"

Everyone nodded solemnly. "In order to prepare ourselves for the ceremony we must be spiritually uplifted. Therefore, we have brought with us the delights of the season."

Archbishop Rugglio observed with satisfaction that all of the boys were comely. All of them were lightly drugged. There would be no opposition tonight. The upcoming ceremony was too important; all must go off without a hitch.

Adolfone raised his staff. "There is one boy for each of us. Enjoy! Fulfill your spiritual lusts and be cleansed for the ceremony."

Each of the participants took one of the boys and had sex with him. After this preparation all of the boys but one were herded out of the room. This boy, naked, was taken by Pietro Adolfone and laid upon the altar. His body was bound with ropes. Everyone chanted, their voices rising. Adolfone slowly approached carrying a long knife. He raised the knife and chanted *"eripuit coelo fulmen sceptrumque tyrannis."* Adolfone's light flashed in the candlelight. The boy's blood flowed and the crescendo of voices climaxed in a unified scream of excitement. These rituals were appalling, but necessary to establish the proper spiritual resonance. Was it not written that "without the shedding of blood there is no forgiveness"?[12] And, "for it is the blood that maketh an atonement for the soul"?[13] Those who were uninitiated couldn't possibly understand the importance of these rituals, thousands of years old, and the vital role they played in ultimately improving the human race. In ancient times, Archbishop Rugglio knew, these ceremonies resulted in ritual sacrifice. The knife would have been plunged into the boy's heart. Today they were far more sophisticated.

Above the group Rugglio saw a shape gradually take form. The participants slowly backed away from the altar, quieting their voices. Their ceremony had worked.

The forbidding figure of the serpent-god, nine feet tall, materialized above the boy, and began to drink his blood. "For the life of the flesh is in the blood: and I have given it to you upon the altar to make an atonement for your souls," he intoned. The others responded. "For it is the blood that maketh an atonement for the soul."

The figure of the serpent-god was utterly terrifying. Rugglio could see the creature reveling in the blood drinking. It horrified him and excited him. Was this creature a projection or the real thing? Was it a demon or a living entity? Whatever it was, it obviously had enormous power. Here he was, at the very apex of power on the planet.

Belial straightened from his position at the altar. The hominids had prepared well, for his projection had solidified nicely. Fresh from his victory in the Hangul over his bitter rival Ubar, Belial was bursting with confidence and vitality. This was how all Tau would feel after the Harvest. A massive infusion of life force, raising the Life Force Indicator of the entire species to unprecedented levels. And ensuring a successful Harvest Mating the following year, increasing the Tau population by several thousands and making the race even stronger. As he surveyed the robed figures who stood back respectfully from the altar, Belial noted with approval that each of the hominids wore the seal of Marduk. His ancestor had given them this seal almost 4,000 years ago in Babylon, and instructed the hominids to display it prominently. And they had. Now for the final execution of the Harvest Plan.

"Initiates!" Belial thundered. "It is time to prepare for the Rapture. The life force of those who do not believe will be harvested. Those remaining will be completely under your dominance. We have won!"

[thunderous applause]

Belial felt their adulation and fed deeply. This was almost as good as feeding from the dying. For a millisecond he considered the idea that keeping the hominids alive to worship him would be even better than sucking away their life force. But that was impossible. For thousands of years they had taught the sacred rituals to the earthians. These ceremonies and the dribbles of galactic technology he had given them all glorified death. This was necessary, for at death the precious life force was most readily available for feeding. The fools! They were preparing the termination of billions of their fellows. When the Harvest was completed the population would be reduced to a more manageable half billion or so, and the cycle could begin again.

Belial felt expansive. "In a special biological laboratory the bioenhancer is being prepared, under our instructions. The antidote for those who understand the Mysteries is also being manufactured. Humans, it is only a little while now before you become the Masters of your planet. Your General will outline for you the final strokes of the Plan. Do not fail your gods!"

Belial faded out. There was a wild babble of excited voices. The voice of Pietro Adolfone quieted the crowd again. "I have received personal instructions from the gods, represented by Belial. The date of our triumph has been revealed, when all of the Biblical prophecies will be fulfilled. The date, of course, has immense esoteric and numerical significance. Those of you who understand will be able to calculate the precise day, month, and year. It is not far off.

"Very soon we will release the cleansing bioenhancer. The result will be a drastic improvement in the human genome, which will benefit our species immensely. The genes of the resultant population will be purified. The human lifespan will increase and disease will be a thing of the past. The population of the earth will be reduced, lessening pollution and saving the environment. We are the liberators of the human race! With the instructions we have received from the gods, the Chosen Ones in this room will usher in a golden age. You will be the Masters of a genetically improved human race."

[wild applause]

"Pay careful attention to the Signs. At the appropriate time, take your antidotes and tell no one. Am I understood?"

All present solemnly nodded.

"Excellent. Proceed to your duties and remember that we are on the cusp of victory!"

Cherry Island bioweapons research laboratory, Montauk, New York

Dr. Simon Huygens examined the incredible chromosome-altering biomaterial at work on a human test subject from behind a thick plastic window. He watched the progress of the invader using a sophisticated imaging system. The immune system was quickly disabled by the new genetic material. He had never seen anything like it. He had seen the report about an unusual tissue sample they were calling "Riley's Scratches," but this stuff was far more sophisticated. This biomaterial had clearly been programmed for specific tasks. It was clear that it had the capability to literally shut down large portions of entire chromosomes, and activate "junk" DNA. It was light years ahead of current knowledge and theory. Huygens saw the prisoner's shoulders sag weakly. The invader was doing its work. In twenty minutes he would know whether another had died.

Dr. Huygens waited impatiently as the patient's skin darkened to a deathly gray. The life force of the test subject seemed to leave the body. He looked down at the ugly green- and black-tiled linoleum floor. He had the primary lab adjacent to the Director's corner office in the facility, a classified installation on a small island in the Atlantic off the coast of Long Island. Cherry Island was a small outfit with three sophisticated testing laboratories. It had been built in the 1960s but was now furnished with state-of-the-art equipment. Each lab had a sealed testing room that was microwaved after each use, killing any residual pathogens.

Twenty-five minutes later he was about to enter the test chamber and remove the body. The prisoner began to move. Three armed guards stood by in case the test subject became violent. This particular case, a man named Forbush Alpers, was on death row for the murder of his business partner in a dispute that had involved over $10 million dollars. After a half-hour or so the subject's skin began to regain a healthy pallor. The man's eyes opened and he smiled. He tried to get up off the table but his body was shackled.

"Hey doc, come in here and let me out!"

Huygens was amazed. Out of the fifty-two patients he had treated only four had survived. This man would be the fifth. Each time, after having their bonds removed, the men had gotten up unassisted. After a few wobbly steps each test subject had demonstrated uncommon vitality and energy. A thorough physical examination had shown each of the subjects to be in perfect health. They had simply walked out of the facility and into a new life.

Huygens shook his head, unbelieving. He had been invited to the project last spring by Director Kelvenbach, who had heard of his work at NIH in Bethesda, Maryland. He was known for his meticulous experimental techniques as well as his discretion. Huygens knew himself to be a silent man, uninterested in gossip. Research was his primary interest in life. He had never married or even dated. His only other interest was his stamp collection.

As he walked into the test chamber he thought about his role in Project New Dawn. Prisoners on death row within the New York state prison system had volunteered to engage in testing. They were warned that the tests could make them much stronger and healthier, or it could kill them. In exchange for their participation in the life-threatening experiments all charges were to be dropped and the individual was to be released back into society. Surprisingly, dozens of men and two women had eagerly agreed to participate in the project. All had all freely signed release forms that stated their understanding and acceptance of the risks they faced. The project was classified, of course. It was one of the things that had attracted him to the work.

The Director had informed the Attorney General and the Legislature about the nature of the testing. The details were hidden under the cloak of national security. There would be a healthy contribution to the state's "rainy day" fund. After being assured that the families of those who died would be handled, the authorities had signed off on the project. They were only too glad to have those responsible handle the obvious repercussions. Executions were unpleasant and the jails were filled. Besides, the purpose of the testing was to improve the human genome and eliminate disease in the human organism. And it was working.

Huygens began his post-op examination, unwilling to release the prisoner's restraining devices. He saw that the man was babbling cheerfully. In every case the survivor seemed to have achieved amazing mental balance and emotional stability. One of the men, a surly double-murderer, had optimistically walked out of the facility whistling, claiming that he had never in his life felt so good. The previous four who had survived the bioenhancer had returned to their families completely whole. They were now free of antisocial behaviors and evil tendencies. The results completely justified the program's existence. The others who did not survive would have died anyway by execution.

Huygens completed his examination. Everything checked out. The man was in perfect physical condition. He unbuckled the thick straps that held the testee's body. As the soon-to-be-free-man rose from the examination table, he held out his hand. "How ya' doin' doc?" he said affably. Huygens shook his head again in disbelief. He said nothing, silently examining the patient, holding both arms at his sides. The testee looked perfectly normal and perfectly cheerful. It was a miracle.

"You are free to go," he said. "The guards will return your personal effects. You will be briefed before you are allowed to leave the facility. After that they will escort you out of the building."

"Well how about that!" the man replied. "The gummint actually keeping its promises. I'm not going to get shot in the back walking out to the parking lot am I?"

Huygens turned away in disgust. If the truth be told, he couldn't stand people. Their emotional outbursts were unpleasant. He didn't understand how their minds worked. He opened the door of the examining room and handed the subject over to the guards. "Thanks doc!" the man said, waving.

Huygens walked to the hallway door and stood frowning, lost in thought. A man approached from the office next door but he didn't see him. He had been working since seven in the morning and it was now well past eight in the evening.

"Dr. Huygens, what are the results of the latest testing?"

Huygens started. "Director!" Director Kelvenbach was a very tall, almost obese man with a large head and a beak nose. He had small but intense black eyes. He looked like a pregnant hawk about to pounce on his prey as he leaned over into Huygens' face. Huygens pointed down the hall at the subject being escorted by the guards. "As you can see, another survivor in this batch of ten."

"That's five survivors so far, correct?" Kelvenbach asked, staring down intently at the smaller man.

"Yes, that's correct."

"Of course you will submit your weekly report, but please briefly summarize the week's work."

Huygens cleared his throat. "We have identified areas in several chromosomes that are directly responsible for shortened lifespan, lower intelligence, and disease susceptibility. The task has been to target this genetic material without harming the organism. Our testing shows, however, that in nine out of ten cases the subjects die. That was confirmed again this week, Director. In about ten percent of the cases the organism survives with the altered genetic material intact."

"Is it established then that ten percent is the maximum survival rate?"

"Yes Director."

Kelvenbach smiled a cold smile. "Excellent. What about the antidote?"

The antidote was a substance that had been invented to quiet the liberals and to soothe political qualms. "The antidote is ineffective, of course. The airborne invader completely overwhelms the immune system and inserts its own genetic coding."

"Satisfactory, doctor. Are you prepared to state that the bioenhancer is at maximum effectiveness?"

"Yes, sir. Marginal improvements may be achieved, but at great expense of time and money."

"And life," the Director added.

"Oh of course sir." Huygens agreed without enthusiasm. "And life."

"Excellent. The biological material can be easily duplicated?"

"Remarkably, yes. The genetic material that was given to me only needs a specific biological additive in order to activate the material. The process can be done by any competent scientist. Where, if I may ask, did it come from?"

The Director frowned, then his brow cleared. What did it matter now? "This genetic material was engineered ... with a little help from our friends."

"Ahh, thank you Director. I suspected as much."

Oh did you? the Director thought. "Very well. Prepare your samples and send them through the service tube. When you are finished ring the buzzer. Then you can go."

Huygens was weary but pleased. He had completed his job successfully. He had two new stamps arriving in the mail and was keen to add them immediately to his collection.

Two hours later the Director heard the sound he was expecting. He secured the samples in their protective case. As he exited the building he pressed a small transponder that locked all of the doors and released a small sample of the bioenhancer into the building. Director Kelvenbach hurriedly left the facility without being seen. As he was driving along the Montauk Point State Parkway on his way to a small airfield, he smiled with satisfaction. *Copiae faciunt, haud minus ac iussi faciunt.*

It had been a long day and he was very tired. He should stop and rest but the case with the bioenhancer samples and the biological activator he carried was too valuable. It was now almost a quarter to midnight. He was right on time. Only twenty more minutes of driving, he told himself, and he'd deliver his cargo. He'd take a rest on the plane. The miles went by monotonously and his head nodded. There was almost no traffic on the road except for a pair of headlights he could barely see in his rear view mirror. His head dropped again and he jerked awake. There was no time for failure now! He opened the window to allow in some cool late August night air. When his head nodded again the Director was asleep at the wheel. The vehicle veered off the side of the road and tumbled into a ditch, rolling over and over. The case with the precious biomaterial tumbled out of the window. With the last of its momentum the car slowly turned over and landed on its wheels.

"He's dead Jim," joked Carlos Quintan.

"He doesn't have a red shirt on does he?" Jim Staars replied.

Quintan peered into the car. "Hard to tell. It's pitch dark. His neck is broken, that's for sure."

Staars shined his powerful flashlight into the vehicle. "Kristophe Kelvenbach," he said as a sort of eulogy, "Director of the Cherry Island Bio Research Facility."

"The very same." Quintan walked around the car, checking for anything that might have been deposited on the ground. Staars pulled on a pair of rubber gloves and pried open the driver's side rear door. He carefully examined the inside of the vehicle. Staars climbed into the front seat and inspected the glove compartment, whose door had been ripped off in the accident. "Nothing in here of any interest," he said, joining his partner. "It's too cold out here."

Staars would have replied with his usual "that southern blood of yours is too thin," but his foot had come into contact with something hard. He shined his flashlight on the object and whistled. "Well, what do we have here?'"

Staars turned the case over with his foot. The distinctive biohazard sign with its three rings and a center ring on a red background was visible in the center. In the bottom right corner was a small symbol of a woman's head, with rays of light coming out from it. "Never saw that before, Carlos. Any idea what it is?"

"Nope. Good looking babe though."

"We have ourselves a little present," Staars said.

"An early Christmas gift from our friend Kelvenbach," Quintan acknowledged. The men looked at each other and sighed.

Quintan verbally expressed what was in each of their thoughts. "This goes right to Serven and we have to do it now."

"How long a drive to the city?" Staars asked.

Quintan checked his dataset. "Two hours, nineteen minutes."

"We'd better get going." Staars walked back to their vehicle and opened the passenger door. "I'll drive for the first hour, you take us in."

"I'm too tired," Quintan said.

"So am I. I'll nap now and you can sleep on my shift."

"OK." Quintan got in the driver's side. Between the two of them, Staars was by far the better and more patient driver.

"There shouldn't be too much traffic on your shift," Staars said.

"There's always too much traffic," Quintan replied.

Department of Homeland Security, Washington D.C.

"We have received our orders!" cried Hans Brubaker. "Directly from Venitti, personal aide to Pietro Adolofone himself."

The others around the small table smiled knowingly, excited and a little afraid of the culmination of their plans. Hans was the nominal leader of a private group within the critical Office of Infrastructure Protection, and assistant to the director of the department. Brubaker was a short man in his mid-thirties, very slight, with a broad forehead, receding hairline, and the demeanor of someone who is fanatically dedicated to a cause.

"We should not be meeting here," Jonathan Lightman said. He looked around the conference room nervously. Lightman was a heavy, blustery man with a florid complexion. He had the squishy, blubbery appearance of an overweight seal. "If Rand should walk in and hear us, all will be lost."

Dorothy Schnellenberger snorted. "Rand is as likely to show up here as Nopalutani." Rand was the director of the OIP and Nopalutani the DHS chief. "I have my secretary keeping watch on the door. She's right across the hall." Schnellenberger was a tall, bony woman with an angular figure and short raspberry-blond hair, a long face, and large black glasses.

"Don't worry," said Draco Smith, who sat at the foot of the table. "Rand is just a career civil servant and Nopalutani is with us. Get on with it."

"I don't like your tone of voice, Smith," Schnellenberger said, her volatile temper getting the best of her. "You're nothing but an errand boy."

Draco bristled. He stared darkly at the tall woman but she met his gaze unflinchingly.

Dorothy snorted again, which never failed to irritate the smaller man. "You're here because you're a snake and can't do anything else. The rest of us do this because we are committed to the cause."

One day when this was over, Draco Smith thought, he would strangle Dorothy Schnellenberger very slowly. He would enjoy the doing of it.

"That's enough," Brubaker said. "Smith, give us the latest report."

Draco Smith calmed himself. "The bioenhancer is being tested as we speak. Soon it will be ready for distribution. In another month or two it will be your job to liaise with our guys. We must ensure that the material finds its way into secure facilities, ready for release at the appropriate time. When it comes there will be a lot of it, so don't blow it."

Dorothy Schnellenberger's eyes lit up. She met the excited eyes of Brubaker. "Glorious!" she said. All knew that the OIP was formally tasked with leading a coordinated national effort to reduce risk to the United States' critical infrastructures and key resources (CIKR) posed by acts of terrorism. Their cell was in perfect position to scout locations and distribute the new biomaterial. But they were a little short of personnel right now and didn't have enough teams in place.

"Ausgezeichnet!" Brubaker cried. "We will be instrumental in the improvement of race genetics. We are on the cusp of the creation of the ubermensch."

"Shut up with that Nazi bullshit," Dorothy replied. Hans constantly referred to his grandfather's position in the old Reinhard Gehlen intelligence organization during WW II in Nazi Germany. As if that was relevant to anything. The man was certifiable, and as irritating as a barking terrier dog. "What is important is that this biomaterial will ensure the improvement of the entire human race. It will avoid inevitable environmental disaster. It is a godsend." Dorothy Schnellenberger knew that she would probably be among the ones who died. She saw herself as a race heroine, sacrificing her own life if need be for the good of humanity. Dorothy was unconscious of how much her personality resembled that of Brubaker's.

"Are your teams ready?" Smith said loudly, cutting off Brubaker. The little man had risen to hotly contest Dorothy's dismissal of him. For once she was thankful for Draco Smith's presence.

"Yes," Lightman rumbled. "I am to report directly to Venetti in Rome after this meeting. I want to report good news."

Brubaker paled for a moment. The thought of Carlo Venetti made him physically ill. He had spoken briefly with the man on his one and only visit to the Vatican. He had been impressed and frightened. Venetti was the right hand man of Pietro Adolfone, a shadowy figure in the Congregation for the Doctrine of the Faith. Formerly the Holy Office of the Inquisition. "I am pleased to report that our inspection teams have already located desirable facilities in over seventy cities. We are ready to store the biomaterial whenever it becomes available."

"Very good," Lightman said, easing back in his chair and patting his ample paunch.

Dorothy wrinkled her nose. Lightman was uglier than Jabba the Hut. How could a man allow himself to get so grossly fat? "We will need extra funding to hire more personnel," she said, correcting Brubaker. She hated prevarication. They weren't ready yet and Brubaker knew it. That's why Draco Smith was here.

Lightman ignored the obvious inconsistency and said nothing. A former bank analyst, he had been recruited last year by Venetti at a meeting of the International Monetary Fund in Washington. He would report that all was on schedule. If these incompetents in DHS weren't ready on time it would be on them. Carlo Venetti was a man who appreciated good news and he was eager to furnish it. Anyway, Draco Smith would know how to keep them in line. Lightman's call to Rome was at 5 p.m. After that he'd eat a fine meal at Escoffier's in Arlington. He glanced at his watch impatiently.

"Funding is all taken care of," Brubaker said. He wished that the big woman would not overstep her authority. He looked over at the fat man. "Lightman has assured me that we will receive all that we need."

Lightman was an errand boy just like Draco Smith but he liked it. He was paid well. He waved his hand in assent.

"Then there is nothing to worry about," Brubaker said.

Dorothy Schnellenberger smiled. If the money was in the pipeline they would not fail. She would see to that despite Brubaker's incompetence.

"You probably have a couple of months before the material will be distributed," Smith commented. "It is being tested now in select locations. When the word comes down from on high you better be ready to get into action fast. You understand?"

Brubaker nodded nervously.

Dorothy Schnellenberger glanced at Draco Smith. The eyes of the two antagonists met for a fraction of a second. Although he was a snake Smith was a competent snake, unlike Brubaker. "To a better humanity and a better planet," she said, raising her water bottle in a toast. The others raised styrofoam cups of coffee. Draco Smith watched.

"To the ubermensch!" Brubaker cried just as the cups began to tip.

Dorothy scowled and drank.

El Dorado St., Chicago

Jemelle Washington sat in his luxuriously appointed apartment with its big screen TV, new carpeting, and state-of-the-art sound system. He was studying a spreadsheet with a summary of the weekly sales reports on his expensive laptop. He heard three taps, followed by a pause, then one tap. The door opened and a skinny 13-year-old, dressed in dark, drab clothing, entered the apartment.

"You goin' to watch the game tonight?" the boy asked.

"What do you think?" Jemelle rose from his desk and faced the boy. "Take off your shoes motherfucker. You get one dirt mark on my new carpet and I'll end you."

Lucius Tyler gazed at the older man with respect bordering on awe. He hastily took off his shoes, placing them on a mat by the front door. Lucius saw a meticulously dressed man of medium height and slender build. Jemelle was dressed in a black suit with a carefully trimmed goatee decorating an intelligent, brown-skinned face with penetrating eyes. They were eyes you could not lie to. The boss was wearing polished black shoes, some kind of cloth in his breast pocket, a gold bracelet on his left wrist, and a Rolex on his right wrist. On his head was a dark blue-gray hat with a black ribbon, one of those old fashioned ones his great-grandpa used to wear. But this hat, on that head, looked totally unbelievable.

"You look great man," Lucius said with frank admiration. "That old-fashioned hat. It's legendary."

Jemelle turned and faced the full length mirror on the wall of his living room, carefully adjusting it. "Yeah, I can't believe how good this looks. I'm wearing this downtown tomorrow night. Gonna start a new fashion."

He turned back to Lucius. "What the fuck you bothering me for?"

"Heard something tonight," the boy said.

Jemelle perked up. This kid was the smartest little fucker he'd ever seen. Lucius seemed to pick up important information by telepathy. Jemelle sat down on his new leather chair. He gestured for Lucius to sit across from him on the old sofa. "Gotta get rid of that old thing," he muttered. But he knew he wouldn't. It was his mom's, God rest her soul. Jemelle made the sign of the cross on his chest and said a prayer for her.

Lucius knew what that was about. He was silent, waiting for the boss to go through his ritual. His own mother was a crackhead and he had no respect for her. Jemelle's mom was a saint. Or so he'd heard.

When Lucius saw that Jemelle was ready, he spoke. "Talked to that stupid bus-boy at the Cats Meow. His brother's uncle works at IRT International. This fucker was over at the kid's mom's house yesterday for dinner. He had too much to drink. Anyway, this guy overheard somebody talking about some top secret shit that came to IRT yesterday. Something that's gonna fuck people up or turn them into super-men."

Jemelle's eyes hardened. "What kind of shit?"

"I don't know. A bio-something or other."

Jemelle's eyes widened. "Yeah, I know what that's about." This was confirmation that what had happened to his dealer was no accident. He rose from the chair. "Good work kid. Come by at 9 and we'll watch the game."

Lucius brightened immediately. "Thanks man!"

Jemelle, still lost in thought, gestured the boy away. Lucius quietly exited the room and went back to the street. After the boy left, Jemelle called the Cats Meow.

The Cats Meow, downtown Chicago

Luca Carcelli sat at his desk in his private office at the Meow. He was watching the Bears game. Above the TV was a bank of monitors that showed the main floor of the Meow, and the activity in the private rooms in back. From here he could keep track of everything that happened in the club. Against the wall on his left was a pull-down bed for sleeping. To the right he had a small bathroom with a shower. The walls were decorated with pictures of strippers from the club.

He was thinking about his ex-wife as the Bears fumbled the ball. The beautiful Angela had walked out on him a long time ago, taking his daughter with her. She said that he was an anger case and that she couldn't live with him. An anger case! So he got mad sometimes. Everybody gets mad! The memory still rankled. He hadn't seen his ex-wife for ten years and he had no idea where his daughter was. It just wasn't right. For the thousandth time he told Angela to go fuck herself. For the thousandth time he told himself that he liked being a bachelor. Sometimes he even believed it.

His phone rang and Luca picked up immediately. "Hey boss, got something unusual goin' on," said Frank Nitti III.

"More problems?"

"Afraid so. I been talkin' to Washington. You know, that fancy pants dealer over on East Garfield. Worst neighborhood in the city and he lives like a king over there. You know we talked about that."

"Yeah." Ever since the Outfit decided to deal they'd had problems with the gangs.

"Washington's been trying to expand his heroin business up in the suburbs. Yesterday one of his guys made a delivery and saw an unmarked van with its windows painted shut off on the side of the road with a flat tire. So he goes over to see if they need help. He hears them talking about some top secret new vaccine they're supposed to deliver to IRT International."

"What's IRT International?" Luca asked.

"Some secure place where they do classified bio-research. Anyway, he walks up to the van. He sees a couple of guys inspecting two big plastic cases with one of those biohazard signs on it."

"Oh yeah?" Carcelli replied.

"This guy goes right up to them and asks them if they need any help. The guy fixing the flat tells him to fuck off and get out of there if he knows what's good for him. This guy was a dolt and asked what they were doing with the plastic cases. One of the guys from the van took out a silenced gun and shot the guy dead right on the side of the street. He kicked the body into a ditch. Just thought you should know."

"People don't get shot delivering vaccines," Luca said. "How'd you find out about this Frank?"

"Washington's guy got curious and streamed the whole thing. Washington got pictures. He says there's something not right about it and we should both sort of watch the streets and keep notes."

"What we should do is rub him out. He's our competition."

Nitti hesitated. "If you want boss. It would cause a lot of problems."

Yeah, Carcelli thought. It might organize the gangs against them. The demolishing of Chicago's public housing had also fragmented the gangs. But organized, they could be even more dangerous. And Jemelle Washington was the leader of the Black Fighters, the biggest gang in the city.

"If the feds are starting to shoot dealers now it might not be a bad idea to cooperate with Washington," Nitti added. "I kinda like the guy. He's got balls and he's smart."

"I don't trust that *mulignan*," Carcelli replied. "But at least he's born and bred in Chicago. All right, tell him that we'll keep our eyes open. Do you know who these fuckin' guys are who brought in that vaccine?"

"Washington doesn't have a clue. They look like people you don't want to mess with. Military, or black ops. Looked like they were wearing body armor vests."

"What's this world coming to Frank?"

Two days later Luca got a call that he never could have imagined in a million years.

His phone told him that someone named Pablo Rodriquez was on the line.

"You're Luca Carcelli?' the Spanish-accented voice asked.

"Who should I be, the Queen of England? You got my private line."

"I'm Pablo Rodriquez and I run a mob in L.A. I got a call from a guy you know. Jemelle Washington, who knows one of our guys. Washington told me about a case of biological material that was delivered to a biolab up there in north Chicago. They're calling it a new vaccine. Is that true?"

Luca pulled the phone away from his ear. Who was this mickey mouse asshole? There was an urgency in his voice. Somebody he knew must have given Rodriquez his number. "Yeah. What about it?"

"We got one too. So did Dallas and Detroit."

"So what?"

The voice mumbled something in Spanish, pissing Luca off. He was about to hang up when Rodriquez began to speak. "The word on the street in L.A. is that this new vaccine is not a vaccine at all, *senor*. It is something deadly that will kill many people."

Luca remembered Nitti's report. "One of Washington's dealers got burned by some guys who were bringing in a vaccine. Feds. Shot the bastard right by the side of the road."

"That is ver' bad, *senor*, ver' bad. It is perhaps even worse than we thought."

"Who gave you this number?"

"Your friend Bobby Battaglia in Dallas asked me to call you. I know him because we both played poker in Las Vegas last year. He told me a Dallas biolab received one of these vaccines in a peculiar dark red case. I became curious and called him. He told me to call you and Brown in Detroit."

"So you called. What the fuck do you want?"

Rodriguez sighed. "Washington said you were stupid."

"You call me stupid you asshole?"

"Look *cabron*, our sources are telling us that something is going to happen to fuck us all up: my people, your people, ever'body. It involves this vaccine that is not a vaccine, *comprende*? We must find out who is doing this. You have to help."

"The fuck I do!" Luca heard a *click!* and the phone went dead.

Incensed, Luca punched in Bobby Battaglia's number. Bobby and him had grown up together fifty years ago in the old country.

The swarthy face of his friend appeared on the screen. "Bobby, what's the idea givin' some asshole my private line?"

"Calm down Luca," Battaglia said. "Rodriquez is a friend of mine."

"All right, so what about this vaccine? Big deal, the feds are doin' more classified research."

"The word is, Luca, that this stuff will kill nine out of every ten people who come in contact with it. It's some sort of contagious airborne biomaterial."

"I don't understand."

"It's like a virus, Luca, *capisci*? A deadly one. The only reason I know is I get a call last night from a guy using a computerized voice. He says there's a top-secret lethal bioweapon being tested in four US cities and that the plan is to release this stuff all over the country."

"So why is he calling you?"

"That's just what I asked him. He says, because organized crime is the only group in the country that has the resources to stop it. So I called Rodriquez in L.A. He says they got one and there's one in Detroit. We know Chicago got one too. That's four cities, just like he said."

"Who was the guy who called?"

"I don't know Luca, his voice was computerized. I believed everything he said."

"Why would anybody want to kill millions of people, Bobby? It don't make much sense and it's bad for business. What can we do about it anyway?"

"I don't know, some kind of big power play maybe. If it's true the feds have gone too far this time. They're fuckin' everything up six ways from Sunday Luca. We're going to find the people behind this and burn them. Are you in?"

Luca was confused but he had always looked up to Battaglia, even when they were kids. "If you say so I'm with you."

Luca folded up his phone. He walked out of his office and down the plush carpet to the main floor, lost in thought. He sat at the main bar drinking Scotch on the rocks and staring at one of the big screen TVs. The White Sox had just lost the game to Detroit on a ninth inning homer. He was out 10 large. Now Kelley Scott was on the CBS evening news talking about budget deficits, racial violencee, and crummy school systems. But no mention of a lethal new vaccine.

Luca Carcelli considered himself and liked what he saw. Sure, he used people for his own ends. But there were limits. He wasn't smart but he wasn't a psycho either like some of the leaders of these drug gangs, and some of the people in Washington. His consigliere, Jason Taubman, once told him he was more like a pork chop at a Bar Mitzvah: distasteful, but not life threatening.

Luca looked at his drink with distaste. He turned on his barstool and stood up. That rat Jake Holden was sitting with some nerd at a table across the room. Luca gulped his whiskey and strode over to the table. He was ready to slug Jake when the nerd stood up.

"Sir, I'd like to request that you don't erase Jake, and let him work with me."

"Who the fuck are you?" Luca said, unclenching his fist. The man before him was unimpressive. An egghead for sure. Something in the man's voice calmed him down.

Jake got up from his chair and cowered. "I'm sorry Luca, I—"

"Shut up!"

The other man motioned for the capo to sit down. Carcelli thought that the nerd was already half in the bag, but his voice was steady. He was thin and his head was a little too big for his body, reminding Luca of a pet toad he had when he was a kid. The nerd wore thin-rimmed glasses and a crumpled suit. Luca decided he was one of those guys who talked and never did anything.

Luca gazed coldly at the nerd.

"My name is Gerald Hutchinson. I'm a mathematician and a historian."

"Whoop-de-fuckin' do." Luca picked up a DVD that was lying on the table. "On the Mat: The Shocking Collapse of the United States."

"What's this?" Luca asked.

Hutchinson looked nervously around the Meow's big main floor. This was definitely not his kind of place. He was terrified of Carcelli. The capo smelled strongly of cologne. Carcelli had his gray hair carefully combed back, accentuating a hard face and cold brown eyes that gave him the aura of an executioner. Hutchinson had drunk half a fifth of whiskey before he could get the nerve to even enter the place. He fumbled quickly for an explanation that would make sense to the mob boss. "Historians are basically dumbasses. They—"

Luca guffawed.

"By that I mean historians don't know math or science, or understand complex adaptive theory." Hutchinson noticed that his voice was rising. He tried to calm himself. "I do. When I used these scientific tools to analyze history I found something everybody in the field missed. And it officially scares the shit out of me."

Luca's eyes widened. He appreciated passion and the toad sounded genuine. He picked up the DVD. Maybe Bobby would be interested in this stuff but he'd slept through his history class in high school.

"Jake here helped me," Hutchinson added. "But we still have a lot of work to do. That's why," he gulped, "I request that you don't kill him."

Luca Carcelli gazed at the two men across the table and suddenly laughed for the first time in three weeks. Jake looked like a rabbit about to go under the butcher knife. The egghead stared at him like a little dog begging for a dish of food.

Jake Holden and Hutchinson exchanged quick glances as the capo banged his fist on the table. Even his laugh was intimidating, Hutchinson thought.

Luca relaxed back in his chair. "You two assholes are funny."

Hutchinson sat innocently, waiting expectantly for Carcelli's answer. Luca waved his hand dismissively. "You can have him, Hutchinson, but I don't see why. Holden couldn't figure out how to wipe his ass."

"Yes sir," Hutchinson replied. What do you call a mob boss, he wondered? "Jake is actually a first-class researcher." He had an idea. Hutchinson slid the DVD across the table. "Why don't you take a look at this, sir. I can see you are a man looking for answers."

"Oh you can, can you?"

"Yes sir," Hutchinson said, big eyed.

"You two guys are as funny as that terrier I saw in the park last month, trying to fuck a goose."

"Yes sir," Hutchinson said. He was losing his nerve and got up quickly. "Let me know if you like the DVD. It's the first of eight. Here's my card."

Luca watched as Jake Holden and the toad scurried out of the Meow. He put the DVD and the card in his suit coat pocket and spotted a girl walking by. He motioned to her to get him a drink.

Quingu Research Corp, Private Bio research Lab, Pache Island, Long Island Sound

"This stuff is amazing and frightening," said Dr. Watney Granger.

"It certainly is," replied Dr. Lois MacDonald.

"Why are we here again?" Watney asked, looking admiringly at the rather plain-looking woman beside him. She might be homely to most men but to him she was a goddess. This was their second day at Pache Island. They were both just getting used to the place.

"Because we're expendable," MacDonald replied. "And because of our besetting vice, our ungovernable curiosity."

Curiosity? Watney thought. Yes, definitely that. But he had come mainly because she had come. She didn't yet know of his obsession about her and would probably be surprised. Dr. MacDonald was the most unconceited woman he had ever met. "Sure, our curiosity."

Lois MacDonald regarded her colleague for a moment. Watney Granger was a thin, ascetic looking man. He looked just what he was: a research scientist. She looked around at the big lab with its specialized equipment for manufacturing the secret biomaterial. The lab was housed in an old metal storage facility on the small, twenty-acre island. The only access was by small plane or by boat. A few of the locals occasionally camped out or hiked out on the island, which could have been a problem. The shore story was that a new startup bioresearch company was setting up shop. Pictures of the old warehouse were shown in the local papers, as well as the renovations to the inside. The building had been open to the public during the summer renovations. Other than a few news reporters and the curious, who occasionally stopped by to see the progress of construction, the new facility was soon forgotten. The specialized equipment had been brought in later, of course. Now it was late September. They had finished testing the equipment with a small sample of the bioenhancer and its activator. All was in readiness for the big delivery, which could happen any day!

Both of them slept here and were not allowed out of the building. The walls were covered with a high-tech soundproofing material, even though the production of the biomaterial didn't make any noise. A pile of equipment was at the back, including a couple of welding torches and a small forklift; probably left over from the construction. Their exercise was taken at a makeshift indoor gym that had been set up in a corner of the building. The structure itself had high windows thirty feet off the ground, covered with plastic, but which let in a little sunlight. There was a small bathroom and a shower, as well as a small combination washer-dryer. Each of the scientists brought in as much clothing as could be contained in a small suitcase or overnight bag.

"This is the most exciting job I have ever had," MacDonald said with a burst of passion that startled him.

"It is?"

"Are you kidding Watney?" she said, staring out at the production equipment with obvious pleasure. "The chance to study an exotic biomaterial that alters the human genome? It's astonishing."

When she lit up like that, Watney thought, she was the most beautiful woman he'd ever seen. Even through those thick black plastic glasses. Kinda round and a little dumpy, but there was something about her that turned him on. "We're not supposed to study it, we're supposed to produce more of it. We're nothing but glorified lab techs."

MacDonald flared. "I intend to study this material and crack it wide open."

Watney Granger snorted. "You're aware of course that our every movement is monitored?"

"Certainly. That's irrelevant."

"We have strict instructions, Lois."

"Sure we do. But we aren't allowed out of this building, so who cares? Any information we gather will stay here."

Granger looked at her, slightly befuddled. "Are you trying to tell me something?"

Lois shook her head, amazed that the man could have been so obtuse. "You don't get it do you?"

"Apparently not."

Lois looked him straight in the eye. "We're never coming out of here, obviously."

Watney stared blankly at her for a moment, certain that the woman was joking. "Ha, ha, not a joke in very good taste, Lois." He was surprised by the authoritative and confident sound of her voice. What did she know that he didn't?

"I'm not joking Watney. It should have been obvious to you that this job was potentially suicidal."

"That's preposterous!"

"Consider. We were both at NIH last year. Word came down through very select channels about a fantastically new but dangerous biomaterial that could alter the human genome and end disease forever. You remember that? A briefing from one of the scientists at CGR."

"Of course, that's how we met. We were both more fascinated by what wasn't said than what was said, even though we knew we'd be working in a place like this." Watney waved his hand in the air at the high-ceilings and the dirty, old-fashioned glass windows that made the place pretty drafty when the wind blew.

"Precisely. We took extensive psychological tests and were grilled for hours by NIH psychologists. We are ideally suited to work in isolation. The aura of secrecy that surrounds this program is excessive, you know that. It became obvious to me just before committing to this project that we may not come out alive."

"But ... you mean they intend to kill us?"

Lois stomped her foot. "Think! You know the rumors."

"Nonsense." Watney was really upset now. "They would have told us about the risks and made us sign release forms."

Lois stared. "You must be daft. There is no paperwork associated with this project at all. No emails, nothing. It has all been done by word of mouth."

Suddenly Watney got it. He staggered backward. Of course! The tests they had taken were evaluated right in the room and had been incinerated, even the marking pencils. All interviews were oral. He knew that in tests on death row inmates only ten percent of those who were exposed to the airborne material survived. If the public ever got wind that here on Long Island Sound, next to one of the most densely populated areas in the country, a fatal airborne biomaterial that could kill millions was being manufactured .... He had been a fool.

"It appears that you have seen the light, Watney. I made my plans as soon as I committed to the project. I intend to expose myself to the material when our work has been completed. I am certain that is the intention of the project managers. This – substance – we're working with is simply too advanced and too dangerous. I thought you understood that."

Watney Granger looked at his goddess in an entirely new light. A goddess all right, but one with a core of steel. "You go ahead. I'll get out of this somehow."

Lois smiled, a smile etched with pity. "Good luck with that. Now it's time to begin the protocols."

"I'll be with you in a minute." Watney seated himself in one of the well-padded office chairs. Fortunately, producing the bio-enhancer was time consuming and slow. He should have time to figure out how to escape this place. The production process itself was mostly automated; their job was to monitor the equipment and analyze the product. The plan was to produce the biomaterial for several months, at which time a small aircraft would land at the facility and pick up the product. The bioenhancer was stored in heavy, dark-red plastic cases that each contained 12 carefully prepared aluminum cylinders. The cylinders were two feet long and eight inches wide, stacked in four rows of three cylinders each. Each of the cylinders had a tiny transponder at one end; probably a release mechanism. They looked like little bombs. Watney shook his head, amazed that he had let his attraction for Lois

MacDonald put him in this position. She was nuts! His only thought now was to get out. The little island was a half-mile offshore and he couldn't swim. Lois couldn't either.

CHAPTER 21

MARCUS was lying next to Darcy in bed in her apartment, twitching. Darcy felt it and snapped wide awake. She saw Marcus' body spasming and was terrified that he might be having a seizure.

"I'll kill you," Marcus muttered, his hand turning into a fist as if he was holding something in it. Suddenly his body stiffened and his arm slashed out in a wide circle, almost hitting her in the face. She could see sweat beading on his forehead. There was a crazy look in his eyes. "Marcus!"

Marcus snapped awake and looked around wildly. He saw Darcy and his face calmed. "God, I had that dream again."

"That's the third time this week. I'm not getting much sleep."

"Neither am I. Give me a break!"

"I'm liking you less and less," Darcy said. "What happened to the sweet Marcus I used to know?"

"You ask me that at 4 in the morning?"

"Shhh, you'll wake Kathleen."

"Fuck Kathleen."

Darcy sat up. "This isn't working anymore. I love you Marcus ? well, I loved the person you used to be anyway, but not the person you've become. You remind me more and more of that friend of Carla's we met that time, what was his name ... Brian Anderson."

Marcus was shocked. "I can't be as bad as that!"

"Sometimes you are, Marcus. I'm afraid of you sometimes. You fly off the handle and do strange things, you swear and curse. In your dream you just said, "I'll kill you.""

"I did?"

"Yes. It scares me."

Marcus shuddered. "I'm sorry Darcy, I really am." He put his hands gently on her shoulders and looked her in the eyes. She saw the old Marcus there.

"Yes, that's the man I love right there," she said.

Marcus sighed. "This dream I have, it's about the fight I had with that demon. I can't tell anybody about it or they'll think I'm crazy and lock me up."

"I wish I could help."

"I can see I have some serious problems. Bethany won't even speak to me. Even Carla thinks I'm crazy, and now I'm upsetting you. The only person who thinks I'm cool is Tom Shapiro at work, and he's a little paranoid. I'll go see Doctor June again. Maybe he has something I can take. After all, the guy's an ET."

Darcy yawned. "All right Marcus. I'm so tired, I have a long day tomorrow."

"OK. I'll try to sleep quietly."

Darcy rolled over and thought: I'm glad we decided not to move in together.

The next day Marcus made an appointment to see Dr. June after work. When he walked into the office, June greeted him like an old friend. "I was wondering when you would show up."

"You were expecting me?"

"Yes Marcus. You've been having dreams, haven't you?"

"Yes. How did you know?"

"It's part of the pattern, Marcus. You are the only human being who has successfully confronted a Tau and come away with his consciousness and personality intact. However, you are now intimately connected to the Tau. Your natural resonance has been overlain with that of a very powerful alien personality. This is naturally causing disturbances in your psyche. Your dreams will continue to be troubled because of your connection with the Tau, through their primary focal point, Belial."

"Wait a minute. That ...demon died in the street! Are you saying it's still alive?"

Dr. June's thin lips pursed. He gazed at Marcus as if to say, "What do you think?"

"But …but …that's impossible."

Dr. June sighed. He was beginning to understand earthian emotions even if he could not fully feel them. "Did you learn nothing from your battle with Belial? The body in the street was just that …a body. That monster's consciousness abandoned the physical container and returned to Tau, just as you returned your consciousness to the trading room after your confrontation."

Marcus knew that what June said was true. He'd known it when he told Darcy that Belial was still alive, even though he didn't want to believe it. Suddenly Marcus' world exploded. His conception of the universe expanded in a quantum leap of understanding.

The Aleph watched, amused, as Marcus' thoughts raced. Comprehension slowly etched itself on his face in a look of wonder and disbelief.

He turned to June. "We're total retards aren't we?"

Dr. June laughed. "I would not say it exactly like that."

"Am I in danger from Belial?" If he was, then so was Darcy.

June frowned. "You are all in danger. The short answer is yes, because you are currently a focal point."

"If I end it with Darcy will she be safe?"

June leaned back in his chair. "That is less certain. There is a strong connection between you even if no physical contact is made. I would say that if you were to disassociate from the female, she would be less likely to become embroiled in the unfolding events."

Marcus made up his mind. "I'll need to break it off with her but I don't know if I can."

June shrugged. "It's your call, as you humans say." He changed the subject. "You wanted to know if there is anything you can take to ease your anxiety, especially at night." June walked over to his lab bench and pulled out a little flask. "This substance will calm your nervous system and induce sleep." The little man handed the flask it to Marcus. "Take two drops just before you lie down for the night. Your sleep should be more restful."

"What's in it?" Marcus recognized a vial similar to the one he'd been given earlier. This one was a deep lavender color. Marcus, looking at the color of it, felt calmer.

"Just filtered water," June replied.

Marcus snorted. "Here doc, take it back. I can get water from the tap."

June smiled. "Oh ye of little faith. The color and shape of the container imprints the water and alters its essence. The substance in the vial will make your sleep more restful."

Marcus stared at the little container, fascinated. It was made of colored glass, about three inches high and less than two inches wide. The flask was rounded, sloping upward in beautiful, intricate curves. The color of the vial was rich and vibrant. A geometric symbol was etched on the front and back of the vial. As he stared into it he began to feel very relaxed and sleepy ... "Wow!"

June smiled. "If you need me again Marcus, you have only to call. You are my most important patient."

That night Marcus went over to Darcy's apartment after work. "Darcy, I have something to tell you."

"Did you see Dr. June?"

"Yes. He said that I am in the middle of some dangerous events. I don't want you to get hurt, so I think it would be best if I didn't see you again."

Darcy's reaction was not at all what he was expecting. She said with a wise smile, "Silly boy, don't you think I understand?"

"What?"

"Do you think you are the only one who can talk to the Aleph? I knew him before you did. We're in this together."

Marcus just stared at her. The tension of the past several months overwhelmed him. He threw himself into Darcy's arms and cried like a baby.

"It's OK Marcus, it's OK," she said, cradling his head on her shoulder. She was crying too. Darcy raised Marcus' head and looked him in the eye.

"A good ending," she said, trying to create the right future.

Marcus got it. "Yes, a good ending. If we both live that long."

The Cat's Meow, Chicago

"Hey boss, you OK?"

It was Bobby the bartender, leaning over and looking concerned. "You was lookin' kinda funny there."

Luca straightened. "Yeah I'm fine Bobby. I was just thinking about the conference tomorrow."

"I think you're doin' a good thing."

His old buddy Battaglia had been as good as his word. Bobby was known for his savvy. His mob was the best organized in the country and he was trusted and respected. Luca had asked around after that call from Pablo Rodriquez. He confirmed that something big was up and that it had to do with a killer bioenhancer. The rumor was that the substance was going to be released in several US cities. When the Outfit confirmed the rumors everybody got pissed off. Battaglia organized a conference of most of the mobs in the entire USA. They were going to compare notes and decide what to do. It was a miracle. Luca looked around the Meow and saw some of the most important gangsters in the country.

From New York John "Fatty" Costigliano; the pockmarked face of Tony Bruno from New Jersey; the Coca brothers from Florida and Harry "The Psycho" Salicio the big Miami boss (he had his boys keeping an eye on that bastard); from Detroit the tall and fashionable Darnell Corwin with his carefully trimmed goatee; his friend from Dallas, Bobby "The Politician" Battaglia, who looked like an NFL linebacker. Tommy Chen was here from San Francisco. Gino Moretti, built like a fire hydrant, from the Hill in St. Louis, was here in his usual black double breasted suit. The Nevada contingent was represented by Greg and Johnny Alito, the twins, in their blue sport coats and white turtlenecks. The west coast was also well represented, with Pablo "Scarface" Rodriquez and Jorge Espinoza from California, among others. These were just a few of the famous names present at his club.

There was plenty of muscle here tonight too. Luca recognized Johnny "Hands" Branco, Paulie "the Butcher" Zambrano, and Vinnie Graziano from New York. The giant Ivan Lezco was here as well. Lezco, it was said, could run the 40 in 4.5 seconds and had once encountered a brown bear and knocked the animal out with one punch. Luca recognized the usual bunch of knockaround guys who had been able to get into the Meow tonight. Everybody was mostly getting along.

Racial and cultural animosities had been pushed away. It would have been unthinkable to get this group together even a year ago. Mob guys sittin' around talking together like the Waltons? Luca didn't get it, but maybe he'd learn something tomorrow. He'd have to stop drinking early tonight because he wanted a clear head in the morning.

Luca rose early from the bed in his private office at the Meow. He ate a good breakfast with plenty of black coffee, brought to him by one of the girls. Nitti drove him down to the large conference room at the Congress Plaza Hotel by Grant Park. As he walked in Luca almost laughed out loud. At least one hundred people crowded the room, representing the biggest collection of murderers, thugs, blackmailers, and drug dealers in the country.

Luca scowled as he walked in and saw a crush of curious media at the back of the room. How did those bastards get here? He moved forward to tell them to leave. The massive figure of Bobby Battaglia walked toward him. Bobby was well over six feet tall and at least 260 pounds, but light on his feet. Bobby was dressed smartly as usual in a dark blue suit with a pale blue shirt and a tan tie. His thick gray-brown hair was combed back to reveal a smooth, wide, olive-complexioned face with high cheekbones and absolutely symmetrical facial features. A handsome man by anybody's standards. Two beautiful girls trailed behind him.

Luca was angry. "Why are these media people here?"

"Calm down Luca. I invited them."

Luca's mouth fell open. "What do we need with publicity? We got serious things to discuss."

"That's the point Luca." Bobby was obviously pleased with himself. "You just sit back and listen. We've been figuring out some stuff and we're going to need public support and participation to pull it off."

"It sounds crazy." Bobby had briefed him about what the feds were doing. Something about a rogue element within the intelligence community, fulfillment of Biblical prophecy, and some really twisted shit. Luca knew his friend wasn't telling him everything.

"Luca, the public has always been fascinated with us," Bobby said. "The Sopranos, Goodfellas, the Godfather, we got what they call a certain cache in the public imagination. If we play our hand right we can get the public on our side."

Luca shrugged.

"You started it. That DVD you sent me, and that website your guy put up, it's better than a crew of Sandmen."

"Oh yeah?" The Sandman was a famous hit man used by the New York crime families. "I never seen it."

"Have your guy show it to you. It names names and who's rotten. *É ora di fargliela vedere, capisci?*"

So Hutchinson had been busy. Maybe the guy wasn't a loser after all. Luca hoped that his old friend knew what he was doing. He noticed that the media had several tables at the back. Their cameras were everywhere. He recognized that smart-ass reporter from the *Tribune*, a skinny kid who had investigated the Courvall killing. That fucker discovered that Costigan's was one of his companies. Luca choked down his anger. He saw a *Chicago Tribune* sitting on one of the tables and opened it up. A big headline said, "Rumored Mob Conference Today – Crooks to Bring Justice?" Probably Bobby's work again.

There were rumors that the feds were going to come in and bust everybody. Luca had sent word that there would be a war if that happened. Nevertheless, he could feel an undercurrent of nervousness in the room. He heard a gavel banging and took his seat at a table at the front and off to the right.

"All right, here we are!" Battaglia announced. Guys in the front were looking behind them, guys on the left were looking to the right. "Hey, relax.! Nobody's going to burn anybody today."

There was nervous laughter and the room gradually quieted. "OK look, we all got businesses to run," Battaglia said. "We don't have a lot of time to fuck around …uh, excuse me. We're here today because of a persistent rumor that's been on the streets for a couple of weeks."

Battaglia paused and a reporter from the *New York Times* perked up. Her cameraman turned to her. "Maybe we'll get something good out of this."

"It's already pretty good," the news reporter replied. "A public gathering of organized crime figures? It's never happened before."

"We've got sources," Battaglia continued, thinking of that eerie voice over the telephone. "Sources in, er, certain places. We've heard that a radical new bioenhancer – that's what it is being called anyway – is being tested that is supposed to improve the human genome. The problem is that it kills nine out of every ten people exposed to it. It kills regardless of race, color, or creed. Our sources tell us that this material is going to be distributed all across the country. And later it's going to be released, if what we're hearing is correct. That aint good."

"Have you heard anything about this?" a reporter from the Tribune asked his colleagues seated at one of the media desks. Everybody shrugged.

"This rumor we've heard may or may not be true, but we think it is. We want you guys" – Battaglia gestured to the reporters against the back wall – "to ask your sources. Verify this thing or squash it."

[cheering]

"Here's something else. I was talking to Luca Carcelli the other day. Luca is part of the Outfit here in Chicago. One day he had a talk with a guy who told him that he had to rub out an alderman because that alderman was going to expose a pedophile ring in Chicago. If he didn't, he wouldn't get his product. This is just the kind of thing we're asking the media to investigate. You know what pedophilia is, having sex with little kids. If any of you in here like that, get the fuck out right now. If we find out you're a pedophile we'll kill you."

[cheering]

The *Times* reporter looked at her cameraman in astonishment. "Headline!" she said. "Drugs Gangster Threatens to Kill Pedophiles."

"What's this about a Chicago pedophile ring?" the cameraman asked.

"We're going to find out," the reporter replied. "I'll talk to a friend of mine at the *Tribune*."

"... Where do Luca's drugs come from? From an airplane outside of Chicago at a private landing strip. Where does that plane come from? From organizations associated with the goddam CIA and their intelligence network. We all know it, it's about time somebody said it."

"These guys are crazy," the cameraman said.

The reporter shrugged. "There was something about that back in the late 1990s. Some guy, Gary Webb I think his name was, from the *San Jose Mercury News*. He claimed that the CIA is running drugs into the country."[14]

"... The intelligence services and Homeland Security are run by assholes at the top who give bad advice and who are fucking everything up. The Fed is destroying the dollar, the banks are bleeding us dry. The politicians are letting it happen because they're all bought and sold. We need a country and some laws and regulations or we can't make any money!"

There were angry shouts. Battaglia let the crowd noise dissipate.

"Now we find out about this so-called experimental vaccine. The situation with the feds is out of control. We want you guys in the media to do your jobs and start investigating this shit, for real. If there is a lethal vaccine we gotta find out who's behind this and stop them."

Shouts of "kill 'em all" and "wipe the slate clean" were heard. Battaglia banged his gavel again. "We can't fight these guys, gentlemen, because we don't even know who they are." Battaglia looked around at the assembled news media, who were looking at each other in astonishment. "It's up to you to help us find out. Do your jobs and investigate this. I'm available, as well as our research group, to give you all of the information we have."

Battaglia paused and looked around the room.

"Everybody in this country is from someplace else. I was born in Sicily. Tommy Chen's family are from China. Darnell Corwin is from Africa. Pablo over here is from Mexico. Some of us have good bloodlines and most of us are mongrels. But we have one strength: we work together now. We love our country and we're not going to see it destroyed."

{cheering}

"Nothin' like this has ever happened in the history of crime," Battaglia continued. "We're all comin' together to work for the common good –" [more cheering] – "so we can get back to business as usual!"

[laughter]

"All right, I'm opening up the floor for questions and suggestions. You've all got the plan we put together. We gotta get 100% agreement on what we're doing before we start."

The next day in the *New York Times*, the following story appeared on the front page, with an 18pt headline:

Organized Crime Fights Back?

By CHRISTINE AMANTOR

Unsubstantiated and irresponsible rumors, conspiracy theories, and a public conference of over one hundred of the most important figures in organized crime. That was the bizarre scene yesterday at the Congress Plaza Hotel near Grant Park in Chicago. The theme: Restoring America.

You might ask with good reason, restoring America to what? The Crims, as they are being called, decided that in order to continue to exploit the masses, sell their heroin and crack, and engage in the nefarious activities of fraud, blackmail, prostitution, and vote buying, it was necessary to restore order to the country. Preposterous, you say? We thought so.

As Bobby Battaglia, Texas crime boss said, "We gotta have some laws or we can't do business."

It's unbelievable. It was even more unbelievable in person.

The impetus for the conference, according to Battaglia, head of the Dallas organized crime syndicate, is a persistent rumor that a radical new airborne biomaterial is being developed and tested on human beings, and will soon be released. This biomaterial supposedly kills nine out of every ten people exposed to it. No sane person would believe such an irresponsible rumor, of course. Even a hint of something like this would immediately provoke a huge outcry. Even so, the *Times* is looking carefully into these allegations.

That wasn't all. Luca Carcelli, one of the heads of the Chicago crime organization, asserted that a shadowy contact demanded the assassination of Alderman Barry Courvall. Courvall had threatened to expose a Chicago pedophile ring whose members, it has been alleged, feature some prominent Illinois politicians and Chicago clerics. Barry Courvall, fifth ward alderman, was killed in a traffic accident three months ago outside a Chicago gas station when a truck driver lost control of his vehicle and smashed into Mr. Courvall's car.

The Crims, in a prepared statement, also asserted that shadowy groups associated with the CIA and what some call the Deep State are running illegal drugs into the United States.

Had enough? All of this seems absurd and unverifiable. The nation's organized crime leaders insist that they have access to inside information and are asking the media to investigate.

When I asked Mr. Carcelli whether his organization was involved with the CIA and if his organization was involved in the death of Mr. Courvall, he replied, "no comment."

This reporter, frankly, does not know what to think. Certainly, the unprecedented gathering of the nation's crime bosses is remarkable and newsworthy. However, the tone of the meeting resembled a collection of conspiracy theorists ranting against "the system."

The website of organized crime, takeourcountryback.com, has been receiving over 50,000 hits per day. The Crims have captured the imagination of a public who are fascinated by the idea that an organized group of hoodlums are working to help solve the country's problems.

The man responsible for the website's content, Gerald Hutchinson, has a double PhD in mathematics and history. He claims to have documentation and research to support the wild claims of the Crims. Hutchinson has produced an 8-DVD revisionist history of the United States.

The question is, what will happen next in this unlikely drama?

CHAPTER 22

"Darcy, come here and look at this."

Darcy walked out of the shower with a towel wrapped around her, trying to get the water out of her ears. She leaned over and looked at Marcus' gigantic laptop.

"Take Our Country Back. Yes I've heard of them," she said. "Gangsters trying to get some publicity."

Marcus leaned back in his swivel chair, grabbed her by the waist, and deposited her on his lap. His hand went to her shoulder and drew the towel down.

"Marcus!" Darcy removed his hand and straightened the towel. "You said you wanted me to look at something."

"Oh yeah I forgot," he said, kissing her neck.

"Down boy."

They were in Darcy's apartment, which she used to share with Kathleen, who had moved in with Albert. It was on 83rd street between 2nd and 3rd Avenue, a walk up studio with one decent size bedroom. Darcy had decided that, for better or for worse, they had to live together again. If it didn't work out this time she'd have to find someone else. At least they didn't have to worry about money. On both their salaries they were able to make the $1400 rent, but living in New York was expensive. In the back of her mind Kathleen's voice said that she always said she'd find someone else and always got back with Marcus anyway. She ignored the voice and told it to eat a lemon meringue pie and then drown itself in the bathtub.

Marcus pointed to an image on the screen that showed Gerald Hutchinson, a researcher for the Crims, sitting next to a skinny, scraggly-looking guy in a big conference room. "Recognize him?"

"Oh my God, that's Jake Holden."

"I thought so," Marcus said. "Look what I got in the mail today."

Marcus opened a small envelope and found eight DVDs and a letter addressed to Darcy. "God Marcus, you read it. I don't even want to touch it."

"Dear Darcy..."

"*Dear* Darcy! The nerve of that little worm."

"Dear Darcy," Marcus continued, "I want to apologize for my actions over the years. I was just a stupid street kid and nobody ever taught me any manners, unlike you who got to live like a queen for Royalty, but that's no matter now. Anyway, I just wanted to write and say I'm sorry and that I'll never bother you again. I met a guy who is straightening me out. His name is Gerald Hutchinson and he's amazingly smart. He's got two doctorates in math and history. He says I'm a great researcher and I have a head for it. So now I have a career and won't have to bother you anymore. As a token of my sincerity I want to offer you a gift of the presentation Dr. Hutchinson and I put together. I understand that these DVDs can't wipe the slate clean between us but we'll probably never see each other again anyway. All the Best, Jake Holden."

"This saves me the trouble of buying them."

"What are they?" Darcy asked.

"Oh, this guy Hutchinson has applied mathematics and complex adaptive theory to history. He's come up with some interesting stuff. The Crims are selling them on their website."

"I don't think I want to see them, if they're what I think they are."

"Why not?"

"There's nothing we can do about it. The problems are too big."

"That's a defeatist attitude."

Darcy pouted. "You're so much different now than you used to be."

"I was just a boy then. Now I'm a man who fought a battle with a dangerous ET and lived to tell about it." Marcus shuddered at the memory of Belial.

"I hope we aren't going to get into another argument."

Marcus forced himself to relax. He was getting tense again. Dr. June told him yesterday that his psychic turbulence would probably continue. "These Tau are persistent creatures when they have been thwarted, Marcus," June told him. "You have to stay as calm as possible. When you feel yourself getting anxious, step back and take a couple of deep breaths."

Marcus breathed in and out. "I'm sorry Darcy. Dr. June told me I would have periods of anxiety. I have to try and calm myself."

Darcy smiled sympathetically. "All right Marcus. I'll watch the presentation if you want me to."

Marcus sighed. "That's OK. I'll look at them. If I see anything I think you should know I'll make you watch it."

Draco Tau

The hot blue-white sun baked the arid landscape. On Draco Tau, the mating season was about to begin. Belial strode confidently into the huge mating cave. Within, hundreds of females awaited his pleasure. It was the duty of the alpha male to spread his genes widely. For the next week Belial would mate with as many females as he could. He would attempt to better the record of 167 matings in the six-day.

Before his ordeal he prepared himself with vital essences that would enhance his male prowess. The planet's chief geneticist greeted him in his personal chamber. Qa-Hrrzl was highly respected for his knowledge of the intricacies of the Harvest plan and was the world's leading authority on the genome of the hominids.

"Are preparations for the Harvest proceeding apace?" Belial inquired.

"Sire, all is in readiness for the glorious moment," Qa-Hrrzl replied. "The planet's societies have been conditioned for the new world order. The population threshold has almost been reached. The bio-enhancer is being prepared and is almost ready to be stored in secure facilities. In a few short months the time will be ripe. The Trigger can be pulled on your order."

Belial was feeling expansive after this rosy report. But underlings always exaggerated. "What assurance is there that our Plan will be executed successfully?"

Qa-Hrrzl bowed. "Sire, everything that can possibility be done is being done." The scientist decided to be brutally honest. "Of course I cannot guarantee success. But I and my minions are working diligently to ensure the best possible outcome. These hominids are vermin, sire, as unpredictable as Argul and as disgusting as Shiga."

Belial nodded. From what little he had seen of the planet, these words rang true. "If all goes as you say, you shall sit in council on the historic day."

Qa-Hrrzl's eyes widened in gratitude. He bowed low. To feed at the exact moment when billions would die! The ecstasy of that moment would be beyond comprehension. The ancient records of the Tau told of these momentous times, when the life force of an entire planet would be transferred into their grids. All Tau would immensely benefit from this transfusion of life-giving energy but those at ground zero would experience the most orgiastic and rapturous excitement. Their cellular structure would be enhanced beyond that of anyone on the planet. They would grow even stronger relative to the rest of the race. These times always presaged a Golden Age of abundance and relative peace on Draco Tau. The energy of the entire planet was raised to a new level and the Life Reading Index of all were augmented. Whoever was Alpha at the time of the Harvest almost always enjoyed an elongated life span and a reign marked by complete subservience. To be invited at the behest of the Belial, the preeminent bloodline, was an honor to be enjoyed for a long lifetime.

Qa-Hrrzl continued his low bow until the Alpha had passed on to the mating chamber, signifying his absolute obedience.

Serven BioLabs, New York City

"Dr. Schultz, please report to BioSecurity immediately. Dr. Premon Schultz, please report to BioSecurity."

Premon Schultz was in the middle of an experiment at his lab bench. He cursed loudly. The call came on his personal dataset, issued to all employees. It was mandatory to carry it everywhere in the building. Such summonses from BioSecurity could be something serious, or nothing. The rule was that you dropped everything and rushed as fast as you could to the basement.

Schultz stepped out of his lab and into the brightly lighted corridor. The entire facility was hospital white except for the black linoleum floor with its gold hexagonal pattern. The elevator was a few hundred feet from the lab. He hurried down the hallway, his white lab coat flying away like a superhero about to take flight. He brushed past a woman with raven black hair who emerged from her office. "BioSecurity?" she asked, and Premon nodded quickly in passing. He was a short, balding man with delicate hands and 15/20 vision. It was said by his peers that his visual acuity was matched only by his talent for observation. He reached the elevator and emerged into a softly lighted corridor that led into the BioHazards lab. Across from it were the offices of the Chief of Security, the notorious Carlton Inge. When he entered the office Inge was at his black marble desk, holding a small glass vial. "I just received your report, Mr. Schultz, on this new biomaterial. It surpasses all explanation."

"Yes, sir." It was best not to offer anything when being interrogated by Inge. Premon said nothing. His analysis of the substance had astonished him, but he was not a curious man. He was paid to do a job and he did it.

"Where did you get this sample?" Inge asked.

"It was driven over two days ago at 3:23 a.m. by two men who wouldn't identify themselves."

"How was the sample packaged?"

"It came in a standard bio-hazard case, dark red, with the symbol of a woman in the lower right corner. Inside the case was an aluminum container shaped like a football."

"Well, well, well," Inge replied, leaning back in his chair. "Now things are beginning to make a little sense."

Schultz raised his eyebrows in inquiry but Inge was lost in thought. "Thank you doctor," he said, waving a hand dismissively in the air.

Premon was grateful for his early dismissal. He didn't want to get involved in any controversy. If he rushed back to the lab he may still be able to save his experiment ...

Carlton Inge sent an encrypted message to Fort Meyer. "LIEUTENANT HAVE POSSESSION OF BIOMATERIAL SAMPLE. MATTER URGENT. INGE"

Fort Meyer

"It's on, Colonel," Lieutenant Mutumbe said to Rodgers. "You've seen my text from Inge?"

"Yes lieutenant." The colonel spoke bleakly. "It's up to us to stop it. There's nobody else."

"But how?" Mutumbe asked. "We don't even know what's going down. Those two rats, Bobo Jacoby and his buddy Draco Smith from Army intelligence are in on it. Those two never show up unless something big is about to happen."

"How did you hear that?"

"I got it from Buzz Metzger, General Jones' aide. Jones is on the staff of the Joint Chiefs. He was at a secret meeting with CIA Director Pantera. Said that Bobo and Draco told the CIA director that something big was about to happen and that Pantera didn't have a need to know."

"Shit. Then it's totally out of hand. What the hell is going on?"

"That's just what DCI Pantera said before he got swept under the rug."

Rodgers' eyes were flint and he met his subordinate's. "Are you in? If you are, it's to the death now."

"I understand sir," Mutumbe replied, totally committed. "We have to find the source of this biomaterial. Unless it's already too late?"

Rodgers grinned harshly. "It's never too late lieutenant. The ball is on our five yard line and there's a minute left in the game. There's still time to score, even if it kills us. But we need allies outside of Washington DC. I don't trust anybody in here."

"Neither do I. The good news is that we're independent anyway, and we have the highest security clearances. We can pretty much go and do what we please."

"Until we step on somebody's toes."

"Oh, we're bound to do that sir."

The colonel's lips thinned. "It's a long shot but I think I know where to start."

CHAPTER 23

M ARCUS woke up early, feeling refreshed. It was amazing what two drops of water will do. *Imprinted* water, Dr. June had said. He was skeptical about that stuff but his physical cravings for cocaine had almost completely subsided now. However, when he remembered those days his body still responded. Part of his anxiety was from the psychological need for the drug. Even now, when he thought about those times with Carla, he felt a sense of sexual excitement and an almost cellular vibration.

Marcus admitted to himself that he missed the excitement and the sex. He was more like Carla than he cared to admit. Darcy was a little boring. God, those were amazing days! Maybe just one more outing with Carla ... he could call Freddy, get a line or two ... it was tempting.

He got out of bed quickly, trying to shake off the impulse. If he didn't move he might pick up his phone. Time to run the stairs. As Marcus made his morning shake he could hardly remember those tranquil days in Midland Illinois. He looked back on himself with disbelief. Darcy was always saying how she liked the old Marcus better, but that guy had been a child. A puffball. He was different now.

Marcus put twelve ounces of milk, two raw eggs, one ounce of a liquid trace-mineral neutraceutical, and one ounce of a liquid vitamin/amino acid neutraceutical into a blender. He drank the mixture and took his herbs. He always woke up with a slightly nauseous stomach but he needed a boost in the morning. This was the only thing he could get down. Marcus filled up a half-gallon water bottle and placed it in his pack along with ten energy bars, and two small one-pound weights with hand grips. He was consuming over 4,000 calories every day and needed every one of them. He was running the stairs during lunch and after work as well. People in the building had gotten used to seeing the strange, giant manchild motoring up and down. Some of them even came out to watch and encourage him. He had completely given up alcohol, which only reactivated the cravings.

Marcus called a cab and left the apartment. Darcy always got up an hour earlier and walked to her work three blocks away. This place was convenient for her but no so convenient for him. When he got to the NYCBank building he strolled quickly through one of the massive carousel glass doors, pushing it aside easily. He went to the red door that marked the stairwell entrance. He tightened his pack with the bulky water bottle and grabbed the weights one in each hand. He placed his right foot on the first stair, pumping his legs methodically at a runner's slow jog, and swinging his arms up and down. There were thirteen steps to each flight and two flights per floor. Marcus felt the familiar pressure of his lungs filling with air and the heat in his thighs as he continued up the unpainted concrete steps. He was now at floor five, getting his rhythm. He could feel his lungs expanding to let in more oxygen. The heat in his legs became more intense. He continued up to floor ten, floor eleven, and floor twelve, still jogging. The pain in his legs was intense now. He was breathing hard; but for the past two weeks he had been able to make it all the way to floor twenty without stopping. The water bottle in his backpack moved slightly back and forth, irritating his skin, but that couldn't be helped. As he reached floor nineteen, his work floor, his legs were agonizing lumps of leaden pain and his lungs were almost bursting. As he turned the corner to the second flight he saw someone coming down from floor twenty. When Marcus tried to brush past the man on the landing his way was blocked. Marcus looked down at a short but barrel-shaped and muscular man about forty years old. He was built like an ape with long arms and big hands.

Uh-oh, Marcus thought. This guy is trouble. "Let me by." He was so tired now the guy could probably have pushed him down the stairs with ease.

"Not until I've told you something kid." The smaller man stood at ease, slightly forward on the balls of his feet with his legs slightly bent. This guy was ready for action and seemed very comfortable with the idea. Marcus realized he was holding the weights and wondered whether he could smash this guy's face in.

The smaller man read Marcus' intent and laughed. "Don't try it Riley." Marcus got the impression that the man was skilled in hand-to-hand combat. He relaxed.

"That's better."

"How do you know my name?" Marcus was till sucking wind.

"Don't be an idiot Riley. You were all over the news a few months ago. Besides I have connections to a friend of yours."

"If he's a friend of yours he's no friend of mine." Marcus disliked the man.

"I don't like you either kid," the man said, feeling Marcus' antipathy. "Here's the message: do your trading and stay out of business that doesn't concern you."

"Fuck off." Marcus activated his web of light without thinking. He would have to trust that those Tau had stopped monitoring him.

The man stepped back, startled. "What's that you're doing?" Marcus could see fear in the man's eyes.

"You mean you can see it?" Marcus was astonished and curious, forgetting for a moment that the man before him probably meant him harm.

"Yeah, it's some kind of light! What are you anyway Riley? A freak?"

Marcus didn't bother to respond. He entered the man's mind and in an instant knew who he was and why he was here. "OK Jacoby, message received." Marcus spoke with an air of superiority and satisfaction.

Jacoby's mind worked swiftly. He could kill Riley right here and he probably should, but he'd have to do it quick and somehow dispose of the body. However, somebody might enter the stairs at any moment. He was under strict orders not to cause the slightest ripple in the public's awareness, or to alert the police. Everything connected with this operation had to be silent and clean. Jacoby glanced up and down the stairwell. He sneered. "You're lucky kid or I'd take you out right now."

"You can't kill me." As soon as he said it he knew it was true.

Jacoby looked him over and anger overcame his better judgment. He moved to strike, incredibly fast, but felt a force block his movement. He stumbled and fell against the wall to the right of his intended victim, bumping his waist painfully against the rounded blue metal handrail. He couldn't move.

"Tell Adolfone that I got his message and that I'll be seeing him some day," Marcus said.

"You goddam freak!" Jacoby was still unable to move but he could breathe OK and he still had possession of his senses.

Keeping his web activated, Marcus backed down the stairs. He kept his eyes on Jacoby, who had a look of astonishment on his face. He could only hope that the man would stay put and not go after him. Marcus knew from reading Jacoby's mind that he was a skilled assassin and would have no trouble with him. Anxiously, he went down the steps until he turned the corner. He quickly entered the hallway to the 19th floor.

Bobo Jacoby stood in the hallway until he felt the energy release him. He had never felt anything like the force field that had overpowered him. He knew it had come from his opponent. He had been as helpless as a child and that scared the shit out of him. This guy Riley was a mutant and he wanted no part of him. Adolfone would have to hear about this personally. He would have to go to Rome again and talk to Venetti. Goddammit, he hated that place. Those Sabbateans were crazy in a dark way that even scared him. Next time they could send somebody else. He forced himself mentally to shake off what had happened, and his training took over. In a few moments he had himself back together.

Bobo Jacoby walked warily down the stairs and almost went through the door marked "19." He'd heard about these banks and their traders. He was curious to see what the place looked like and if there were any good-looking women. Especially that Carla Waverley everybody talked about. What a piece of ass she was supposed to be! But he was out of place here and knew it. He sure as hell didn't want to see that freak kid again. Jacoby continued down the stairs, walked out of a door on the far right side of the building, and entered an unmarked car standing at the curb.

After work Marcus waited around in Dr. June's office until his other appointments had left. He reported about the morning's events. They had agreed that Marcus should report to him at least once per week, and after any unusual development. "Very well Marcus, thank you. Are you sleeping better?"

"Yes doctor, thank you. That water really works."

The Aleph smiled, a bit pitifully. These humans had so much potential. The entire race was being kept ignorant and held back from their development. To not understand the simple process of geometric imprinting! At least their own race, while atrophied, had control of its destiny.

"Did you say that you prevented the Jacoby intruder from attacking you?" June asked.

"Yes. I used my web of light to get into his head. Then I got scared and was able to make him ... stand still."

"The other human recognized the energy you were projecting?"

"Yes."

June was shocked. "I believe that the Tau will have to press their Trigger sooner than they anticipated. We are almost at the critical moment."

"Trigger?"

"It's best you don't know."

Marcus saw that June wanted to say something else. "You might as well tell me doctor. You already said before that the cat was out of the bag."

June smiled thinly. "There may be hope yet. If even a fellow like Jacoby can see your web, it means that the Light Codes within your species are being activated."

June explained that every race contained programming that naturally led it up the ladder of evolution to greater awareness and a higher Life Reading Index. "The Tau will have to be very careful now. That just makes them more unpredictable."

June checked him over and pronounced him fit for duty. After the earthian had left the Aleph removed a small disk from his left ear, closed his office, and exited the building. He met his contact and handed over the disk, which was a faithful recording of everything that had happened to him during the past 24 hours. He was tired again. The 24 hour earthian day was 5 hours longer than the 19 hour day on Epsilon. Nevertheless, he wouldn't trade his field mission here for anything.

That evening Marcus received a video call from Thom Madigan.

"Thom Madigan! I haven't heard from you in a while."

"Yes, well, Holderness Parkinson wanted me to call you."

"Parkinson? Isn't he the guy who turned Darcy into a glorified whore?"

Madigan scowled. "That's not like you Marcus, to talk about Darcy like that."

"I'm sorry Thom. I'm not a nice guy anymore. New York does that to you."

"Not to everyone," Thom replied sharply. "Only to those who lack character."

Marcus flared and was about to hang up. What the fuck did Madigan know about his life in New York? Not a damn thing, the arrogant bastard. Something inside Marcus told him that Thom was right. He stared at the image of the older man, who looked back at him unflinchingly. Marcus took a couple of deep breaths and tried to calm himself.

"You're right. But you don't know what's happened to me so I have an excuse."

"There's always an excuse, Marcus." The older man spoke without rancor.

"Yeah I guess so. What does Holderness Parkinson have to do with all of this?"

"He wants you to call him."

"Why?"

"I don't know Marcus, but it's pretty important. He said to tell you that it's about those DVDs you watched, and your recent experiences."

"How would he know anything about my recent experiences?"

"Let's just say that Parkinson is knowledgeable."

Marcus thought for a few moments. "All right. I'll call him."

Madigan brightened. "Good. Now that we've gotten business out of the way, I'd like to buy you guys dinner and catch up. Expense is no barrier. You can choose the best restaurant in town."

"Hey that's great! I've been watching what I eat lately, and I usually just get something from the cafeteria at work, or the local sandwich place. It will be a nice change of pace."

Madigan was pleased. He really didn't care all that much about Marcus, but he was concerned for Darcy's happiness. He thought of her almost as his daughter. Even more than that: as someone he could confide in. "All right then, how about this Friday? Call me tomorrow and I'll make the reservations."

Marcus hung up. He was about to call Parkinson when Darcy walked in, looking elegant as usual.

"You look great." Marcus rose from the table in their small kitchen and gave her a hug. He was still thinking about what Madigan said about character. Was his fatally flawed?

"I just had a call from Thom Madigan. He wants to take us out to the most expensive restaurant in town."

Darcy clapped her hands in delight. "Wonderful! Audrey has a new creation that I'm dying to wear in a formal setting. I'm tired of bistro food."

"Darcy, am I ... do I have a flawed character?" Marcus blurted.

Darcy tilted her head to the right, thinking.

Marcus was a little upset because she hadn't denied it. There must be some truth to what Thom had said.

"I'd say that your temperament has certainly changed for the worse," Darcy said finally. "You used to be so kind and loving. Now you're sharp, coarse, and vulgar at times. You're more impatient and angry."

Marcus objected immediately. "That's just New York! It happens to everybody." He wondered whether she'd say the same thing as Madigan.

Darcy regarded him coolly. "Does it?" She stood there so calm and collected. Marcus realized that she hadn't changed at all. She was still the same person. But that was bad; she wasn't growing. You needed to change to grow, didn't you? "But ..."

Darcy let him cogitate for a while. She could see the wheels turning around in his head.

Marcus thought out loud. "What does character mean anyhow? Always being the same in every situation? Trading has taught me that you have to change with changing conditions. This city admires people who are aggressive and get what they want. It's—" He suddenly had a realization. Character was being true to the person you really were. Like Darcy, and Holderness Parkinson, and even that mob guy Nitti. And Carla. It didn't matter what you *did*. It was about what you were *being*. But who was he? He hadn't the slightest idea.

Marcus sat down and put his head on the table with his arms circling his head. "Fuck." People who had character were happy. Or at least not miserable. In his mind's eye Marcus looked at the people in his life and counted them down. All of them knew who they were and where they were going. He was the only one who didn't, and he was emotionally unstable. Even Freddy was happy, the same guy who once told him that he wanted to be the most reliable supplier of cocaine and drugs to the New York jet set. For God's sake, where was he? He didn't have a goal at work other than to make money and pay the bills and have a little fun trading. He'd lost that feeling of looking for the deep patterns, of looking for meaning in life. His relationship with Darcy sucked. Everybody else except Dr. June thought he was a wacko. Maybe even June thought so too. His character had changed because he had fought that demon ET. That was it of course. It had changed his personality, Dr. June even said so.

Marcus contemplated that and rejected it. No, that was just an excuse. Something had happened to him and he didn't know what it was. Darcy could see it and so could everyone else.

Marcus raised his head off the table. "What am I supposed to do?"

Darcy smiled. "Don't feel so bad honey. You are the most complex person I have ever met. Maybe that's part of it."

She got him. He didn't have to explain anything. She could tell what he was feeling. "God, you're amazing," he said with feeling. "Even though I know that complex is just another word for fucked up."

Darcy just smiled and said nothing.

Marcus sighed appreciatively. She knows that saying anything will just set me off again. She was smiling to let him know she cared. He sat up and patted his legs with his hands. "Come here."

Darcy sat down on his lap. She smelled really, really good. She felt good too. "I don't understand who I am," he announced.

Darcy laughed; a bright, full laugh that put a smile on Marcus' face. "When you figure it out you tell me."

Marcus frowned. "You mean you don't know who you are?" That was wrong somehow. He thought she had it figured out.

"I've never thought about it. I guess I'm a person who likes elegance and I like things to be peaceful and serene if I can get it."

Marcus looked at her and agreed. That was Darcy. In a crisis she was pretty good and didn't get rattled. Marcus remembered those confrontations with Carla. Darcy had kept calm and defused the tension. "That's it? That's who you are?"

Darcy smiled up at him. "I guess so. Who are you, Marcus?"

"That's the question I've been sitting here trying to comprehend. I used to know a long time ago. I don't now."

Darcy queried him with her eyes and Marcus thought some more. "I really don't. I couldn't even give you a vague answer."

Darcy rose. "You'll figure it out. Remember you said that Thom invited us out for dinner. What's that about?"

"Oh yeah." Marcus remembered he had to call Parkinson. "Thom says he'll take us to the most expensive restaurant in town. Your choice."

"Great! I'll decide and text him." She went off into the bedroom with her phone.

"Hey Darcy, what's Holderness Parkinson's number?"

Darcy reappeared in the kitchen. "Holderness? Why do you want to call him?"

"I don't. Madigan said that he wanted me to call him."

Darcy was a little hurt that he hadn't wanted to speak to her. "You don't even know him."

"Yeah I know. I'll just get it over with I guess." Darcy gave him the number and he punched it in.

"Chantelle Hudson, Royalty Services, how can I help you?"

"Uh, hello Chantelle. My name is Marcus Riley. I—"

"One moment please. I'll send you through."

In a moment Marcus' mobile showed an office filled with dark paneling, old wood furniture, paintings on the wall, a plush carpet, and figurines of crystal and gold. A large man with white hair, dressed formally, sat behind a massive oak desk. "Wow. It's 1850!"

The man at the desk laughed in a rich baritone. "Yes, it's rather old-fashioned in here. I like it that way."

So this is the great Holderness Parkinson. "I'm very curious why you wanted me to call you," Marcus said. "I should have thought you'd want to speak to Darcy."

"I would love to speak to Darcy but the matter is rather urgent and primarily concerns you."

"Holderness!" Darcy cried, grabbing Marcus' device and placing it in front of her. "You are looking well."

Marcus saw the old man's eyes light up. "Damme, Darcy my dear, if you aren't the most beautiful and elegant woman I have ever seen."

Marcus laughed. Parkinson was frankly admiring without vulgarity. Darcy's face turned red.

Marcus retrieved his phone. "If you talk to her like that Mr. Parkinson, you'll spoil her."

"She deserves to be spoiled my boy. You are taking good care of her I presume?"

Marcus felt a sense of great power emanating from the man, but no hostility or the slightest bit of criticism. This was a man who commanded instant respect. Now that was character! He felt guilty. It must have shown on his face because the old man frowned very slightly.

"After our business is over, perhaps we can talk about that." To Marcus this suggestion felt like a command. Where did this guy learn to be so confident and certain? It was a bit irritating.

"And now to the business at hand," Holderness said. Darcy was leaning over to see the screen. She put her head on Marcus' shoulder. "A pretty picture. Marcus, I want to talk to you about a Dr. June, with whom you have had several conversations, and about those scratches you got on your face."

Marcus felt his face. The scratches had healed but had left three faint scars along his right cheek.

"There's this guy at NYCBank, his name is Doctor Aleph June."

"Go ahead, Marcus, you can tell me." Parkinson spoke quietly, inviting a response.

Oh really? Marcus thought. You presume a lot, old man. "Dr. June treated my face and sent the samples to a biolab. He told me that the DNA of the samples was … not something found on earth."

"Did he tell you anything else?" .

Marcus felt uncomfortable but Holdernesss Parkinson just smiled. "He said something bizarre about a bunch of ETs who are going to release a toxin that will kill off most of the human race. Of course it's just stupid nonsense. The guy must be crazy."

"It is not. What Aleph 209 told you is exactly correct. It is the primary reason I wanted you to call. We know about the Alephs Marcus, Dr. June is one of them.

Darcy met one of them several years ago at a party we threw for one of our, ah, clients."

"If you already knew, why did you ask me?" Marcus' irritation was increasing. He felt like a child in the presence of this man.

Darcy raised her eyebrows as if to say, 'forgive him, Holderness.'

"Who are you anyway?" Marcus asked. He remembered how Royalty had taken Darcy off the streets and made her into a high-priced whore. "I thought you were just a guy who owns a fancy brothel."

"Marcus!" Darcy shrieked. "Have you no manners?"

Marcus realized that he was over the mark. "I'm sorry sir."

"Two days ago I received a call from a Gerald Hutchinson," Parkinson replied, ignoring Marcus' rudeness. "If you saw the 'Take Our Country Back' DVDs you know who he is. I know him because one of my former contacts is now his associate."

"That rat Jake Holden," Darcy interjected.

Parkinson inclined his big head forward in acknowledgment. "Just so Darcy. May I add that you no longer have to worry about that gentleman? Mr. Hutchinson has got him firmly in hand."

"That's a relief," Darcy replied. "But Jake Holden is not a gentleman."

Parkinson raised his eyebrows slightly. Darcy knew the gesture well, when Holderness wanted to depress pretension. "You should see him now my dear. That is no matter. We have strayed somewhat off-topic."

"All right then, get to it," Marcus said. The big man in the chair had superb manners but his self-assurance was almost overwhelming, like a conceited person who thought all his opinions were facts.

"We have, in the last couple of days, become aware of the manufacture of an exotic biomaterial that directly alters the human genome. It is our belief that this biomaterial will soon be distributed to secure facilities around the country, and perhaps all over the world."

Something Marcus had gotten from Belial's mind clicked into place. "Ah, yes, I understand."

Parkinson noted with approval that the boy did not flinch.

"What are you talking about?" Darcy was mystified and a little afraid.

Holderness saw the look on Darcy's face and looked pained. "That is why, Marcus, I wanted you to call me, and not Darcy." He glanced at Marcus. "You can tell her if you want to."

"Don't treat me like a child."

"We'll move on," Parkinson said. Darcy pouted. "We have to stop the distribution of this biomaterial."

"I don't understand," Marcus said. He was trying not to show his irritation. "What can an insignificant trader like me do against those guys? I assume that this biomaterial is connected with some top-secret organizations."

"That is what I called you about. We have got ourselves a little team. Your Colonel Rodgers and his aide, Lieutenant Mutumbe, and some military white hats, CIA Director Pantera and some of the white hats in the intelligence services. Luca Carcelli with his mob organization, which everyone knows about now. We're all coming together." That wasn't entirely true, for he hadn't yet talked to Carcelli. But Holderness was pretty sure the mob boss would want in.

"That's great!" Marcus was genuinely pleased. "What does that have to do with me?"

"You're the key Marcus." Parkinson spoke solemnly and nodded his great white head slowly up and down. "When you were at Fort Meyer, you were told that the scientists could not analyze your web of light and didn't know where it came from. That was not quite the truth."

Marcus bolted upright. "What? You mean that lieutenant lied to us?"

"I'm afraid so Marcus. It was for your own good."

Darcy was indignant. "I always thought Mutumbe was a creep. Why, after all that prodding and questioning he just dumped us off at a hotel and told us to find a ride home."

"Yes dear." Parkinson was indulgent. "It was necessary."

"Men are stupid and vulgar," Darcy replied. "Except you of course, Holderness."

"I am relieved to hear it Darcy. May we resume our conversation?" The big man was perfectly tranquil.

Darcy sighed, knowing well that Holderness was imperturbable. "Very well."

"Marcus, the scientists at Fort Meyer discovered that the origin of your 'bio force field' lies within certain identifiable sequences in a very specific region of your non-coding DNA."

"Huh?" Marcus said. "I don't know anything about biology."

"Neither do I. I'm just repeating from my brief. You need to know this information. Human genes are essentially just coded sequences of DNA that make up proteins. In humans this is less than 10% of the total amount of DNA. It turns out that many types of non-coding DNA sequences do have known biological functions, and the other non-coding sequences have as-yet undetermined functions.

When the Fort Meyer scientists analyzed your DNA they found that over 10% of it was coded in a new way they couldn't understand and had never seen before. Your DNA, Marcus, is self-organizing. This is a fancy way of saying that you are ... evolving."

Marcus looked at his body. "I don't feel any different."

Parkinson shrugged. "The point is that you probably have abilities you don't even recognize yet. That makes you valuable to the team. The team of good guys."

"What's your role in this Mr. Parkinson?"

"I am somewhat of a coordinator."

"You mean you're running the show," Marcus suggested.

Holderness Parkinson threw back his head and laughed. "You might say that my boy. You see Marcus ? and Darcy I want you to hear this as well ? my company, Royalty Services, acts as a sort of confessional."

Darcy was shocked. "Do you mean, sir, that Royalty Services is an elaborate information network?" She couldn't wrap her mind around it. Dear kind Holderness ... she couldn't believe it.

"In short, yes. Our service caters to the people who really hold power in the world: major executives of the most important banks and corporations, presidents and prime ministers and other top government officials, decision-makers in the world's military, intelligence, and police agencies. Many of them have used our service but we have to disguise what we are doing. We have to exercise the utmost subtlety and discretion." Parkinson puffed out his chest a little. "And I must say, Darcy, that we have been enormously successful. Not one of the people who have used our service over the past thirty years has ever suspected that we are, simply, collecting information. I am in a position to state that with confidence."

Darcy looked at her mentor with amazement. "What is your position in this information network, dear Holderness?"

"I'm on the white team," Parkinson replied, taking a sip of a limited-edition cognac from a crystal glass on his desk. The cuvee, and he was enjoying it at $2,500 the bottle.

"Are you an ET?" Marcus blurted.

Holderness Parkinson laughed again. "No Marcus. A highly trained intelligence officer."

"Oh my," Darcy said. "I thought I knew you."

"You do know me, my dear. Now you know a little more."

"You've blown your cover," Marcus suggested. "You're telling us this over an unsecured line. Anybody could tap in."

"Yes, that's right, but it no longer matters now. The gloves are coming off and the actors are jockeying for position in the final battle that will decide the future of the world."

"So there really is an Armageddon, like it says in Revelations?" Darcy asked.

"Let's just say that the world is a lot different place than you learned in school, or if you listen to the news."

"I'll say," Marcus said. "I've already met three ETs. They're everywhere!"

Parkinson chuckled. "That's a refreshingly novel attitude, Marcus."

"What do we do?" Marcus asked.

"I have your number," Parkinson said. "Continue your life as usual and wait for instructions. There are plans being made right now to stop the release of the bio-material. We may need your help. Stay in the city; under no circumstances should you or Darcy leave Manhattan. Is that clear?"

"Yes," Marcus replied.

"All right Holderness," Darcy agreed.

The screen went blank.

Marcus and Darcy turned and stared at each other. Darcy muttered another French phrase she had learned from Aubrey, whenever there was trouble. "*Nous sommes maintenant en difficulté*," she said.

The Cats Meow, Chicago Illinois

Luca Carcelli sat in his private office at the nightclub. His private line rang and he switched on. "Luca."

"Luca Carcelli, this is Holderness Parkinson."

"Holderness Parkinson? What the fuck do you want?" This was the second asshole who had called him on his private line.

"Now now, Luca, calm down. We have to talk about those DVDs you made, the website you put up, and other matters."

"You didn't answer my question, asswipe. How did you get this number?"

Parkinson removed the phone from his ear in disgust. He would have to talk to this man in his own language. "Listen dimwit, you have no idea what's going on. Neither did your friend Joey."

Luca Carcelli exploded. "What do you know about Joey! You goddam pimp!"

"I know a lot more than you think, Carcelli, and I'm your friend. If you weren't so stupid you might calm down and learn something."

Luca had his mouth open for an angry reply when he realized that somebody who knew Joey was probably a player. "OK, then talk."

"Joey was a low-level operative," Holderness began. "But I represent—"

"You're just a pimp!" Carcelli interrupted.

"—I represent a white hat faction within the intelligence services that are loyal to the constitution and the United States."

"You do?" Carcelli was dumbfounded. Everybody knew Parkinson owned a really fancy cathouse, but that was all it was.

"I do. You've done a good thing with this Crims movement. If you keep your head you can help us to get that so-called vaccine out of Chicago."

"We don't need your help."

"Think about it Carcelli. We know that there are four biocases of this stuff already in Chicago. All four are probably at secure facilities. Even if you knew where they were, how are you going to get them? And when you get them what are you going to do with them?"

Luca hesitated. "We're workin' on it."

"Yes you are, but you're not getting anywhere. If you work with us, we've got people on the inside. We're going to find this dangerous biomaterial and destroy it. Our team has got the skills to do it." Parkinson paused. "Carcelli, the problem is a lot bigger than a harmful vaccine. We must also identify and remove the people behind it."

Luca was flabbergasted and impressed. "That's the kind of talk I like. But how do you know about Joey?"

"Joey was murdered by an operative from the Sabbatean faction. The Sabbatean's are a fanatical bloodline that is determined to make Biblical prophecy come true. They are planning an Armageddon for the human race and hope to rule the survivors. If you want Biblical references, you can find them in John, 16:16. Armageddon, a place where the kings of the earth under demonic leadership will wage war on the forces of God at the end of history. Look in Matthew, 24:5-7,11; Revelation 13:16-17, II Timothy 3:1-5,7. Especially the passages that refer to wars, earthquakes, famines, and false prophets."

"That's nuts. All that end-of-the-world stuff is over. 2012 and all that crap – what a bunch of bullshit."

"I'm afraid not Carcelli. 2012 was just a diversion. The biocases – you know about the one at IRT – are the real deal. The game of who controls the world – the good guys or the sociopaths – is still on." Holderness explained that the White Hat alliance consisted of individuals from the military, intelligence services, scientists in the 'black' programs, a few politicians, and others. "We've got some muscle behind us. We could use you for an important operation."

"Why do you need us?" Luca asked.

"Because you're already organized and set up in every city in the country that matters. Because you have a certain public awareness and sympathy. You have started something with your website and DVDs that the public is getting excited about. We need you to help us locate those damn biocases!"

Parkinson explained and Luca's eyes lit up. "I think I can get the boys to go for it if you explain it simple. In language we can understand."

"I can do that," Parkinson replied. *"Ai mali estremi, mali rimedi,* eh? Extreme conditions require extreme remedies."

"Chi non fa, non falla!" Luca responded. Maybe this pimp wasn't such a bad guy after all.

Holderness arranged the details with Carcelli. Then he pressed a small button under his desk and a small table rose up from the floor, with an old-fashioned red plastic phone fastened securely to it. He called Fort Meyer. "Mutumbe? It's Parkinson."

"Long time, sir. How are you?"

"Good, Lieutenant, good. Red Cantaloupe."

"That bad, eh?"

"Indeed. Are you ready?"

"Yes sir."

"Good. I'll be expecting to see you soon."

Holderness hung up the phone and made several more calls. Then he tapped the button lightly with his foot and the table receded back into the floor.

CHAPTER **24**

AT Daniel that Friday Thom Madigan was curious. He had already taken his seat and watched Marcus arrive with Darcy. Darcy's quiet, unconscious elegance turned heads as she walked toward his table. She wore a dark blue creation from the boutique with a classic square bodice. He felt a sense of pride that she was coming to him. He waited to see whether Marcus would seat her; he didn't. Darcy was astonishingly beautiful. She was wasted on Marcus. His heart ached for her but she was beyond him and he accepted it. Tonight he could provide her with an evening in a setting that would match her own refinement.

"Oh Thom, this is wonderful." Darcy gave him her full attention and the smile that always melted him.

"Thank you Darcy." Thom smiled back as if her smile was a favor conferred upon him. "It is always a pleasure to see you."

"The pleasure is mine," Darcy replied correctly.

Marcus watched the tête-à-tête and frowned. What was going on here?

Thom turned to Marcus and noticed the three scratches on his face. "You look different. You've been working out."

"I have," Marcus said, pleased. "I've been running the stairs at the NYCBank building three times a day, twenty floors."

"*Running* twenty floors?" Thom was astonished.

"I can go up now without stopping," Marcus said proudly.

After this politeness Thom ignored Marcus and concentrated on Darcy throughout the meal. It was his payment for taking them to a four-star restaurant. Darcy opened up to him and he found out all about her life since arriving in New York. Marcus didn't mind because he didn't know half the stuff she was doing or what had happened to her. He felt guilty. He was supposed to be her boyfriend. Was Thom doing this on purpose? He looked carefully at the two, engaged in conversation. He could see only deep interest on Thom's face and a pleased smile on Darcy's. Should he be jealous of this guy?

"Excuse me Tom, I need to use the ladies room," Darcy said. She waited for his acknowledgment.

After Darcy left Thom turned to Marcus. "What's this I hear about an alliance?"

"How did you know about that?"

"I was talking to Parkinson yesterday. He mentioned it in passing."

"Are you in it?" Marcus asked bluntly, implying that Thom wasn't fit.

Madigan forced down his irritation. "No one has invited me, if that's what you mean."

Marcus took a sip of brandy. "Wow, this is good." Thom was afraid he'd ask how much it cost, but Marcus said, "I don't know too much about it either. Apparently Parkinson is one of the leaders. He told me to go about my life and wait for instructions."

Madigan was satisfied. Things must not be at a crisis yet. He'd call Parkinson tomorrow and hope he could get through.

When Darcy and Marcus returned to their walk-up apartment on 83rd, she was glowing. "I haven't had that much fun in a long time!" She was sparkling.

"You spent almost all of it talking to Madigan," Marcus complained.

"I'm sorry Marcus but Thom is so interesting."

"And I'm not?"

Darcy's bright smile faded. "No Marcus, you're not."

Marcus was shocked. He had expected an apology. Did this relate back to his lack of character? "Really Darcy?"

"Yes Marcus, really. I love you, you know that, but you never pay attention to me. You never notice what I'm doing, you're not interested in my activities. To you I'm just an accoutrement, an article of occasional pleasure. I have been seriously thinking of leaving you. I love you but I can't live like this."

Marcus stumbled backward, grabbed the chair, and lowered himself into it. His first reaction was to protest. After a few moments of thought he knew she was right. He had been neglecting Darcy ever since they came to New York. But that was her fault. She was the one who left him back in Midland! Marcus remembered what Thom Madigan had said about his lack of character.

He knew he was brilliant. Was he selfish as well? Maybe that was his character flaw. He didn't value Darcy because she wasn't educated. Despite her training and refinement he had always regarded her as just a high-priced call girl. However, Darcy was highly skilled in social situations. That was a valuable skill, as she had shown him a number of times. So why did he undervalue her? Of course. Holderness Parkinson and Jake Holden and the porn film. His prejudice against Holderness Parkinson and his brothel had unfairly tainted his view of Darcy. Yet Royalty had provided Darcy not only with impeccable training but also an excellent, if informal, education. She had no knowledge of mathematics or finance, which was his area of strength and interest. But she was just as skilled as he was in her own area. He had never gone to college either; his own education was not broad enough.

Did he really want Darcy? Should he find another girlfriend? Maybe he should go back to Carla if she'd have him. Life was sure a lot simpler with her. They'd work together, go out at night and get fucked up, have lots of sex. It was a great life, uncomplicated. A part of him really wanted it. Screw Holderness Parkinson.

Darcy could almost read the thoughts in his head. She felt very sad. Every time it looked like Marcus was OK he'd turn away from her. With sudden mental clarity she knew this was the turning point for her. If he didn't come to her enthusiastically she would have to break the connection right now and never see him again.

Chapter **25**

T EN minutes went by. Darcy waited silently. Marcus' face was clouded over. It was obvious he was going through some kind of difficult life decision. She was sad that it was taking him so long to make up his mind. Didn't he want her after all?

Just as she was about to break the silence Marcus' face cleared and he smiled. He stood up and put his hands on her shoulders.

For the first time since they both came to New York he really saw her. Marcus really liked what he saw. "I'm sorry Darcy. You're right, I've been totally into me and my work, and this crazy stuff with the ETs. I'm going to try to make it like it was when we were in Midland."

Darcy brightened immediately.

God, she's beautiful Marcus thought. *And loving, and kind.*

"Really Marcus? I've longed for what we had back then ever since we came here."

Marcus lowered his head. "Yeah, you've said that all along sweetheart."

"Oh Marcus, am I really your sweetheart? You never said that before." *You have never told me you love me either.*

"Uh, I guess you are," he said, grinning. He had seen so many beautiful and talented women in New York. They were desirable sex partners and social acquaintances, but not someone to live with. That little lady from Orpheus Analytics, Sarah Blaisdell, she was intriguing. Would he want to spend his life with her? Marcus understood that he was really a one-woman man. It was fun to play the field but basically he was a homebody. What really excited him wasn't travel or adventure, but the search for knowledge. The mental excitement of trading was a part of that. He'd never met anyone he liked as much as Darcy, despite their divergent interests.

Darcy felt wonderful again. She was happiest when she was with Marcus and that's the way it would always be. For better or for worse. But she had to be sure. "Really?"

Marcus tightened his grip on her shoulders and looked into her eyes. "Yes."

"Good. Then I'll stay."

CHAPTER **26**

Fort Meyer

LIEUTENANT Mutumbe sat at his desk. It was 2:30 in the morning after a long day. He was reading over documents in a folder labeled "Red Cantelope." At 9 o'clock in the morning Colonel Rodgers had walked into the office and handed him the folder. It was over two inches thick.

"You're in the loop now Lieutenant," Rodgers said. "I want you to read everything in the folder and absorb it as soon as possible. Don't stop unless you have to eat or shit."

"Yes, sir. But why the hard copy?"

"To the guys we're dealing with, everything on a computer, any computer, is the same as broadcasting it over the public airwaves. Read this folder in this portable Faraday cage."

Mutumbe raised his eyebrows.

"Lieutenant, the people in these documents are using ET technology that has been twisted to the dark side. They can read any computer anywhere in the world and extract information from it. Nothing is safe anymore. I erased almost everything we have on our personal network and printed it. That's the folder. Now get to it. We have a busy day tomorrow."

"Yes sir." Mutumbe got busy. He spent hours reading about exotic technology in hidden programs. Apparently, a field of spinning neutrinos at the earth's Schumann resonance created a vortex, and what Dr. Edward Teller called "divided space," completely separate from universal spacetime. These bubbles of spacetime were inertialess and could travel anywhere in space or in time. That means we already have anti-gravity. And time travel. And teleportation. He began to get madder and madder as he realized that this technology was unavailable to the United States military.

Another large document called "Black Hats" described a private, highly organized, trans-national network of military, corporate, and intelligence personnel. They had their own private army and air force and were using this advanced technology, which had been reverse-engineered from downed ETVs. Mutumbe twigged on that. "So that's where that stuff is going." He and Rodgers were usually first on the scene at these crash events, but never knew what happened to the craft after they had checked it over and made their report. Their work had led them into some dark and hidden corridors. They knew that a lot of brilliant people had been reverse-engineering these craft for decades, trying to extract their secrets.

Apparently there were multiple private Black Hat factions, competing against each other. Each was dedicated to fucking up the human race in order to grab power. Over half the folder was about the White Hat Network, a hastily assembled group of military and intelligence officers, and people who had also worked in black projects for outfits like SAIC, Lockheed Skunk Works, Mitre, and other private military contractors. These people were sick about how the new technology was being misused. So it was White Hats against Black Hats. The game was crossing corporate, governmental, and national boundaries.

Sixteen hours later Mutumbe was mentally numb as he finally finished the folder. He could only make one conclusion: the White Hats were way behind. He fell asleep in his chair, exhausted.

"We gotta move fast," Colonel Rodgers said. He shook the slumped-over body of Lieutenant Mutumbe, still at his desk. It was 6 a.m. and time to start the day.

"What's up sir?" Mutumbe asked. Every one of his muscles ached and his head felt like an overcooked marshmallow over a fire. He needed something to eat.

Rodgers walked over to his workstation and brought up a map of the United States. A red star had been placed over Long Island Sound. There were 24 smaller black stars over major cities all over the country. Rodgers pointed to the red star.

"Here's where the biomaterial is being manufactured. The black stars are what we think are the targeted release cities."

Rodgers brought up a picture of an opened, dark-red plastic case with twelve silvery objects packed carefully inside. "The biomaterial is packed in these specially prepared aluminum cylinders. Apparently a private network within DHS has already been set up to distribute the material. It won't take much time to send a few plastic cases around the country."

"What the hell sir?" Mutumbe was still fuzzy from lack of sleep. His mouth felt like the inside of a septic tank. "Biomaterial?"

"You read the Black Hat documents?" Rodgers asked.

"Yes sir. I never read anything about any bioenhancer."

"You did read about the eschatological group of nutsoids that are trying to make Biblical prophecy come true. This is their Final Solution for humanity, where they will take over the planet."

Mutumbe shook his head. "For God's sake colonel. It's so insane I didn't think it could be true."

"Yes Lieutenant. No one would believe it and that's why they've had such good cover. Our involvement in the ET issue puts us in the perfect position to understand how they've been able to maintain their edge. It's behind all of the secrecy on the planet, all the black programs. It hides the exotic new technology you read about in the folder. It puts the Black Hats years ahead of us technologically."

Lietenant Mutumbe shrugged. "If this new technology is so good why haven't we used it to kick ass in Iraq and Afghanistan, or to just take over the world ourselves?"

"Because, lieutenant, it would lead to disclosure of the entire ET issue and the release of exotic technology that would completely destroy the hundred trillion dollar fossil fuel empire. Do you get it? This technology must remain hidden."

"Yeah, of course. I never thought of that." The stuff he'd read about would completely change the economies of the world if it were developed commercially. Clean, free energy from the vacuum, antigravity, quantum leaps in medicine and physics. Technology from the stars!

"So their plan is to release some harmful biomaterial?" Mutumbe was appalled.

Rodgers nodded. "According to the most recent information it's a highly advanced DNA enhancer. The problem is that it kills nine out of every ten people exposed to it."

"But why do they want to kill so many people?"

Colonel Rodgers ground his teeth. "It's simple. The Twelve recognize that their fossil fuel empire cannot continue much longer on a planet with over seven billion human beings consuming scarce resources. It's their insane way of reducing the population and keeping the status quo."

"What happens to the survivors of this bioenhancer?"

Rodgers frowned. "According to the reports I've read they become completely immune to disease, more intelligent, and have a sense of heightened mental and emotional equilibrium. Dammit, this stuff really is beneficial! That's what's so frustrating. You can almost understand how the bastards can claim they are benefiting humanity."

Mutumbe shuddered. His African ancestry, with its strong sense of community and sharing, rebelled at the idea.

Rodgers turned and pointed to the red star on the screen. "We now know where the stuff is being manufactured: Pache Island, Long Island Sound. They've had a plant up for months and are almost ready to distribute."

"How could we not know about this?"

Rodgers shrugged. "We had no idea. Two of our guys found a plastic case with twelve samples of the biomaterial on the Montauk Point State Parkway, next to a car that had overturned. Apparently the stuff came from the Cherry Island research facility. We had the stuff analyzed at Serven Labs. The guys who did the analysis couldn't believe what they were seeing. It took us three months to figure out that the clever bastards had set up a manufacturing plant almost right next door! They opened everything up to the public during construction. Looked like another routine construction project. We didn't follow up. We got played."

"What do we do?"

"We can't destroy the plant. The toxin is designed as an airborne material that will quickly spread over a radius of at least 40 miles and the entire New York City area. Taking the plant out would serve their purpose just as well."

"We have to interdict," Mutumbe said.

"Yes, that's correct. Look at this." Rodgers pulled up images of the Pache Island facility where the biomaterial was being manufactured. A small airstrip was visible right next to the building. Otherwise, the place was surrounded by woods. A small pier jutted out into a little harbor, which was only 200 feet wide and 100 feet long.

"Can't get much in or out of there," Mutumbe said. "Adequate cover for a good sized force though."

Rodgers clicked on another image, infrared, taken at night, of the inside of the building. "These were taken by one of our guys in a plane with a super-sensitive infrared camera. The image has been enhanced. You can see some specialized equipment against the far wall."

"Any protection?"

"Nothing, they don't need it. There are two civilian scientists there, monitoring the production. That's it."

"It's damn clever, sir."

"Diabolical. Our only hope is to stop the stuff from coming out of there. Failing that, we have to intercept the material at the release points. The problem is that we haven't identified the target cities for sure. They could be anywhere. If we knew for certain we might have a chance to intercept the toxin before it is released."

Mutumbe shook his head. "It's no good sir. We can't possibly—"

Just then a red light flashed at Rodgers' workstation. "Encrypted message," Rodgers said. He opened his translator program. WHITE HAT NETWORK: OPERATION INTERDICT 0230 THIS MORNING IN PROGRESS. DO OR DIE NOW. REPORT FORTHCOMING

Both men looked at each other and clenched their fists.

"I take it we're part of this network sir?"

"Yes Lieutenant."

"Who are we fighting?"

Rodgers sighed. "That's the hell of it. These people are so well concealed. Their agents are caught but the principals remain unidentified. For example, we know the two scientists who are producing the bioweapon and where they are located. We know who recruited and examined them and put them in the facility. Everyone connected with the project has been questioned but no one can identify a person behind it. In every case we were able to intercept a few emails on official letterheads but the servers could not be traced. We can't figure it out, even though we've got contacts now at the highest levels."

"What about Bobo Jacoby and Draco Smith?"

"Just errand boys. This is a private operation and its control center is outside the country. Apparently the United States is the guinea pig."

"Screw that sir," Mutumbe said.

"Amen," Rodgers replied.

Chicago

"Don't fuck with us, Parkinson."

Holderness Parkinson had just picked up the red phone from its platform under the floor. He recognized the voice immediately. "What do you want Conte?"

The voice on the other end chuckled. "I'd like to invite you to Utah for a little demonstration."

"Are you behind the release of this biomaterial?"

"Nope. Different bloodline, different faction. The Sabbateans think they're hot shit but we have other plans. They're a lot better."

Irritated, Parkinson said nothing. These crazy, inbred bloodline families were fighting a private war that crossed governmental and national boundaries. He could never keep track of who was fighting whom.

"I'm not going to Dugway unless it's an emergency."

Conte chuckled appreciatively. "Not bad old man. So you know what this is about. Don't get your quills up Holderness." Conte spoke sarcastically, using Parkinson's first name. He knew it would irritate the old man. "This is just a courtesy call. We're inviting you over to see what's going to happen in the near future, if Plan A doesn't work. We're what you might call psychics!" Parkinson heard the man guffawing coarsely.

Psychics! Psychos, Parkinson thought. "This doesn't have to do with man-made ARVs and satellites in space projecting holographic 'alien' ships, does it?"

"Congratulations. You win the prize." Conte laughed. "Another War of the Worlds but a lot realer this time. Parkinson, you're going to want to see this." The man spoke like an eager teenager excited about his first car. Parkinson hesitated.

"No need to worry old man. Nothing is going to happen to you. You're too valuable to us alive. We just want you to know what you're dealing with."

Parkinson believed him. Conte had a reputation for being vulgar but not vindictive. He simply believed that ruling over the rest of humanity was his divine right, just like the other crazies in the Twelve group. Parkinson put down the phone and considered. His research showed that approximately two percent of humanity was either mildly or severely antisocial, and that a minority of those were psychopaths. Unfortunately the genetic inbreeding associated with the major bloodlines resulted in a much higher percentage of anti-social behavior within these groups. Their penchant for secrecy kept them below the radar of public awareness. "All right Conte, you know where I am."

Holderness knew what would happen next. In a few minutes an unmarked vehicle would drive up in front of the building. He would be driven to a private airfield. There he'd board a jet and in less than two hours he'd be in the desert. He knew that whatever Admiral Conte had to show him would probably not be in the best interests of the citizens of planet earth. As an intelligence officer it was his duty to observe and report.

After he hung up Admiral Conte beamed with satisfaction. He was sitting in the control center underneath the Utah desert with Captain York. This underground base was one-quarter mile on each side. It had been hollowed out of the earth with huge earth-burrowing machines using advanced technology. It was shaped like a bent dumbbell with an elaborate command and control center at one end, barracks and living quarters at the other end, connected by a large L-shaped corridor over 200 feet wide. Within the structure a small hangar contained five intelligent antigrav spacecraft. He couldn't wait to show the fat man what he could do.

Conte looked at the Main Board and regarded his aide, a skinny but brilliant officer with a doctorate in physics. Captain York had come up through the ranks without ever having seen combat. He had been assigned to him as a sort of techno-troubleshooter. Conte generally had no use for geeks like York but the man had proven his usefulness time and again, giving him sensible advice and moderating his rash and sometimes self-destructive impulses. Conte knew York didn't like him. But York was loyal. Loyalty, the refuge of many stupid men, was something Conte understood.

Conte and Captain York waited around for Parkinson's arrival. The meaty, barrel-chested Conte gloated. "The program is simple, captain. The Sabbateans and their stupid bioenhancer will fail. Then our bloodline will launch the simulated 'alien invasion' from right here in this base."

Conte swung his arm around to indicate a vast and sophisticated array of panels, each of which was directly connected to the Main Board. The visuals were handled by a large display about six feet wide and three feet deep, surrounded by ultra high-res 3-D display tanks suspended from the ceiling. "How many of the ARVs do we have now?" York asked.

"Thousands. They are all stored in several underground bases in the United States, Britain, and Australia."

That was news to York, but he said nothing. Conte drew his finger over a green blister on the main board. The hangar door, about 100 feet to their left, opened.

Captain York stared. Five beautiful spacecraft sat on the concrete floor. He had heard rumors about them but had never actually seen one up close. The craft resembled the ones in science fiction movies like Star Wars, and were about 100 feet long. "Who made these things?" York was astonished.

"We did!" Conte was cheerful. All of these wonderful toys were *his*. "Where do you think all those billions that disappeared into the black budget went to?" Conte stared admiringly at the sleek looking craft. "Aren't they beautiful?"

"There are only five here, admiral."

Conte snorted. "These are intelligent ARVs, capable of being piloted by a human being. The only five in the world. The rest of them are drones."

Captain York was amazed. He wondered why he, a nobody, was being treated to insider information. His experience with the Twelve bloodline factions had clearly demonstrated their secretive paranoia. Probably Conte was just eager to show off.

"You understand what we're doing, don't you captain?"

"Vaguely."

"After we launch thousands of these realistic-looking drones over the world's major cities we'll activate the holographic motherships. These displays will be created from satellites launched during the SDI program. You've seen the images."

Conte brought up an image of a gigantic spacecraft 10 miles in length and 4 miles wide, on one of the huge 3D display tanks hanging from the ceiling. "These 'motherships' will appear in the lower ionosphere, well above the range of the world's fighter aircraft. There they will hover, threatening, while the governments of the world will be forced to declare martial law in order to combat the threat from space."[15]

Captain York was awed. "They look absolutely genuine. Totally convincing." And totally overwhelming, York thought. How would he react if one morning he woke up and saw one of those things hovering over his city? He'd be scared out of his mind.

Conte checked his dataset for the time; Parkinson should be here in an hour. He could hardly wait to see the look on the fat man's face when he saw what he was up against. "The whole thing is a fake but it will scare the living shit out of everyone. It will be picked up on the net and the mass media. Panic will spread quickly," the admiral said cheerfully. "We can get the drones up fast because they are inertialess, and neutralize gravity."

Captain York at least knew the theoretical capability of these craft. In a few short minutes they could traverse one end of the world to the other.

Conte played a demo of the attack and watched the face of his aide to see his reaction. As the simulated attack unfolded Conte saw York's jaw drop. "My God, admiral, will it really look like this?"

"The real thing will be even better. You see, captain, projections are one thing but actual spacecraft" – he pointed to the hangar door – "will be undeniable evidence of an attack by evil aliens. The internet kooks and the conspiracy nuts, and the mass media of course, will help us spread chaos all over the world. Then we step in as the saviors of humanity, declare martial law, and take control. Captain York, this program is infallible. It can't possibly fail!"

Captain York thought this plan was insane. Conte was clearly a nutcase. He'd taken this job because it promised access to super high technology and he wasn't disappointed. York gulped as he saw the drones quickly take their positions over the world's major cities. When the motherships made their appearance in the skies he almost shit his pants. It was the coup de grace.

"When Parkinson sees what we can do he and his gang of do-gooders will be completely demoralized. So will that arrogant Pietro Adolfone."

Captain York was convinced. If the real thing was half as good as the demo no one would have the slightest doubt that the earth was being invaded. He regarded his commanding officer. For Conte to talk of arrogance was like Alec Baldwin lecturing on humility. York observed a fanatical gleam in the admiral's eyes. Crazy he might be, but Conte was undeniably an organizational genius. It was due to his efforts that this Command and Control Center existed. York had to admit that the base, and this setup, was impressive. He was standing within the very hub of the Terrestrial Space Command.

A part of him was disgusted with the misuse of this technology for nefarious ends. Yet he admitted to himself that he wanted to see this system in action. It would be the most spectacular thing in the skies in world history. Captain York wanted to be on the winning side.

Pache Island

Watney Granger got up from his bunk against the wall opposite the manufacturing equipment. It was almost 2:15 in the morning. He heard the steady breathing of Lois MacDonald sixty feet away. Great care must be taken, for even the slightest sound was magnified across the hard concrete floor. Lois had moved her bunk close to the biomaterial, Granger thought bitterly, as close as she could get to her precious little babies. He had gradually realized after several weeks that MacDonald was a psycho. He wanted nothing more to do with her. Soon an aircraft would come to pick up the biomaterial, stacked on pallets. He wanted to be out of here before the action started.

An hour ago he had quietly opened the single door that provided the facility's only entrance and exit. There was a small canoe floating beside the small pier about 200 feet away, directly in front of the building. Finally, the break he needed! For almost three months, as the weather grew colder, he had checked the area every night while MacDonald was sleeping. He had quietly walked around the facility, familiarizing himself with the area by moonlight. Even if he had a boat he might not be able to make it if the sea was choppy and the wind was up. But Watney was determined to leave before it was too late. Now, tonight, he would take his chance, rough seas or not. Fortunately it was very warm and dry for December, although the water would be very cold. Fortunately the sea was unusually calm after this balmy day. His luck only had to hold for another hour. He walked in his sock feet back to his bunk and grabbed his overnight bag, which contained underwear and socks, a couple of shirts and slacks, and his toiletries. He put on his waterproof boots and a heavy leather coat.

Watney Granger exited the facility and tossed his bag into the canoe. He grabbed the two oars clumsily and began rowing as fast as he could toward the opposite shore. After he had gone a quarter mile the seas began to roughen. In the darkness he thought he heard other craft approaching on the water. He turned toward shore and saw an aircraft land in back of the building. Several men got out and rushed into the facility. They were going to see him! He pulled even more frantically until his boat was going around in circles. Panic! He had to settle down. He stopped rowing. A big wave came toward his little canoe and almost capsized it. With both hands he began to throw water out of the little boat, which was almost one-third full. The shore was still a long way away. Another big wave came and overturned the boat, and it began to sink. As he held on for dear life the canoe, with his clothing, disappeared under the waves and he began to go under. Just as he was about to gulp seawater into his lungs he felt hands grasping him. His body was hauled over the side to solidity and safety.

Two silent Special Forces Rigid Inflatables with their diesels turned off dropped twenty Navy Seals into the water, a quarter-mile from Pache Island. Infrared showed several men already inside the building. Several armed men were outside guarding the perimeter.

Watney Granger was hauled over the side, coughing, and the pilot struck him over the head. Too damn much noise! What was this civilian doing here anyway? Either he was one of the locals or one of the scientists at the place. The pilot covered the man's mouth with duct tape and let the boat drift. As the Seals swam toward shore in the cold Atlantic sea water, the pilot could not discern any unusual movement on the water's surface. Hopefully they were not too late because the transport plane had landed several minutes ago.

The Seals were equipped with infrared headgear and knew that another force was already on land and had probably spotted their positions. As one the men stopped, still under water, spread out, and launched themselves onto the beach in a surprise attack. It was important that the invaders be stopped before they could escape with the bioenhancer. Under no circumstances, their orders stated, was any weapon to be fired inside the facility. Their orders were to secure the facility and then call in one of the White Hat aircraft to pick up the product. When a Seal gets his orders he obeys them to the letter, and his life not factored into the equation.

Five of the men on shore dropped to the ground under Seal fire just as two large palettes were wheeled out of the building.

One of the men from the building, much larger than the others, waved everyone to the ground and issued commands. Shots rang out. Two of the Seals, now lifeless, dropped their weapons. The palettes were quickly wheeled back into the building. In a minute the Seals smelled burning metal. The Black Hats were cutting an opening at the back of the building! The Seals were now pinned down from enemy fire but the men rushed the perimeter with guns blazing, heading toward the aircraft. Five of them were hit but took the men defending the plane with them, even as the palettes were wheeled out to the waiting aircraft under covering fire. Desperate, the remaining Seals knew they had only one chance to prevent the airplane from taking off: a suicide rush. There was no hesitation as the men yelled battle cries and began firing at the aircraft, still under fire from the others defending the building.

The Seals were not successful. The big man and three survivors got the palettes loaded and the aircraft took off into the night.

Minot AFB, Minot North Dakota, two weeks later

"What is a Gulfstream 200 landing here for?" Technical Sergeant Bailey said as he watched a civilian aircraft landing on the airstrip in the early morning, a half-hour after dawn.

Sergeant Bailey squinted eastward into the rising sun. He saw several figures hurrying out to unload something from the civilian plane. Puff balls of water vapor came out of their mouths.

"I don't know sergeant," Lieutenant Nikata replied. "It doesn't look authorized."

It was cold, North Dakota cold in January. Both men were outside inspecting one of the B-52H Stratofortresses that belonged to the base's 5th Wing.

Lieutenant Nikata was born in Anchorage Alaska and was used to the cold, but Sergeant Bailey was from Arizona and cursed the weather up here. Nikata was slightly overweight and often referred jokingly to his "blubber." His dark, almost aboriginal face was in contrast to the pale countenance of Bailey, who was freezing his ass off as usual. Bailey wanted to finish their inspection as quickly as possible.

Bailey cursed. "Fuckin' idiots! Remember the time somebody tried to take some nukes out of here? Five of us almost died."

"I'm with you sergeant but the base commander said that there might be some unusual things happening around here."

"To hell with that, sir," Bailey said. "The chain of command is breaking down. I don't trust my orders anymore." Nikata's eyes glinted.

The two men looked at each other. "Secure your weapon, Sergeant," Nikata ordered. "We're going out there to take a look."

"Yes *sir!*" Bailey replied enthusiastically. Minot was an Air Force base, not a dumping ground for civilian cargo. Something fishy was going on.

The two men ran out toward the landing strip and the airplane. Lieutenant Nikata saw six men dressed in black combat fatigues unloading heavy plastic cases onto a truck. He didn't recognize any of the men and they were not in uniform. "What the hell are you doing here?" he barked at one of the men.

"Get those pallets loaded!" a voice boomed from the inside of the plane.

Lieutenant Nikata walked up to the cargo entrance, which was located in the middle of the aircraft. He could see that the old Gulfstream had been modified. All of the seats had been taken out, leaving room for cargo. A cargo door had been inserted in the middle of the fuselage. Straps had been secured to the inside of the fuselage, which the men would use to secure themselves. He looked up. Confronting him was a huge man, not in uniform. "Get out of here sonny. You're in way over your head."

"Who are you?" Nikata said, trying to keep his composure. The man was almost seven feet tall and moved with the easy grace of one who had seen a lot of action.

"One more time," the man replied easily. "Leave now and everything will be jake."

"I want to know what you are doing," Nikita answered stubbornly. Nikita was holding his gun at his side and Bailey was behind him. The man before him wasn't worried. If he wasn't concerned, it meant that he could get into action mighty fast.

"You don't have a need to know son," the man said, leaping lightly onto the tarmac. "Ask your base commander."

"Stay with me Sergeant," Nikita said to Bailey. "We're going to see what these guys are up to."

The big man heard and turned. "Do what you want but stay out of the way."

Nikita called the base commander. "Do you know what's happening out here sir?"

"Yes Lieutenant. I am incapacitated at the moment. Don't interfere with those men, they'll be out of here in twenty minutes."

Nikita and the sergeant were freezing their asses off. The two men ran over to the base commander's office. Through the frosted windows they saw that the staff area was surrounded by men in black, form-fitting clothing. Their weapons were drawn. "Private army, goddamit," Nikita said.

"This has gone too far sir," Bailey said. He ran back to the Gulfstream and inspected the markings on the aircraft. There was nothing except a strange symbol of a woman's head on the tail of the plane. Rays of light came out of her head. Bailey didn't recognize the symbol even though he was an expert on military decals.

The two men watched as the intruders completed the unloading of the plastic cases. One of the men ran over to a couple of modified F-22s sitting on the landing strip, ready for takeoff. "What are those things doing here?" Bailey said. "This is the 5th bomber wing!" The planes looked like modified F-22 Ds, but the fuselage was much wider. Not much storage space in there. The invaders were wheeling both pallets, one to each of the aircraft.

The men quickly loaded the F-22s. Two of the black-clad men got in and the planes took off. The other men ran out of the staff building and piled into the Gulfstream, which took off into the clear morning sky.

Nikata and Sergeant Bailey walked quickly over to the staff area and burst in. "What just happened here, sir?" Nikita demanded.

"What do you think just happened, lieutenant?" Commander Dawkins shouted. "For thirty minutes my Air Force base was taken over by a private army! They caught us totally unprepared," he sputtered.

"Who's they, sir?" Sergeant Bailey asked.

"I have no idea, sergeant. My orders came through as usual. I was told that a team would unload several pallets of classified material and take off from here using modified F-22s that were to be left on the tarmac. When the bastards came in and I asked them what they were doing, they turned on us."

"Sir!" Lieutenant Nikata said. "Respectfully request that we find out just what the hell is going on. Sir!"

Dawkins looked gloomily at his energized subordinates. "Request granted lieutenant," he said as cheerfully as he could. "Report back to me when you find anything."

"Yes sir! Sergeant Bailey here will assist me."

"I took pictures sir," Bailey said, producing a small phone in one of his big hands. "Nobody even saw me."

Dawkins looked at Bailey, sizing him up. "Good work Sergeant. Carry on lieutenant."

Dawkins sent everyone out of his office and sat at his desk, severely shaken. He knew precisely what had happened. It meant failure.

Manhattan

Two days later Marcus was walking out of the NYC Bank building at 7 p.m. after running the stairs. He had gotten up twenty flights for the first time without feeling like he was going to keel over. He felt great! His lung capacity was getting bigger and his legs were now solid rocks of muscle. It was time to go home and get ready for the president's State of the Union speech. For some reason Darcy wanted to watch it. Marcus didn't mind because they'd sit on the couch together and maybe something good might happen.

When he got home he opened a can of spaghetti and ate it cold. The trading was good today. He had personally made a tweak to one of their algos which made the company some more money. Carla's old man had personally sent him a commendation. It had gone on his record and he got his first raise. He hadn't had to use his web of light in weeks. That was good because he still feared Belial might get him again.

An hour later Darcy walked into the living room and sat down on the couch, patting the space to her left. "Come here Marcus."

Marcus was only too glad to do so. He recognized the signs that she might be interested. If the president didn't put her to sleep. Darcy put her head on Marcus' shoulder and felt very comfortable. "I wish we had a fireplace," she sighed.

President Foley gave his speech. He looked preoccupied, as if he was avoiding things that were a lot more important than the stuff he was talking about. Marcus saw that Darcy wasn't even paying attention. He wondered why she wanted to sit here and do nothing. Then he noticed that she had a blissful smile on her face and her arm around him. Oh. She didn't care about the speech, she just wanted to be with him. Marcus smiled and felt pretty good about that. He tried not to move and disturb Darcy even though his left leg was cramping up.

After the speech ended the reporters gathered around Senator Fazio, from New York, the leading Democratic candidate for president. Marcus was just about to flip the remote off when he noticed something strange about Fazio. He looked closer. Although Fazio was fairly good-looking, something black and ugly surrounded his body; as if there was a sickness attached to him. Marcus blinked and looked closer. Yes, there was definitely something there.

Marcus pointed to Senator Fazio. "Darcy, do you recognize that guy?"

Darcy raised her head from his shoulder and looked at the TV. "Yes, he's evil." She told him about what she had seen at his fundraising party.

"Do you see anything different about him?"

Darcy looked closely. "No. But I don't like him."

Marcus shrugged. "OK. I'm probably just tired. I thought I saw something." He wondered whether Fazio knew anything about those Tau. If he did he was a real scumbag. He'd have to ask Parkinson about him.

When he turned to look at Darcy Marcus turned on his web of light. He could see a halo around her. It was utterly gorgeous, about ten feet in diameter, dominated by pale blues, greens, and yellows. There was a column of beautiful dark purple that ran down from over her head to her feet. She had no black in her halo, like Fazio, except for a black area over the top of her heart.

"What's the matter Marcus?" Darcy asked. He was staring at her but also through her. The look on his face was one of astonishment and admiration.

"Wow, you are really beautiful Darcy."

She got up from the couch and pirouetted. "That's refreshing! What's happened to bring on this sudden burst of appreciation?"

"Uh, I've been sort of seeing things."

Darcy shook her head slightly and laughed, her eyes twinkling. Marcus was a nut but every now and then he surprised her. "What sorts of things, Marcus?"

Marcus sometimes felt that she was a hundred years old and he was just a little kid. "This is kinda hard to say. I can see halos around people."

"Halos? Like around my head?" Darcy looked up and tried to see hers.

"Yeah, but around the whole body. It goes out at least ten feet," Marcus said.

"You aren't just teasing me, are you dear?"

"No Darcy, I swear, no kidding around. You have some really beautiful colors in your halo." Marcus was excited. He described what he saw. When he mentioned the black area around her heart Darcy teared up quickly.

"Geez I'm sorry Darcy." Marcus rose from the chair and took her in his arms.

She looked up at him almost in awe. "How did you know about that?"

"About what?"

Darcy lowered her head. "That's where I keep all of the things that have hurt me."

"Wow. I'm not just seeing things."

"What else do you see Marcus?"

Marcus squinted into the black area. A bunch of images popped into his head. "I see a rundown house and a drunken guy walking into a bedroom. There's a girl there, probably about 15 or so ... shit! That's you Darcy! Is that scumbag your old man? He's going after you! He— "

"Oh Marcus, stop!" Darcy cried. "I still can't face that memory." She sat down. Marcus could see how upset she was.

"I'm sorry Darcy. I didn't mean to—"

She stopped him by putting a hand on his shoulder as he sat down beside her on the couch. Tears were running down her face. Marcus felt that the situation was too delicate to do anything or say anything, so he just sat there. After about thirty seconds or so Marcus could see that she was happier, even though tears kept running down her cheeks. He thought: I obviously don't understand women. "It's OK Marcus," Darcy said. "For some reason I feel ... comforted. Some of the emotional upset has left. I feel better."

"You mean just by me looking at whatever that was, it made you feel better?"

"I don't know, maybe it was you pointing it out to me and me looking at it. I can see what happened more clearly now. It's like you uncovered something inside me and then I was able to see it better. I can see it from both sides. I—" Darcy stopped, startled.

"Yes?"

"I can even see it from my father's point of view now. He was so pathetic Marcus, but now I see the burdens he was carrying."

Darcy looked better now and Marcus decided to leave it alone. He wasn't good at this interpersonal stuff. From now on he should just keep his mouth shut. "Let's go to bed Darcy. I'm too tired to keep my eyes open." Especially after that boring speech.

Parkinson said he was evolving and maybe he had some new ability now. He got up and went into the bathroom, looking at himself in the mirror. Nothing was different.

The next morning at work Marcus turned on the web of light. He could see all of the traders' halos. Carla's had a lot of bright, splashy colors, mostly red and yellow, with a lot of gray around the heart area. He also noticed a black spot on one of her kidneys.

After work he spoke to her. "Hey boss, how are you feeling?"

Carla looked him over. "Funny you should mention that. I've been having back pain, and a fever."

"Go see the doctor and have him take a picture of your right kidney."

Carla was surprised but felt his concern. "What are you now, a doctor?"

"Just do it," Marcus said firmly. That was the only way to deal with Carla. "Have him take a picture of your right kidney." He walked over to the elevator and got in, wondering if his perception was correct. He'd ask Carla about it later.

When he finished jogging the stairs Marcus walked outside into the cold winter air. It was seven o'clock and the wind was blowing. He walked down Park and crossed 48th, looking for a taxi. A yellow cab suddenly swerved into the intersection and a door opened. A friendly face leaned out of the window and said, "Get in! Looking for a ride, aren't you?"

Marcus shrugged. Pretty unusual behavior for a cabbie but he was getting cold. The cabby got out, flipped open the driver's side back door, and Marcus got in. He felt a prick on his left wrist as the cabbie moved around him and got back in the cab. "82nd and 2nd Ave, right?" the driver said, smiling into the rear view mirror.

"Yeah, how did you know?"

Marcus leaned over, looking for the operator's cab license and picture. There was no identification.

"I recognized you from the news. You're that Marcus Riley guy, right?"

Marcus groaned. An autograph seeker! "Uh, I'm not that famous that you should know where I live."

The cabbie laughed softly. "Sure, it's easy. I just looked you up on the people finder site." The cabbie maintained a flow of conversation as the streets went by. Marcus grunted appropriately when necessary. He was getting really tired and he didn't feel so good. His head was swimming and he broke out in a cold sweat.

"What's the matter Riley?" the cabbie said. Marcus couldn't tell whether he was being sarcastic because he was having trouble seeing. The cab was going in the wrong direction.

"Hey, where are you taking me?" Marcus heard the words slur.

The cabbie laughed. "Somewhere you can't cause any trouble, boy. By the time you wake up you'll either be dead or a superman." The cabbie laughed at his joke. "Get it? When you wake up you might be dead!"

Bobo Jacoby saw that Marcus was out cold. Now we'll see how tough he is. He wanted to take off his latex face mask but he still had one more job to do. He was on east 110th, close to Jefferson Park in East Harlem. Perfect. He turned left onto 1st Ave and parked the cab to the side. Nobody was around except a couple of shivering dopers. Jacoby opened the back door and dragged Marcus out. He was a strong man but the kid's dead weight was really heavy.

"What's the matter with him?" one of the dopers asked.

"Ah, he's either drunk or really sick. Tried to puke all over my cab," Jacoby replied. "He doesn't have any money, the bastard."

The man laughed raucously. "Take his credit card. Or leave it for me."

"This piece of garbage is all yours. I think he might be contagious." Stupid fucking druggies, they don't deserve anything. A bunch of useless eaters. Jacoby dropped Marcus' body on the frozen ground, walked back to his cab, and drove away. He glanced out of the passenger side window. The two dopers were going over the body.

Twenty minutes later Marcus woke up, shivering with cold. Something was wrong with his normally responsive body. He was being rearranged from the inside out but something was going terribly wrong. He gagged and threw up, spasming. He was cold, so cold ... "Darcy!" he cried. With the last of his energy he struggled to his knees. He knew he wasn't going to make it. "Darcy ... I love you ..."

Marcus collapsed and his head hit the ground with a smack. The body spasmed for a minute. Gradually his limbs relaxed and he lay sprawled out as the warmth slowly trickled out of his body into the cold night air.

CHAPTER **27**

I T was midnight and Marcus still had not come home. Darcy was worried because they were supposed to have gone out to a cute little bistro that Marcus liked. What could be keeping him?

Suddenly she thought: Carla Waverley! Oh, if he was with her, she'd never forgive him. She dialed, Carla answered impatiently. "This is a bad time Regier. What do you want?"

"Is Marcus with you?"

"No. Why should he be?"

"He didn't come home tonight and I wondered ..."

"Forget it. I haven't seen him since he left after our post-trade meeting." She was about to ring off when she had a thought. "Darcy? Are you still there?" Carla's voice softened.

"Yes."

"Tell Marcus thanks."

"For what?"

"He told me to have an x-ray of my right kidney. They found a small tumor on it."

Despite her dislike of the woman, Darcy gasped. "Oh no!"

Carla knew Darcy hated her. Even so, the woman's fundamental humanity and concern was refreshing. "Not to worry, I'm going in for surgery tomorrow. The doctor says I should make a complete recovery."

Darcy was relieved. "That's good. But I need to find Marcus."

"I'll call around. Maybe somebody from work saw where he went. If I find out anything I'll call you back."

It was now 12:30 in the morning. Darcy wanted to call Thom Madigan but Thom probably couldn't do anything and she knew he went to bed early. Then she thought of Holderness. Would the police be better? She couldn't decide what to do. A cold fear pierced her stomach. Somehow she knew Marcus was in serious trouble. Oh God, don't let anything happen to him.

Her phone rang. "Darcy, this is Carla. One of our traders saw Marcus get into a cab on 48th heading uptown on Park, a little after seven."

"Thanks Carla."

"Are you going to call the police?"

Darcy hesitated. "No," she said, making up her mind. "I'm going to call an old friend who I think can help."

"OK, good. If you don't get any results call me back. My father knows a lot of people in New York. We'll find him."

Darcy's eyes were tearing. "Thank you Carla." As she hung up the phone her hands began to shake. Clumsily she dialed Holderness' private number, which he had given her after she'd left Royalty.

Holderness Parkinson was in bed when he heard the phone ring in his office next door. He was a light sleeper and always kept the door open in case of emergencies. He padded out of bed and stepped on the floor switch. The little stand with the old-fashioned corded red phone was already out of the floor. Its sharp ring sounded shrill and anxious in the silence. A horn honked out on the street as he picked up the receiver.

"Holderness?"

"Is that you Darcy?" Parkinson spoke calmly, quickly switching the feed to his big desktop monitor.

"Yes. Oh, thank God you answered. Something has happened to Marcus." The older man's composure settled her nerves a bit. "I think he's either dead or dying."

"Yes my dear. Please give me any information that could help me locate him."

Darcy sighed gratefully. It was like Holderness not to ask questions. She needed help and he was there for her. She told him about their plans and what Carla had told her.

Holderness Parkinson's mind worked swiftly. This was the third life-threatening situation involving Marcus Riley. First, the incident in midtown, then the attack on the stairs, and now this. He should have seen that somehow Marcus was at the center of this crisis even though the main events seemed to be flowing around him. Even a trained intelligence officer makes mistakes. He'd have to bring Marcus in. "All right Darcy, we'll find him."

"But what will you do?"

"I have contacts in New York my dear, people who will be able to locate Marcus. Don't worry." He could see that her lovely face was strained and her eyes were bloodshot. He smiled. "Try to get some sleep Darcy. As soon as we find him I'll call you."

"I don't care what time it is, call me."

"Yes, certainly. I have to ring off now and set things in motion."

"All right Holderness." Darcy had never felt so mournful in her life.

Parkinson broke the connection and called the New York office of Homeland Security. This office liaised with the NYPD and other law enforcement agencies in the city. "Barney, it's Holderness."

Barney Jacobsen had trained with Parkinson thirty years ago at the Agency. "Hello Holderness. I assume this isn't a social call."

"Indeed not. This is White Hat business. We have to find a young male, twenty one years of age, six feet six inches tall, with black hair. Images to follow. Last seen in a Yellow cab at 7 p.m. last evening on Park and 48th, heading uptown." Parkinson sent the images of Marcus.

"Yes of course," Jacobsen said. "We know precisely who he is. We've been keeping tabs on him ever since that little incident in midtown. I think I might have a general idea where he's at."

"Excellent Barney! I knew I could count on you. When you find him, bring him in. I'm pretty sure he's the key to this mess." In the back of each man's mind was the question: when would the bioenhancer be released? It had now been over forty-eight hours since the incident at Minot.

At two-thirty in the morning Darcy's phone rang. She was reading a book on the couch but hadn't turned more than three pages. "Darcy Regier?" a voice asked.

"Yes!" she screamed. "I'm sorry, yes, this is Darcy Regier."

"Please come to Lenox Hill Hospital, room 108," the voice ordered. "A driver is waiting outside your apartment."

Darcy hurriedly threw on her coat and raced down the stairs of their walkup. Sure enough, a car was waiting at the curb, its headlights providing enough light for her to see through the frozen night air. On the side door was a decal that read "Goldman Driving Service." She opened the passenger door and took her seat.

"Holderness Parkinson sends his regards," the driver said. "I'm Patrick." He was uniformed, wearing a dark cap with a gold headband around it.

"Is he all right?" Darcy asked, afraid to hear the answer.

"We don't know ma'am," Patrick replied. "The hospital says he's in pretty bad shape."

Darcy clutched her purse, sick with fear for Marcus. She said nothing as the car pulled out into traffic. She felt safe with this man. In less than five minutes the driver stopped at 100 East 77th. He got out and walked with her to the hospital entrance. "Thank you so much," she said gratefully. Patrick nodded, approving the girl's good manners.

They walked up to the desk and the man flashed his identification. "This way please," the nurse said, and led them about one hundred feet down a hallway. "He's in here."

Darcy entered the room and saw Marcus hooked up to a lot of medical equipment. His face was gray in the pallor of death. He was completely motionless. Her purse dropped to the floor and she raised her hands to her face. She turned to the nurse. "May I hold his hand?"

The nurse smiled. "It couldn't hurt. Please be silent. The doctors have examined him and they don't know what is going on inside his system. All we can do is provide fluids and monitor his progress. He's fighting for his life, obviously, but he's young and strong."

Darcy sought for reassurance. "Will he make it?"

"We don't know. Having you here should help." The girl would do a better job than she ever could. "If you notice any response call me right away."

Darcy turned to the driver. "I'd like you to stay. Would you mind, oh please?" She noticed that Patrick was small and wiry, built like a gymnast.

Patrick smiled. He felt protective toward this girl; her quiet beauty made him feel like helping her. He moved a chair over to the right of the door so he could guard the entrance. His orders were to keep the target safe and terminate any intruder. He was to assume that any entry, unless hospital personnel, was hostile.

Darcy walked slowly over to Marcus' bed and gently took his hand. It was so cold! He was barely breathing. Darcy felt that if she squeezed his hand too tightly she would lose him. Darcy had never prayed before in her life, but she prayed now. Patrick sat silently in the chair against the wall by the door. His quiet presence comforted her. She flashed him a smile and whispered "thank you."

Darcy waited, hour after hour, but Marcus did not awaken. She wondered whether his spirit had left his body; whether the hand she held was just the shell of the essence of the man she loved. She was not a religious person. Now she understood what religion was really about. It was about love and life and the precious and sacred nature of existence.

Patrick sat silently, watching the woman. She exuded an almost palpable aura of love and concern. His heart ached. To have a woman like that! What would it be like? He hoped this guy was worth it. Occasionally, the nurse walked the corridors and looked in. Other than an occasional sound from the street, the building was silent. Patrick carefully withdrew his weapon, checking the loads. Rumors were that Bobo Jacoby was in the field and had already tried once to eliminate Marcus Riley. Time dragged on. He would have to keep alert ... his eyes closed.

He jerked awake. Movement! Silently Patrick got out of his chair, crouching low just inside the doorway. In order to enter the room an intruder would have to turn to the right. He had the position covered without exposing himself. The door was open, inward against the wall. To his left he heard the faintest rustling of clothing in the hallway and estimated the distance at twenty feet. There was nobody on duty except the nurse at the front desk. He would assume that a hostile was approaching.

As Bobo Jacoby approached the door he sensed the presence of others inside the room. There were no windows, he was guessing, but his instincts were good. His orders, direct from Venetti himself, were to make sure of Riley. But if there were others in the room it could get messy. He was irritated. He could have easily killed Riley this evening. This operation was sloppy and he didn't like it: a sloppy commander can get you killed. Maybe it was time to go back to Brazil. He had a little house there, on the Atlantic, near Sao Luis ... his mind was wandering. That was another bad sign. He would have to concentrate.

The door to the room was open. Reflected in the glass he could see, in the very dim light from the fluorescents at the front desk, the vague outlines of Riley, a woman sitting next to him, and a shadowy figure crouching about six feet from the door. The fool! Didn't he know better than to expose himself like that?

Jacoby was ten feet from the door when he made up his mind. He could kill everyone in the room in a few seconds. That might arouse the duty nurse and get the police involved. He should have eliminated the stupid woman but he had not been able to find her. Damn that Riley. He had the devil's own luck. He would withdraw and trust to that stuff he injected to kill the kid.

Patrick heard the faint sounds of someone withdrawing back down the hall-way and breathed a sigh of relief. The woman was still sitting there, her head bowed, probably asleep. He would stay with her until she was ready to leave. He waited, completely motionless, for five minutes without hearing anything. Patrick cautiously edged out into the hallway. All clear. As he approached the door he saw that it was angled just right to mirror the faint reflection of its occupants. He froze. The intruder could have had all of them! He cursed himself under his breath. An amateur's mistake. He should have closed the door. Shaking, Patrick entered the room, shut the door, and resumed his post.

An hour later Darcy woke up. Was Marcus' hand just a little warmer? Or was that warmth from her own hand? No, the icy coldness was definitely thawing. She looked into his face and saw that its pallor had faded, and was just a little less gray. Encouraged, she squeezed his hand very softly and thought she felt a faint response. She looked back. The driver was still in his seat near the door. Darcy gave him a grateful smile.

Half an hour later the nurse made her final round of the night. "Looks like he's slightly better. You've been doing a good job."

Darcy sniffed and smiled forlornly. "I hope so."

"The doctor will make his rounds in an hour or so." She looked at Patrick. "You don't have to stay here."

"I'll stay."

Fifteen minutes later Marcus' eyes fluttered and he groaned. Darcy almost screamed with anxiety. She said as calmly as she could, "Patrick, will you get the nurse please?"

"Where am I?" Marcus mumbled. Life was returning to his features, Darcy noticed, and his breathing was deeper. Darcy watched as Marcus took a few slow, deep breaths.

"How do you feel young man?" the nurse asked.

"I'm totally exhausted," Marcus said. He was having a hard time speaking, as if he had never done it before. "But there's a good feeling inside me, instead of that ... blackness."

"I'll get the doctor," the nurse said.

A few minutes later a very tall man in a white lab coat with large hands and feet entered the room. "Hi, I'm Dr. Russell."

Darcy hoped he wasn't clumsy. Those big paws looked like they belonged to a basketball player instead of a medical professional. She need not have worried.

The man's movements were practiced and gentle. He quickly checked Marcus' vital signs and examined him. "You'll do, Marcus Riley," he said with satisfaction.

Darcy clapped her hands in delight. "Is he going to make it?"

"Yes. In fact, I've never seen anyone who has readings like this guy. It's probably due to my consummate skill as a physician."

Darcy saw that the color had completely returned to Marcus' flesh. A glow of health surrounded him. "That's impossible. Half an hour ago he was basically dead."

"I told you I was good," Dr. Russell joked. "Seriously folks, I've never seen anything like it. We received a call from a guy who called himself Barney at Homeland Security. He said we had an important patient that would either die or make a miraculous recovery."

Holderness! Darcy thought. He must have been behind all this. She moved away from the bed as the doctor unhooked Marcus. "How do you feel?"

Marcus stretched. "Inside I feel fantastic. But I don't know how to use my muscles anymore, like I was ... reprogrammed or something."

"Try to sit up," the doctor suggested.

Marcus felt like a little child. Clumsily, he got his arms underneath him and sat up. He waved his arms around and moved the muscles in his fingers, testing them. "OK so far."

Darcy noticed that Marcus was different, in a good way. Whatever the darkness was that had surrounded him for so long was gone now. He looked even better than the old Marcus.

"Darcy!" Marcus noticed her for the first time. He tried to get out of bed and fell to the floor. His legs didn't have the right muscle memory.

"Oh Marcus, are you all right?"

Marcus laughed. "Never better Darcy. I just don't seem to be able to remember how to use my body."

He didn't seem worried and neither did Dr. Russell. Marcus struggled to his feet and stood, a little unsteadily. "Try to walk," Russell said.

Marcus clumsily raised his leg and put one foot in front of the other. "One step!" he said cheerfully. He raised his other leg and put it in front of the other. "Two steps!" In a couple of minutes he was walking around the small room normally. He looked up at Dr. Russell, who was three inches taller than he was. "Wow, did you play basketball?"

"Yes I did, at Alcorn State, forward. I didn't have the talent to make it in the Association. So here I am."

"A better use of your abilities, doctor," Darcy said. "You saved his life."

Dr. Russell grinned. "I did no such thing. We have no idea what caused Marcus' illness and we have no clue how he recovered."

A voice came from the back of the room. "Maybe it was the power of love." Patrick was looking at Darcy.

Darcy flushed and looked into Marcus' eyes. They were happy eyes, for the first time in a long time. Marcus took Darcy awkwardly in his arms. "Maybe it was."

As they were leaving the hospital Marcus thought: I'm going to find the motherfucker who tried to kill me.

C‍HAPTER **28**

A‍DMIRAL Randall James sat at his desk in the Joint Staff area in the Pentagon.

His two year term was almost up and he couldn't wait to get the hell out of DC and back to his old job.

He still had not forgotten that meeting last year with Blair and Pantera, the CIA director. He was out of the loop at the NSC and so was the Joint Chiefs of Staff and everybody else except for Oleg Brentkowski, the NSC advisor. The National Security Council was supposed to advise and assist the president on national security and foreign policy. Lately Brentkowski was giving the orders and everybody else was just nodding their heads. General Dickson, the JCS chairman, had assigned him the task of finding out who was behind Brentkowski. It was hopeless. Something was about to go down and the highest military advisory board in the country was clueless.

He'd had another conversation with that dickhead Draco Smith last month in his private office. Smith seemed to be an important liaison for some shadowy group outside the chain of command. This group appeared to be behind the NSC Advisor. James was skillful at extracting information from general conversation but Smith was close-mouthed and he didn't find out anything useful.

"Admiral James," Smith had said. "There are some wild rumors going around the Pentagon, you've probably heard them, but they're nonsense of course. This loose talk has even gotten to the White House, and State. We want you to hold the fort over there at the NSC. Brentkowski is counting on you to squelch any, uh, inappropriate suggestions."

James was angry. "Who are you guys? I'm the Vice-Chairman of the JCS. How do you presume to give orders to me? You are way out of line."

Smith smiled but it wasn't really a smile. "I'm not here to answer questions, admiral. Let's just say it would be a good idea if you were to calm the waters."

James was getting more and more irritated. He took a deep breath and tried to relax. "Look Smith, I know that you're a member of some private group outside normal channels. You are involved in something that could affect the national security. If you level with me and tell me what's going on, I might be able to help."

Draco Smith sighed. "Unfortunately for you, admiral, there's a new chain of command and you're not part of it. It would be better for you to do as I suggest."

At that Admiral James exploded. "Is that a threat you little punk? Who the hell do you think you are?"

Smith smiled sadly. "The world is changing too fast for you to understand admiral. It's out of your hands now, and the JCS, and the Agency too. Just do as you're told or you know what will happen."

James was appalled. This little shit was threatening his family! He rushed Smith but the younger man stepped easily and lithely out of the way. "Hold on there old man, don't start something you can't finish." Then Smith opened the door and walked out.

There was a knock on the door, interrupting his reverie. Captain Borgess, his personal aide, walked in. "Sir, I just received this but I don't know what it means." He handed over a printed message in the form of an old telegram:

WHITE HAT NETWORK

YOU MUST INFORM THE PRESIDENT OF THE THREAT TO THE COUNTRY AT THE NEXT NSC MEETING. THE PRESIDENT IS WILLING TO ACT BUT HE NEEDS YOUR SUPPORT. TALK TO PANTERA ...

James read the rest of the message and felt a sense of dread. He couldn't believe what was happening to the United States of America.

CIA Director Felix Pantera received the same message on his secure private line. "Talk to Admiral James," it said. Pantera slammed the printout down on his desk and swore. Telling the president was futile. The man had no power; he was just a figurehead now.

The next day Captain Borgess met Felix Pantera after he testified before the Senate Intelligence Committee in the Hart building, in room 219. "Excuse me sir, may I have a word?"

Pantera looked nervously about. As usual a few reporters hung around, hoping to get some information about the closed hearing. The CIA director didn't feel like discussing anything in front of them. He nodded and said, "Come with me."

Borgess followed him down the hallway, trailed by a couple of curious media with cameramen. Pantera couldn't blame the nosy bastards. This was supposed to be a democracy and they were just doing their jobs. If they only knew the real situation. He was a man with cataracts trying to inform the blind.

Pantera led the way outside the building and into a government limo. Borgess got in beside the CIA director. Pantera signaled the driver to raise the soundproof partition. "What's this all about?"

Borgess unlocked his briefcase and brought out the White Hat telegram. Pantera groaned. "So you got it too."

"Yes," Borgess said. "Admiral James suggests that one of us tell the president in private."

Felix Pantera shook his head. "That won't do captain. If we tell the president privately he's out on a limb and that could be dangerous for him. We're supposed to be defending the country. If we do this it has to be out in the open."

Borgess agreed wholeheartedly, but he knew that Admiral James was under extreme pressure not to rock the boat. Borgess was hoping the DCI would volunteer. "That's true DCI Pantera. Someone has to inform the president, but Admiral James feels constrained."

Pantera flared silently. "Yes captain, all right. I'll do it at the next NSC meeting." He knew he was going to make himself very unpopular with NSC director Oleg Brentkowski and his pals. He remembered Draco Smith's warning to smooth the waters at the last inter-agency meeting. Was Brentkowski part of that shadowy group? What would happen to him if he told the president?

Captain Borgess confirmed his fears. "Sir, I suggest that you protect yourself."

Pantera grinned. "Thank you captain, but screw that. If I'm going down it will be in a blaze of glory."

Captain Borgess was impressed. You never knew about a guy until the bullets began to fly. The DCI had stepped up and was going to take one for the team if necessary. His eyes widened in respect and he held out his hand. "You're a winner sir, and thank you. If you need anything from me let me know."

Felix Pantera took the hand and shook it firmly. He felt the euphoria that comes with volunteering for a dangerous mission. It would be like the good old days when he was the youngest station chief in history, back in Kabul. During the time he was there it was the most dangerous place in the world. He pulled down the partition and instructed his driver to drop the captain off at the Pentagon. Then he went home and took a long, hot shower.

Chicago

Marcus had made no progress whatsoever finding his attempted murderer. One of the bank's employees had seen him enter the cab but no one had gotten the license plate number. The son-of-a-bitch had gotten clean away. He would have to give it up, but it rankled.

Now he was sitting on the couch in the suite he and Darcy shared at Royalty Services, re-reading the Harry Potter series. He was very bored and didn't know why he was in Chicago. In a couple of hours he'd go to dinner with Darcy and Parkinson. Like the Madigan dinner at Daniel in New York, the evening would be for Darcy and not for him.

Their suite had three rooms. A sitting room with a TV and a stereo system with a nice view of downtown Chicago, a bathroom, and a bedroom. Darcy was in the bedroom parading around, trying on clothes. Marcus didn't want to go in there because he'd want to take them off. That was for later. The Royalty building ? owned by Parkinson ? was an old-fashioned brownstone with eight stories, all of them occupied by Royalty personnel. He hadn't realized what a large operation the old man had put together. It was pretty impressive.

After his brush with death in New York, Holderness Parkinson had moved both of them out of the city. Parkinson insisted that Marcus' life was too valuable to risk. Marcus suspected that his concern was more for Darcy than for him. It was impossible to argue with the older man. He had arranged things with NYCBank and also with the little modiste, Audrey Quenioux. The old man found her a nice location in a fashionable section of downtown Chicago. She was setting up another Audrey's and planned to keep Darcy as busy here as she had been in New York. Holderness had refused to let Marcus out of the building.

Parkinson had called him two days ago at their New York walkup and told them he and Darcy must leave New York. "I'm sorry Mr. Parkinson, but that's impossible. I'm a valuable employee for NYCBank and I'd leave a big hole if I left. My boss would think I'm a traitor."

The big man had smiled knowingly. "I've had a talk with Carl and he's cleared it with NYC."

Carl? Oh yeah, he must mean Carl Waverley, Carla's father. "I don't want to leave New York. I like it here." Marcus had no intention of abandoning Carla and her crew in Equities Services. He was an important member of the team now. He was getting better and better at his job. Even Bethany accepted him as one of the team.

Parkinson laughed. "I admire your youthful courage Marcus but there have been three attempts on your life so far. At the very least, I'd like you and Darcy to come to Chicago this weekend as my guest."

"Do you know anything about the guy who injected me with that poison?"

"Not yet. We're looking into it."

Marcus brightened. He'd only have to miss one day of work if he went for the weekend. Maybe the old man could find out something. "I could sure use a vacation. What will we do in Chicago?"

Parkinson smiled. He had no intention of letting Marcus out in the city except for dinner on Friday night. "On Friday night we'll eat at Alinea. The squabs there are to die for. On Saturday I'll take Darcy out shopping on State Street. On Sunday there's the Bears playoff game at Soldier Field."

"That's great!" Marcus wasn't a big football fan but he'd sure like to see an NFL game live. "How will we get there?"

"I'll send my private jet out there tomorrow. A driver will pick you up at 7 p.m. Make sure you're back from work on time."

When Darcy came home at 9 p.m. after another long day, Marcus told her about their weekend. "Marcus, I can't. We're having a show on Friday night and I have to be there."

"Call Parkinson," he ordered. For Darcy, her old boss was the final authority on everything.

Marcus had loved being picked up in the limo, and Parkinson's private jet was a revelation. White-gloved waiters served them champagne and a five course meal during the flight. When they landed at O'Hare another driver met them.

"I could get used to this," Marcus exclaimed on the ride downtown. He had his arm around Darcy. Her beautiful blond head lie on his shoulder.

"It's like old times."

"Do you miss it?" Marcus was a little alarmed at her enthusiasm for her old life.

Darcy raised her head. "I miss the luxury, the refinement in everything, but not the other stuff."

"Good. Because nobody else can have you. You're mine."

Darcy was thrilled. Marcus had never been possessive. She had always wondered whether he really wanted her. Maybe that horrible bioenhancer had worn those drugs off for good and cleaned him out. She looked him in the eyes. "And you're mine Marcus." This time he didn't flinch or flush up.

When Parkinson personally ushered them into their suite, Darcy clapped her hands in excitement. "My old rooms!" Darcy was delighted.

The old man's face softened. He really did care for her. Marcus wondered what would have happened if he had continued down the road of drugs and sex. What would Parkinson have done if he had hurt Darcy? He gazed at the bulky old man standing there in the doorway. Marcus realized that Holderness Parkinson was probably a dangerous man to fall foul of. He was a bear, and experienced in the affairs of the world. Hell, he probably ran the world. "We have reservations for 10 at Alinea," Parkinson rumbled. His eyes twinkled. "Look your best."

Darcy smiled and walked over to the closet. Her clothes were all there, hung up perfectly. Her other stuff was folded neatly in her old dresser. "Oh Holderness, I'm going to enjoy myself tonight." Darcy looked impish.

"That was my intention, my dear," Parkinson replied with contentment. Just to look at her made him feel thirty years younger. The boy was coming around as well. He looked ... enhanced in some way. He'd heard about the injection and knew that Marcus was lucky to have survived the bioenhancer. He knew the boy wanted to discover who injected him and hoped that Marcus would cooperate in his own investigation. Tomorrow morning would be the real test.

Marcus, half asleep, was startled out of his memories by the sharp thud of a book dropping on the hardwood floor. A familiar bass voice said, "Harry Potter."

"Yes," Marcus said. He was reading Harry Potter and the Deathly Hallows. It was an oldie but a goodie, and he always forgot plots. "I've always been fascinated by magic. These books provide a fascinating possible reality." Marcus hoped the old man would go away, for Harry and Hermione were in trouble again. They didn't have to leave for another twenty minutes.

Parkinson nodded. "That author is clever on many levels."

Marcus looked up. "What do you mean?"

"The entire series describes a battle of bloodlines."

Marcus straightened. "Does it?"

"What's the first thing that happens when Harry enters Hogwarts?"

Marcus thought a moment. "The sorting hat."

"That's right. The hat sorts according to bloodline. The Slytherins are the group most concerned with bloodline purity."

"Yes that's right," Marcus acknowledged grudgingly, "but so what?" As usual, Parkinson was too deep for him.

"The Slytherins are all crazy are they not?"

"Well yeah, I guess."

"That group represents an inbred genetic line with little diversity. They are obsessed with eliminating the 'mudbloods,' those who have a lot of genetic diversity. Their leader, the dark lord Voldemort, is certifiably insane. Voldemort is a destructive psychotic with no conception of the higher truths of humanity. He lacks compassion and integrity and has no soul. That is the result of inbreeding in the name of genetic purity. The sane people in the book are those with the despised 'mudblood' heritage, like Harry and Hermione."

"I suppose so. But aren't you reading too much into this story?" Marcus flipped the book over and read the back cover. "Supposedly J. K. Rowling wrote it for her little son."

Parkinson smiled knowingly. "Indeed Marcus, perhaps I am."

Marcus wanted to know more but just then Darcy opened the door from the bedroom. "Holderness! It's nice to see you."

The old man's eyes softened. "You look wonderful tonight my dear."

Darcy smiled. "You have a way of making a woman feel cherished and appreciated, dear Holderness."

The older man glanced at Marcus and winked. Marcus didn't feel the need to flatter Darcy all the time but he could see the advantages if it was done with sincerity.

Parkinson looked at his watch. "It's time to go."

Marcus enjoyed his dinner at Alinea. The food was fantastic, and Darcy sparkled. Parkinson told them about the White Hat network and asked Marcus to be in his private office at 9 a.m. the following morning.

"That's Saturday," Marcus protested. "I want to do the town."

Parkinson chuckled. "You and I have something more important to do than that." Parkinson spoke mysteriously.

Marcus felt like a child next to this guy. The note of natural authority in his voice created an air of unquestioned obedience. Marcus felt he must agree. The guy was shelling out a lot of time and money on them and his hospitality was generosity itself. "All right." Marcus grumbled, a little petulantly. "I want to find the asshole who injected me with that biotoxin."

"We just might find out something about that tomorrow," Parkinson hinted, and walked down the hall to the elevator.

Saturday morning at 9 a.m. Marcus was still lying in bed. Darcy had left an hour earlier to look at clothes with Audrey Quenioux. There was a knock on the door. Marcus knew it was Parkinson. "All right! I'm getting ready!"

Marcus heard a rumbling chuckle outside the door. He got dressed quickly and within ten minutes stood outside the bedroom door looking down at the old man, who had taken a seat on the couch. "I thought we'd take a drive over to Soldier Field," Parkinson said.

"Why bother? We'll be there tomorrow."

"Humor me Marcus. I have something to show you."

Parkinson took him to the basement of the old building, where a number of fancy limos were parked. They got in and the driver nodded. "Hello Marcus, I'm Richard."

Marcus looked closely. "Darcy used to talk about a Richard at Royalty Services."

So this is the famous Marcus, Richard thought, studying the image in his rear view mirror. "You are taking good care of her aren't you?" Parkinson wanted to know the same thing. He turned his head slightly toward Marcus.

Marcus summarized their relationship in one sentence. "I did at first, then I didn't, now I am,"

Richard scrutinized him in the rear view mirror for several seconds, and then relaxed. "OK. Because a lot of people care about Darcy, including me."

Parkinson nodded his head a millimeter. Botsford had expressed his sentiments completely.

"All right, I get the message." Marcus felt like the little kid on the playground just before he got thrown into the dumpster.

The limo came out of the basement garage and on to N. Cleveland, then took a left on N. Lincoln. Just as their vehicle was about to turn onto Clark three automobiles approached with their tires screeching. One came north on Wells; the other two from opposite directions on Clark.

"It's Nitti!" Parkinson shouted. It was the first time Marcus had ever seen him flustered. "Richard, drive like hell if you can." Parkinson quickly grabbed his phone.

It was too late. The three vehicles surrounded the limo. Horns were sounding as Nitti's vehicles blocked the three-way intersection. A man raced out of one of the vehicles, brandishing an automatic weapon. He smashed the glass with it and poked the weapon to the head of the driver. A police siren sounded in the distance and the intruder mouthed an obscenity. "Get your ass back here!" a voice cried. The intruder ran back to the vehicle. All three of them took off in different directions.

"The traitors!" Parkinson bellowed. "I thought we had an agreement with Carcelli."

"What?" Marcus cried as the three cars disappeared. "Who's Carcelli?"

"The mob boss, head of the Crims in Chicago." Parkinson was calm now. "We have to act fast."

He looked over at Marcus from his position to the left of the manchild. "I need to know where Nitti's vehicle is going. Can you do that?"

Marcus eyes him suspiciously. "Why would you think I'd be able to?"

"There is no time for idle chit-chat my boy. Tell me where that vehicle is going. The one that took off south on Clark." Parkinson spoke in his command voice.

Marcus stifled his irritation at the old codger. This was supposed to be a vacation! He activated his web. He didn't feel any malevolent presence, so those demons on Tau must have stopped monitoring him. In his mind he saw a map of the city in real-time.

Parkinson saw Marcus looking intently out in front of him, about five feet away, into the front of the limousine. The boy's eyes moved slightly as if following a moving object.

"Got it. There's a car with three guys in it heading south down Wells. One of them has hairy arms – probably Nitti – and the other two are his goons." Marcus played back the scene in front of him, as if it were on a recording and his mind a 3-D viewing screen. He saw the three vehicles moving backwards along the timeline, meeting at the intersection, and moving away. He fast-rewound the mental image and knew that all three vehicles had come from a downtown nightclub. He rotated his perspective to the front of the place and saw a red neon sign with an outline of a shapely female figure. "They all came from a place called the Cat's Meow."

Parkinson's reaction was nothing like Marcus had expected. The old man sat back on the plush leather seat, radiating satisfaction.

"Aren't we going to go get the bastards?" Marcus said.

"This was just a test, Marcus. Nitti is part of our network."

"What? Those mobsters?"

Parkinson chuckled. "Yes. Luca Carcelli, the Chicago mobster, is one of our strongest supporters."

Marcus was flabbergasted. He'd heard about the Crims, of course, but the idea of a bunch of murderers and drug dealers on the good side didn't make a lot of sense. Then he had a realization. "So that's why you wanted me to come to Chicago. That other stuff was just bullshit, about going to the game."

Parkinson was unruffled. "I'm afraid so. You see Marcus, we have much bigger fish to fry."

"What kind of fish?"

"We're going to stop the Slytherin psychopaths who have been running our planet for the past several centuries. You might just be our secret weapon."

Felix Pantera got a call on his mobile the evening after talking to Captain Borgess.

"Felix, don't do anything stupid."

"Who is this?"

"You know damn well who it is Pantera. And you know why I'm calling." He heard a click.

So Draco Smith knew about his meeting with Borgess this afternoon. It was clear to him what would happen if he opened his mouth at the next NSC meeting.

CHAPTER 29

White House Situation Room. Meeting of the National Security Council

THE Vice President, Robert Sensenbaugh; Secretary of State Marianne Hilton; James Gaitner, Secretary of the Treasury; Gary Colbert, Secretary of Defense; National Security Advisor Oleg Brentkowski; Vice-Chairman of the Joint Chiefs of Staff Admiral Randall James; DNI Gen. Blair Dennis; CIA Director Felix Pantera; and President Martin Foley sat around a long rectangular table in the Situation Room of the White House. A stack of papers had been placed at each seat, meticulously sorted and arranged. Foley was an old-fashioned guy, Pantera thought, insisting that all business conducted at the NSC be done with hardcopies. He was also a neat-freak.

Felix Pantera pulled out a sheaf of papers from his briefcase and tapped them with his index finger, meeting Admiral James' eyes. James nodded back as the president began the meeting. Pantera knew that he had James' backing, but he would have to do the heavy lifting. The CIA director looked sympathetically across the table at the president. The poor guy, he's trying to do his job the best he can but he doesn't even suspect how events are flowing around him. Today he's going to get a punch in the mouth and we'll see what he's made of.

"The first item on the agenda is the situation in Bolivia," the president said. "Insurgents have attacked La Paz and are threatening to overthrow the government and nationalize the oil and gas industries. As you know, Bolivia is the second largest oil producer in South America. We see a dangerous tendency for the country to fall into Venezuela's orbit. I want everyone's input and a firm decision about what to do before we leave this meeting."

Two capital cities in Bolivia, Pantera thought. What a mess! Probably why Foley was so involved. The president was fascinated with political science and foreign relations. He thought that Foley should have been a diplomat, or an academic.

Pantera listened with half an ear as everyone deferred to Brentkowski. An hour later he was ready to rock the boat.

"I believe that concludes our meeting today gentlemen," President Foley said, shuffling papers. "Oleg, if you'll coordinate with Marianne and Gary, we can get the ball rolling."

Everyone rose to go. Felix remained seated.

"One moment Mr. President."

All eyes turned to Pantera, surprised. Admiral James said, "That's right Mr. President. Felix has something important to tell you." Brentkowski must have suspected something because he moved quickly to herd the president out of the room in good-old-boy fashion. He placed his left arm firmly around the president's shoulders and turned his body so that his back faced toward Pantera. "Agenda complete," Brentkowski said heartily. "And a very good decision it was, Mr. President." Over his shoulder he threw the CIA director a black look.

"Mr. President!" Foley turned around, facing the CIA director, shaking off the thinner Brentkowski's grip.

"Yes Felix?" Foley was irritated.

Pantera knew that the president had a press conference today, and needed to be briefed. He made it quick. "There is a grave security threat to the United States that has not even been mentioned in your briefing papers, sir."

Brentkowski turned around. He was a thin, nattily dressed man in a perfectly tailored suit. Coldly intelligent and emotionally sterile, he exuded an air of cultured refinement.

Brentkowski spoke sharply. "Watch it Felix! Don't tread in waters that are too deep for you." So Oleg Brentkowski knew about the bioenhancer. Was he also involved with Draco Smith and Bobo Jacoby and their group?

"What's this all about?" Foley asked, confused. He was a man who liked order. Above all he liked information.

"Approximately five days ago a deadly bioenhancer was shipped out of a research laboratory on Long Island to at least two dozen American cities ..."

"How do you know that?" Brentkowski shouted.

"... and is scheduled for release sometime in the near future. It is being described as a new test vaccine but in actuality it is a dangerous airborne gene alterer with the potential to kill nine out of every ten people who come in contact with it." There. It was out. He was a dead man walking.

"Don't listen to this man," the NSC Advisor said firmly, glaring hard at Pantera. "I think the pressures of his job have finally gotten to our CIA Director."

The room went silent. Everyone was looking at him strangely, as if he had just announced the landing of aliens on the White House lawn. Brentkowski stared down everyone in the room as if to say, "You don't really believe this crazy story, do you?" Secretary of State Hilton laughed nervously. Secretary of Defense Colbert fidgeted, drumming his fingers impatiently on the table. The vice-president coughed and Treasury secretary Gaitner walked to the door, ready to leave. The others were about to follow suit. Felix realized that Brentkowski's strong personality was dominating the room and turning sentiment against him. He found his voice again.

"Mr. President, if you want confirmation, call Minot AFB and ask for Commander Dawkins." Felix was upset that he'd used his hole card and endangered Dawkins, but millions of lives were at stake.

"Close that door!" Brentkowski barked, startling everyone.

"I agree with the president," Admiral James said in support. James moved closer to Pantera, standing beside him. "What's this about, Felix? A black program gone out of control?"

Brentkowski whipped his head around and growled at James.

Felix nodded gratefully to the admiral. "Mr. President, I have a briefing paper." He held it out to Foley. "It's a fairly long document but I'd like you to study it tonight. It tells the story of precisely what Admiral James has mentioned: a black program that has gone seriously off the rails. It contains a summary of a secret covert operation that has subverted the chain of command."

"Interesting you should say that Felix," President Foley said. "Lately I have not been satisfied with the quality of my daily briefs."

Oleg Brentkowski saw his position slipping. "Give me that paper," he ordered, holding out his hand to President Foley like a teacher demanding a homework assignment.

The president bristled and turned to his national security advisor. "Why shouldn't I read Pantera's document? He's the head of our intelligence network."

Brentkowski turned on Pantera and James. "You know what will happen now."

The president's eyes widened. It was a thinly veiled threat and had no place here. "Oleg, what are you saying?"

Brentkowski forced a smile. "I'm sorry Mr. President. You've known me long enough to know that I sometimes say things I don't really mean."

President Foley relaxed a little. The group waited to see what the president would do. Out of the corner of his eye the president saw Admiral James's shocked expression as he met the eyes of the CIA director. In that look was anger, sympathy, and fear. Why was Admiral James afraid of Oleg? The president made a quick decision. He smiled and clapped Brentkowski on the back with his right hand. It was a gesture completely out of character. Foley tried to guide Brentkowski out of the room. "Not a problem Oleg. You get busy with that Bolivian situation."

Brentkowski stopped short and his gaze sharpened. He studied the face of his nominal superior, wondering how much he knew. One thing was clear: he had to get his hands on that paper. He turned and smiled, confronting Pantera. "I'll take that Felix," he said smoothly. "Sounds like a very important national security matter. I'll look it over and brief the president tonight."

Pantera couldn't resist. "I'm sorry. This document is for the president's eyes only. You don't have a need-to-know."

Brentkowski's eye lit up and he bristled with anger. "*I* don't have a need to know? Who do you think you are Pantera?"

"This nation's coordinator of intelligence, Oleg." Felix answered using the familiar, which he knew would irritate Brentkowski. Pantera knew that the hidden meaning behind their little play was beyond everyone else in the group except maybe Treasury Secretary Gaitner and DNI Blair Dennis. Gaitner had already walked out.

"This is a national security matter!" Brentkowski barked. He spoke very calmly and coldly. "Give me the paper, Felix, and all will be well."

Despite himself Pantera shuddered. That was the same phrase Draco Smith had used to him after he had been threatened. Felix tried to keep his voice from shaking. He turned toward the president. "Here's your document sir." Felix placed it into his hand, waiting to see what Brentkowski would do.

The National Security Advisor forced a smile and faced Foley. "Mr. President, if you have any questions about that document don't hesitate to call me. I have not seen it." He turned and looked at the front page. "The White Hat Network indeed.

Mr. President, there have been a lot of unsubstantiated rumors flying about lately. We've told you about them in your briefing papers." He glanced at Admiral James and the CIA Director. "Certain individuals who should know better are being foolish beyond permission and are abandoning institutional rigor. I'll call on you this evening and present a more rational and objective assessment of the information."

The White House

President Martin Foley was beat. He had worked a full day, given a press conference, appeared at a Democratic fundraiser, and spoke on behalf of the Washington Kiwanis at the University Club. Now, in his private study in the White House, he pulled out Pantera's document from his briefcase and groaned. Over 200 pages of data. The president got to work and was immediately absorbed. He grew more and more angry as the hours slipped by. President Foley was reading the same data passed around to all White Hat operatives, and it contained the most sensitive information. It was almost midnight when he completed the document and heard a knock on the door.

"Mr. President!" Oleg Brentkowski entered the room with his most disarming smile. Profoundly irritated that his Secret Service agents had let the man through, the president nevertheless fell victim to the man's real charm.

"It's a bit late."

"I'm afraid not Mr. President. We have a serious national security issue when our DCI and the VC of the Joint Chiefs are running around spreading unsubstantiated rumors."

Foley was very tired and he decided to be blunt. "Has a bioenhancer been distributed within the United States?"

Brentkowski thought quickly. "Of course. It's an exciting new biomaterial that we're sending to a number of research facilities for testing." His eyes brightened. "This new biomaterial has the potential to end disease forever in the human organism."

Foley could see that the man was clearly excited. "Is it true that this material kills nine out of every ten subjects?"

Brentkowski frowned. Obviously the information in that paper was of high quality. If that were so, what else was in it? How much did the president know? He pasted on a smile. "At the moment it does. But the material simply needs more research and testing. Is it credible that we would abandon such a promising new biotech discovery? One that could literally change the future of the human race?"

Foley nodded his head. "Of course not Oleg."

Brentkowski was torn. James had told the president to call Commander Dawkins at Minot. Had he done so? It had been ten hours since the NSC meeting. If he had, the game was up and the timetable for release would have to be accelerated. That would not go over well with Adolfone, of whom he was deathly afraid. He raged inwardly as he sat across from the president, who was seated at his desk. This stupid man, supposedly representing democracy. What a sham! Close on half a billion rabble scratching and clawing at each other, when a ruler was needed to keep them in line.

"Have you talked to Commander Dawkins, Mr. President?"

Foley almost jumped out of his chair. "Of course! I can confirm this report with a simple phone call."

Brentkowski was relieved. If only the man would wait until morning... "I'm sorry sir, I can see that you're very tired. You can call Dawkins first thing tomorrow. Then we'll talk."

The president nodded. He was very weary. "All right Oleg, I'll go to bed. I have another long day tomorrow." Yes, he thought, and the second item on his agenda tomorrow was a long talk with Felix Pantera. Or maybe the first item.

Brentkowski smiled. "As do we all, sir. Good night."

The Pentagon, JCS Staff Area

The next morning at 6 a.m. President Foley called Minot AFB in North Dakota. Sitting presidents don't call commanders in the field. However Buzz Metzger, aide to Air Force General June Jones, arranged everything from his office in the Pentagon. Admiral James and President Foley both saw a harassed and excited female sergeant at her desk. "Mr. President. I'm afraid we've had a series of unfortunate and unexplainable accidents this morning."

"Please explain."

"Commander Dawkins, Lieutenant Nikata, and Sergeant Bailey were all found dead in their beds this morning."

Admiral James' face went white.

"Please explain sergeant," the president said.

"Staff Sergeant Ellis Jordan, sir. Neither Commander Dawkins nor Lieutenant Nikata showed up for the morning briefing. Sergeant Bailey failed to report for duty. We found all three of them in their beds, faces and bodies contorted. Medical staff reports that all three men died from brain aneurysms. All four arteries to the

Circle of Willis at the base of the brain were ruptured. It's impossible sir, simply impossible. Security swears no one entered the sleeping quarters of the three men. There is no explainable cause for their deaths."

"Thank you sergeant." The president was completely numb. "Please give my condolences to the families, and carry on with your duties." The president eyes teared up and when he spoke his voice was heavy with emotion. "Understand that all of you in the military have my full, unqualified support and admiration."

"Yes sir," Sergeant Jordan mumbled. She began to cry.

"Buck up sergeant. This is a sad loss for me personally as well but we must carry on for the good of the country."

"Yes sir."

"Please call this number any time there are further developments. Leave a message if I don't answer." President Foley gave her the number to his private office.

"Yes sir, and thank you."

"Thank you sergeant."

Foley hung up and met the eyes of Admiral James. The president told James about Brentkowski's visit last night. "Do you think Oleg had anything to do with this? He was acting very strangely at the NSC meeting yesterday."

James frowned. "I don't know sir. My impression is that Oleg is aligned somehow with ... the Black Hats, I'd guess you'd call them."

"I don't understand why this Nikata and Bailey were killed. And why Commander Dawkins? Unless ..."

"Yes sir," James acknowledged. They had both been briefed on the details of the incident at Minot several weeks ago, when an unauthorized military force had taken over the base for half an hour.

"Are you part of this White Hat network? What is it? What possibly could have caused these deaths?"

"I'm only nominally involved, sir. Your best bet is to talk to DCI Pantera."

"Have you seen this document admiral?" Foley asked, holding it up in the air.

"No sir. The first I heard of it was when Felix brought it into the Situation Room yesterday."

"Very well." The president held out his hand. "Thank you for your cooperation admiral. I'm beginning to suspect that you've placed yourself in danger. I appreciate it."

James took Foley's hand and felt a strong clasp. The man's hands were dry as well, indicating that he wasn't panicking. "Now is the time for all good men to come to the aid of their country."

The president smiled. "Indeed admiral. My next agenda item is to speak to Pantera."

"I can help you with that sir." James picked up his comm device. "Felix? This is James. The president wants to speak to you."

Pantera appeared on the screen in a rumpled suit. "Did you get any sleep last night Felix?" Foley asked. The DCI ran his hand through his bushy gray hair. "Not much Mr. President. But I have some information. A Colonel Rodgers called from Fort Meyer and said that three of the principals involved in the distribution of the bioenhancer have been killed at Minot AFB under very suspicious circumstances."

"Yes, we know about that."

"You do?"

"Yes Felix. My question is, how was it done? There's something in that document you gave me about that."

Felix was glad the president was in the loop now. "Scalar weaponry. Yes sir, very sophisticated stuff. Apparently the Black Hats can target selected persons with harmful vibrations that can cause disease and even death."

"For God's sake!"

"Yes sir, apparently the technology was reverse-engineered from downed ET spacecraft. That information comes from Colonel Rodgers, who is the military's top investigator into ETV crashes and ETs. Apparently the technology is being misused. Those who use the weapon for harmful purposes are themselves killed."

"That science-fiction report you sent me is true?"

"I'm not sure how much of it is true, sir. Colonel Rodgers swears that the description of the new scalar technologies is spot-on."

"From now on I want all communications from the White Hat network hand-delivered to me personally, in my private office," Foley ordered.

"Yes sir!"

"It's great to have you on board sir," Admiral James interjected.

"It's great to actually have some reliable information," the president replied. "Now gentlemen, I have to ask you whether Oleg Brentkowski has anything to do with this."

"Unknown sir," Pantera replied. "I know that he's had dealings with some pretty shady characters from Army and Air Force intel. We have no actual evidence that he's involved in activities harmful to the United States."

"I agree sir," James affirmed.

"Your assessment of the reliability of information from Oleg," the president asked.

"I don't trust him," the DCI said matter-of-factly. "However, I have no evidence upon which to base my opinion. Just personal dislike."

The president sighed. "Felix, where do my briefing papers come from?"

Pantera laughed softly. "Excuse me sir, but I haven't the faintest fucking idea."

"I thought so. From now on I want you to personally brief me."

Pantera looked shocked for a moment. "I ... well ... I'm not sure of the reliability of *my* information."

The president winced. "All right. Who and what is this White Hat network?"

"You might not like this sir," Pantera replied.

"Go ahead."

"As far as I know it's run by a senior intelligence officer who works out of a brothel in Chicago. We're —" Pantera noticed he had identified himself with the group, and accepted it. "We're allied with organized crime groups throughout the United States who are helping us track the whereabouts of this bioenhancer. The Crims, you've probably heard of them. We're building a network of military, intelligence, corporate, and government people who are sick and tired of the direction the country has been going in."

The President of the United States listened in open-mouthed astonishment. "You're joking of course."

"I'm afraid not sir," Pantera replied. "I can tell you all about it at our first briefing."

The president sighed. "I've been completely in the dark, haven't I Felix?"

"You aren't the only one." Admiral James beside him concurred.

"Brentkowski isn't going to like not briefing you," Pantera said. "Especially when he finds out it's me. I suggest that you continue your daily briefs with him. We can go over what he said and compare the two information streams. I'll give you the straight dope."

President Foley raised his eyebrows. "The straight dope?"

"Sorry sir, a little expression I picked up from my time as station chief in Kabul."

Foley smiled. "I know a little bit about what went on there."

"Yes sir."

President Foley looked at his watch. "Speaking of daily briefs, I'm late for Oleg. Why don't you come to my private White House office every night at 11 p.m.? We'll go over everything that happened during the day."

"All right, but you might not get much sleep afterward."

The president shrugged. "I don't sleep much anyway. Alice usually kicks me out of bed because I'm mumbling all the time."

Pantera laughed. "I'll tell you about my night life sometime."

As Felix left the president he wondered whether he would wind up like Commander Dawkins.

The White House

President Foley decided to be completely objective.

When Oleg Brentkowski strolled into his office at 8 a.m. he greeted the man with his usual affability. He brought up something relatively uncontroversial. "What's the latest in Bolivia?"

Brentkowski seemed startled. "Oh yes, that. The station chief down there has offered the rebels ten million dollars and a guarantee that their lands will not be attacked by government troops. That just might do it."

"That's all well and good. But what about that ambitious president, who says he wants to consolidate and unify Bolivia under one government?"

The NSC advisor became irritated. These petty little disputes! He stifled his anger and waved his hand negligently. "Not to worry, Mr. President. A little greasing of the wheels and Rosario will cooperate."

Now that he had an idea about hidden background events, the president was able to read Brentkowski a lot better. He could see that the man wanted to discuss other issues. Oleg's breeding and upbringing in a wealthy family favored a subtle and nuanced approach to social situations, even in private. He decided to be blunt. "Did you have those three men at Minot killed?"

A split-second look of shock and then rage appeared on his advisor's face, which was quickly smoothed over. Brentkowski studied the president carefully. "Why would you ask a question like that, Martin?" he asked with genuine concern.

Foley was disgusted with himself. Brentkowski was now showing his charming side and masking his real feelings. "Did you?"

Brentkowski sat silently.

"I know about the exotic technology and how Commander Dawkins was killed," Foley remarked.

It was as if he'd fired a gun at him, Foley thought afterward. Brentkowski shot from his chair. He spoke with suppressed rage. "Mr. President, I strongly advise you to keep to the affairs of state. Leave national security matters to me."

President Foley was himself outraged but he kept his cool. He had never faced danger in his life except for a couple of playground fights. He was pleased to be able to keep calm while his opposite lost his unruffled demeanor. This was the second time in two days that Oleg had reacted like this. Perhaps the real Oleg Brentkowski was the unstable anger case, his outward calm merely a mask. "You haven't answered my question Oleg."

Oleg Brentkowski realized that the game was up. It was too bad. Just another few months and the timing would have been perfect. He could see that he'd lost the president now. "What if I did?"

Despite himself, the president's eyes widened. "It was a stupid thing to do, was it not? You have just verified that a dangerous bioenhancer was moved out of Minot. You have also confirmed that the substance is a threat to the national security of the United States."

Brentkowski shrugged, his eyes gray steel. "No one will ever be able to confirm it."

The president paused for a few moments. "Why, Oleg?"

That night, President Foley described to Felix Pantera what happened to the national security advisor. "It was as if another person, or thing, was controlling him. His face twisted and his body shook. His voice even sounded different. He mumbled something guttural I couldn't understand. He told me that I wasn't among the chosen and would die with all the rest. Then he left. I was so shocked I sat there for half an hour. He scared me half to death I'll tell you. I couldn't believe it."

"Jesus Christ," Pantera said. "Did he look like one of those creatures in the Alien movies?"

The president nodded. "Yes. Just like that. Positively demonic."

"What do we do now?" Pantera asked. The lines of authority seemed to have dissolved. Here he was talking to the president like they were just buddies.

President Foley swallowed hard. "I know what I have to do." He leaned over and whispered something in the DCI's ear. "Just in case this place is bugged, you understand."

Pantera nodded. "That will really shake things up sir. Are you sure you want to do it?"

Was he sure? He knew he couldn't tell a soul, and certainly not his wife. "Yes," said the President of the United States. "I'm the only one who can."

Chapter **30**

Draco Tau

Belial fumed. He continued to personally monitor the hominid Mar-cus Ri-ley, and still hoped to kill the creature who had humiliated him. Unfortunately Ri-ley was not accessible unless he turned on his mental device. The hominid had already proven that he could not be killed in this way. It frustrated Belial that he did not know how the hominid did this, or how he had survived their battle. Even more upsetting, it appeared that events on the hominid planet were now evolving in an unsatisfactory way.

Belial picked up his communication device and summoned his chief scientist, Qa-Hrrzl, to meet him in his private chamber.

Belial's order did not find the planet's chief geneticist in a sanguine mood. As he entered the chamber of Belial he bowed low in obeisance to the great one.

"What is this I hear about the target date being moved forward?" Belial spoke softly. That was a bad sign. Qa-Hrrzl would have much preferred a satisfying roar.

"Sire, I know that you have little patience for tiresome explanations and excuses."

Belial nodded. Qa-Hrrzl felt a little relief, for he had precisely identified Belial's mood. "With your permission I would like to explain the exact situation to you." He knew that if he attempted to make excuses or justifications he might be killed where he stood.

Belial sat silently, unmoving.

"Sire, my calculations are constantly being upset by the volatility and unpredictability of over eight billion of the hominids. It is similar to tracking the flight of the Shiga as it swings randomly to and fro in the sky. Therefore the Harvest target date, once so perfectly established, is now fluctuating on the timeline as events move with startling rapidity. As the Harvest time approaches the situation becomes more chaotic as information spreads widely amongst the target population. It is always so, sire. As the hunted become aware of their plight they squirm and squeal and run quickly in all directions like frightened Argul."

Surprisingly, Belial laughed. "You have a way of putting things, scientist," Belial acknowledged. "But failure is unpardonable."

These words chilled Qa-Hrrzl. Was Belial suggesting an execution? Or even the unthinkable Zorghal? His skin tightened and he felt cold inside.

Belial saw this and nodded with satisfaction. "You understand the situation then. Either sit with us at the feeding in glory, or face ignominy."

Qa-Hrrzl bowed low once more. He exited the chamber and walked slowly back to his laboratory, lost in thought. The large-scale socio-behavioral data on the earthians had indicated a most precipitous date in the northern summer of the planet's rotation, during the third week of their July month. At any time during this period the life force readings of the hominids would be at their maximum. Any deviation from this interval would mean a less successful Harvest. Of course he, Qa-Hrrzl, had little control over events on the earthian planet. But he would be blamed if the plan went awry.

Belial would never understand the biological science behind the determination of the target date. The Life Force Index of the planet fluctuated with current events. The emotion of fear not only consolidated the earthian life force readings but also enabled it for release. Unfortunately the earthians, unlike the Xorg, did not stabilize properly in this emotional bandwidth. For the first time Qa-Hrrzl asked himself why the earthians seemed to move naturally toward the higher emotions. Higher emotions represent greater life force. Were these hominids superior? It was a heretical question. After a little thought Qa-Hrrzl dismissed this idea as too radical. What difference would it make? The entire Tau race needed and expected periodic Harvests for their survival.

As matters stood now the Trigger would occur sometime in late May, three weeks early. An acceptable Harvest was still guaranteed if further deterioration in the earthian socio-event matrix was avoided. Otherwise it was certain death for him. Qa-Hrrzl would have to light a fire underneath Ad-ol-fon-e tonight during their scheduled ritual. The hominid was losing control of his subjects.

Qa-Hrrzl shuddered with excitement, for the time of feeding was rapidly approaching.

The Cats Meow, Chicago

Luca Carcelli had finally established a working relationship with Holderness Parkinson. Their organized crime network was monitoring, as best as it could, suspicious activity in seventy targeted cities. They were working mainly with Colonel Rodgers at Fort Meyer, who knew some important people in the restricted programs who could identify the location of the bioenhencer cases. Unfortunately no one knew for sure how much of the biomaterial there was and where it was. Colonel Rodgers was doing the best he could to track Black Hat movements. Luca was focused on burning the assholes behind the distribution of the so-called vaccine. He didn't believe that 90% of the population could be wiped out. That was crazy. But he didn't like the feds, or whoever they were, fucking around in his city.

Luca remembered the first talk he'd had with Rodgers and Mutumbe, at Parkinson's insistence. It was a conference call moderated by Parkinson. He couldn't understand why a bunch of UFO flakes were involved. Colonel Rodgers had grave misgivings about "working with criminal scumbags." Each side was reassured by Parkinson, whose credentials and huge personality kept everybody on the same page. It took them a long time, but they had reluctantly agreed to work together. They didn't have any choice.

"That ET stuff is a load of crap," Luca said at first, when Colonel Rodgers told him that they investigated ETV's. "What does that have to do with tracking down this vaccine?"

Rodgers and Mutumbe told him some harrowing and unbelievable stories about their ETV investigations. "Carcelli, we think that there are non-terrestrials behind the people who are distributing this new biomaterial."

Luca just shook his head. Rodgers told him the story about his daughter and the reptile, and about what really happened in mid-town Manhattan. Luca's mouth dropped open. He recorded the conversation so he could show it to the boys.

"We're skilled investigators and we know a lot of people," Rodgers said. "We've still got above top-secret classification so we can go just about anywhere and talk to almost anybody. Hopefully, we can discover where the bioenhancer is going. Your …organizations …can help us to recover it before it's too late."

"Explain to me and the boys why no one in the media is talking about this damn bioenhancer or whatever it is." Luca was angry. "A threat to 350 million people and no one is talking?"

"Your friend Joey told you all about that," Rodgers replied. "It's too shocking to be believed. If you talk about ETs people think you are a lunatic."

"You knew Joey too?"

"Yeah. He was one of us. By that I mean he was, at least peripherally, involved in ET issues."

"That's one of the reasons we're in," Mutumbe interjected. "We're going to fuck up the people who killed our guy. Those motherfuckers are going out of this world as soon as we can send them to hell where they belong."

Luca's face lit up. After that he had no problem with Colonel Rodgers and Lieutenant Mutumbe. "That's the kind of talk I want to hear!"

"Now you tell me something Carcelli," Rodgers said. "Why should we work with a bunch of crooks like you? We can recruit combat-trained, honest personnel we can trust."

Parkinson was about to interrupt when Carcelli spoke. "Because time is running out, number one; and number two, because our guys can do the dirty work and nobody will suspect anything. It will just be business as usual. And number three, there are thousands of us already in place all over the country. We aint combat trained but we've seen combat if you know what I mean. When the bullets fly we know what to do. We're organized and we've got a nation-wide network already set up. *Capisci*?"

Colonel Rodgers was exasperated. "For God's sake Parkinson. What have you done?"

"Relax colonel," Parkinson replied. "I've talked with Luca here, and Battaglia in Dallas, and we've worked it all out. Like he says, we don't have much time. We're forced to be strange bedfellows. Here is how I want you to work together …"

Parkinson spelled it all out. He showed them the dark-red plastic cases with the biohazard stamp and the image of the Babylonian goddess Semiramis at the bottom right. "These are the cases in which the airborne bioenhancer is stored." He showed them the twelve aluminum cylinders in each case, each with their transponders at the tip. "If your boys see any of these things report it immediately." The Crims would be the civilian intelligence-gathering arm of the White Hats in the matter of the bioenhancer. Their organizations would monitor all targeted cities for hints that a cache existed in the city, and where it was. They'd keep their ears to the streets and report back anything of interest. Whenever possible the Crims would recover as many of the cases as they could. Rodgers, Mutumbe, and their network would keep tabs on the black hats and recruit as many white hats as they could. The plan was to recover every one of the cases and send them to a biolab for irradiation. "The only way to kill this stuff is by severe UV light and microwave radiation."

"How much of it is there?" Mutumbe asked.

"Unknown, lieutenant," Parkinson replied. "The latest intelligence is that several hundred cases have already been distributed and are being stored in secure locations. And not just in the United States."

"We're in the dark Parkinson," Luca said. "We gotta know where this stuff is before we can do anything."

Rodgers and Mutumbe agreed. "Our network can keep tabs on the black programs we know about. When we discover a cache or a shipment we'll let Carcelli and Battaglia know. But we can only get a fraction of them."

"Don't worry gentlemen," Parkinson said. "I think we might have an ace up our sleeve."

It was clear that Marcus Riley had remote sensing capabilities. The boy had proven himself in a real situation out on the streets of Chicago.

Royalty Services, Chicago

Darcy looked up at Marcus just before going to bed. "Marcus you look better than ever."

"I do feel fantastic even though I haven't exercised at all for several days." It didn't seem to matter. His body had unlimited quantities of energy now. Marcus' anger at the person who tried to kill him had evaporated. If he ever met the guy he would thank him.

Darcy noticed that the darkness that had been a part of him in New York was completely gone now. As much as she hated the people who had injected him with the biomaterial, she had to be thankful. There must be a good side even to evil people. Marcus didn't swear much anymore and he was deeper, but childlike. And really, really, sexy. "You better tone down a little. When you go out on the street you're going to be mobbed by women."

"I am? Wow, that might be cool."

Darcy frowned. "No it's not cool Marcus. You promised!"

Marcus laughed and took her in his arms. "I'm just teasing you Darcy." His eyes were sparkling. "I don't need drugs or casual sex like I used to. That was interesting but it's not a part of me anymore."

"OK," she said. "Then kiss me ..."

Afterwards they lay in bed talking. "Tell me about the adventure you had this morning."

"God you're beautiful," Marcus replied.

"Thank you Marcus. That's a non-sequitur, as Holderness would say."

Marcus laughed. "All right, here's what happened." He told her everything, and about his new ability. "Holderness said something about me being a secret weapon. Tomorrow morning he's going to test me."

"Test you? How?"

Marcus shrugged. "I don't know. I just hope it doesn't hurt."

The next morning Marcus found out what was in the complex and devious mind of Holderness Parkinson. The guy was like a computer except better. He never forgot anything. The old man's pattern recognition skills were almost as good as his. But above all he knew people. He could look at somebody for a few seconds and tell you their personality and temperament.

Marcus walked into his office and saw the old boy talking to someone in San Francisco. He practically told Marcus the guy's life story.

"An old friend, eh?"

"No Marcus. I just met Mr. Stargell ten minutes ago."

"Then how do you know so much about him?"

"Observation and deduction, mostly, and my knowledge of people. I've hired him to do a little snooping for us out there."

"But how do you know you're right about Mr. Stargell?"

Parkinson studied him from his big chair at the large oak desk. "How did you know where those cars were going yesterday?"

"You mean you have a mental viewer too?"

Parkinson laughed. "No my boy, I just know. I'm glad you came in because it is time for your test."

"I'm not a boy, just for your information. I'm almost 22 now."

Parkinson guffawed and began to shake with laughter.

Marcus frowned disapprovingly. "It's not *that* funny."

"O ho! It certainly is."

When he laughed like that his whole body shook like a vast pile of good-natured gelatin. The older man got up and walked into his private office. He punched a button and an elevator door opened up.

"Hey that's cool," Marcus piped, strolling over and stepping in.

Parkinson stepped in next to Marcus and gazed up at the manchild standing next to him. Whatever had happened to him that last day in New York had done the boy a lot of good. The bioenhancer, whatever its dangers, clearly had a beneficial effect on whoever survived it. That's what the reports said, and here was living proof. It seemed that Marcus' personality had even altered for the better. The boy positively exuded vitality and health. Right then he made up his mind. If the white hats won, no matter what happened, the psychopaths who were responsible would not be killed. Some kind of Truth and Reconciliation Commission would have to be established to draw out their poison, and make their deeds known to the people. They would have to be forgiven because the positive aspects of this biomaterial could not be ignored.

The elevator door opened to a basement filled with big screen monitors, servers, and other sophisticated computer and communications equipment.

"Wow." Marcus stepped out onto a black-painted floor that gripped the soles of his shoes, even though it was perfectly smooth. "This is almost as good as our octagon trading room at NYC. What's all this stuff for?"

"This is my workroom," Parkinson said, waving his arm. The rectangular basement was huge. Marcus guessed that on one side it was the size of the building's foundation, and half that size on the other side. The garage housing the limos must occupy the other half. The office, if you could call it that, was crisscrossed with I-beams on the ceiling and support poles on the floor, one every 30 feet or so. "I told you I was an intelligence agent. I spend most of my time down here." He patted his ample midsection. "In my younger days I was a field agent." Parkinson spoke wistfully. "Saw action in Iran, Lebanon, and Southeast Asia. Now I'm confined to my desk."

Marcus looked around. There were windows every twenty feet or so, with blinds that could be lowered or raised. This morning the blinds were up and beams of sunlight shone down like yellow searchlights in the dimly lit darkness. A series of eight monitors, each about ten feet wide and six feet long, had been suspended from the ceiling. The displays were arranged in a big circle around a central desk. At least two dozen others were working. They all greeted Parkinson as he escorted Marcus to the big desk in the middle of the room.

Parkinson sat down and put on a headset. Immediately, the images on the monitors changed.

"How did you do that?" Marcus asked.

"We've been able to get some of the suppressed black technology down here," Parkinson replied. "These interfaces are standard-issue in many of the hidden programs; low-tech stuff."

"What's the test?" Marcus asked, trying to count how many people were in the big room.

Parkinson pointed up. "Look at what's on these monitors and try to commit the information to memory."

On the monitor numbered "1" was a map of the United States, with black stars next to a number of cities. Another monitor displayed a list of bioresearch facilities and other secure facilities across the country. Red dots indicated each individual location and green stars for those in the same city.

On the third and fourth monitors the images swapped out, about one every five seconds. The images displayed the inside of laboratories with the name of the facility appearing in the upper right corner.

On the fifth and sixth monitors, images of the outside were shown, presumably the external view of each of the facilities.

On the seventh monitor a list of names was presented. Underneath the name was a picture of a person and a list of facilities he was associated with. Some names had multiple facilities.

The eighth monitor showed a dark red plastic case with a red biohazard symbol in the middle. In the bottom right corner of the case a small yellow symbol of a woman's head with rays of light emerging from it was displayed. A silver-colored metal canister that looked like a little rocket, about two feet long and eight inches wide, sat next to the case. Next to that was an opened case, with twelve of the gleaming canisters stacked in four rows of three cylinders each.

Marcus stared at the huge displays. His head shifted from side to side and his chair moved around on the noise-deadening floor. It helped that the text was displayed over an extremely large area, creating easy readability. The resolution of the images was so detailed that memorization was enhanced. After ten minutes or so Parkinson said, "OK Marcus."

"What am I supposed to do?"

"Examine monitor eight with its dark-red plastic case and the cylinders. These are the actual cases and canisters which contain the deadly biomaterial."

The stuff that had practically killed him. "All right."

"I want you to use the same procedure you used to track those cars of Nitti's. Tell me where on the map of the United States they are. The most likely places are displayed on monitors 3 through 6, but they don't have to be there. Take all the time you need. My people are here to help. If you need anything, ask."

Marcus activated his mental remote viewer and placed the images on monitor 8 into it. Then he loaded in the map of the US. Almost immediately, lines appeared in his web of light on the map. All of the lines branched out from an island off the coast of New York. Most of them then went to someplace in North Dakota before moving off to over 100 cities and towns on the map. Fifty-seven of the destination cities were not marked on the map. Marcus chose one of the cities and zoomed in. He immediately experienced vertigo and felt himself crashing into a building. He backed off, sweat running down his forehead.

"What's the matter?" Parkinson asked.

"I have to be careful with this thing," Marcus muttered, unaware of anything except his new ability. "I'll go slower this time." Marcus moved in from the air gradually to the ground. It was weird, floating above the clouds without being inside an airplane. He felt naked in the sky and wondered how he kept breathing with the wind blowing so hard around him. Then he understood that his perception was just a projection of his consciousness. Similar to his fight with Belial, his body was still in a chair in Royalty's basement. This was happening all inside his head! Or was it? Was he really out there or was he just seeing it in his mind? Or both? Marcus didn't have a clue. If he followed the little projection line he'd be at the MedTech building in San Francisco.

Marcus' consciousness floated down through the roof and into a clean room. One of the red plastic cases was sitting within a sealed chamber.

He punched a mental button and froze the image. "I've identified one of the cases and its location."

Parkinson slapped both palms on the thick wooden desk, scaring the crap out of Marcus. "Eureka! He's got it!"

The man looked like an overstuffed Humpty-Dumpty who had eaten too many marshmallows. Hopefully, like Archimedes, he wouldn't throw off his clothes and run out of the building.

Marcus unfroze his image and tracked the case back to New York. He ran the worldline backwards from there and saw the firefight between the Seals and some military guys in a Gulfstream. He traced the canister back to a factory in Charleston, West Virginia. He saw the case delivered to the Cherry Island lab on Long Island Sound where two scientists in white lab coats loaded cylinders into it. With a little probing he went outside the worldline of the plastic case and into the facility. MacDonald and Granger were talking and arguing. It was like having a built-in time machine in his own mind. Apparently he could move at will through time and space as long as he had an identifiable object or location to focus on.

"We need you to trace every one of the cases and their locations," Parkinson said. Marcus could tell the old guy was really excited.

"I can do it but it's going to take time."

"You have the con Mr. Spock," Parkinson said, getting out of his chair.

Marcus laughed. "Are you turning over control of the ship to your first officer, Captain Kirk?"

"Yes Marcus. Have at it. I'm going upstairs to have breakfast. All of this excitement is making me hungry." Parkinson walked over to the elevator and got in. They all heard the whoosh as it took off.

Marcus was too excited to think of food, and glanced at the clock. "I want to see how many of these I can get before 5 o'clock." Everybody in the office began to make side bets, and crowded around the whiz-kid. A good looking brunette sidled up to Marcus' chair. "When the cat's away the mice will play."

Marcus activated his mental view screen and decided to tag the cases that had gone out of North Dakota first. There were 77 of them. He picked the biggest bunch, a group of three, and began to follow their worldliness. These cases had been sent to Dallas, Texas, and were each housed in different facilities. He turned his mental screen to pause and asked the woman who stood next to him how to work the computer.

"My name is Barbara. There's no need to do that." She regarded Marcus with obvious interest. "You tell me the data and I'll enter it." Barbara put on one of the headsets and Marcus gave her the data. He looked up to see that the information on the monitors changed. "That is totally amazing. I'd like to learn how to use those."

"I'll show you sometime," Barbara said.

"I'd better not." Marcus was a little flustered. Even though he didn't want to sleep around anymore this woman was making his heart beat faster.

Barbara smiled. "All right then, I respect that. I know you're going with Darcy Regier. The boss wouldn't appreciate anyone messing that up."

"Thanks." Marcus relaxed and Barbara laughed. She knew she had gotten to this big manchild, and that was enough.

"Now for the next batch." He turned on his mental screen again and discovered that he could move it outside his head and make it bigger. The other workers saw Marcus staring out into space about five feet in front of his head. "What are you looking at?" Barbara asked.

"It's like having a high-definition 3D viewer that you can program with your thoughts. I don't know how it works but I can see anything I want and track its history."

Barbara held up one of the headphones. "This thing works the same way. I just think into it and the information device – it's not a computer at all, really – responds."

Marcus went back to work. Another batch of three had gone to Los Angeles. As he followed their trajectory through spacetime he felt a pulse of attacking energy. He instantly recognized Belial and felt his hatred. "Mar-cus Ri-ley, what are you doing?"

Belial was a malevolent monster. He should be terrified. For some reason he felt no fear now, only pity. With his halo-sensing ability he could see how the life force around the creature was distorted and twisted.

"I am tracking down the location of all your bioenhancer cases," Marcus said without rancor. As fellow combatants, he almost felt a bond with this creature. Was he nuts?

"So it is *you*!" Belial roared. "*You* who are destroying plans for the Harvest. I will kill you now."

Marcus placed a protective blue bubble around his mind, blocking Belial's thrust. As the creature railed and attacked Marcus was able to fully enter Belial's mind. He understood now exactly what Belial meant by a "Harvest" and why it was necessary. Marcus did not fight back but allowed Belial to expend all his energy. Finally, muttering the most vile oaths and imprecations, the creature vanished. Belial was obviously psychotic and stupid. It should have been clear by now that neither could harm the other, yet Belial continued to threaten and rave. Holderness was right when he talked about what they were facing. If Belial was behind these crazy bloodlines on earth, no wonder everything was so messed up.

Marcus felt people shaking him. He turned off his viewer and saw that Barbara and three others had their hands on him. "Are you OK?" Barbara asked.

"Never better," Marcus replied, lying as cheerfully as he could.

"What was that all about?" said a guy with gold round-rimmed glasses. "All of a sudden you broke out in a sweat and your body started to shake."

Marcus decided that discretion was the better part of valor. "Sometimes I have trouble with my remote-viewing ability. But I think it's OK now." Belial was like Chuck Norris in a bad movie: you kept killing him and he kept coming back.

Nine hours later, completely exhausted, Marcus had identified the locations of 109 more of the cases. The number that had shipped from the Pache Island facility totaled 711. At this rate it would take him a week to locate the others. It was tough work. Using his mental viewer consumed a lot of energy and he'd had nothing to eat all day.

The elevator doors opened. Holderness Parkinson strolled into the room just as Marcus was about to walk over to the elevator. "Well done my boy. You deserve a reward."

"Yes I do," Marcus replied. "I need to get something to eat and then I need to see Darcy."

"O ho! So that's the way it is."

Barbara smiled. She was a little envious as the manchild rose to his full height. He was magnificent.

"That desk is yours now until this crisis is over," Parkinson said. "We'll need you to lock down the locations of every biocase. Continue to monitor the locations in case they change. Choose someone for your assistant."

Marcus was so tired he didn't care. "Her," he said, pointing to Barbara. "We seem to work together OK."

Barbara was delighted. Parkinson led Marcus up to his room. Darcy was there and they had a wonderful dinner. He felt better after he'd eaten. Darcy chatted brightly about her day in town; Marcus told her about his Sunday. Finally, all the food he'd eaten made him sleepy. He took off his shoes and fell into bed. The last thing he thought before he lost consciousness made him panic. He had told Belial that he knew the locations of all of the cases. Idiot! Now they'd all be moved and..... He tried to force himself out of bed to call Parkinson but he fell back into unconsciousness and didn't wake up until Monday afternoon.

The Vatican

Pietro Adolfone donned his black robe with the serpent-god Marduk prominently displayed on the front. He went through the Purification Ritual, preparing himself with the incantations that would summon the minions of Belial. He exited his quarters and walked down a marbled Vatican corridor to an elevator that took him to a hidden suite of rooms that were used for communication with the gods. He was now ritually prepared. Next he must establish the proper communication frequency. This routine ceremony did not require human blood; only animal sacrifice. He was deathly afraid but, as always, ecstatic. To have such esoteric knowledge! To communicate directly with the gods who had established human civilization on earth!

To call this "black magic" was preposterous. Only the unschooled would think such a thing. But then, of course, they will soon be cleansed from the earth in the great purification ritual. To hear the great serpent-god Belial describe this event was so uplifting it brought tears to his eyes. That, and the awesome terrible malevolence of the great god, made him shiver with delight. To It he was an insect to be pinned to the wall, squirming in his death throes. He often imagined being ravished by the great god, feeling It engulfing him, absorbing him, as his life force ebbed away. He felt faint and almost stumbled into the stone altar, which was stained with blood. He gathered himself. Tonight there would be much more mundane matters. His report, and the weekly instructions. The addictive power of the Purification Ritual never failed to enthrall him.

Before him, on the altar, a bloody chicken heart rested, still warm from the animal he had sacrificed. Candles, and a knife, lay beside it. He abased himself and repeated the ritual incantation, over and over: "Take me, take me, I am your slave. I call upon you, O great Belial, god of gods, giver of life, destroyer of evil, fulfiller of prophecy, devour me. I am yours to command."

As he chanted Adolfone felt his life force weaken and another presence made itself known. He completed the incantation by plunging the knife into the chicken heart, spurting a little of the life-giving blood over the altar, his robe, and his face and hands. Magically a great, dark-green entity appeared over the altar and in front of the replicas of the gods that lined the back of the chamber. Adolfone shuddered in anticipation: would the Great One appear, or only the assistant?

"Ad-ol-fon-e," Qa-Hrrzl rumbled. "Why are the locations of our Purification Substance being discovered?"

Like Abi-ramu over 3,500 years ago, Adolfone cowered in the presence of the serpent-god. This was news to him. "O great one, all of our biomaterial cases are in place, safe and secure, just as I reported last week."

"They are not!" Qa-Hrrzl roared. Adolfone almost fainted. Qa-Hrrzl observed this and became even more irritated. This vermin! His life was on the line, and his participation in the feeding. "Ad-ol-fon-e," Qa-Hrrzl spoke balefully in his sibilant, hissing language which he, Pietro Adolfone, could somehow understand. The creature's serpent-tongue moved in and out of his mouth. "The miscreant Mar-cus Ri-ley has learned how to identify the locations of every one of your cases. They must be moved at once to different, secure locations."

Pietro Adolfone's knees gave way. Spittle moved out of his mouth and down his cheek. "But great one," he blubbered, "that is impossible. There are only so many secure facilities available."

"You dare to gainsay *me*?" Qa-Hrrzl bellowed. "Malignant! Due to your error the glorious event has been, by necessity, moved forward. If the date changes again, failure is possible." The thought of failure caused Qa-Hrrzl to feel particularly malevolent toward this ugly, hairy little hominid. His voice turned cold. He whispered, sending the earthian into paralyzing, slack-jawed fear. "You have two of your earth weeks to rectify the situation. You must move the cases and kill the hominid Mar-cus Ri-ley. Do you understand?"

Through his terror, Adolfone managed to nod his head affirmatively.

"Ad-ol-fon-e. If you fail in your task I promise I will suck the brains from your head."

Qa-Hrrzl saw the little hominid collapse and hit his head on the altar. He fell to the floor. The great god looked at him with contempt. How could he have ever thought these weaklings superior?

The last thing Pietro Adolfone saw and heard before he lost consciousness was a baleful laugh and the fading projection of Qa-Hrrzl, a sneering, lizard-faced Cheshire Cat. Adolfone was found an hour later by one of the altar boys, who cleaned up nightly after scheduled ceremonies. When he awoke he stumbled back to his quarters and called his secret contact in the Curia about Marcus Riley. He set in motion the procedure to redistribute the biomaterial. Then he prayed for his own salvation.

Amsterdam

Nils van Bergen's phone buzzed. "What do you want?" Van Bergen recognized the caller's face very well.

"Are you sober?"

"What difference does that make? Who do you want dead?"

The man's face wrinkled in disgust. "You are a very good operative, Nils, but you are also a barbarian."

"I'm a man with the bark on," Nils said, employing an American expression he had learned while on a job in Wyoming. "I say things like I mean them."

The man's eyebrows raised slightly. "Oh really? Since when did that occur?"

Nils was about ready to switch off.

"Marcus Riley, Chicago, Royalty Services building on West Grant. I don't anticipate any difficulties."

Nils was irritated. "What would you know about it?" Garcia, the Curia's man, was a Spanish aristocrat, pure Castilian, from a noble family that could trace its heritage back over a thousand years. His inbred arrogance rankled.

"This must be quick," Garcia said. "'Therefore the job comes with a premium." Nils noticed the faintest hint of fear in the man's voice. Garcia? Afraid? He was legendary for his emotionless demeanor.

"I don't do quick." His bank account was in good shape. He didn't like Garcia or those murderers in Rome. "I'm sorry."

"$300,000," Garcia said quickly.

"Who is this guy?"

Garcia's normally impassive face flushed slightly. "He's a 22-year-old boy. Should be easy."

Nils said nothing, letting his silence demand more information. "This is a special job," Garcia explained. "There is nothing special about the target, however. The boy has information – sensitive information – that could be very dangerous to certain parties. That is why we want him out of this world within the next 48 hours. If you are successful the money will be deposited in a special Vatican Bank account. I will supply you with the number when you have successfully completed your mission."

"No. Switzerland. Or you can find somebody else. Half right now and half when the job is done."

Garcia's eyes narrowed. "Someday, Nils van Bergen, I shall have you killed."

Nils grinned. "That's more like it Phillip." Nils had the satisfaction of seeing the man's thin, aristocratic nose narrow and his eyes flash. He had deliberately provoked Felipe. The man had a thing about his family and his name.

Garcia smiled thinly and leaned back in his chair. "Someday, my friend, you will outlive your usefulness."

Nils read the man in the chair. Even over the phone it was easy. High-strung and temperamental behind his mask of uncaring coldness. Overbred. That was the perfect word to describe Felipe Garcia; a man who must have his own way even in trivial matters. A man who was incapable of seeing a point of view other than his own. Atrophied on the dynamics of life other than his own selfish interests. Almost soulless. A textbook psychopath. The problem with being a criminal is the company you have to keep.

Nils made up his mind. After this job he was through. He'd get plastic surgery on his face and head down New Zealand way and make a new life.

Nils checked his Swiss bank account. "Garcia, I don't see a change in my balance."

He saw Garcia make some hand movements and the figures changed. Nils spoke softly. "Felipe, you'd better not be playing tricks with me."

Garcia's eyes glinted. The nerve of this mongrel! But Garcia was himself afraid, for van Bergen's skills were legendary. He would not play the screen-switch game with this one. "All is well Nils. Report back to me when the work is done. Your time begins now."

"Forty-eight hours plus travel time," Nils said.

"You have eight hours to get to Chicago. Fifty-six hours from now." The screen went black.

Felipe Garcia always had to have the last word.

Chicago, two days later

"I'm going for a walk," Marcus said.

"Oh no you're not," Barbara replied. Everyone looked up from their desks. Several shook their heads in rejection. It was clear that Parkinson had put Marcus in his chair so that his activities could be monitored.

Marcus got up and stretched. "I'm afraid I am, ladies and gentlemen. There isn't anything you can do about it."

Barbara looked up at Marcus, startled. Today he felt indomitable. His body was now much stronger and more vital after surviving the bio-injection even though he had been sitting in a chair for weeks. Barbara saw that the manchild fairly glowed with energy. He seemed to her almost superhuman.

"If you're going I'm going to," Barbara said. She punched the app that would warn Parkinson that something was amiss with Marcus.

Marcus pulled his coat from the hanger by the wall, walked up the stairs, and out the front door of Royalty Services. Barbara followed close behind him. He couldn't seem to shake this good-looking woman, who had worked as Parkinson's database programmer for ten years. Darcy was at work downtown with Audrey (modeling clothes of course). He had spent an exhausting sixteen hours on Monday. So far he had identified over 300 more of the bioenhancer cases. He wasn't going to burn himself out today. Ten hours today and tomorrow should finish the work. Then he could get out of here and have some fun in Chicago. Parkinson was working with his network and the Crims on a plan to steal the cases and irradiate them.

Marcus turned right on the sidewalk in front of the Royalty brownstone. A man crossed the street and walked toward them. The day was cold. The man, about six feet tall, wore a dark polar-tek coat. He had blond hair sticking out of a woolen cap. He sauntered casually along the sidewalk.

As Nils approached the target he almost laughed out loud. This was probably the easiest job he would ever do. The street was empty. His needle was filled with the drug of his choice: a lethal, fast-acting, and completely painless barbiturate dissolved in ordinary drinking water. Three to four minutes after injection, the target falls into a peaceful sleep and dies without leaving a residual trail of chemicals. Frozen carbon dioxide bullets would not work here. Metal bullets were messy and traceable, and the sure sign of an amateur. Marcus Riley would leave the world today but he would do so without needless suffering. Nils van Bergen was a compassionate workman.

Nils approached Marcus from the left. Barbara moved to the target's right, placing her in perfect position. She would see nothing.

For the second time Marcus felt a prick on his wrist. He turned quickly but the man had passed him on the sidewalk and stopped under a lamppost with his back to them. He was lighting a cigarette. Suddenly Marcus felt very tired. His body told him that he had been injected with a deadly substance. It also informed him that his immune system was on the job and that the pathogen would not be fatal. He must avoid movement for a few minutes. Marcus eased himself down to the frozen grass beside the cold pavement. Barbara, now a few steps ahead of him, turned back.

"Are you all right Marcus?"

"Just a little tired is all. I need to rest here for a little bit."

"Come now Marcus. It's too cold to sit on the sidewalk."

Marcus wasn't listening. He turned on his mental viewer and placed the man at the lamppost in it. He quickly traced Nils van Bergen's worldline to Amsterdam. He reviewed the man's conversation with Felipe Garcia and knew that Nils had come to Chicago to take him out. Marcus was very tired now, and weak, but his body informed him that all would be well shortly.

Nils van Bergen enjoyed his cigarette. In four minutes he would turn around, phone in hand, ready to call emergency services. 911, they called it here. The body would be off the streets within the hour and the poison would never be identified. The cause of death would not be determined with certainty. It would be written off as just another mysterious death in a metropolitan area of ten million people. And he would be $300,000 richer. He waited, casually puffing, seeing his breath mix with the smoke. When he got back to Europe he'd take a ski trip in the Alps and then have his plastic surgery.

Van Bergen turned complacently, expecting to see a dead body. Marcus Riley was slowly getting up off the sidewalk. Shocked, Nils could only stare. The woman was beside him, helping Riley to rise, castigating him for being a silly boy. Marcus walked toward Nils with his hand out. "Nice try, Nils van Bergen."

Nils took the hand mechanically. This job was not proceeding the way it should! Nils felt he was in a bad dream. "How do you know my name?" he asked stupidly. This man should be dead.

Marcus smiled. "I know a great deal about you Mr. van Bergen. I know about your little conversation with Felipe Garcia, who paid you $300,000 to do this job."

Barbara stood there, uncomprehending. "What's this all about Marcus?"

Nils was shocked again but recovered quickly. He read Marcus and felt no animosity but the woman had seen his face. That was unfortunate. He had slipped badly and now two would have to die. For sure, this was his last job. His karma had finally caught up with him.

Nils always carried a weapon and he reached for it now. "I wouldn't do that if I were you," Marcus said.

Nils felt an odd euphoria and his muscles involuntarily relaxed. Strangely, he didn't feel like killing anyone now. He tried to move his legs but he couldn't. His arms were pinned at his side. Nils looked up at the big manchild who was smiling down at him.

"You'd be a good operative for the White Hats."

"The White Hats?"

Marcus used his web of light to get into Nils' mind. In an instant he knew van Bergen's life story. A street kid, highly intelligent, Nils had avoided school. He had been picked up by a Dutch intelligence operative looking for children who displayed unusual abilities. He had been essentially kidnapped and trained at the Binnenlandse Veiligheidsdienst (BVD) for highly sensitive field operations. He had never failed in a mission until now. Nils spoke five languages fluently, and had a wide knowledge of world affairs and covert operations.

Nils saw the humor in his situation. He felt a not unpleasant paralysis. Fortunately his breathing was unaffected. He knew that the source of his condition was the boy, Marcus Riley, who seemed completely unconcerned that Nils had attempted twice to kill him. It was an impossible situation.

"Well?" Marcus asked.

"Well …what?" Nils replied, thinking that he would now have to return Garcia's funds. That rankled.

"Do you want to join us?"

Nils was able to mumble a response. "I don't want to do anything except go back to Europe and do a little skiing."

Marcus tried to see the man's future. He'd never tried this before. He turned his time sense forward and immediately saw five branches, five probable outcomes, for Nils' life. Marcus thought out loud. "There are five possible futures for you, Nils van Bergen, from this worldline. In one, you die in a skiing accident shortly after returning to Amsterdam. In another you abandon your former profession and go to New Zealand, leading a very boring life, and eventually drink yourself to death. A third potential worldline shows you returning to your Dutch handlers and becoming a trainer for the Dutch Military and Intelligence Service. The fourth and fifth worldliness are much vaguer, like a slightly out-of-focus camera. These are the timelines associated with your decision to stay in the United States." Marcus paused for a moment. In the most probable timeline, Marcus saw Nils talking with Holderness Parkinson and marrying Barbara. Marcus thought he might be able to solve two problems all at once. He assumed his best Holderness Parkinson voice. "These outcomes are more fortuitous. My dear fellow, I'd like you to talk with a friend of mine. I think you will like him very much; you have a lot in common."

This manchild spoke assuredly, as if he could actually read the future like a computer printout. Nils was horrified and intrigued.

Barbara walked up to the two men and studied van Bergen. "Do you know this man?" she asked.

"Quite well, in fact," Marcus said truthfully. And he did, even though he had only met this stranger ten minutes ago. The power of his web of light had been improved by the bioenhancer. "Nils van Bergen, meet Barbara …?"

"Napier," she said.

"Nils is a brilliant man, Barbara, highly capable. He has been involved in very dangerous government work for over twenty years." Marcus presented van Bergen in the best possible light. "See that scar across his cheekbone? That was made by a bullet from a Libyan gun during their civil war."

Barbara looked Nils over. A good looking man for sure, she thought. Older, but very handsome. She still had no idea what was going on though, and she intended to get some answers after they got back inside. The man in front of her was definitely worth a second look. Well set up, ruggedly handsome. And she loved blondes.

"A dashing fellow in all respects," Marcus added, seeing her interest.

"He's a bit shy though, don't you think Marcus?" Barbara was concerned that Nils was a little slow mentally. The man simply stood there, unmoving. She noticed that his eyes were animatedly looking her over.

"Nils is, er, incapacitated at the moment Barbara. No doubt blown away by your beauty."

Barbara looked sharply at Marcus, sensing that she was being made fun of. The manchild's face and his demeanor showed no signs of satire. Marcus was having lots of fun playing Holderness Parkinson. His suggestion was a good one: Parkinson would definitely want to talk to this guy. He was thinking like the old boy now and he liked it.

Barbara studied Nils. "Perhaps we can go out for coffee," she suggested.

Nils managed to nod his head.

Marcus sent Nils a mental question. 'If I release you, will you behave yourself?' He was inside Nils' mind now; he *was* Nils van Bergen, and Nils knew it.

There could be no lies to this young giant. Nils relaxed. He had learned during his BVD training that human potential was far higher than had ever been imagined. He knew that the Dutch were working with other covert groups to develop that potential. Perhaps this guy was a product of that development. Nils accepted this. He knew now that Marcus could immobilize him, perhaps even at a distance, any time he wanted. Not being one to waste time on hopeless outcomes, he agreed.

Marcus released his field of energy and Nils turned to Barbara. He liked what he saw. Nils made a leg. "Nils van Bergen at your service, my lady."

Barbara's eyes brightened. "How gallant!"

Marcus walked between the pair, placing one arm around each of them. He turned his head to van Bergen. "Nils, I want you to talk to a very experienced and high-level operative, my friend Holderness Parkinson." He turned to Barbara. "And you, my dear, should get back to work."

Barbara was amazed. Marcus seemed to have grown twenty years older in fifteen minutes. "All right Marcus." She understood that the manchild was completely in control of the situation. "Our building is right ahead."

Marcus freed his arms and let Nils walk ahead with Barbara. Playing Holderness had gotten him into the old boy's mindset. He had picked up on a little of his confidence and sophisticated swagger. Marcus had talked with Parkinson many times but he had never tried to get into his mind. Something told him that if he tried he might not succeed.

After the three entered the Royalty building, Marcus escorted van Bergen to Parkinson's office. "Nice place," van Bergen remarked as he walked down the hallway with its plush dark-green carpets and artwork on the walls.

Marcus led Nils into Parkinson's office. "Mr. Parkinson is a man who enjoys luxury."

Holderness looked up from his monitor. "Ahh, no harm done I see."

Marcus was amused. "How do you know that sir?"

Parkinson turned the monitor. Marcus saw a view of the outside front of the Royalty building.

"You saw and heard the whole thing then?"

Holderness folded his hands over his ample midsection. "Indeed I did."

"Sir, let me introduce Nils van Bergen, a man of the world, highly capable, and fantastic in a crisis."

"Thank you Marcus, that was excellent work. Now please get back to work."

Marcus groaned. "I'm feeling very tired sir. All work and no play makes Marcus a dull boy."

"Perhaps you are forgetting the nature of this crisis, Marcus. This isn't a video game you're playing. We're talking about the potential deaths of 90% of the population."

"Yes sir, of course. I'd like to remind you that I just survived another death threat."

Parkinson ignored him. "I believe you'll find quite a bit of work awaiting you. Some of the cases are being moved. Your workload will be even more substantial." He looked up at Marcus and smiled. "Try not to leave the building again my boy. Now, if you'll excuse me, I'd like a few words with Mr. van Bergen."

It was a subtle reminder that he had violated orders. Marcus shrugged and left the room. If the biocases were on the move it meant that the monster Belial had gotten word to the Black Hats. And it was his fault. Marcus raced down the hallway to the stairwell and took the stairs three at a time down to the basement.

Nils van Bergen faced Holderness Parkinson across the older man's thick oak desk. Nils knew immediately that he was in the presence of a master. Like Parkinson, Nils was infallible at judging a man's capabilities and his character. This ability had saved his life at least twice in the field. The man facing him was very large and big-boned, with a huge head that seemed to fit his body. Nils had met two men in his career like the one across from him. The first was his instructor at the Dutch

BVD and the other the Iraqi ambassador to the Netherlands. He had turned down that job. These men had large bodies because they were large-souled, and needed a very large physical container to hold their élan vital. Nils knew about these things because he had faced death many times in the field, and because of his training and study of extrasensory phenomena at the BVD. When your life was on the line your perceptions became enhanced and you expanded your awareness. You saw things beyond the five human senses. Although Nils was ten feet away he felt that Parkinson controlled the entire room. Most important, this guy felt comfortable.

"Mr. Nils van Bergen, I have an assignment for you."

Nils grinned. In that one sentence Parkinson conveyed a world of meaning and subtle nuance. He'd told him: "Yes, I am large-souled and can handle you. I know who you are and you know who I am. We have a very important mission to accomplish together and you are the man who can do it."

"Very well then sir, I was about to retire anyway. I have no more commitments. What do you want me to do?"

The White House

President Foley sat in his office, angry and frightened. It was late. Felix Pantera had just left after his daily briefing. Alice was calling him from the bedroom, urging him to stop work and come to bed.

"I'll be there in a minute honey!" He would lie down even though he knew he wouldn't sleep. The disparities between the information from his NSC morning briefing and his nightly one were profoundly disturbing. Brentkowski knew the president was seeing Pantera after hours and it didn't seem to bother him. Oleg had never mentioned his angry outburst. The president concluded that the man himself wasn't even aware he had done it.

Brentkowski's concerns were all about Bolivia, Iranian saber-rattling, and the deficit. Real world stuff. Whereas Pantera's were about suppressed technologies and their cover-up, the imminent release of a deadly bioenhancer, and the criminal activities of a private organization he called the Black Hats. Covert stuff. Which briefing was the real one? Until the last NSC meeting he had trusted Oleg implicitly and had only occasionally talked with his DCI. But now he wasn't sure who to trust. When he mentioned suppressed energy technology, for example, Oleg had laughed. "You've been talking to Pantera again, with his false Black Hat – White Hat dichotomy. Certainly we are working on some exotic new energy technologies but their practical implementation is still several decades away." Oleg said it so nonchalantly he was believable. And similarly for all of his other questions: there was always a sensible and plausible response. He had begun now to doubt Pantera's veracity.

President Foley dialed the private number of Admiral James. "Mr. President! What can I do for you? Not an emergency I hope?"

"No admiral, nothing like that. I'm sorry to bother you so late. I am confused." He explained his problem. "Whom do I trust?"

"Mr. President, let me tell you a story. Two years ago I called a man I know who used to work for Lockheed Skunk Works. They are a defense contractor working on exotic technologies. His job was the development of electrogravitic craft that can travel at fantastic speeds. This man said we have had them since the 1960s, that we knew how to extract energy from the quantum vacuum. I just laughed, but he was serious. He said that everyone in these programs knew that the universe was connected, every single particle of it, and that we could already do things people wrote about in science-fiction books. Well, Mr. President, I was ticked off. If this was true why didn't a man in my position know about this stuff? This man gave me a name in one of the deep black programs and told me to ask him for a briefing. So I did. The man on the phone was very polite. 'I'm sorry Admiral James, but we can't divulge any of that information.' I said, 'I'm the fucking Vice-Chairman of the Joint Chiefs of Staff! What do you mean you can't divulge that information? Who are you?' The man said, 'Admiral James, you simply do not have a need to know.' And then he hung up."

President Foley stared at his monitor and said nothing for several minutes.

"Mr. President, are you all right?"

"No admiral, I am not. Clearly, if you do not have the credentials to know this information, then neither do I."

"Yes Mr. President. From what little I know, I'd say we have a *Seven Days in May* situation."

The president was shaken. "Thank you admiral."

That's it then. President Foley made a decision. Tomorrow was his regularly scheduled meeting with the press. Tomorrow, he would blow the lid off.

Chicago

Darcy and Marcus sat on the couch in their living room watching TV. "And now, stay tuned for President Foley's monthly news conference. The White House has informed the press that President Foley has an important announcement after his press briefing."

Darcy looked at Marcus. "Do you have any idea what that will be?" She snuggled deeper into Marcus' arms.

Marcus mussed her hair. "No honey, I don't. I think Parkinson does though."

Darcy loved it when he called her honey. "Holderness knows everything," she said matter-of-factly.

Marcus laughed. "Is Holderness Parkinson omniscient my dear?"

Darcy sat up. "Are you teasing me, Marcus Riley? If you are I'll have to do something about that."

Marcus squeaked. He was enormously ticklish. Darcy had just discovered that a week ago and now used it to get her way in everything. "That's not fair!" Marcus pouted.

"It certainly is. Why, you're a foot taller than I am and much stronger. A girl has to fight back somehow."

Marcus pointed to the TV. "Look, the news conference is starting."

Darcy settled back in but looked up with eyes twinkling. "You'll get yours for that, Marcus."

Marcus groaned. He knew she'd attack him later that night and have him on the floor in a fetal position.

President Foley went through his statement, reading from the teleprompter. Darcy was heartily bored but Marcus was interested in what Foley had to say. It would tell him how much the president really knew. The briefing was about the usual crap on the news until Foley said, "And now, my fellow Americans, I have something important to tell you. I have been thinking about what I want to say all day because there is so much to tell. I don't have a lot of time so I will make this brief."

The president paused. Marcus saw that his face had turned gray. "Ladies and gentlemen, I have discovered something very disturbing. As you know, there are many hidden classified programs within the national security establishment. At least one of these programs, and the people in them, have gone rogue and threaten the security of this country. In brief— "

A voice was heard off-camera, interrupting the president.

"President Foley, please change the direction of this news conference immediately."

President Foley's face first registered shock, then anger. "Who are you? How dare you interrupt my—"

The screen went black. After a few seconds an old re-run was shown.

Darcy turned to Marcus on the couch. "What just happened Marcus?"

Darcy's phone rang. It was Kathleen. "Did you see that news conference?" she asked. "They cut the president right off! I'm watching ABC and they've got some basketball game on now."

Oleg Brentkowski then appeared on the screen. "I am OLeg Brentkowski, the president's National Security Advisor. We apologize for the interruption. The president has suddenly taken ill and cannot continue his news conference. I have just spoken with President Foley's personal physician, who assures me that the president will make a full recovery. Please stay tuned to this channel for further updates."

A babble of voices was heard behind the speaker. People were running around in the audience. A group of people bent over the stage, where a body lay. Someone knocked into a camera and the image went spinning dizzily. "Get the president out of here!" Brentkowski demanded. Then the re-run resumed.

"Did you see that Kathleen?" Darcy asked. "What have they done with the president?"

"I know one way to find out," Marcus said. He led Darcy to Parkinson's office on the top floor.

As Darcy and Marcus entered Parkinson held up a hand and then pointed downward with his thumb. He was looking at four different monitors and was apparently in a meeting. Marcus and Darcy left.

"Now what?" she said.

"I have to go to work," Marcus said.

Darcy smiled and put her arms around him. "What are we going to do about the president?"

"I think Parkinson has got his claws into that."

Draco Tau

Qa-Hrrzl sat dejectedly before the magnificent throne of Belial, his head bowed. The foolish actions of the hominid president had moved the calculated Harvest date forward once again. It was inexplicable. The man had been compliant ever since taking office.

The trick was to pull the Trigger just before Threshold, when the Life Index Reading of the planet was at its highest. The idea was to constrain the hominid energy and like a contained gas that has been heated, release only when the system reached maximum pressure. Every time suppressed information was released, however, the pressure inside the system relaxed and the LRI lowered, requiring an earlier and earlier Harvest date. He had failed to guarantee Harvest apogee. He would die before ever tasting the delicious life substance.

"Sire, I am forced to recommend release of the Purification Substance as soon as possible. We must move the Harvest date forward once again."

Belial's response was deathly cold. "You informed me not thirty rotations ago, miscreant, that all was on schedule."

Qa-Hrrzl bowed his head in submission. "Yes sire. My explanations are meaningless now. I have done my best and it wasn't good enough." Qa-Hrrzl found courage and spoke with passion. "Before I go, sire, I ask permission to suck the brains of the impotent derelict Ad-ol-fon-e, the reprobate hominid who has ruined our plans with his incompetence!"

To his surprise Belial chuckled. "Scientist, I like your attitude. Permission granted." Belial paused. "A great chief must be intelligent enough to realize when events have cycled out of control." The alpha's voice, usually stern and unyielding, almost softened. "I have, of course, been monitoring you. All reports have indicated your diligence and cleverness. Never before has our race harvested a planet with so many dominant life forms. You have done well."

Qa-Hrrzl dared to glance up. Belial was truly imposing and awe-inspiring. The face of his master showed unusual contentment. Belial spoke confidentially. "I have been secretly hoping for an early Harvest. I am pleased. I want you to direct the release of our Purification Substance at the soonest possible moment."

Qa-Hrrzl nodded, ecstatic. "Yes sire." He boldly met the eyes of the dominant Tau. "Sire, even with the reduced feeding and an early Harvest there are so many of these little scum that we shall still gorge satisfactorily."

Belial laughed. This scientist amused him; his words mirrored his own thoughts. "Scientist, I am not able to act alone. The Council must have adequate evidence before a Harvest is initiated."

"Yes sire." Qa-Hrrzl was quick to understand Belial's implied meaning. He should arrange his report to show the necessity for an early Harvest.

Belial was already anticipating the glorious feeding and it made him magnanimous. "My offer still stands. If you manage correctly you shall sit with us at the feeding."

Qa-Hrrzl effaced himself. "Your legacy will shine far above the greatest in racial memory."

Belial, pleased, agreed. His face hardened. "But remember! A failed Harvest is insupportable."

Qa-Hrrzl froze for an instant before backing out of Belial's chamber.

Belial closed his eyes and allowed himself to fantasize about the feeding. Now that the event was imminent he felt the eager excitement of something glorious that had always been a dream, but was now close to manifesting. His little warning would, of course, motivate that scoundrel Qa-Hrrzl to do even better.

Qa-Hrrzl excitedly walked to his laboratory. He was terrified yet jubilant. He would sit in Council! IF he was successful. There was much work to do of course. First he would allow himself the pleasure of dealing with Ad-ol-fon-e.

Chapter 31

MedTech Building, San Francisco

AT 8 a.m. Dr. Frank O'Leary parked his car at the side of the MedTech building, about ten feet from the big refuse container. This was cause for suspicion, but it couldn't be helped. He carried a plastic biohazard case that closely resembled the heavy, dark-red plastic case in the classified biohazard area. It sat underneath his camping equipment in the trunk. Dr. O'Leary walked around to the front and entered the building normally, undergoing the usual security scan.

Frank O'Leary worked a normal day, supervising MedTech's classified research. Tonight he had an important after-hours task to perform. It was one of many, he had reason to believe, that would occur at dozens of different locations across the country.

At 6:45 p.m. Frank walked to the biohazard area and glanced again at the heavy plastic case in its special sealed container. The thing had suddenly appeared two weeks ago, under armed guard. The word from Roger Burress was not to ask questions about it but Frank O'Leary's Irish temperament would not let that happen.

Three weeks ago, an old associate in Mitre's Public Health department had recruited him to the White Hats. Frank O'Leary was senior administrator for the

MedTech facility. His job was to run the place but he had no power, really. That pissed him off because he had joined MedTech to do exciting work. Unfortunately all of the classified work went through that idiot Burress and he never got to work with the exciting new stuff. He had been warned about the red plastic biocase from his contact and knew what it was. It was his job to take that case, replace it with a dummy, and hope no one would notice the difference.

Obsessive secrecy did not sit well with him. Burress had told him nothing about the case's contents, keeping the senior administrator in the dark. The container sat openly within the biohazard area behind thick, bullet-proof plastic. Of course a guard was posted but at night security was more lax. He made it his business to talk to all four of the guards, who worked for a private security contractor called ACTP Group. Tonight, Larry Donahue was supposed to be posted; a man friendly to him. The shift change was at 7 p.m.

At 7 p.m. Frank was at his desk in the classified executive area. To prevent casual gossip and maintain security all MedTech employees with a security classification were segregated from the clerical staff, and had a separate cafeteria and restrooms. The door opened; his secretary's head popped in. "Will you need me for anything else Dr. O'Leary?"

"No Bob, thank you." Bob Chatham was his eager-beaver personal research assistant, an intern of sorts working on his doctorate in microbiology. Bob was entirely devoted to him.

The building was practically empty now but he needed a break. He had to get in there without suspicion. Frank walked out of his office and down the corridor to the biohazard area. This small room was fifty feet from his office and enclosed in clear, bullet-proof plastic. The day shift guy was still guarding the room.

"Larry sick tonight?" he asked.

The man shrugged. He was uniformed in dark blue and black, with an "ACTP Group" logo in yellow across his chest. "I sure hope not because I've got plans."

Frank didn't know what to say so he walked back to his office. He sat drumming his fingers on the desk, worried about his car. It was probably sitting exposed now that the other employees had left the building. What if one of the outside guards looked in the trunk?

Frank waited impatiently until 8 p.m. and walked out again. Still no Larry. "Dr. O'Leary!" the guard said. "Would you watch this for a minute? I gotta take a dump real bad."

Frank thought quickly. Larry might never show up tonight and he had to get the cases switched tonight. The nearest employee bathroom was two corridors down in the non-classified area. "Sure, take your time." He probably had ten minutes to get in and out, but then thought of a better plan. "Could you open up for a minute? There's a sample in there I need to test."

"Sure." The guard fumbled with his imprint and stood bowlegged with his sphincter muscles straining. When you gotta go, you gotta go, Frank thought. The guard looked like a man who'd had too much to eat at the Texas Chili Cookoff. This guy sometimes went to the john and smoked on his break, so he might just have enough time. The guard hurriedly placed his security imprint on the scanner. The lock on the thick plastic door opened a few inches. "Make sure you close this, OK?" The guard turned and walked swiftly down the hallway.

Frank grinned and walked in, leaving the door slightly ajar. He walked over to the case and lifted it. Of course it was locked, but they'd figure a way to open it later. Unfortunately the thing was extremely heavy and bulky. He tested the weight and estimated about eighty pounds. Was he strong enough to carry the case by its reinforced plastic handle?

"What are you doing in there Frank?" a voice asked. O'Leary, startled, dropped the case and it landed awkwardly on its platform, almost teetering off and onto the floor.

Frank whirled to face the director. He was dead meat now and he had to think fast. "Roger, I want to know what's in this goddam case."

"No one knows. I don't know. It's not your business."

"The hell it isn't. I'm responsible for everything that comes into and goes out of this place."

Roger Burress frowned. "Not this item."

"Come on Roger. Level with me."

Burress sighed, understanding O'Leary's insatiable curiosity and his persistence. It was never difficult to distinguish between an angry Irishman and a ray of sunshine. "It's the truth Frank. I don't know what's in that case."

"Then what is it doing here?"

"I'm sorry Frank, what you are doing is out of the question." A look of fear crossed the man's features.

"What are you afraid of Roger?"

Burress didn't reply. O'Leary remained silent. "The unknown, I guess," Burress finally said. "Something is going to happen in the next couple of days." The older man pointed to the case. "I'm not sure what it is. It's out of my hands."

"Nonsense. I'm going to look inside that thing, Roger. Tonight."

Burress started. "No! Frank, if you do that we're both in serious trouble."

"You had nothing to do with it. I never talked to you about anything. The only person who knows I looked at the case is you. If you get in a spot tell them you saw me take it."

Frank was sweating bullets because the guard could come out at any time. He had wasted five minutes already talking to Burress. He thought he heard footsteps. He reached in and grabbed the case, barely able to lift it. He grabbed the thing with both hands and held on.

"O'Leary, what do you think you're doing?"

"Shut up Roger. I have to act fast. The guard is coming back soon."

Frank O'Leary shoved the door open with his left shoulder and walked slowly out of the biohazard area, struggling with the case.

"Where are you going Frank? You can't just walk out with that thing."

Frank lowered the container to the floor and placed two fingers to his lips in a ssshhhh gesture. "I have an exact replica, Roger. It's out in my car. Let me go or the security guard will come back from the bathroom and we'll both be sunk like a lead life-jacket."

Roger Burress watched helplessly as the fitter and taller man picked up the case. The fool! How will he get past the outside guards? He agreed with Dr. Frank O'Leary but he wasn't willing to get in trouble for it. He should stop the man but his muscles felt oddly sluggish. He watched, almost mesmerized, as his assistant hustled the case awkwardly down the corridor. What did the man propose to do with it? Burress knew the shift change was late and the guard was in the head. It was already too late now; he should have at least tried to stop O'Leary. He was committed. Burress decided to post himself in front of the public lavatory and watch the door. When he stopped in front of the men's room he smelled cigarette smoke.

Frank O'Leary turned right at the exit sign and went to the back door. He opened it and looked around. Three guards walked the perimeter every night but sometimes, when it was cold, two of them played cards in a little alcove next to the delivery ramp about 50 feet from the back door. It was cold tonight. Frank cracked open the door and heard muffled voices.

"Full house! That beats your straight."

"That's six hands in row Henry! Where did you learn to play like that?"

"Online poker baby, that's the ticket."

"I owe you two hundred now."

Frank knew from his talks with Larry that the third guard was always at the front. He should be safe. Frank launched himself out of the doorway, trying not to make too much noise. Sound traveled clearly in the cold. Fortunately it was only forty feet to the side of the building and forty more around the corner where his car was parked. He made it to the corner, turning toward his car. The front guard was moving past the end of the building about 200 feet away. If the guard saw him the game was up. Frank stopped and knelt to the asphalt, motionless, dropping the case. He needed to stop anyway; his arms were killing him. The case made a harsh crack as it hit the ground. The guard turned and faced him. Frank was only twenty feet from his car. The guard's flashlight beam was sweeping from right to left, toward him. He sank down to the cold asphalt and crawled forward, abandoning the case and increasing his chances. He hoped the car's shadow would block the light. Frank looked back and froze. The goddam case was sitting out there, totally exposed.

The beam passed, hitting his car and throwing a shadow just inches to his right. Now he knew what deer felt like. The guard's beam passed through both car windows but there was a dark space a few feet wide as the light was blocked by the metal between the doors. The case was right in the middle of that shadow. The beam hesitated for a moment, then moved on. The guard turned and walked out of sight. Frank hurried back to pick up the case and muscled it over to his trunk. As quietly as he could he sprang the latch and lifted it in to the trunk, removing the substitute case. Frantically he covered the thing with his tent and closed the trunk door.

Now he had another problem. He'd left the biohazard area at least ten minutes ago. The guard might already be sounding the alarm. Just then a vehicle, driving fast, approaching the building from Bluette road. God, what now? If that was Larry he might still make it.

Inside the building Roger Burress was panicking. Larry was late for his shift change. He was still in front of the bathroom door. He had to stall the guard until O'Leary got back with the substitute case. He heard a toilet flush and the sounds of a stall door opening. Burress stepped back from the door and walked a few paces toward the classified section. He turned around and walked slowly back. The bathroom door opened and the guard stepped out. The door to the biohazard was open, wasn't it? Burress had planned to face the guard, hoping he wouldn't be able to see around his corpulent body.

"Guard!" he heard himself saying. He wasn't good with words so he'd have to channel O'Leary.

"Uh, hello sir," the guard said. "I know I'm off-post but I've got Dr. O'Leary watching the area." His face flushed. "I really had to take a crap, sir, I'm sorry."

Roger thanked his lucky stars that this man was so compliant. Sometimes with these PSCs you got hardened military types who scared him to death. This guy looked like an out-of-shape desk sergeant. He knew he had to get the man out of the hallway, and pronto. O'Leary could be coming back any second. He had an idea. "Would you come into my office for a moment? I need to ask you a few questions."

The guard, anxious, agreed. He hoped his dereliction of duty wouldn't go down in the director's weekly report.

Burress turned and walked ahead of the guard and slightly to his left, hoping to block his view of the biohazard door. It hung slightly open. If the guard saw the open door he would have to investigate. Burress, his senses amplified by fear, heard the sound of a door latch turning and a door opening behind him. O'Leary! Burress heard a car pull up in front.

Panicking, Roger turned and motioned quickly toward his office door. The guard, fearful for his job, had his head down, expecting a severe berating. The two men entered the director's office and Burress closed the door. Burress, his legs shaking, made it to his chair and collapsed into it. "Is something wrong sir?" the guard asked.

"Uh, no ... well, I haven't been sleeping very well and I'm very tired."

"You should go home Mr. Burress," the man said sympathetically. "You work too hard."

Roger looked up. "I do work too hard!" He struggled to his feet. "I'm getting too old for this." He was stalling, trying to think of what to do next.

"You going to report this?" the guard asked.

It was all Roger could do to pause for a few moments. He wanted to scream his relief. "No, we'll let it slide this time. You know the procedure if you have to leave your post."

The man sighed with relief. "Yes director. I'll be more careful."

By this time O'Leary, substitute case in hand, had entered the L-shaped corridor from the back. Frank heard a door shut around the corner, and then voices. They were too muffled to identify anyone. He stopped. What was it this time? He walked and peeked around the corner. No one. He'd have to hope that Burress had covered for him. Frank took the case and walked as silently as he could down the corridor. When he reached the director's door he crouched low. Fortunately the window was over four feet from the bottom of the door, and he made it past. Just as he walked into the biohazard area with the substitute case a man came running down the corridor from the lobby.

Shite! Frank didn't know what to do. Was this Larry? He fumbled with the case and placed it on its clear plastic stand. The weight wasn't the same. The substitute was lighter because they didn't know how heavy the original was. Oh well, he was screwed anyway. Sweat dripped off his forehead and onto the case but Frank didn't see it. The man had stopped in the corridor and he'd seen everything.

Unthinkingly, Frank wiped his oily palms on the case. He got out his handkerchief and wiped his sweat-soaked forehead just as the director and the other guard came down the hallway.

"Larry!" the guard cried. "About time you got here you piece of shit."

"Sorry man. I had a flat on the way over."

"You could of phoned me."

"Then I'd have been more late. I drove forty over."

"All set Larry?" O'Leary asked, trying to sound casual and hoping his voice wouldn't crack.

"Yes sir, thank you sir." Larry Donahue took up his post at the door, thankful that no one had asked any questions.

As O'Leary walked out he was stopped by the other guard, who had walked a few steps down the corridor. "Where is your sample?" he asked.

Frank panicked. "Sample? What sample?" Had the guard noticed the switch?

"Is there something wrong Dr. O'Leary? You said you had to test a sample."

Frank was so relieved he almost fell over. He slapped his head and said, "For God's sake, I must be tired. Yes, I need to see that culture, labeled PL-243-7A." He walked over to the sample shelf and retrieved the sample, steadying himself. The guard walked quickly to the exit.

O'Leary walked back to his office followed closely by Burress. "That was the stupidest thing I have ever seen," Burress hissed. "What am I going to say on my report?"

O'Leary didn't reply. He walked as casually as he could to the lab, which was up the hallway fifty feet from his office and across the hall from the director's office. When the two men entered the lab Burress closed the door. The two men walked over to one of the lab benches. O'Leary grinned and spoke with admiration. "That was good work Roger."

"Good work! Your stupidity is going to cost us more than our jobs."

"No Roger. Relax. If you'll come with me to my office I'll show you something that might cheer you up."

"I'm going home," Roger said. "I'm tired."

"Larry is one of us."

Roger Burress was disgusted. "What the bleep is that supposed to mean?"

"I know you want to get home Roger, and I have an urgent errand to run. Larry saw me handling the case but he's on our side."

Burress' eyebrows went up. "One of us? What does that mean?"

Frank made it quick. "Larry and I are members of a group called the White Hats."

Burress held up his arms and walked backwards, hitting one of the wheeled lab chairs. The chair rolled several feet and smacked up against an adjacent lab table. "More spy vs. spy nonsense. No thanks. It's what I'm trying to get away from."

"What are you afraid of, Roger?" The man's attitude baffled him.

Burress studied O'Leary carefully. "Look Frank, you know I was the CEO of Martindale for almost twenty years. I came here because I wanted more freedom." Burress grimaced. "It turns out that I'm still faced with the same crap here as I did there. I was told to place a guard on that damn biocase 24 hours a day. I asked the fellows who brought it what it was. They said, 'that is a question better left unasked, Mr. Burress.' Then they left."

Frank grinned and leaned his right hip against the table. "No problem Roger. You're out of it now because Larry is the only one who knows besides us."

"What if he talks?"

Frank snorted. "Who is he going to talk to? Roger, events are moving way too fast now. In a matter of days this issue will have been resolved, for better or worse." Frank decided that he wouldn't brief Burress. The man was too fragile.

"I should fire you and the guard right now and call security. You know what that means."

Frank shrugged. If Roger finked on him neither the case nor himself would make it into the city. "You can of course. But you'll be doing your country, and me, a disservice."

Roger Burress groaned and plopped himself into the chair he'd bumped into. Only six months left on his employment contract and now this! He should have retired two years ago. Damn Frank O'Leary. The man was an excellent administrator, but too volatile. He looked up. Frank was waiting for his response. "I'm dammed if I do and dammed if I don't. I'll have to lie on my report and that will make me liable if anyone finds out."

Frank looked down sympathetically at the older man, who resembled an overfed cage turkey resigned to its fate. "I really am sorry Roger. I never would have placed you in this position if it wasn't absolutely necessary."

"What's this all about Frank? Some kind of national crisis?"

"Precisely. I can't tell you unless you want to be in. And if you're in it's to the death. All or nothing."

Burress blanched. "I thought so. Rumors about a potentially lethal pandemic. I've heard whispers all over the place."

"Correct Roger." Frank was excited because if Burress had heard the rumors then everyone had. Roger was the sort of fellow who avoided trouble and controversy. "You're already involved and so are about eight billion others by the way. This isn't just the United States, it's worldwide."

"Oh My God. So it's true then. Some kind of Armageddon."

Frank was cheerful. "Yes. The sooner I can get that case into the city the better our chances are."

Roger opened his mouth and then closed it. "All right Frank, go ahead. I want no part of it."

In over 70 cities across the United States similar vignettes were occurring as the White Hat network desperately tried to locate and neutralize the bioenhancer. There were still several hundred of the cases with unidentified locations safely in place.

Chicago

"God this is boring," Marcus said. "And hopeless."

Darcy was sitting next to him at Parkinson's basement desk. "Not even when I'm here?"

Marcus smiled. "Of course sweetheart. You make it all bearable."

This peroration made Darcy feel much better. She was, in fact, surprised with herself. She had an exciting career and lots of work. Yesterday she'd come home and gone down into the basement to see Marcus. He and the beautiful Barbara were working together like old chums. Darcy felt jealous. The woman was good looking but everyone here was good looking, especially the consorts. Many of the women made no secret of their preference for Marcus. Especially Barbara, even though she was sort of going with that new guy Nils van Bergen. That leggy brunette in suite 404 was particularly attentive. Darcy knew Marcus had a preference for tall, intelligent women like that insufferable Carla Waverley. She felt like taking that damn poison herself, if only to make her so attractive that he would never look at anyone else.

So, for the past two days, Darcy left work early to come spy. But she had to admit that nothing was amiss. And compared to her job Marcus' was horrible. Staring at those monitors all day, exhausting himself, constantly keeping track of those biocases. For the past week he'd not had more than five hours of sleep a night and was on call twenty-four hours a day. Marcus was more Royalty's than hers. Particularly Barbara's, and the bitch knew it. She saw how Barbara touched Marcus' arm just a little too long, handing him a printout. Wipe that satisfied smile off your face, bitch!

How could she worry about something so trivial when the world was about to end? Because she trusted Holderness and Marcus. The two men were superhuman. She felt there was nothing they couldn't do together.

"I'm so happy that you and Holderness are getting along so well," she said out loud.

"What was that?" Marcus replied cheerfully.

Darcy knew she committed a faux pas because Barbara looked irritated. Good.

"Perhaps you could save your reminiscing for later." Barbara was condescendingly sweet.

Darcy was about to pull out her claws when Marcus raised his eyebrows a quarter inch. Barbara flushed. She had taught him that! Marcus patted Darcy's arm. "Time for another check." Darcy saw his attention go inward for a moment. His eyes focus about six feet in front of the desk. "453, still in position. 456 on the move. In a white Mercedes-Benz van moving north down Granz avenue." Barbara took the data and concentrated, using the headphones. One of the monitors updated its information. At the same time she typed on the keyboard, entering the data in a database. Barbara called upstairs. "Holderness, get the Crims in Cleveland to intercept a white Mercedes van going north on Granz."

Darcy noticed a hole in one of the windows that had been patched with masking tape. "What's that?' she asked.

"Bullet hole," someone said from an adjacent desk. "Rifle shot."

Darcy was shocked but knew better than to say anything about it. Apparently the Black Hats knew about Marcus and where he was. She appreciated why Holderness wouldn't let him out of the building, and forbade him to stand by any windows. Holderness never went anywhere except his private office and occasionally the basement these days. The old man was as safe as he could be.

A few minutes later the elevator door opened and Holderness Parkinson stepped into the room. In one glance he summed up the situation between the three young people. "Status report!" he commanded softly.

"136 of the biocases are in motion, 277 remain in place," Marcus said. "298 have been located and destroyed."

"We'll never get them all," Parkinson muttered.

"My thoughts exactly. It's hopeless."

"I'm afraid people will die. We must be vigilant and save all we can."

Marcus shuddered. Nobody knew how many of the cases had been manufactured and shipped worldwide. He felt sorry for countries that had no sophisticated communications network. Parkinson told him that a number of the Alephs had come in from Draco Epsilon. The Epsilons were working with the Asians, the Africans, and the South Americans. Apparently the Alephs also had the ability to track the biomaterial.

"Holderness!" Darcy was disconcerted by this information.

Parkinson smiled. "You thought I was infallible my dear. I'm not."

"No, of course not." Suddenly the crisis became very real to her. After the president had been silenced last week all hell broke loose in the media. Almost everyone now knew about the rumors of worldwide danger to humanity. Even so, the majority ignored the information because the danger was presented as a potential pandemic that could result from a new strain of virus. It was diabolical.

Parkinson had explained it to her last night. "The Slytherin cover story is almost perfect because there have been outbreaks before: AIDS, SARS, the Ebola virus, the Hanta virus, H1N1, and others."

"But that's silly. This is a world wide conspiracy to kill billions of people. It's all over the internet. People should be marching on Washington, demanding action."

Holderness smiled. "What would happen if you told people that?"

Darcy remembered what Kathleen had said yesterday at work. Darcy tried to explain to her what was going on behind the scenes. "Oh I don't believe it. I've seen that stuff on the net and it's too preposterous. No one can be that crazy." Audrey had said essentially the same thing. "Even if it's true, what can I do about it? If I'm going to die I'm going to die. Meanwhile I have wonderful clothes to design and another show in New York next month." Darcy hadn't argued with either of them. Their reactions were precisely what that odious Lieutenant Mutumbe told them last summer.

"A potential cataclysmic event like this threatens the foundations of people's belief systems," Holderness said. "They don't confront it. The best way to handle the situation is to keep pouring out information." The *Take Back the Country* website of the Crims was now getting five million hits each day worldwide. He was sending data in every two hours. However, five million hits daily was only a fraction of the total human population.

Darcy glanced over at the window with the piece of tape over the bullet hole. She froze in fear, her other concerns forgotten. Somebody was trying to kill Marcus.

Soldier Field, Chicago

When Frank Nitti III heard that a biocase had been planted underneath the stands at Soldier Field he called Holderness Parkinson. "Who put that goddam thing there?" Nitti demanded. "I know that kid of yours has got powers. You tell me because Guido and Benny and me are going to string them up by their balls."

"Relax Frank." Parkinson knew that Nitti was a die-hard Chicago Bears fan. "Your face is as shiny as the rear end of a bus driver's pants."

"Hah, hah, didn't know you was a jokester. You tell me who these scumbags are and I'll take care of them."

"That's P.D. Wodehouse for your information," Parkinson replied. "We have bigger fish to fry, Frank. We don't want the errand boys. We want the assholes who sent them." Parkinson chuckled to himself. He was getting better at speaking Nitti's lingo. "Every case we find saves hundreds of thousands of lives and gets us closer to whoever is behind this."

"All right, all right. What should we do with this thing?"

"Standard procedure. Bring it in and I'll send it for irradiation."

"How many of them are there and how many have we destroyed?" Nitti asked.

"So far we have found and destroyed 198 cases. As far as we know there are 711 total within the mainland 48 states." There was something about these people, Parkinson thought. They were crazy about numerology. The numbers 7 and 11 had significance to the Sabbateans but he wasn't sure why. If you add the 7 and the two 1s in the 11 you get 9, and then the 11 made 9/11. These psychopaths might be trying to re-enact another crisis similar to the September 11, 2001 incident, this time on a worldwide scale.

Nitti interrupted his thoughts. "Are they making any more?"

"We don't know. We were able to destroy that manufacturing facility on Pache Island after they took the bioenhancer out of there."

"How much time have we got?"

"I don't know Frank. We have to act as if there is only a minute left in the game."

"Whoever is doing this is nuts."

"I agree Frank. Keep on your toes and tell your people to be careful. The people behind this are clearly insane. You never know what they will do."

The bioenhancer cases were being moved quietly. Apparently the Black Hats didn't want any firefights. That would surely make the news and mobilize millions of people all over the country. That was an advantage for the White Hats. Equally frustrating for the White Hats was an odd public apathy. Images of the cases and their diabolical purpose had been posted all over the internet. Yet the vast majority of people were content to let others do the searching, with the philosophy that nothing could be done. The mainstream news outlets simply presented the situation as a potential pandemic that public health authorities were working hard to prevent. People seemed satisfied with that, which made internet and other cable outlets appear as crazies. Apparently President Foley had been frightened into silence. Holderness wondered how the rest of the world was doing. He hoped it was better than his efforts in the United States.

Suddenly he had an idea and looked at his watch. It was not quite 8 p.m. and Marcus should still be downstairs.

That night Marcus sat in bed with Darcy, reading. He decided to test Parkinson's hypothesis. At the end of a very long day Parkinson asked him a question. "Marcus, do you think you could use your mental viewer to determine the people who made the biomaterial? We know it was manufactured on Pache Island but there is genius far beyond the two scientists there."

Marcus put his book down, took two deep breaths, and turned on his mental viewer. He sent himself to Pache Island and pushed the "rewind" button. Images began to flood into his head. Before he'd only checked to see that a plane had arrived with the plastic cases. Where did that plane come from? Marcus put the plane in his viewer and rewound its worldline. The plane had taken off from a small hidden airstrip in West Virginia, in the Bowden Cave System. Bowden is ten miles east of Elkins on US Rt. 33, in the Monongahela National Forest.

His mental viewer was becoming more sophisticated. Before, he could track the worldline of a single case. Now, at the cave, he could see the entire history of the cave as far back as he wanted. Wow!

"What are you doing, Marcus?" Darcy asked. He was staring intently at something several feet in front of him. Marcus heard her voice in the distance like an enthralled movie-goer might hear someone talking beside him. "I'm tracking these damn biocases to see who made them."

Darcy put her hand on Marcus' arm and saw him smile.

Marcus traced back the images and saw two men get out of the same Gulfstream aircraft that had landed on Pache. What he saw next blew him away. He rewound his viewer and saw the men enter the cave, walk in about fifty feet and turn left. There they were, all stacked neatly in rows. When he moved back an hour, they weren't there. "Huh?"

"What's the matter?" Darcy asked.

"How did hundreds of those things get delivered and stacked in an hour?" He slowly moved his viewer forward, five minutes … nothing. Ten minutes, twenty minutes … *poof!* "That's impossible."

Darcy put her book down. Marcus was much more interesting than the adventures of her fictional heroine. She pinged his arm with her finger like a bus rider would signal the driver. "The cases just magically appeared."

"Things don't just appear out of thin air," Darcy remarked.

"They're not supposed to." Marcus ran his viewer back a couple of seconds, then slowly forward. One second the cave was empty, the next second it was filled. "How fine can I get this thing?" He moved back and then forward again in millisecond increments. He didn't know how or why his viewer worked but when he needed a finer delta on the time, he just thought about it and it happened. After several minutes of fiddling Marcus discovered a vague shimmering in the cave a few milliseconds before the cases appeared. He fine-tuned the image even further and saw the image of another cave in the background. He moved the worldline slightly backward and saw that the cases had been transferred almost instantaneously from this other cave, which looked a little fuzzy. But how? And where was that other cave? He focused on it in his viewer.

Marcus felt a wrenching in the pit of his stomach as if someone with a giant set of channel-locks had grabbed his insides and was pulling his guts out. Marcus jolted forward on the bed and fell to the floor. He ran into the bathroom and placed his head above the toilet, severely nauseous.

"Marcus!" Darcy could see he didn't hear her.

Marcus' consciousness hovered out in space somewhere. He looked around at the star field but the constellations didn't make sense. His stomach tried to come out of his mouth a couple of times. He steadied his breathing and felt a little better. He was out in the middle of infinity with no reference points, and couldn't get his bearings. Vertigo! He was losing it; he had to turn his viewer off but if he did would he make it back to his body? Marcus panicked. He felt a hand on his shoulder.

"Marcus!"

"Put your arms around me Darcy," he mumbled, really afraid for the first time since that thug had injected him in New York. "I'm going crazy."

"What's happening? I'm going to call an ambulance."

"Don't you dare leave me right now!" Marcus shouted. Nobody could possibly understand what it was like out here except maybe an astronaut. But they had the comforting solidity of their space capsules. "I'm just going to talk my way through this. Hang on to me OK?"

"OK, but I'm frightened."

"So am I Darcy. Just keep in physical contact."

Darcy hugged herself to his back as tightly as she could and rested her head against him as they sat on the small bathroom floor. They were squeezed together like lizards in an M. C. Escher drawing.

Marcus thought out loud. He tried to express his emotions and drain them out of his system. Darcy acknowledged him or squeezed him to let him know she understood.

"God Darcy, there aren't any boundaries out here at all...." He felt a million times worse than when he'd first flew across the country to Dallas. At least he could see the ground and the blue sky over his head and he knew where he was and where he was going. Marcus fought down his vertigo. Out in space there was a vast, terrifying nothingness; no solidity; nothing to grab hold of. As far as he could see, to infinity, just a petrifying blackness and emptiness punctuated with tiny points of light. He turned slightly and saw a bigger object, about the size of a ball bearing, shining brightly. A sun! He turned again and looked down. A bottomless abyss lay beneath his feet and he was falling into it .... Marcus saw a purple planet about the size of a basketball rushing past and grabbed wildly for it like a drowning swimmer reaching for the rock that will save him. Marcus plunged through the atmosphere toward an arid, rocky surface. There it was, the cave.

He stopped himself just in time, hovered just above the cave, and looked up. This place had a thin purple sky. The sun high overhead was bluish-white, smaller than the sun above earth and much brighter. The ground was dotted with small stones and boulders. Outcroppings of rock jutted above the surface, ten to twenty feet high. A cave system, probably, mirroring the one in West Virginia. If this was midday this planet was a lot darker than earth. The scene looked like an oversaturated image with the brightness and gamma turned way down. Blacks, grays, and deep browns dominated the landscape. A deep purple sky on the horizon moderated to a mid-violet overhead. A group of animals moved slowly in the distance.

"God Darcy, this planet is totally alien. It's awful, but beautiful too. It looks like a high desert scene on earth just before sunset. It's probably Belial's planet, no wonder the guy is such a retard. There's nothing here except rock, stone, and sand. Oh no."

"What?" Darcy didn't know if Marcus could come to harm using his mental viewer. It sure seemed so.

"There's a guy moving down there." A figure moved across the rocky surface, his head glimmering in the sun's glare, heading for one of the cave openings. "It's one of those reptiles."

"Get out of there Marcus."

Marcus moved through the top of the cave like a ghost. Finally he realized that he didn't have his body with him. "I keep forgetting that I'm just a mental projection here."

"Be careful."

Marcus found himself inside a huge cave about twenty feet high and a hundred feet in diameter. The entire cave was stacked with biocases, in neat rows. He looked toward the entrance and saw someone enter, a reptilian figure about eight feet tall. Was it Belial, and would the monster see him? Marcus closed his eyes and hoped.

The creature spoke, its tongue slithering in and out of its mouth. "Mar-cus Ri-ley!" it hissed. "What are you doing here?"

This creature wasn't Belial; he was smaller and his head was larger. "Who are you?" Marcus asked, startled. He must not be invisible.

Marcus felt the creature probing his mind.

"I am Qa-Hrrzl. Hominid, I perceive that you must be from my future."

Marcus thought quickly. Of course: his mental viewer was now several months in the past. How could Qa-Hrrzl know that? And how could he communicate with someone from his past? "You are very perceptive," Marcus said, hoping that flattery was the universal language of social progress.

Qa-Hrrzl studied Marcus for a moment. "I am our planet's chief exo-biogeneticist."

Marcus pointed to the cases. "Did you design this hideous biological material?"

Qa-Hrrzl spoke proudly. "Indeed I did. This genetic material is designed specifically for the earthian hominids. All it needs to be effective is a biological activator, which must be placed into the material on the earthian planet."

That must have been what they were doing at Pache Island. Parkinson would want to know that.

Qa-Hrrzl waited for a few moments, observing as Marcus processed the information. "Your mind is much more sophisticated than the other hominids on your planet." The creature spoke approvingly. "Are you a separate sub-species?"

Marcus analyzed Qa-Hrrzl's communication sidebands and saw Pietro Adolfone and his cohorts and their disgusting communication rituals. His consciousness exploded in comprehension.

"So you guys *are* the rats behind our dark arts and demonology and all the rest."

Qa-Hrrzl nodded, pleased at Marcus' quick understanding. On Tau the only ones he could talk to intelligently were his fellow scientists, and they were a small minority of the population. "Of course. You did not answer my question."

"No, I am not a separate sub-species. The idiots you communicate with are recidivist morons with no understanding."

Qa-Hrrzl stared, flabbergasted. This hominid had precisely identified his thoughts about the earthian scum he was forced to work with. Mar-cus Ri-ley apparently understood his greatest problem when working with the hominid bloodlines: genetic purity also meant genetic stagnation. Qa-Hrrzl's curiosity got the better of him.

"Do you mean to say that the majority of your race has a mind like yours?"

Marcus was honest. "No. But almost all of us are smarter than the people you are dealing with."

"Open your mind, Mar-cus Ri-ley," Qa-Hrrzl said. "I wish to verify your assertions."

Marcus shrugged mentally. If he could defeat Belial he wasn't worried too much about this guy.

Marcus opened up and let Qa-Hrrzl enter. The creature's mind was vast and powerful like an elaborate information network. Emotionless, but fairly sane. Or at least saner than that psycho Belial. While Qa-Hrrzl examined him Marcus did the same. Qa-Hrrzl's greatest excitement was scientific pursuit and the coming Harvest ... so this guy was also involved in that sickening enterprise.

He heard Darcy's voice from a great distance. "Marcus, who are you talking to?"

Marcus was able to use a small compartment of his mind to reply. He could still feel her arms around his body even though his consciousness was in the cave. "The creature in the cave. He's a bit friendlier than Belial."

"Oh Marcus I hope so."

Marcus saw Qa-Hrrzl examine his mental image of Darcy. "Your female?" he asked.

"Yes."

Qa-Hrrzl was not interested. After a few more moments he spoke. "I am satisfied, Mar-cus Ri-ley. My impression of your planet has been skewed. I must reevaluate."

Qa-Hrrzl turned his attention to the cases and walked right through him. "This is weird Darcy. That guy just walked right into me like I wasn't even here."

"How do you feel?"

"Scared out of my mind. But I want to find out how those cases got to earth."

Qa-Hrrzl walked back about 100 feet and grabbed a pair of headphones that looked like the ones Barbara wore. "OK, this reptile guy is putting on some headphones," Marcus narrated. "Wow! The air in here is literally shimmering." Marcus saw a huge white cube form around the cases and then they disappeared in an instant. Qa-Hrrzl walked out of the cave and glanced perfunctorily upward at Marcus, whose projection hovered about two feet off the ground.

"Now I have a problem," Marcus realized, staring into the empty cave.

"What?"

"How do I get back? There's no way I'm going through that space travel again."

"Just shut off your viewer," Darcy suggested.

Marcus shook his head. "My consciousness might be stuck here with no way back."

He thought for a few moments. "I'll try to visualize the cave on earth where I started. Maybe I can project my consciousness directly to the cave without going back out into space. Hang onto me Darcy."

Darcy hugged him tighter. Marcus used the viewer to get an image of the West Virginia cave. He imagined himself back in it.

"Hey that was easy. I made it!" Marcus noticed that the cave was empty. He had arrived back on the worldline of this cave at the same time he left. "OK, I'm back in the original cave just before the transfer."

"Good. Now what?"

Marcus flipped the viewer forward and saw the cave on Belial's planet shimmer. The cave on earth did the same and the cases were transferred. He was careful to keep his awareness on this side. "I made a mistake by projecting myself to the other cave too fast," Marcus remarked. "It scared the crap out of me."

"I'll say. You scared me too."

Marcus shut off his viewer and turned to Darcy, who was staring at him, fascinated. "I thought I saw a cave and a brilliant white star," she said.

"You could see what was in my head?"

"Maybe it wasn't in your head. Maybe you were projecting the images."

Marcus scratched his chin, which had a black stubble; he'd forgotten to shave. "Yeah, maybe. Those cases came from Belial's planet. The planet of those damn reptiles."

"How did they get here?"

"Some kind of transporter. The technology must be really sophisticated because I didn't see any instrumentation."

"Let's go back to the couch," she suggested. "This bathroom floor is getting uncomfortable."

They walked slowly back to the living room and sat down.

"So what have we learned?" Darcy asked.

"Nothing much, after all that. All we know is that some crazy Slytherin group, backed by a bunch of psycho aliens, are trying to kill us. That doesn't solve any of our problems."

"Maybe Holderness can make something of it," Darcy suggested.

"Yeah, but probably not. Apparently the cases I saw in that cave were only for the United States. Did they also send them to other places in the world? Damn, I forgot to ask Qa-Hrrzl that."

Darcy gasped. "It's ... it's abominable. You'd better make a report while the events are still fresh in your mind."

"God I'm tired, and sweaty. I want to take a shower and sleep."

"First make your report," Darcy ordered.

"It's two in the morning. If I have to work at this time of night I'm going to need special compensation later," he hinted.

Darcy laughed. "Go make your report. I'm not going anywhere."

Marcus didn't finish his report until after 7. By that time Darcy was already up and about.

"All that work for nothing!"

"For nothing?"

"Yeah, I wanted to make love to you last night."

"We have plenty of time for that Marcus. You're needed downstairs in less than an hour." Darcy walked out into the hallway.

Marcus groaned. Life wasn't fair.

Draco Tau

Qa-Hrrzl returned to his laboratory, disturbed. The conversation with the hominid Ri-ley had just revealed itself in his awareness, even though their discussion had occurred more than two months ago. This was a disturbing anomaly. It indicated influence on his personal worldline from a future event, which also indicated a paradox within the earthian socio-event matrix. A paradox was a build up of temporal energy around a future probability that now had unexpected variables. This signified an imbalance in the matrix and in his Harvest calculations. Qa-Hrrzl reviewed the latest data from the earthian planet, and was shocked. Many of the locations of their Purification Substance had been identified and the substance itself was being destroyed. But how? He reviewed his conversation with the hominid and discovered that Ri-ley himself had been responsible. They had tried to kill him several times but he was beyond their reach now. Fortunately, Ri-ley only knew the locations within the United States, which had only four percent of the world's population. There was still a chance.

Qa-Hrrzl backtracked his socio-event model and discovered that a critical event had been the United States president's announcement. This ill-fated occurrence had caused the system to trend too rapidly toward the edge of chaos. Something would have to be done, and quickly, to stop the momentum toward the chaotic state. The hominid president had somehow maneuvered himself outside the control of Brent-kow-ski, his handler. The personality matrix of Fo-ley, a mild-mannered individual, should not have reacted in this way. Qa-Hrrzl checked the variables surrounding the Event Matrix and discovered that he had made an error. The combination of the actors Pan-ter-a, James, and others, had all contributed small but subtle momentum and tripped the personality matrix of Fo-ley. Hurriedly, he moved the model forward in time. Yes. Fo-ley was temporarily the sociological centroid of a divergent Event Matrix, one that would move the system chaotically and ensure a failed Harvest. Now that Fo-ley's activity threshold had been reached he was capable of even more unfavorable acts. He must be stopped, but how?

Then he knew.

Chicago

Rumors were swirling around Washington DC. As Darcy and Marcus watched the CBS Evening News, Kelley Scott concluded, "Ever since President Foley took ill at his press conference two days ago, strange and unsubstantiated rumors have been coming out of the White House. The president hasn't been seen in public or spoken since then. Conspiracy theories have been circulating on the net. One is that President Foley is under armed guard, that he's been taken seriously ill, and that little green men have taken him away in a UFO. You know, you can't believe everything you see on the web. And that's the news for today."

Marcus called Parkinson on the Royalty intranet. "Did you see CBS news?"

"Yes Marcus."

"What do you think?"

"That one of those three unsubstantiated rumors is true."

"What?" Darcy said. "I thought they lied most of the time."

Parkinson chuckled. "No Darcy, that wouldn't work. The Black Hats only lie in the media when they absolutely have to. Almost always they do tell the truth, but obfuscate it."

"How?" Marcus asked.

"My guess is that either the first or the second rumor is true. The third one debunks the first two. As you know, interest in UFOs and extraterrestrials has been very high for the past year. However, surveys show that most people believe these topics are for fruitcakes, or they don't care. To mention them in the same sentence as the truth devalues it, and listeners dismiss the entire sentence. Notice that the information was prefaced with the keywords 'conspiracy theory.' These two words indicate mental imbalance and tend to debunk everything said after it. The result is confusion."

"It's very clever," Darcy said.

"Yes dear. We're dealing with inbred crazies but some of them aren't stupid."

The White House

Just after President Foley's nightly briefing with DCI Pantera two nights after his news conference, he heard voices and a scuffle outside the bedroom door. One of the secret service agents opened the door and stuck his head in. "I'm sorry Mr. President. There's someone out here who needs to see you."

Alice was already in bed and asleep. "Tell him to come back tomorrow morning Henry," Foley replied, still at his bedroom desk. "I'm tired."

"I'm afraid this won't wait, Mr. President." Martin Foley saw a smallish man with hard blue eyes and a brush cut blow past the guards and walk purposefully into the room. He wore a sidearm and was followed by two armed men.

"Who are you?" the president asked, profoundly irritated. "Henry and Jorge, come in here."

The two secret servicemen entered the room and stood behind the intruders. "Who are these men?" the president asked.

"The Secret Service has discovered a plot against your life and recommended a personal bodyguard," the intruder said. "These two gentlemen will confirm it."

Jorge and Henry nodded their heads but said nothing. The other man was clearly in command.

"That is patent nonsense," the president replied. "Pantera has said nothing of it, nor Oleg, in my daily briefings."

"They didn't want to frighten you, Mr. President." The intruder met the president's eyes insolently. Martin Foley felt like Nikolai Alexandrovich, the last Russian tsar, after his family had been captured by the Bolsheviks in the 1917 Russian Revolution. The two other intruders stared into space but looked ready for action.

"Martin, what's happening?" Alice asked, waking.

The intruder's eyes blasted a warning. He was clearly on edge and gripped his weapon tightly. "These gentlemen were sent here to watch over us," the president said calmly. "Not to worry."

The man gestured to the two secret servicemen. "You may leave us. I need a few words with the president and his wife." The men left without a word.

The intruder nodded grimly as if to say, "Play along and don't be a hero."

Martin Foley didn't feel heroic at all. He felt like one of those ornamental statues in a public park that dogs urinated on.

"Explain this, whoever you are, and it better be good," Foley said, finding courage. "This is the United States not Paraguay. Is this a coup d'état?"

The man smiled coldly. "We're here just to make sure you don't do anything stupid."

The president was entirely clear on the man's meaning. President Foley gestured to the armed men. "Get those thugs out of here."

The intruder hesitated for several seconds and then gestured. The armed men left. "We are intelligent men. I'm hoping that this little performance won't have to be repeated."

"I understand," the president said.

"I'll be with you from now on Mr. President," the intruder said. "In the background of course. Your little performance two evenings ago isn't to be repeated. Is that clear?"

Alice Foley was now sitting up in bed, thoroughly shocked and angry. "Martin, he can't say those things to the President of the United States!"

"Apparently he can, Alice," Foley said. "Please don't say or do anything out of the ordinary."

"That's good advice," the intruder said. "It applies to both of you."

"Does Oleg know about this?" Foley asked.

The man shrugged. "Certainly. Brentkowski is very concerned. I'm here on his orders to ensure your future safety."

So that's how it is! All is to go back to normal. With the caveat that he, the President of the United States, toe the line. "If I asked who you represented would you tell me?"

"I represent a group of concerned patriots who see the country going in the wrong direction."

The president laughed out loud. "All right, if that's the way you want it."

"Remember Mr. President," the man said, glancing at Alice. "Even if you can't see me I'm with you. We have others watching your family."

President Foley's face hardened. "I understand, you degenerate. Get out of my bedroom."

As he walked back to the bed and confronted his shocked wife, the president understood that he had no real decision-making power at all. A bunch of thugs had just marched past two Secret Service agents. His guys had quietly deferred.

"Martin, that man just threatened you and our family. It's outrageous."

The president sat on the bed and ran his fingers through his thinning white hair. "I'm afraid it is dear."

"What will you do?"

"I'm going to have a long talk with Oleg tomorrow morning. If he doesn't give me satisfactory answers I'm going to step down as president."

Alice's jaw dropped. "Step down? Why, that will put you in the same class as Nixon!"

President Foley yawned involuntarily. "Not at all Alice. Nixon resigned because he was engaged in illegal activities and got caught. I don't want to be a muppet but apparently that's what I am now." The president lay down in bed and pulled the covers up. "God I'm tired, bone tired. I'm going to sleep."

Darcy and Audrey Quenioux walked from the office of "Audrey's Creations," on State Street between Adams and Jackson, to a little restaurant across the street. The location was perfect for her boutique. The landlord had heard of her New York shop. He was suitably impressed when the two women, impeccably dressed, entered his downtown office. An introductory letter from Holderness Parkinson had also been well received. Audrey, a shrewd bargainer, talked down the rent. She insisted that her boutique, with its fashionable cache, would raise the tone of every business in the building. Audrey and Darcy, excitedly discussing their upcoming show (and very hungry) entered the little sandwich shop. Eating and serving food didn't seem to be foremost on anyone's mind. Servers, staff, and patrons all crowded around the TV as anxious reporters listened to the White House Press Secretary.

"What's ado?" Audrey asked.

"President Foley has resigned!" a woman said.

"Shhhhhh!"

"'... the president told me this morning that he no longer feels capable of assuming the duties of his office. That's all I can tell you Bill."

"Is he sick?"

"He's in good health. Due to intimate personal reasons, which will not be divulged to the press, President Foley this morning submitted his formal resignation to Secretary of State Hilton. Vice President Sensenbaugh will take over as president until the new elections next year. I'm sorry ladies and gentlemen. It is not my job to speculate and I will not do so. I only know what was printed on the president's formal resignation statement. I have distributed copies to all of you. You know as much as I do. As of ten o'clock this morning, the new president is Mr. Sensenbaugh."

"I'm not hungry anymore," Darcy said.

"Neither am I," Audrey replied. *"Nous a laissés partir."*

Draco Tau

Qa-Hrrzl was in his personal laboratory, gazing into his three-dimensional holographic simulator. The simulator contained the results of the latest data he had fed into the socio-event event matrix of the earthian planet. He saw clearly that the resignation of the hominid president in the United States had thrown the entire system past the edge of chaos and almost completely out of reach of their influence. His action to salvage the situation had only made it worse. He summoned his chief assistant, Qa-Jbbt.

When Qa-Jbbt arrived Qa-Hrzzl showed him the simulator and asked for his analysis.

"The hominid planet is now self-organizing to a new level," Qa-Jbbt said.

Qa-Hrzzl bristled. His minion's assessment could be interpreted as an insult. But the scientist in him saw the truth.

"The key actor is now Mar-cus Ri-ley," Qa-Jbbt said. "No. There is someone behind Riley, someone in the background."

Suddenly Qa-Hrzzl saw it. "It is that one, the hominid Ri-ley calls Par-kinson. And Roy-al-ty."

"Yes," Qa-Jbbt agreed. "This hominid's configuration space now shows linkage with more of the important opposition actors than any other. This is the true epicenter of the matrix imbalance."

Qa-Hrzzl was almost admiring. "Subtle and clever, shielding himself inside an earthian brothel. Like me the hominid Par-kin-son remains aloof, directing the flow of events from behind the scenes."

"We will check the staff list and re-inspect the worldliness emanating from Roy-al-ty," Qa-Hrzzl ordered. Both scientists worked silently. "Yes, this is the new nexus of instability," Qa-Hrzzl concluded. "It will have to be eliminated."

"It is amazing how rapidly events on the earthian planet have changed, sir," Qa-Jbbt said.

"All of the important worldlines are organizing but not to my own vectors." Qa-Hrzzl frowned. "Despite thousands of years of preparation, an invisible hand is apparently guiding the important earthian actors and the population as a whole, according to an unknown but self-organizing principle." Qa-Hrzzl studied the hominid event matrix and saw its beauty, but also the very real probability of a failed Harvest. "The immense earthian population of over 8 billion has created too many actors. We have bitten off, as the hominids would say, more than we can chew."

"Too much information is being released sir," Qa-Jbbt said.

Qa-Hrzzl gnashed his teeth in frustration. "The carefully constructed meme structures that keep the earthians thinking and acting within the correct boundaries is imploding. At the critical time juncture when all should be in readiness, too many of our containers are being located and destroyed."

Qa-Hrzzl made his decision. "The Trigger must be pulled immediately. It is that or complete failure."

Qa-Jbbt bowed low in submission, thankful that he was not responsible for the fiasco on the hominid planet. Qa-Hrzzl dismissed him with a wave of his hand. His blood ran cold as he contemplated the disgrace and dishonor of *Zorghal*. What had Belial said? "A failed Harvest is insupportable." He had said it twice. His entire bloodline – males, females, and children – would die a humiliating death. Even more egregious, his bloodline would be permanently stricken from Tau genealogy.

There was still the slimmest of chances, however, for a glorious resolution. He would have to act boldly, heroically. He must himself go to earth and personally kill Par-kin-son and his staff. And if he had the chance he would kill the irritant Mar-cus Ri-ley as well. Without the backing and the guidance of Par-kin-son, Ri-ley would become an ineffective element. That might just provide the needed jolt. When a socio-event matrix entered the zone of chaos, shocking the system could sometimes re-balance it, just as an electric shock to the brain could sometimes restore neurological balance.

Qa-Hrrzl wasted no more time bemoaning his situation. He would inform the Council that in 36 earthian hours, the Purification Substance must be released and the Harvest begun. That would barely give him time to complete his mission. After, he would find refuge in the desert of the American southwest, where he could be comfortable. He knew exactly where to go. An ancient transportal existed forty miles south of Sedona Arizona.

Chapter **32**

Cave of the Mounds near Madison, Wisconsin

Agigantic hooded figure shrouded in heavy clothing gazed into the pitch-black parking lot from the cave entrance. The sharp yellow eyes of the waiting figure could see well enough. A short distance away, the bulk of a transportation vehicle loomed. His hominid contact had been successful then.

Qa-Hrrzl was cold. The northern hemisphere of this planet was in spring and the weather was warming. The temperatures were still much too low for his reptilian biology. He had known the risks, however. Was he not the Tau's chief geneticist? He had developed a serum that would temporarily raise his metabolic rate and thin his blood. He planned to stay on the earthian planet only as long as it took to complete his mission. A suicide mission, but one worthy of a true race hero.

Confidently (for caution was unknown to any Tau) Qa-Hrrzl strode to the waiting monstrosity. He cursed. The hard substance beneath his leathery feet was so cold he had to hurry, offending his reptilian dignity. Even though no one was watching he had been made to look ridiculous. These hominids would pay dearly for that.

Now, how to enter this primitive thing? A piece of metal protruded and he pushed inward. The door swung open to a cockpit containing a large wheel, pedals on the floor, and an instrument panel. He swung his eight-foot bulk slowly into the cramped device. On the seat he saw his instruction sheet. The paper had diagrams in the Tau language for the vehicle's operation. Next to the instructions was a basket. He opened the basket to find raw meat, iced to preserve its freshness. Qa-Hrrzl shuddered. Meat should be eaten warm and fresh-killed, with its blood. This substance was dry but its odor was not unappetizing. He needed five pounds of meat each planetary rotation. This flesh would suffice for the time being. Underneath the seat opposite was a special surprise for the hominids at Roy-al-ty.

Qa-Hrrzl turned his attention to the instruction chart and studied it carefully for several seconds, noting with satisfaction that the vehicle had a heating unit. Qa-Hrrzl reached for a handle in front of the seat, moving it back as far as it would go. His knees bumped against the wheel. He manipulated the steering column upward, providing some comfort. He lowered the seat as far as it would go but his head still bumped against the ceiling.

How to activate this primitive vehicle? He inspected the wheel and its environs and discovered a button. He placed one of his long leathery fingers on the thing and pushed down. Instantly he felt the vehicle come alive, and smelled something repulsive through the still open door. Hydrocarbons. He remembered that the vehicle had a fuel storage tank. Qa-Hrrzl checked the indicator on the instrument panel, which pointed to "F." Excellent. From here to the hominid hive of Chi-ca-go, and Par-kin-son, was approximately 180 earthian miles. This device should allow him to reach the earthian hive without refueling. His night vision was excellent but these hominids were blind in the dark. He had been warned that the vehicle's lighting system must be enabled. Looking on the sheet beside him, he saw the proper control.

The guidance system had already been programmed. Qa-Hrrzl turned jerkily from the parking lot onto Cave of the Mounds road. This primitive vehicle was sluggish and slow but the positioning system guided him. He would take the 90 thoroughfare all the way into the city. He had been lucky. The nearest transportal was located not far from the target city of Chi-ca-go, in a cave. Unfortunately the cave was in an inhabited area, and the cave itself had been turned into a tourist attraction. On this night the site was devoid of hominids.

For some reason, many of the earthian stargates were in caves. This one had only recently become available for use less than a century ago when limestone quarry workers blasted a section of the quarry and exposed an opening to the cave. Fortunately, knowledge of the naturally occurring stargates had been hidden from these primitives.

Qa-Hrrzl traveled down the hard surface of the interstate with his heating unit on maximum. The sky was becoming faintly lighter. He must make it to the earthian hive of Chi-ca-go before the rising of the planet's sun. Hunched over, he might pass for an unusually tall hominid in the dark. Daylight would expose him. Qa-Hrrzl pushed down upon the fuel pedal. He was not sure how quickly the vehicle would go; but he would keep the velocity of this machine at its maximum. As he passed other vehicles he noticed something peculiar: the sky was filled with moisture accumulation. On Tau, when the sun came over the horizon, the effect was instantaneous. The sky was always clear. Here, the light overhead remained dull and diffused. The atmosphere of the hominid planet was thicker and higher in oxygen. Moisture actually fell from the skies!

Qa-Hrrzl drove for some time, easily maneuvering his vehicle around other slower-moving ones. He heard a noise behind him and saw flashing lights. Qa-Hrrzl gazed down into a small mounted mirror and saw a hominid in an official vehicle behind him, pointing to the upcoming exit. He turned off the highway onto a smaller, deserted road. He was curious. These earthian police departments were linked with the more secretive intelligence agencies, which in turn were directed by Tau operatives. Now he could determine the efficiency of their field workers at the end of the chain of command, at the level of citizen contact.

Qa-Hrrzl stopped the vehicle and watched as a little earthian approached, carrying a firearm at his side. Good. Intimidation was important for establishing fear and correct behavior. Qa-Hrrzl laughed as the earthian squinted, trying to see into the vehicle. Apparently his windows were one-way only. Qa-Hrrzl marked down another point for his hominid contact as the little earthian pounded his hand on the window. This was well. The average citizen would by this time be willing to obey any command.

As the officer continued to beat upon the side of his vehicle Qa-Hrrzl became irritated, for he could not locate the button to open the transparency. The hominid now began to shout and the tone of its voice became threatening. It banged even harder. The effrontery of this scum! Qa-Hrrz's reptilian emotions got the better of him. His blood began to boil and he finally discovered the window mechanism, thrust out his great reptilian head, and roared.

Officer Grady was tired after a long shift. He hated traffic duty and the abuse he got from angry motorists. Grady could almost sympathize with them, for the state had increased traffic fines considerably. But this asshole had been going over 100 mph, weaving in and out of traffic. He was going to take him in. As the window opened a huge repulsive head thrust forward and roared like a dragon. The goddam creature from the black lagoon! Frightened and appalled, his muscles would not work right. Grady reached for his weapon, feeling like a fly trapped in coagulating butter. A gigantic figure draped in blankets emerged from the vehicle and stretched to its full height, unsheathing its claws. Grady tried to scream but his mouth opened and nothing came out. Two long, leathery, green-colored arms reached out for him. He closed his eyes, waiting for something terrible. Grady heard a hissing sound and opened his eyes. The ugly, sickly-green creature was easily eight feet tall. It was bent over him with arms curled, a long tongue slithering in and out of its mouth. Suddenly the creature straightened, leaned back, and bellowed. The damn thing was laughing at him!

He should kill it right now but he was too scared. Could this be some sort of bizarre performance test? Grady ran back to his vehicle and turned on his camera, hoping that it wasn't too dark to record. The boys weren't going to believe this. Another one of those science-fiction creatures, like that one in New York! The thing roared again and ran toward his vehicle, its great feet pounding like Godzilla ready to eat Tokyo. Officer Grady floored it, trying to run over the repulsive creature. His bumper struck it a glancing blow and an arm smashed through the driver's-side window, spraying glass all over. Grady grabbed his gun and fired but he had already moved past the creature. His bullet went wide. The gun slipped from his hand and fell to the ground but he was too frightened to retrieve it. The monster behind him was still moving forward with increasing speed like King Kong on amphetamines.

The hominid's vehicle raced away, tires screeching. Qa-Hrrzl detected the obnoxious odor of burning rubber. A short distance down the road he saw the hominid's firearm. His feet were becoming frozen on the cold asphalt road surface but he wanted to prove he had been on the earthian planet so he walked toward it. On the way he inspected his knee but it was unharmed. Qa-Hrrzl picked up the weapon and strode quickly back to his vehicle. The antics of the little hominid policeman made him bellow with laughter. Earthian humor was something he wanted to understand but did not. His race had no sense of the ridiculous and was poorer for it. Perhaps, exposed to the earthian environment and its memes, he may be developing a sense of humor. There was a potential for expansion in these hominids, primitive as they were, that his race did not possess. Perhaps the Tau genetic alterations of the species had not fully suppressed those mysterious "light codes" of this dimension's ancient seeder race.

Qa-Hrrzl shook off those unproductive thoughts. There was important work to be done now and his time was severely limited. The elimination of Par-kin-son was imperative if he were ever to return to Tau and ensure a moderately successful

Harvest. Every moment wasted was one more moment for the socio-event matrix to fall further into an even more chaotic and irreversible pattern.

He checked his chronometer. In 33 hours the Purification Substance would be released. The Chi-ca-go area was one of the prime targets.

Qa-Hrrzl settled down into his uncomfortable seat and followed the directions of the guidance unit. Apparently he must travel at the same speed as the others. But now he knew no one could see inside the vehicle, so he need not worry until he reached Roy-al-ty. He would kill Par-kin-son and the hominid pest Marcus Ri-ley. Two hominids killed with one blow. Qa-Hrrzl bellowed again. He had made a joke!

Chicago, Cadillac Place Theater

The evening before Qa-Hrrzl transported to the Cave of the Mountains, Darcy and Marcus went out for the first time in weeks.

"Marcus, that was wonderful." Darcy and Marcus were walking out of the Cadillac Palace on Randolph and LaSalle. A crowd of well dressed people surged around them. "It was like going back into the 18th century."

"The seats were even big enough." Marcus replied.

"You're such a rustic Marcus," Darcy teased. "Why, this theater was modeled on the palaces of Fontainebleau and Versailles. Did you see all that breche violet and the white marble, and the gold leaf? And the mirrors in the lobby. It was spectacular."

"A lot you know," Marcus retorted playfully. "You got all that from Parkinson."

Darcy pouted. "I've been in Paris many times. I've seen the Louvre and have even been to the Paris Opera. I can appreciate beauty."

Marcus felt his playful devil. "You didn't even mention the play. Was it any good?"

Darcy bristled. "Of course it was good. You probably slept through the whole thing."

"I must admit that when they started singing about diamonds and jewelry I did nod off a time or two."

Darcy straightened. "A rustic, Marcus." She looked up at his tall handsome figure. "But you do look wonderful in that tux."

"Yes I do," Marcus said. "I've had to fight off the women all night during the intermissions."

Darcy's eyes flashed. "I saw that hussy with the black hair ogling you. And you ogled her back!"

"Sure I did," Marcus said, wanting to see how far he could go. "I couldn't disappoint any of my fans."

"*Parbleau,*" Darcy said, her lips thinning. Sometimes people stopped him in the street, recognizing him from the news. "I have more fans than you and they are much more exclusive."

Marcus grinned. "If I'm a rustic, Darcy, you're a snob."

Darcy held her head up. "I prefer the latter to the former."

Marcus laughed. He could see that her mood was changing for the worse so he stopped and picked her up in his arms. He was jostled a bit but he held his ground.

"Marcus! Put me down."

"No my dear," he said, planting a kiss firmly on her lips.

Darcy relaxed into the kiss, thoroughly enjoying herself. In the midst of her pleasure she wondered whether this was the surprise he'd promised her tonight.

Several women stopped and one of them sighed. "How romantic!" she breathed.

Marcus finally put Darcy down and looked around. "There. Did I do that right?"

Darcy began brushing her disheveled curls.

"Oh yes," a pretty blond replied. "If you'd like to practice some more ..."

Darcy stepped in, placing her arm around Marcus' waist. She tried to pull him away. "He's not really that good."

The other women laughed. "Don't bet on it honey," the blond said, observing Darcy's flushed face and her heavy breathing. "That's a beautiful man you have there."

Darcy decided to be magnanimous. "He certainly is." She couldn't help adding, "But he's a bit of a clod."

Marcus watched, amused, at the interplay between the women.

"If you get tired of him you can give him my phone number," said a copper-haired woman with freckles around her nose.

Darcy laughed. "All right Marcus, we'd better find that limo."

By this time the crowd had dispersed. Marcus and Darcy moved toward the curb along with the women who had stopped to observe the kiss. A few cabs were still waiting. Marcus saw their limo, with Richard driving. "Royalty Services!" someone cried behind them. An older woman, expensively dressed, moved swiftly forward and stood in front of Darcy. "You're Darcy Regier. Of Audrey's Creations."

"That's right." Darcy was pleased and held out her hand. The woman had the look and the air of wealth and sophistication. "We're having an exclusive private showing at the Silversmith Hotel next Wednesday evening. Would you like to attend?"

"Oh, would I!" the woman replied.

"Well then," Darcy said, looking in her purse. "Here is a ticket. We'll be showing in the Sterling Room from 7 p.m. until 10 p.m."

"I'll be there." The woman hurried away to find a taxi.

Darcy was smug as she walked with Marcus to the waiting Royalty limo. "I have fans too."

"You certainly do," Marcus replied. "She probably has money. My fans are just young and beautiful normal people."

Darcy thrust deep. "But they only want you for your body Marcus."

Marcus playfully fell back a step. "Touche. You win this round."

Darcy, pleased with herself, grabbed Marcus's hand and they stepped into the limo.

Marcus loved riding in the luxury limousine. They had been dropped off and picked up, and didn't have to think about anything except enjoying themselves. Nils van Bergen had been guarding them tonight, supposedly. "Have you seen Nils?" Marcus asked.

"No I haven't, all night. Wasn't he supposed to be watching over us?"

"I think Parkinson is a little paranoid."

"I don't care. I'm so glad we could finally have a night out together." Darcy sighed. "What has he got you doing tomorrow?"

"I'm tracking down bio-cases outside the US. I'm working ten times harder than before."

"We both have been so busy we've hardly had time to say two words to each other. The world hasn't fallen apart yet, so I assume that you are both keeping things from going over the cliff?"

"It's the damndest thing," Marcus replied, relapsing into old habits of speech. "Last week Nils van Bergen brought in several of the cursed biocases and told the old man that I should be able to trace down some of them outside the United States. And would I try. Now instead of working 16 hours a day I'm working 18."

"Marcus, you can't possibly identify every single one of them in the whole world."

"Of course not honey. Fortunately I'm not the only one who has the remote viewing ability. There are several people in Europe and China and a few others in

Asia and Russia who can do it, and one or two in Brazil. Apparently the development of psychic and extra-sensory abilities has been a high priority in some other countries. The Alephs are helping too. But I still have to do a lot of the work because it takes a while to train new people."

Darcy brightened. "The world is going to escape then?"

"Not according to the old fellow upstairs. He says there are several hundred we haven't located. But the anticipated death toll is down from the billions to the hundreds of millions."

Darcy was shocked. "Hundreds of millions? That's terrible!"

"What we can't figure out is why the bastards haven't set them off yet. It doesn't make sense."

"The entire situation makes no sense." Darcy was outraged. "What kind of evil people would want to kill billions of people? And why?"

"That's what the old boy tried to explain to you before," Marcus said.

"Well, I don't believe it. Harvest indeed. It's preposterous. No sane person would believe it."

Marcus agreed. "The universe isn't anything like we've been told Darcy. The entire situation is like a bad dream, except the dream is real. Those biocases are real. Belial and Qa-Hrzzl are real. Even though I deal with this stuff every day I can hardly believe it myself. It goes beyond anything we have been taught about the world."

They sat in silence for a few moments.

Darcy couldn't focus on unpleasantness for very long before her good nature turned to something more agreeable. She was pleased that she had been kissed very thoroughly in public. She was also a little disappointed because she had not gotten her surprise. Which brought her mind to something she'd been thinking about more and more lately.

"Marcus ..."

"Yes?"

"Do you think we should get married?" she blurted.

"Funny you should mention that." Marcus calmly reached into an inside pocket and drew out a small but very elegant velvet case rimmed around with gold.

Darcy's hands covered her mouth. "Oh!" She looked up at him shyly. "Is this for me?"

"Well of course it is, silly girl. Who else would it be for?"

Darcy carefully took the case and opened it slowly. Inside was a bright diamond ring, set in silver, with a gold band. "Marcus, it's beautiful. Silver, gold, and diamonds all in one!" She gazed up at him wide-eyed, her face looking so angelic and innocent that his heart melted.

"I thought you'd like it."

Darcy waited expectantly.

Marcus realized that he was forgetting something but he couldn't remember what.

Darcy smiled indulgently, as one might to a recalcitrant puppy. Marcus got it.

"Oh yeah, now I remember. Will you marry me Darcy?"

"Yes Marcus, I *will* marry you. I *will* be your wife."

Marcus laughed. "Moonstruck. After Johnny Camereri proposes to Cher."

"And you called me a silly girl. When a man proposes to a woman he should get down on his knees. *Capisci?*"

Marcus got off the seat and put one knee on the floor. "Gimme that ring back."

Darcy handed him the ring.

"Darcy Regier, will you marry me?" Marcus handed her the little velvet case. "And don't tell me it's just a stupid pinky ring."

Darcy laughed. "No Marcus, this is fine." She smiled mischievously. "Do you love her Marcus?"

Marcus knew his cue. "I love her awful."

"Oh, that's too bad," Darcy deadpanned.

In front, Richard sighed and turned his head. "A good bachelor customer!" he moaned. All three of the riders cracked up.

That night Marcus got lucky.

Royalty Services, 5 a.m. the next morning

"Holderness?"

"Speaking." He already knew it was his contact at DHS Chicago. He'd heard the red phone on the first ring and jumped out of bed as fast as his aging body could get him into his private office. "Is there news Rodney?"

"Chicago police report an incident with an eight foot tall reptile during a routine traffic stop. The vehicle is a Ford Super Duty truck. It was headed east down I-90 at over 100 mph. Thought you should know."

Holderness smiled. "That's excellent work Rod. We'll be ready." Parkinson hung up the phone and thought: the network is coming together nicely.

A dark blue Ford Super Duty pickup with tinted windows arrived in front of the Royalty Services building just before 8 a.m. Nils van Bergen, on duty since 5 a.m., duly noted its arrival. The vehicle's engine shut off and no movement was seen inside.

Nils spoke into his headset. "Potential trouble outside."

Holderness Parkinson acknowledged. "Keep an eye out Nils, and be ready. You know what to do."

Nils van Bergen put down his headset and walked the stairs down to the lobby, carrying a specially designed air gun. He took a seat at the back of the room just to the right of the big picture window. He could see the truck and the street and most of the path that led to the front door. He should not be noticed from the outside. Nils sat completely motionless and watched. He could sit this way quite comfortably for hours and remain alert. In the Royalty building there was no lobby receptionist; all appointments were privately arranged by Chantelle Hudson. Nils was alone.

Qa-Hrrzl, his knees hunched up in the cockpit, planned his attack. He removed the meat container's top and pushed it under the heating orifice. As he chewed he reviewed the floor plan of this building, which he had seen from his monitoring station on Tau. He knew that Mar-cus Ri-ley usually came down to the basement at 8 of the earthian clock. Par-kin-son always showed up punctually at 8 for the morning staff briefing. He checked the chronometer on the instrument panel. It read 7:54. He would wait until 8:05, break down the front door if necessary, and enter the waiting area. The basement access point was to the right, approximately twenty earthian feet from the door. The descending consisted of two sets of thirteen footings, with a small platform separating them. Par-kin-son and Ri-ley would be at the central desk approximately thirty earthian feet from the bottom footing. Perfect. He could easily cover that distance in three strides and be upon the hominids before they could react. He knew that neither Ri-ley nor any of the staff carried weapons, but that Par-kin-son sometimes had a firearm. He reached into the compartment under the dash and pulled out the little weapon he'd picked up from the hominid policeman. It was tiny in his huge hand, but serviceable. He retrieved the capsule under the seat and wrapped it underneath his clothing.

Qa-Hrrrzl was not nervous. He simply waited, envisioning his actions and programming them into his muscle memory. He developed contingency plans for all unexpected events. Satisfied, he glanced at the chronometer. One minute. At this time period few hominids were likely to occupy the walking path or be upon the road. Nevertheless, he placed his cloth coverings around him to conceal his form as much as possible. Qa-Hrrzl calmly exited the vehicle and approached the three footings that led to the front door. He reached into his bundled blankets and quickly threw the silver-colored container into the nearest enclosure around one of the basement windows. He saw it land softly and sink into a pile of debris from the grotesque things earthians called "trees." He noticed with satisfaction that Belial's little surprise was almost completely buried. Qa-Hrrzl continued his progress, walking slowly up the stairs. He pressed down on the handle of the door and it opened easily.

Nils van Bergen saw a gigantic figure, covered in black blankets and a hood, walk around the front of the truck and slowly come forward. What the hell? The thing was at least eight feet tall. Nils shut down his clamoring mind and stood twenty feet behind the door, rifle at the ready. He saw it open slowly to his left. When the figure saw him it leaped forward with amazing quickness. Van Bergen's reactions were equal to the task. He quickly emptied his magazine, pumping six vials of a fast-acting tranquilizer into the body of the gigantic figure. As it fell forward, twitching, the thing's unsheathed claws pierced his shoulder. Nils fell to the floor with a heavy thump. He quickly removed his shirt and tied it around his shoulder, staunching the flow of blood. He inspected the figure lying face first on the floor. One long arm and a six-fingered hand with claws curled open were stretched out. What in God's name was this? He had given the thing enough tranquilizer to fell an elephant and hoped he hadn't overdosed. Parkinson would definitely want to talk to this ... creature, if possible.

Nils gingerly stripped the clothing from the monster. It had dark green, hairless leathery skin and an ugly lizard-like face with wide thin lips, a shallow nose with wide nostrils, and huge yellow cat's eyes. Its feet were blocky like a hippopotamus and had six digits. The creature's claws were like a cat's. An alien for sure. He called Parkinson and told him to come down to the lobby.

Holderness looked down at the body. "By gad, it's true then."

"Excuse me sir?"

Parkinson pointed at the prostrate figure. "Colonel Rodgers asserts that our human conflicts and difficulties have, to a large extent, been manipulated by these fellows. How's your shoulder?"

Nils ignored him. "Let's turn him over," Nils suggested.

"All right. As soon as we're done here I'll have a doctor tend to you."

"Don't baby me, it's just a scratch!" Nils was irritated. He'd experienced a lot worse in his career.

"Such heat! I never do anything unless it's necessary. Our friend Marcus also received a scratch from one of these creatures and it became infected. After that I engaged a man I can trust in our network to look after all of our, ah, employees."

"Sorry sir, I spoke without thinking."

"A bad habit indeed," Parkinson acknowledged.

"Look sir," Nils said, opening the clawed paw. "This is a police revolver."

Parkinson opened his mobile and called downstairs. "Theresa, check the police reports in the area and let me know if there has been anything unusual reported. Also check to see if any of our brave officers has lost a weapon."

"What are we going to do with this monster?" Nils asked.

"The first thing to do is secure him. Call Marcus and remove this fellow to that storage room in the basement. Turn the heat up in there."

"Sir?"

"It's over 50 out there and this thing is wrapped for winter. Perhaps this gentleman comes from a much warmer environment. When you're done come upstairs."

"Gentleman my arse!" Nils exclaimed. He went downstairs to get Marcus. When Barbara saw him she cried out. "Nils! What happened?"

Nils hated people to fuss over him, especially women. "It's nothing. Marcus, please come upstairs. We've got a small job to do."

Marcus could think of nothing better. He needed a break.

When they reached the lobby Marcus pointed. "Qa-Hrrzl!"

"Qua what?"

"That's the name of this guy. He's a Tau from the star system Draco. Human reptile, chief geneticist to Belial, their leader. These guys like blood and guts; conflict and war. Bad fellows all around, especially that Belial. This one's better than most. I think."

Nils stood with his mouth open. "How do you know so much?"

"I'm the world's foremost authority on the Tau," he said simply. "I've fought them and talked to them. Well, to two of them anyway. The two most important dudes."

Nils looked at Marcus with new respect. "You *fought* one of these guys and lived?"

"In a manner of speaking. It was like a battle in the Matrix. Stylized. Both of us had weapons and nobody won. I couldn't kill him. I didn't want to actually, but he couldn't kill me." Marcus paused, looking down at Qa-Hrrzl. "His boss Belial thinks I'm a vermin."

Nils burst out laughing. "Belial is it? This creature looks enough like a demon." Nils had a thought. "Say, you don't think that—"

Marcus nodded. "Yup. A lot of our history is tied in with the Tau. Lot's of stuff to read up on that. I can show you some of it if you're interested."

"I am. But first we have to get Qa-Hrrzl here down to the storage room, Parkinson's orders. Let's use the elevator. He probably weighs four hundred pounds at least."

The two men dragged the creature into the elevator. Unfortunately the storage room was on the other side of the room. Nils grabbed one leathery foot and Marcus the other. The two men dragged the body across the floor.

"This guy is so heavy the scale says, 'to be continued …'" Marcus joked. "Thank god this floor is smooth and hard."

"Yeah, we'd need a forklift on carpet," Nils agreed.

The staff gathered around in amazement. Barbara put her hands to her face. "Is that the thing who injured you?" she asked as Nils passed by her desk.

"Yes it is. If you want to know who he is ask Marcus."

"He's ugly," a woman remarked.

"Positively devilish," a man agreed. "He doesn't have a tail."

"He probably thinks we're ugly too," Nils said.

Marcus stopped pulling on the body. "No, I already told you. We're vermin to them." He inspected Qa-Hrrzl's anatomy. "Looks like he's got a vestigial tail though."

"All right, let's get this over with," Nils said, grabbing a leg.

The two men dragged the Tau into the mostly empty storage room. It was carved from the stone of the foundation and was about ten feet by twenty feet, and contained computer accessories. It had a thick, solid-core oak door that would hopefully hold the monster if he decided to break out. "He should be able to stand up in there when he wakes up," Nils remarked. "I wonder what he eats?"

"Raw meat." Marcus replied. "The bloodier the better."

Nils saw a space heater and turned it on.

"Yeah, good idea. His planet is very arid and hot."

Nils shook his head in amazement. "What *don't* you know?"

"Compared to Parkinson I'm a low-grade moron."

"Well, my young giant, let us go up and see what the oracle wants to do with this Brobdingnagian."

As soon as Nils said this Parkinson came round the corner with another man carrying a medical bag. "Good work gentlemen," the older man said. He looked at Nils. "How long until he wakes up?"

"I'm not sure. I gave him all six injections. That would have killed a normal human. He's already been out for half an hour. I'd estimate another 30 minutes at least. If he's not dead, which I don't think he is."

"All right. Marcus you can get back to work, but stay downstairs. You'll be needed when this fellow wakes up. Nils, you stand guard while Doctor Emminger looks at that shoulder."

"What are you going to do?' Marcus asked.

"I'm going to stay right here until I – or rather you, Marcus – can talk to the Tau."

"Me? Why me?"

Parkinson looked deprecatingly at Marcus. "All right sir, but I don't know if I'll be able to control this alien. Their minds are a lot more powerful than a human's."

"I think you'll be able to brush through tolerably well, my boy."

How could Parkinson possibly know that? Was he just expressing confidence in him or did he have some hidden knowledge? "Whatever you say sir." Marcus always said 'sir' when he wanted to express his disapproval to the old man. "Let me know when you need me."

An hour later, Nils walked over to Marcus at the central desk. "You'd better get over here. That monster is waking up."

Marcus was in the middle of tracking down another of the cursed biocases on the move in Boston. He already had his web of light out as he walked over to the storage room. Inside Marcus, Nils, and Holderness heard strange hissing noises and thumps.

"Probably talking to himself," Marcus muttered.

The door came crashing open. A huge, eight-foot reptoid launched himself into the room. The staff rushed from their desks and Barbara screamed "Nils!" Qa-Hrrzl, frustrated and angry, bellowed a warrior's cry. Here were the very hominids he had come to kill! Holderness Parkinson stood back, behind Marcus. Both men were about fifteen feet from the door, to the left. Van Bergen stood directly in front of the creature, holding his air rifle. Qa-Hrrzl lunged suddenly to his right at Marcus and Parkinson. Nils realized he was too late! The monster was almost on the two men already and his weapon was not in firing position. Suddenly the huge figure froze in mid-air and tumbled to the floor, smashing against a desk. Wood splinters, metal, and computer parts flew into the air. Nils heard the thing grunt and hiss. A forked tongue slithered out of its mouth.

"*Men kan van een kale kip geen veren plukken,*" Nils muttered, staring at his gun. He had failed to get off a shot.

"I have him," Marcus said. His face was etched with tension. "But just barely. His mind is even stronger than Belial's."

Qa-Hrrzl, lying immobilized on the smooth hard surface, immediately understood two things. Mar-cus Ri-ley's mind was powerful but untrained. What kind of trick had this hominid used? Qa-Hrrzl now realized that Belial's report on his confrontation with the earthian was entirely fictitious. The great fool, falsifying data! And secondly, he knew that he would not be able to kill Par-kin-son or Ri-ley. However, the Trigger was set to be pulled in less than 30 earthian hours, or 1.25 rotations of this planet. He must get to the desert as quickly as possible or his own life would be forfeit. The Purification Substance, although designed specifically for hominid genetics, was also deadly to Tau biology. He must concoct a plausible story to tell these earthians because he needed their help reaching his hideaway. Ri-ley hominid's mind was immensely powerful but unsophisticated. It would be child's play to hide his true intentions.

Still immobilized, Qa-Hrrzl relaxed his mind and released his mental shields.

Marcus felt Qa-Hrrzl's thoughts and wondered if this creature was honorable. If I release him would he promise not to be violent?

"Hominid, you dare to question my word? I am not like that scum Belial."

"Belial is now a scum?" Marcus brought up a number of events in the Tau's mind. "You seemed to be quite happy to work with him."

"It was my duty. You understand that I cannot now go back. I have failed in my instructions to achieve a successful Harvest. My former life, with its obligations, is now void."

Marcus explored Qa-Hrrzl's mind and was satisfied. The Tau operated on a rigid command structure where obedience was paramount. "All right then, give me your word of honor that you will not harm any human being and I will release you."

Qa-Hrrzl now employed a tactic the Tau had taught to their minions for centuries: the doctrine of mental reservation. A being gave his word of honor while at the same time mentally agreeing to something completely different. This allowed one to break one's promise on the verbal agreement. That a Tau should be compelled to pledge his word to one of these hominids! It was insupportable. One might as well sign a contract with an Argul.

Reading no duplicity in the Tau's mind, Marcus released his mental grip. The giant reptile rose to his full height. Someone screamed. Qa-Hrrzl was about to swat the frightened creatures with one of his great paws. He noted with satisfaction that six thousand years of mental programming and Tau genetic alterations to the earthian DNA had done their work. These little creatures regarded him as a fearful god, just as in their old testament Bible. Staring balefully at the assembled earthians, he carefully considered his position. Qa-Hrrzl reluctantly admitted that anyone who could mentally defeat himself and Belial must be given grudging respect. He had no doubt that if he attempted to harm any of these humans, the hominid Ri-ley would again constrain him. It was galling. As a scientist he was able to think rationally and overcome his baser reptilian emotions. He was also intrigued. He began to wonder how the Tau genetic alterations had failed. These hominids should not have the capabilities demonstrated by Ri-ley. As he towered over the little creatures Qa-Hrrzl studied the huddling figures. Five out of the twenty present were standing their ground. That percentage was drastically higher than expected. These earthians had built-in psychic triggers to fear and obey all Tau, who closely resembled the dragon- and serpent-like creatures in their mythology. He would have to very carefully study the genetic codes of these creatures and determine the genetic mutations. To do this he would have to return temporarily to Tau through the desert portal and retrieve his laboratory.

Marcus saw that the reptile was now hissing and grunting. Through his web of light Marcus picked up on his communication. "Qa-Hrrzl says that in his vehicle is a translation device. Will one of you go out to the truck parked in front of the building and retrieve a dull-gray device about one foot square?"

Marcus heard someone running up the stairs. In a moment the device was in his hand. He could see no mechanical or electronic functionality. It was a flat rectangle about twelve inches long and ten inches wide, almost weightless. The thing glowed very softly. Marcus tossed the device to Qa-Hrrzl. The reptile caught it easily in his big hand.

"Vermin!" Qa-Hrrzl precisely expressed his sentiments toward the huddling humanity before him. The voice was deep and guttural. Whenever he pronounced a consonant it sounded like the bass from a boom-box. "I am now a prisoner on your planet. Because of hominid incompetence at the highest levels, and my own error, I cannot return to Tau. Therefore I request transportation to an area of your planet that is arid and hot, preferably with a cave system. I have identified a suitable location in a remote area of your southwest desert." Unspoken was his desire to remain safe from the coming Armageddon. So many of these hominids would die, but there were eight billion of them! Even if several billion were to perish, billions more would survive. Of those, ten percent would have superior genetics. When these bred the race would improve drastically. Therefore, the Tau were doing these undeserving hominids a great service. This planet was grossly overpopulated and environmentally endangered. These hominids were not good stewards for their planet. Precious biological resources were being destroyed during every planetary rotation.

Marcus saw fear etched on every face, even Parkinson's. Qa-Hrrzl's bass voice boomed and echoed menacingly in the enclosed room. Marcus interpreted, not understanding that the Tau's mind was much deeper than he suspected. "His name is Qa-Hrrzl. He is the chief geneticist on the planet Tau, in the Draco system, many light years from earth. Compared to us he has an IQ of about 300, but his genes are retrograde. Look at him as an emotionally retarded but brilliant scientist, a sort of brainiac Incredible Hulk. He has agreed not to harm any of us. Once a Tau gives his word he will never break it. So let's all relax a little."

Qa-Hrrzl was pleased. He had convinced Ri-ley of his honorable intentions. The fool.

Marcus sent a mental note to Qa-Hrrzl to increase the frequency and raise the pitch of his broadcast.

Holderness Parkinson gulped and stepped forward. "We are prepared to take you to a place of your choosing if you agree to help us." The thick leathery skin around Qa-Hrzzl's head folded over in a frown. By gad, this creature is repulsive.

"I cannot betray my race," Qa-Hrrzl said, his voice sounding much more normal. "I agree to help only if my actions do not threaten the Tau."

Parkinson almost laughed. "Agreed." According to Marcus the earth had about as much chance of harming the Tau as a tree squirrel against a battle tank. "In exchange, we require—"

Despite his need to cooperate Qa-Hrrzl's was angered. The temerity of these vermin. "You require! I require a vehicle and a driver!"

Parkinson nodded. "You shall have them, Qa-Hrrzl. We require that you make a statement to the people of earth and identify for us all containers of your toxic substance."

Identify all of the containers? After all the work he had done to ensure a successful Harvest? It would be an act of sedition and result in the elimination of his entire bloodline from the race genealogy. Qa-Hrrzl's anger intensified at the arrogance of these hominids. He felt his blood beginning to boil. With a great effort of will he calmed himself. He had less than thirty hours before the Harvest and must proceed immediately to the desert and his transportal. He noticed that one of the hominids had a weapon trained on him. From his devious reptilian mind a brilliant strategy was born. He would simply give false locations for the remaining containers. When the hominids discovered his error he would claim that the locations were factual but that the containers had been moved. "I agree. Let the hominid Mar-cus Ri-ley present his mind to me."

"Force it out of him," Nils suggested.

"Don't underestimate this guy. He's brilliant and ruthless. He could probably hide anything he wanted from me in that huge mind of his." Marcus wondered about that. Was this creature concealing something from him? Should he try a deep probe into the alien's mind? No, that would be sacrilegious, and Marcus wondered why. His mind skittered over the issue and he thought no more of it.

Qa-Hrrzl smirked and opened up a compartment of his great mind to let the hominid enter. He exhibited a surface map of the hominid planet and the locations of every container. The Tau had an eidetic memory and the ability to display a wide variety of images and data within it. It was a simple matter to alter the positions of most of the targeted locations. Qa-Hrrzl was careful to suppress any information about the imminent release of the Purification Substance. He was pleased to see that the hominid Ri-ley had no suspicion that by the end of the day tomorrow, most of his fellow vermin would be dead.

Mar-cus Ri-ley assimilated the data given to him by Qa-Hrrzl from one compartment of his mind. The major portion of Qa-Hrrzl's mind was engaged in furious calculation. Like any brilliant scientist, he was uneasy concerning his Harvest miscalculations. His pride and self-confidence had suffered a huge blow. How had he failed? He could not doubt that he had calculated and acted correctly. Some other factor, completely out of his control, must be responsible for his missteps in the Harvest plan. It was imperative that he discover this other variable for it might ruin the Tau Harvest on other planets as well. He MUST find that transportal and reestablish his genetic laboratory.

Probing the alien's mind, Marcus read the locations and made a mental image of the map with his web of light. He discovered that Qa-Hrrzl was responsible for the manufacture of the toxin both on Tau and on earth. Only the required amount had been made. He almost laughed out loud when he reviewed Qa-Hrrzl's conversation with Belial's drone. Like many an earth criminal, the warrior-caste on Tau always assumed a smooth and errorless path to success for their schemes. Since the Tau dealt only with underdeveloped species their technology was always superior. They had never before experienced failure. Qa-Hrrzl's suggestion that a sizable reserve be created (while attempting to show Belial's menial his calculations) was met with scorn. It would be far too costly and time consuming, the drone said. The drone's dismissal was accompanied by a not-so-veiled suggestion of his incompetence and a warning not to fail.

"Good news, sir," Marcus said, having discovered this information in a split-second. "The Tau have only manufactured just enough of the bioenhancer, assuming that their plan would succeed without error. There are no other manufacturing facilities on earth or on Tau."

"That is well," Parkinson replied. "We just might get them all."

Qa-Hrrzl sneered mentally. These earthians were as trusting as little hatchlings. He said nothing but was almost certain that Belial and the Council had hidden more of the Purification Substance than even he had knowledge of.

"There's something else sir," Marcus said, glancing up at Qa-Hrrzl. The Tau stood unmoving, listening with his translation device to their conversation. "The point man for one of the most powerful Black Hat factions is a man named Pietro Adolphone. You mentioned him to me once."

Parkinson's face lit up. "Adolphone! Why ... but of course. He is the Jesuit General." He nodded in satisfaction. "So my assessment of that order was not inaccurate."

At the mention of Adolphone's name the giant creature standing beside them growled. "A-dol-fon-e!" Qa-Hrrzl rumbled gutturally in his hissing speech. "That scoundrel! I have promised to eat his brains."

"An unappetizing meal," Parkinson quipped. "A shriveled and warped intellect, and not to be trusted."

For the second time Qa-Hrrzl was astonished to find himself in complete agreement with a hominid he had planned to kill just a short while ago. "Precisely!" he boomed, startling both men and causing the group of listeners to shrink back. "That hominid's incompetence in carrying out my instructions was one of the primary factors for my failure."

Parkinson and the others looked at him for clarification. Marcus decided that to reveal Qa-Hrrzl's involvement in the Harvest would not quite be the thing, as Parkinson might say. "I'll explain it later," Marcus whispered to the older man. "For now I think we should remove Qa-Hrrzl here as quickly as possible from this building and into his desert stronghold. He's much too dangerous."

Parkinson responded quickly and turned to his employees. "I agree. Ladies and gentlemen, as you may have guessed, our guest here is not from earth. In order to return him to his planet we must drive him to a special, er, area, where he will be able to ... board a spacecraft that will take him back to his home planet."

"And who better for that job than the intrepid Nils van Bergen?" Marcus was looking at van Bergen, whose weapon was still trained on the reptile.

Barbara screamed. Nils gasped. "Me?"

Parkinson grinned. "Yes you. You are a man of action and vast experience in the world. You shall have an assistant who will carry a weapon and keep an eye on our ... guest."

Qa-Hrrzl was indifferent. He would have no trouble escaping from these hominids, should he choose to do so. He spoke. "I know the precise area. All that is required is a hominid driver and someone to procure my meat during the journey. From this location I estimate a total of 28 hours of driving at an average speed of 60 of your miles each hour." The Trigger by that time would have been pulled, but he planned to avoid all large hominid population clusters.

Nils shrugged. "If all I have to do is drive and fuel, and this creature behaves himself and doesn't try to eat me, I'll do it."

Qa-Hrrzl almost laughed. "Hominid flesh is not tasty. Would you eat refuse?" He had made another joke!

"Very well then," Nils said. "I suggest that we lower the back seats. You can lie in the rear and have a little more room. But I warn you. If you try any tricks we'll fill you full of tranquilizer. Or bullets."

"Agreed," Qa-Hrrzl said. He was shivering now in the relative cold of the room. "Let us proceed immediately."

Parkinson interrupted. "The streets are alive now. You must help us make a video of your presence here on earth. You shall leave tonight after sunset."

Qa-Hrrzl, frustrated to be on his way, roared. "I have given my word of honor and so it shall be!" he thundered, sending the humans rushing backward again in fear. The Tau found nothing amiss in his anger at having his word of honor questioned even when he had already decided to break it. Such is the reptilian brain. "Bring your recording equipment to me. I shall stand in the storage area with the heating unit at maximum."

The recording was made. To the earthians it was momentous; proof of the existence of what they called extraterrestrials. Qa-Hrrzl was incredibly bored throughout and thought the entire procedure farcical. Of course the galaxy was teeming with life. Equally obvious was that the planet had been quarantined for millennia, causing an incredibly limited and parochial worldview. This had suited the Tau very well. These earthians had no idea what they faced out there in the galaxy. These hominids were like little children at a complex diplomatic negotiation. Their planet was already a pawn in game far outpacing their understanding. But they certainly were interesting specimens.

After the video was made Qa-Hrrzl put on his blankets and was escorted, hunched over, to the Super-Duty. Nils van Bergen and one of Parkinson's men, a former Marine on loan from Colonel Rodgers, accompanied the Tau. The giant reptile scrunched himself into the cargo area. The Marine held a machine pistol and entered the passenger side. Nils carried a sidearm in a shoulder holster and his tranquilizer gun. Nils gave the marine his tranquilizer gun and took his place at the wheel. The entire Royalty crew watched as the vehicle drove down Grant and turned onto Cleveland.

On Draco Tau, Belial was preparing the Council for the Harvest.

Draco Tau

Belial assembled the High Council of Qrrk-Hazur, in preparation for feeding. The ritual cave had a very high ceiling and the floor had been leveled and decorated with Tau symbolism. The cave was centered within the planet's primary and most powerful transportal. It operated like an earthian "hotspot" for the transmission of life force substance. The stone floor, polished by millions of feet over the eons, reflected its contents like a smooth, undisturbed pool of water. Each of the thirty-three participants, representing the Tau bloodlines, wore body paint. They proudly displayed their symbols in variegated colors and geometric designs. These symbols had been handed down from generation to generation for hundreds of thousands of years of racial history.

The rest of the Tau population had gathered within the other transportals which dotted the planet's surface, ready to receive the precious life substance from the main portal. The Purification Substance would be released as soon as Belial gave the word.

Belial, however, was steaming. He had read the last report of Qa-Hrrzl before he had transported to the hominid planet. He now knew the identity of the two hominids most responsible for the curtailed Harvest. One of them was the scum Mar-cus Ri-ley. He looked about him at the thirty Council members, all waiting expectantly, and calmed himself.

The activation of the Purification Substance was simplicity itself. For reasons unknown to any on Tau, the earthian planet had tens of thousands of transportals, far more in one small area than anywhere in the galaxy. It was the primary reason for so much interest in the obscure little planet. Transportals were invisible, programmable gateways to anywhere in the universe. The hominids were unaware of their existence except for popular misconceptions like the "Bermuda Triangle," and other anomalies. Fortunately, in the rest of the galaxy, identifying these stargates and programming them was a fairly simple business. Thousands of them existed in or around earthian cities. To activate the Purification Substance required only the activation of a tuned signal through the Tau's primary transportal. The transponders on each of the units was tuned to this signal, and would open when the proper frequency was detected. The bio-material, according to Qa-Hrrzl, was a particularly hardy and virulent airborne substance that immediately attached itself to hominid biology. Within a single planetary rotation almost every hominid within a large city would become infected.

Belial's humor was restored with these thoughts. He considered the Trigger before him. The Trigger was a standard galactic communication device, a sort of portable tesseract. He unfolded the device and placed it before him. A real-time image of the hominid planet floated within it. The activating impulse was programmed into his personal communicator. Qa-Hrrzl had tuned the device to the transponders on the bio-material containers.

Belial's anticipation grew as he felt the tension and the excitement in the Council chamber. After he gave the signal the entire cave would function as a massive receiver, siphoning off the precious life substance to the other transportals. All Tau would feed but here, at the center, the life force would be at its strongest and most delicious.

Belial, energized now beyond endurance, activated the Trigger.

Royalty Services

"Marcus I'm not feeling well." Darcy was standing in the living room of their suite at Royalty. "Does something smell funny around here?"

Marcus sniffed the air. Yes, there was a faint odor. Suddenly he remembered. "Oh my God!" It was the same odor he had smelled in that taxi just after he was injected. The Harvest. That fiend Belial must finally have acted.

"Wait here honey!" Marcus ran to the hall and up the stairs. Darcy groaned and lay down on the bed.

Taking the stairs three at a time, Marcus burst into Parkinson's office. "Holderness! Those goddam Tau have released the bioenhancer!"

Parkinson, in the middle of a conversation, glanced up quickly. "Are you sure?"

"Darcy is getting sick. If you smell the air around here you can detect a faint, bittersweet odor. It's the same smell I remember when I was injected in New York by that asshole Bobo Jacoby."

Parkinson raised his bulk from his office chair and walked quickly into his private office, emerging with a leather case. "Assemble the staff and all of our consorts and guests immediately in the first floor conference room. Quickly now."

Marcus rushed down to the basement and to his desk, grabbing the intercom. "Attention all Royalty staff. Code Tau, I repeat, code Tau. This is not a drill. You have five minutes to appear in the first floor conference room. On the double. Your life could depend on it."

Barbara and the staff in the basement rushed to Marcus, asking questions. "There's no time. You have four minutes thirty seconds. Get your asses up to the first floor!"

Twenty people stampeded up the stairs as fast as their legs would carry them. Men stepped aside to let the women go first. After their experience with the horrid alien everyone was prepared for the worst.

Marcus ran into the large conference room and saw all staff and consorts, as well as several guests, assembled. There were about eighty persons total. Parkinson was at the wide lectern, fumbling with glass vials of some milky liquid. Beside him was one of the Alephs, who looked just like Dr. June. Marcus couldn't tell because all of them were clones.

Marcus realized Darcy wasn't present. "Parkinson! I have to get Darcy." He raced out of the room and up the stairs once again. He burst into their bedroom and saw that Darcy's face was already gray. Her breathing was stertorous, although she was still conscious. He gently raised her body off the bed and carried her into the elevator. A minute later he walked into the conference room with Darcy in his arms. He gently lowered her to one of the couches along the side wall and stood helplessly beside it. The tension in the room was palpable. The atmosphere was one of gloomy acceptance of a proclamation of inevitable doom. Marcus waited tensely for Parkinson to begin speaking.

Finally Parkinson spoke. "These are experimental antidotes to the bioenhancer, developed by our friends the Alephs." Holderness held up several small vials of liquid. "We haven't time for questions. Many of you know of the danger and the consequences. It has now arrived. Everyone here is already infected. You have but one choice: take the antidote and you may live a normal life, or risk the invasion. If you are one of the lucky ten percent you will emerge like Marcus here: genetically superior and free forever from all sickness and disease, with possibly an elongated life span. If you do not choose the antidote, nine out of ten of you will be dead within the next few hours."

The Aleph was already distributing the little vials. "This serum is administered orally," Parkinson announced. "Just open the top and drink the liquid. You may feel nauseous for the next hour, but do not worry. If you remain conscious the antidote is working." Marcus could see that Holderness had already tipped his own vial into his mouth. "I have already lived 77 years. My decision is easy."

The Aleph reached Darcy, slumped on the couch. He bent over her, handing her an open vial. "Mr. Gemmi!" she said weakly, taking the little bottle. "What are you doing here?"

The Aleph explained everything to her in a gentle but firm voice. "It's your decision Darcy Regier." Darcy and Marcus exchanged agonized glances. "Please don't die, Darcy." Marcus cried. "Take the liquid."

But Darcy had suddenly slipped into unconsciousness. The little glass bottle fell from her hand and hit the floor, wetting the carpet.

Marcus was stunned. He gazed pitifully at the Aleph. "But Darcy can't die!

Aleph 139 smiled as sympathetically as he could.

Marcus ran over to the leather bag on the podium and got another vial. "It's probably too late now Marcus," the Aleph said when he returned. Marcus opened Darcy's mouth and slowly emptied its contents. He watched her swallow involuntarily, more afraid than he had ever been in his life. To lose her would be unthinkable. He had taken her for granted but now he knew just how precious she was to him. s he held her hand it grew slowly colder. Her beautiful face was now a ghastly gray. He could feel her life force fading ...

All over the world people suddenly fell ill. The same thing happened during the influenza pandemic of 1918–1919, when almost 50 million died worldwide. Instant messaging created panic as those in the know texted and posted online. The word quickly spread all over the planet, garbled and mistranslated, that a deadly virus was spreading uncontrollably.

The Tau High Council, on Draco Tau, saw the panic spreading and was delighted. A fearful death provided the most satisfying feed. Within a few hours after release the Purification Substance would have done its work. Hundreds of millions would perish at the same time, creating planetary ecstasy on Tau. Belial surveyed his handiwork and saw that it was good.

Chapter **33**

Marcus sat on the floor next to the couch holding Darcy's cold and lifeless hand. He couldn't tell whether she was breathing. Parkinson finished his briefing and everyone left. Before he went the Aleph told him what to expect.

"She'll be like this for several hours, Marcus. After that, if she recovers, she will very gradually begin to improve. If her body is unable to process the biomaterial her skin color will gradually darken and her features will begin to shrivel. At death the body will be almost unrecognizable. If you see no change for the worse after three or four hours she will probably recover."

Aleph 139 saw the earthian's pain and felt some of his sadness. He was secretly elated. His emotional response meant that their race's unfortunate evolutionary choice, over 30,000 years ago, was on the way to being mended. The Alephs had chosen the way of technology, assimilating their biology with electronics in the hope of elongated lifespans and the elimination of disease. After 10,000 years it had become apparent that this choice was an evolutionary dead-end. Their race's Life Reading Index had plummeted, threatening their viability.

In retrospect Aleph 139 could see that this decision was clearly irrational. In the excitement of creating a new and improved race the consequences of failure had been brushed aside. The only choice had been to gradually eliminate their biological dependence on artificial assistance. The race's only remaining option was cloning. The vitality and the quantity of their biological material had atrophied over the millennia just as a muscle weakens when no longer used. It had soon become clear, after another fifty generations, that cloning was also a biological dead-end. They had been forced to augment their genetics with sample biological material from younger, immature races not yet admitted to galactic society. In this way their genetic experiments could be completed without interference from civilized society.

As he gazed at the anguished features of the young earthian, Aleph 139 was amazed at their race's progress. Planets like earth were backwaters (often visited by the scaff and raff of the galaxy) and the rules of engagement were much different. But here, unexpectedly, they had struck genetic gold. The Epsilon were recovering their racial virility. They had learned the hard way that biological evolution was superior. Soon, perhaps, sexual reproduction would be possible! As an experiment, Aleph 139 attempted to soothe the earthian. Could he muster enough genuine emotion to do so?

Aleph 139 gently placed his smooth, hairless hand on Marcus' shoulder. He employed one of the earthian expressions he had learned. "So far so good."

"Do you think so?" Marcus replied anxiously.

These earthians! Their expressions of emotion were overwhelmingly powerful. It was difficult for him to comfortably absorb Marcus' nervous fretfulness. Aleph 139 had gradually learned that the emotional responses of these earthians was not the issue. It was the Epsilon's lack of emotional depth that caused his discomfort. Aleph 139 schooled his features, letting Marcus' disturbing responses penetrate his body and his being. He felt a not-unpleasant buzzing inside his stomach. "Yes," Aleph 139 replied. "It has been one hour. Although Darcy has not regained consciousness she has not regressed. This is a good sign."

Aleph 139 saw Marcus sigh and turn toward him with infinite relief. The golden-skinned ET was amazed at the power and poignancy of his expression. Marcus' grateful reaction brought forth a faint feeling of love within him. This emotion he had never experienced before. It was a rare gift indeed, and another indication of his race's progress. They were developing what the earthians called heart-felt reactions. He began to understand, vaguely, the power of compassion and care for another. It was both terrifying and delightful. He also discovered the power of physical contact. It appeared that his touching of the earthian enhanced Marcus' emotional experience.

He explained gently that the Alephs, in their laboratories on Draco Epsilon, had only very recently discovered a possible antidote to the bioenhancer. It had just begun to be distributed to a few select locations. Aleph 139 explained briefly about Darcy's service to the Epsilon and the importance of their work at Royalty Services in defeating the Tau. "So you see, Marcus, Chicago was one of the first places we came to share our antidote."

Marcus' laugh was brittle. "Apparently somebody planted some of the bioenhancer right next to our building. Nils spotted something when he walked out with Qa-Hrrzl. He didn't know what it was and didn't report it until a few minutes ago, when Parkinson called him."

"Qa-Hrrzl!" Aleph 139 exclaimed. "Qa-Hrrzl was here?"

"Yes, didn't you know?"

"Not in the least!" Aleph 139 was as astonished as was possible for one of his kind. "Qa-Hrrzl is the second most influential entity on Tau. If this being took the extraordinary measure of personally coming to earth it was he who placed the substance."

Marcus released Darcy's hand. "That traitor! He swore not to harm any of us."

Aleph 139 shook his head solemnly. "These creatures have no concept of personal integrity. That is why their race is so dangerous and why their planet is shunned within civilized society."

"Qa-Hrrzl said he was going forty miles southwest of Sedona Arizona. He said something about a transportal there."

"Thank you Marcus. I will report these developments. Now I must go, for I have other important stops to make today."

An alien Hanukah Harry distributing life-giving serum, Marcus thought, as he grasped Darcy's hand. He would not leave Darcy's side until the issue was resolved. He'd put his own life force into her even if it killed him. He grasped her dead, unresponsive hands in his and began to feed energy into her body. He would place his vitality into her, and will her to live.

Forty miles south of Sedona, Arizona

"Stop!" Qa-Hrrzl commanded. The Super Duty was whizzing by another mesa, dust swirling.

Nils was weary of the alien's peremptory commands and condescending behavior, but he obeyed. He looked over at his companion, the ex-Marine Ray Hertzel, and rolled his eyes. Ray grinned understandingly.

On their 26 hour journey they had gotten to know the monster far better than they ever wanted to. Ray, bored out of his mind, checked the news reports from the radio and the net every hour. Mysterious deaths were occurring all over the world. Qa-Hrrzl was quiet and almost unmoving in his uncomfortable spot at the back of the Super Duty. The Tau acknowledged these reports with an affirmative and satisfied nod of his ugly head. Whenever this happened Ray would turn around, growling, and point his MAC-10 machine pistol at the ugly creature. Qa-Hrrzl merely grunted unconcernedly and hissed, which the two men eventually learned was suppressed laughter. This infuriated Ray even more. Nils wondered whether the creature knew how many times he had come close to death. Parkinson's videos of the creature were circulating on the world net. Ray thought that by now a War of the Worlds panic would be underway. But strangely, the mainstream media were assigning the unexplained deaths to a new pandemic virus that had unexpectedly developed from natural causes.

Qa-Hrrzl would bellow with laughter whenever he saw himself surrounded by the little hominids in the video. Those who were feeding would, even as he rode in this primitive vehicle, be experiencing ecstasy! Eventually, out of boredom, Qa-Hrrzl began to talk through his translation device about himself, his planet, and the situation on earth. Nils and Ray soon discovered that the Tau had no conception of ethics or morals. Qa-Hrrzl's race were myopically self-centered. The creature was intellectually brilliant but emotionally retarded. What Qa-Hrrzl told them about the Harvest and the other Tau disgusted both men. "An unregenerate devil," was Ray's pithy comment. Nils agreed.

After the Super Duty came to a stop Qa-Hrrzl let the dust settle and then opened the tailgate. He got out, straightening himself, and welcomed the intense, blasting heat of the desert. He began to walk. The extreme heat felt good on the pads of his feet. Yes, he could survive here if necessary. He looked up at the blazing sun and thought that the radiation from this planet's type G star was nothing like the burning ultraviolet of Draco Tau. His blood would not boil here. He could and should stay outside for most of the day, absorbing the weak but necessary ultraviolet radiation. The light from this sun was distinctly yellow as opposed to the harsh blue-white light from Draco Tau.

Soon he spotted a cave system underneath the rock of the mesa and headed toward it. An animal scurried by. Qa-Hrrzl wondered whether its flesh was tasty. For too long he had not been able to drink warm blood from a fresh kill.

It would grow much colder here than on Tau after the pale sun had set, but he would line the cave with heat-trapping materials from Tau. Qa-Hrzzl was certain that the portal was somewhere close by. Once his laboratory was established here he would have an independent base on the earthian planet. He would be free from the control of Belial and the Qrrk-Hazur! From his secure base he might even challenge the power of the Great One himself, if he was clever enough.

Meanwhile, Nils opened the hood of the truck and inspected the air filter. He'd already had to shake it out once and decided to do so again. Ray stood with his sound suppressed MAC-10 casually pointed at the alien, proceeding with huge strides to the shadow of the rock underneath the mesa. It was all he could do to stop himself from opening fire on the disgusting creature. A monster for sure. Without his training in Colonel Rodgers' ET detail he never would have believed that such repulsive beings could exist. "I'm glad," Ray remarked as Nils shook the filter of sand and debris.

Nils didn't have to ask. "It's almost over Ray. I never want to see that dirtbag again."

"Yeah." Ray raised his weapon. "It's fuckin' hot out here." The alien was now almost two hundred yards away but Ray's accuracy with the machine pistol was legendary. He decided on the automatic because it could reliably fire over one thousand rounds per minute. He might have needed to put a lot of lead into Qa-Hrrzl in a hurry. "Should I?"

Nils knew that Parkinson wouldn't like it, but he was past caring. "Might as well scare the shit out of him."

Ray wiped the sweat from his forehead and pulled the trigger, firing off a burst. He wasn't really aiming but if a few hit .... Qa-Hrrzl seemed unconcerned as the bullets went wide. Ray grinned and fired another burst at the rock toward which the alien was moving. He heard ricochets. Qa-Hrrzl did not react, ducking his head and entering the rock underneath the mesa. Ray shrugged. "The asshole has balls anyway." He looked up at Nils, who had just closed the hood. Their eyes met. Both men laughed, releasing the tension that had been building for the past day and a half. They pounded each other on the back and finally entered the vehicle.

"It stinks in here," Nils commented.

"Yeah," Ray agreed. "Smelly bastard."

"Let's go get a drink. I know a bar in Sedona."

"You're on! I want to get wasted tonight. And laid."

"We're almost out of gas," Nils commented as he turned up the air conditioner full-blast.

"Yeah, fuck it," Ray replied. "We've only got forty miles to go."

"Throw the rest of that bloody meat out of here," Nils said.

Ray reached back, grabbed the cooler, and threw it out of the truck. It landed with a puff of dust and the lid came off. "If I ever see that shit stick again I'll shoot him – it – on sight."

Nils grinned in acknowledgment. He programmed the GPS for Sedona. He gunned the Super Duty, both men singing a raucous drinking song.

Royalty Services, Chicago

It was now four hours after the bioenhancer had infected the building. Marcus still sat on the floor, holding Darcy's hand. There was no change in her condition. He heard people coming in from outdoors and snatches of conversation. Several people lay dead on the street in front of the building, and who knows how many more inside.

Parkinson entered the conference room. "No change?"

"No." He was angry and frustrated. "If Darcy dies, Parkinson, I'm going to kill Belial." He would personally send his mind to Tau and destroy that big bastard. He knew how to do it. Marcus was confident he could overcome the creature. He had done it before at NYCBank, but only defended himself that time.

The older man walked over to the couch. "It's time to get Darcy to the hospital."

"Hospital? What can they do? Better to get that Aleph back here."

"I just had a talk with one of them, a Mr. Nye. He suggested it."

Marcus looked down at the once lovely face that was now grayed-over with death. A fierce anger sped upward from under his belly-button. "I'll kill that fucktard," Marcus said grimly, like a warrior about to face a decisive battle. "I'll kill him."

Parkinson was shocked. He'd seen warrior types before and their hardened battle-faces. Marcus exuded a power and determination that was frightening. He backed off a step and gulped. "She can't stay here. We don't have the facilities or the knowledge to do something if she begins to slip."

Marcus released Darcy's hand and straightened. "All right." He looked into Parkinson's eyes. Marcus' gaze was like a cold laser; Parkinson felt like a little mouse about to be pounced upon by a hungry cat. "If she isn't better by tomorrow morning I'm going after Belial."

Parkinson decided not to object. Another glance into those eyes and he began to feel sorry for the object of Marcus' wrath. "Do what you have to do Marcus. But there is some relatively good news. It looks like the total death count is around 350 million or so worldwide. That's terrible but not as bad as we feared. We have done an amazing job locating the biomaterial."

"How many in Chicago?" Marcus asked.

"Approximately 20,000 so far, directly around this building. Apparently this was the only bioweapon left in the city we didn't get."

Marcus' eyes hardened even more and the planes of his face flattened down. "Qa-Hrrzl. I'll kill him too." Three hundred fifty million! He couldn't believe it. He had never really cared for people all that much. But the idea of so many of his fellow humans dying at the hands of these monsters made him physically ill. And really, really, mad.

"He helped us with the video," Parkinson suggested. "It's causing a sensation and bringing more people to an understanding of the situation. The panic has stopped and we're recovering our balance now."

Just then, three gloved paramedics stepped into the room wearing white jackets. "We're ready to transport the patient."

Marcus whirled to face them. "Aren't all the hospitals full?" he asked.

A woman smiled grimly. "Only the morgues for now. You either die from this stuff or you recover within hours, completely healthy."

Marcus nodded. "I'm coming with you."

Draco Tau

The Harvest was over. The Council, drunk with ecstasy and revitalized from the release of life force energy, was enthusiastic. "Approximately three hundred fifty million of the hominids perished, sire," said Qa-Jbbt, Qa-Hrrzl's chief assistant. "Although a small fraction of what was anticipated, it is still far more than the entire population of Tau. He nodded respectfully to the giant reptile seated on his throne at the head of the table. "Sire, it is my opinion that more deaths would not have further increased our Life Reading Index. Our ability to absorb the excess life force is limited." Whether that was true or not, Qa-Jbbt saw his opportunity to move up in status. It was clear to Qa-Jbbt that Belial's consequence was as great as his bulk. He would massage it.

Belial nodded with satisfaction, appreciating Qa-Jbbt's political savvy. His place in the genealogy would not be compromised. His historian would write of a glorious and successful conclusion, backed by scientific corroboration. And if the earthian planet remained in their sphere it could be harvested again, and again, and again. Something told Belial that the Tau should avoid that noisome and troublesome planet. There were plenty of other undeveloped planets to harvest. These earthian hominids were too unpredictable.

"We will have nothing to do in future with that planet of vermin," he announced. But he still had some unfinished personal business. There was the matter of the traitor and miscreant Qa-Hrrzl, who had disappeared to the earthian planet shortly after recommending that the Trigger be pulled. He would deal with that scoundrel personally.

No one dared to speak. The always formidable Belial, after the feeding, had increased his power considerably. He was even more unapproachable. This one, Qa-Jbbt thought, would rule unchallenged for decades. His own position would also be secure if he attached himself to that power.

Belial spoke. "I will kill the traitor Qa-Hrrzl. He has deserted to the hominid planet and is cooperating with the race enemies Ri-ley and Par-kin-son." All Tau had seen the ridiculous video, which was now circulating around the planet. "Afterward, I shall devote my time to disseminating my seed." Belial looked around the room at the Council. "It is time I considered my legacy."

Qa-Jbbt perceived that Belial was gazing particularly at him, as if expecting an acknowledgment. He glanced quickly around the chamber at the others. Seeing their acquiescence, Qa-Jbbt took it upon himself to nod affirmatively. "Yes, sire." He spoke as one giving approval from the entire Council.

Belial was content. "It is well!" He took the ceremonial rod and banged it upon the ancient gong, an oval of rock inset with precious stones and covered with thick Argul skin. A lackey appeared at the entrance and bowed, kneeling and touching his head to the floor. "Your command, sire."

"Prepare my personal transportal for contact with the traitor Qa-Hrrzl. Summon my personal historian and have him in readiness in my chambers within the hour."

The drone exited quickly. Belial let his large yellow reptilian eyes examine the Council members, one by one. His pointed to Qa-Jbbt. "You are now our chief geneticist and chief of the Qrrk-Ytil. You will receive my orders after I have dealt with your superior."

Qa-Jbbt lowered his head to the table, fully aware of the honor done him. This Belial moved quickly and even quixotically. He must be very careful. "Yes sire. All shall be as you desire."

Belial rose quickly and strode out of the Council chamber. All present stood and bowed low.

Prentice Women's Hospital, Chicago

Marcus held Darcy's hand throughout the night and into the morning. There was no change in her condition. Her breathing was very shallow; a mirror held to her mouth barely registered.

The duty nurse walked in at 5 a.m. "How is she?"

"No change," Marcus said. The nurse noticed that Marcus had not shifted his position even an inch since he had arrived at 6 p.m. the previous evening. To have someone so dedicated! He looked like a black-haired Jesus preparing to raise the dead, but who didn't know how. She went to check the patient's vitals and surprised a look of anguish in the young manchild's eyes. "Is she going to live?" he asked in a hopeful but fatally discouraged tone.

"You're right, no change. No news is good news."

Marcus looked his question, still holding the gray, cold hand.

"We're learning more about this ... disease ... every hour," the nurse replied. "The longer the patient can hang on the better are her chances."

Marcus let out his breath in a sigh of relief. "If she dies ..." he said menacingly.

"Yes?" She wondered whether Marcus was a romantic, and whether he had an enemy to slay. She noticed a faint blue glow around the manchild's body and shook her head. "I must be just too tired."

"Yeah I'm tired too." Marcus looked at her name tag, which said "Jenny." He could just read it in soft glow of the hospital room's night light.

"You're glowing," Jenny said.

"Yeah, I do that. I'm trying to send some of my life force into Darcy."

"I can see it."

"It doesn't seem to be doing any good."

"How do you do it?"

"Anybody can do it I think. Imagine that there's a big, invisible pool of healing energy in this room. You just tap into it and let it flow through you and into the other person." That wasn't it at all but he didn't want to waste time trying to tell her about his web of light.

Jenny tried it. After several minutes she could feel something moving through her body and out of her hands. She placed her hands on the patient, hoping that the doctor wouldn't come in. She smiled: Jesus and Mary Magdalene at the patient's bedside.

"Holy crap. You're glowing too."

"I am?" Jenny was startled but pleased.

"Your color is light green."

Marcus thought he detected the slightest movement in Darcy's body. "Did you feel that?"

"No, but I really like this feeling. How come nobody ever told me I could do this?"

At that moment Darcy's hand under his definitely moved.

"Stay here," Marcus commanded.

"I can only do this for another minute. I have other patients to check on."

"Fuck the other patients," Marcus replied, grinning at her. "You're staying here, woman."

Jenny colored, strangely pleased by this command. There was something about this manchild she really liked. "I can stay for a few more minutes."

Five minutes later Marcus noticed a lightening of Darcy's skin tone. "She's getting better."

Jenny took her pulse and temperature and checked the monitor. "Her pulse is getting stronger and her temperature is up a half-degree."

"Come back here and put your hands on her again," Marcus ordered. Jenny stood by the side of the bed, consciously trying to tap into whatever this stuff was. She could definitely feel a sort of soft energy moving through her body. It felt really good.

"Wow, you are really glowing bright now."

Jenny couldn't see anything around her body, but maybe her glow wasn't as strong as the manchild's. Suddenly Darcy's eyes fluttered and then opened. She smiled wanly. "Oh Marcus, I feel so exhausted."

Marcus gently placed his arms around her and gave her a squeeze, willing his own energy into her body. "God Darcy I'm so glad you're back."

"Where am I?" she said, clinging weakly to Marcus.

Marcus released her. Jenny checked her pulse again. "She's making a remarkably fast recovery now. I think she's past the crisis point although we won't know for sure until the doctor examines her."

"You're at Prentice Women's Hospital," Marcus said. "Parkinson sent you here for special treatment."

"Dear Holderness," Darcy replied. She was barely able to keep her eyes open. "I feel really sleepy. I think I'll rest now."

"OK honey. I'll be here when you wake up."

Jenny sighed. "Are you married?"

"As good as. Engaged."

Jenny smiled. Marcus released Darcy's hand and stood up, stretching. "I want you to do something for me."

Just then the doctor walked in, her hair disheveled and her face a mask of exhaustion. "Nurse, finish your round. You're behind."

"Yes doctor."

"Wait a minute," Marcus said. "Jenny, I want you to do what you did to Darcy to the other patients."

Jenny nodded quickly and departed.

"You need some rest doctor," Marcus said. "You're dead on your feet."

"Try telling that to all these poor patients. The hospital is jammed and we're all working triple shifts." She moved swiftly, checking her instruments and the patient. "Good, she's past it now." The doctor turned to Marcus. "Don't order my nurses around."

Marcus smiled, turning on his charm. It seemed to work on Darcy, maybe it would work on this woman, who looked about in her mid-thirties. "Jenny has a special talent. Don't discourage her."

Despite her tiredness something in her responded to the young man's male charm. "Sure. Wait a minute, you're that Marcus Riley aren't you? The financial analyst from New York."

"That's right. This is my girlfriend Darcy Regier."

"All right Marcus Riley, we'll soon have your Darcy out of here. If she's like the rest she'll sleep for two or three hours and wake up healthier than a priest in a porn shop."

Marcus grinned. "Good one doc."

"When she's ready you can just walk out. Check in with the floor duty nurse and she'll mark you off."

A little over an hour later Darcy awakened and sat up in bed. "Marcus, I feel tired, but ... wonderful."

Marcus kissed her. "You'll never get sick again. Now let's get out of this depressing place."

Darcy gathered up her purse and her coat and they began to walk down the hall. As they passed one of the rooms Marcus looked in and saw Jenny with her hands on a patient. "It seems to be working."

Marcus gave the nurse a thumbs-up. "What's working?" Darcy asked.

"I'll tell you later." He opened his phone and called a cab. "I want to get you home first."

Ten miles south of Dugway Proving Grounds

Admiral Frank Conte sat in his private office in the underground ARV control center beneath the Utah desert. Reports had been coming in for three days. It was clear now that those crazy Sabbateans had failed in their attempt to gain control of a depopulated earth. He gave silent thanks to Marcus Riley and Holderness Parkinson, who were almost single-handedly responsible for the failure of their enemies in the Twelve.

Now it was their turn. The only problem was that Adolfone and his faction scared the living crap out of him. Their contact with fucked-up reptiles and their insane demonic rituals gave them a certain power. Conte thought about the history of the Twelve, who had always been at each other's throats. His bloodline, the Artosh, had competed for rule in Germany with the Sabbateans. The Sabbateans attempted to exercise control through their demonic rituals. The Artosh faction conducted searches for ancient lost technology during the world war, and developed exotic technology after the war. These were the two most powerful factions in the Twelve. Their battleground was transnational and encompassed politics, religion, secret societies, banking, and commerce. The Sabbateans had failed, for they always went too far. Most of them were possessed by their alien "handlers." Crazy bastards!

After the fall of Germany competition between the two primary bloodlines continued. The conflict took place mainly within the Soviet Union and the United States, then the new world power. The Sabbateans used the Church of Rome as their base. Their agent Stalin had ruthlessly murdered Artosh agents within Russia, but in the United States the Artosh had found a home. The National Security Act of 1947 was the beginning, allowing the gradual creation of "special access" programs beyond government control. Decades of work reverse-engineering ET spacecraft at Groom Lake had provided them with the technological edge to finally assert their authority. In a few short days they would implement Plan B. When he, Admiral Frank Conte, had control of the Twelve his first act would be to shoot Pietro Adolfone and Carlo Venetti in the head.

Part V – SOVEREIGNTY

CHAPTER **34**

Royalty Services

Holderness Parkinson and Nils van Bergen sat in Parkinson's private office one week after the end of the crisis.

"I don't understand, sir," Nils said. "Three hundred fifty million people dead. Total panic for three days. Now everything is almost back to normal like nothing ever happened."

"Not in China," Parkinson responded. "Elder Li Qiang tells me that over 80 million died there. The Chinese are devastated."

"Why was China heavily targeted and India so lightly?" Nils asked. "Both are the most populated countries on earth."

Parkinson shrugged. "Why was the United States targeted, with only 4% of the world's population? We simply don't know. The entire episode is a study in insanity."

"On CBS last night the deaths were explained as a horrible pandemic that has been bravely borne but was now under control. No one even mentioned the involvement of the people who manufactured and distributed this plague. Those Tau monsters were conveniently ignored as well."

419

"I think our fellow human beings can be forgiven," Holderness replied. "We have been so close to the real action we forget that the vast majority of people have no understanding of The Twelve, the Tau, or the Alephs. For them the pandemic explanation seems to fit."

"It's being explained as similar to the pandemic of 1918-1919, a natural phenomenon. People seem satisfied with that."

Parkinson was looking at the latest brief from the White Hat Network. "Only a relative handful of the population was involved in the search and destruction of the biomaterial. The mainstream media has consistently ignored the issue. Tens of millions have been following alternative websites that explained the true nature of the catastrophe, but this is still a small fraction of the planetary population."

"And that video we made. Dismissed as a clever hoax."

Parkinson nodded. Nils could see that the old man was tiring. He rose from the chair in front of the big oak desk. "Perhaps you should take a nap sir. You're looking a bit tired."

Parkinson summoned a smile. "I think I might do that." After Nils had gone Holderness leaned back in his comfortable leather chair. Perhaps the human race was hopeless. Perhaps we deserve to be powerless. If we cannot stand sovereign and united we will be easily taken advantage of by more sophisticated beings like the Tau. Humanity had really had a very narrow escape but next time it might be different. And then there was Conte and his faction. He had not forgotten about the little demonstration in the desert. It was time for Conte to make his play, but he had little energy left to deal with the admiral.

Even though he had survived the bioenhancer he was very tired now. Perhaps his genes were too aged to have survived the effects of the biomaterial, even with the antidote. Holderness closed his eyes and a wave of exhaustion swept through his body. It might be nice to just let go and see what happens. He had pushed himself hard for decades. There was still too much to do, but he felt like a performer after his last act. He had done all that he could.... Soon he was asleep in his chair.

Sedona, Arizona

Qa-Hrrzl entered the small cave underneath the mesa and took out his portable transportal. This device not only acted as a portal activator but as a data set that held all of his personal information and research. He walked back into the cave, which had a sandy floor interspersed with tiny pebbles. These caves were similar in appearance to those on Tau except for the sand. He preferred hard stone but this would do. The sand was cool and soft underneath the hardened skin of his reptilian feet.

Qa-Hrrzl opened the device and scanned the area. There was game here, enough to keep him alive until he could get back to Tau. He needed fresh-killed meat, which limited his time on this planet unless he could find his contact. There was no sign of human life until the nearest humanoid city. They called it Se-do-na. That was when he spotted the vortex.

"Hola! Here is the transportal." Qa-Hrzzl saw through his transportal a party of humanoids chanting within a large cave. These ignorant hominids were trying to access the subtle energy in the vortex, but they were too dull to understand what they were dealing with. The little vermin! He waited for over two earthian hours until the silly hominids trooped out of the cave. He set up his tesseract and pro- grammed it to access the portal energy.

Just then he heard a babble of voices. More of the little earthians were ap- proaching! They would be on him before he could set up his tesseract and program his return to Tau and retrieve his laboratory. He roared his frustration just as one of the female vermin rounded the corner and saw him. The group of hominids be- hind pushed into the female and she lost her balance, crying out. Qa-Hrrzl cursed. At that moment he saw a shimmering in the air.

Becky Margold dusted herself off. She saw a gigantic reptoid, eight feet tall, fussing with a device that looked like a sophisticated erector set. It was made of a smooth white substance that glowed softly in the subdued light of the cave. Fas- cinated and horrified, Becky stared at the gigantic creature as he worked with his strange device. He was ugly and repulsive with sickly, dark green skin and a terri- fying lizard face with sharp teeth in a wide mouth. His yellow eyes had pupils like slits. His arms and legs were powerful and his hands were clawed. She had the dis- tinct impression that had this monster not been busy he would be happy to have her for his lunch. Her blood chilled while the frozen group behind her, who had come for a meditation, looked on silently. The reptile finished with his fiddling. Becky saw that a large cube had been constructed on the floor of the cave. Just as the reptile was about to step into it he looked up and into her eyes.

Her thoughts froze. She felt completely helpless. Should this creature give her a command she would be hypnotically compelled to obey. The reptile licked his jowls with a long, narrow forked tongue and hissed. Becky fainted.

Qa-Hrrzl knew that the shimmering in the air meant a visitor, probably from Tau. But who? He was set up now and could leave this place, but he was curious.

A figure materialized into the space not fifteen feet from him, at his back. Qa-Hrrzl whirled quickly and confronted Belial.

"Miscreant!" the alpha Tau roared. "You dare to abandon your mission and your sacred duty?"

Qa-Hrrzl knew there was no arguing with the giant. Weaponless, he simply charged Belial and surprised him, managing to knock him over. The two enormous reptoids began fighting, grunting loudly, slashing, and puncturing each other with their enormous clawed hands. Their bodies collided with great thumps. When they fell, struggling, the ground seemed to shake. As the fight continued Becky regained consciousness. She was appalled at the spectacle of the two aliens and their violence and turned on her dataset. Behind her the group was recording the fight and sending it all over the net. Within minutes thousands, and then millions, watched the fight live.

Chicago

Kathleen, Darcy's old roommate in New York, called her just as she was about to leave for work. "Darcy! You have to see this." Darcy opened the phone and saw two gigantic reptiles locked in combat. "Marcus, come in here and look at this."

"Huh?" Marcus rolled over in bed. He had found a job with a Chicago insurance company two days ago and had put in a long day trading yesterday.

Darcy ran into their bedroom and thrust the imager into his face. Marcus sat up abruptly. "What the fuck?"

"That big one is the same one who scratched you."

"Belial!" Marcus exclaimed. What was that monster doing back on earth? Marcus pointed excitedly to the other reptoid. "That's Qa-Hrrzl. He's their chief geneticist and the designer of that bioenhancer."

"That's the fiend who killed so many of us? He deserves to die."

Marcus smiled grimly. "They are both supposedly more evolved than we are but they aren't really. They're a degraded race. They just have some fancy gadgets and technology we don't know about yet."

"What are they doing?"

"Fighting, obviously," Marcus said, engrossed. "But why?"

Marcus sat up in bed and Darcy put her head next to his, still holding her phone. There was something ancient and primal about the scene, as if two malevolent gods were battling it out for control of the human race. Something within her psyche and her DNA quaked. "It's like a nightmare or a bad fairy tale."

"I agree." The next moment Belial rose up and impaled Qa-Hrrzl. His long, sharpened claws went directly in at the smaller reptile's vulnerable soft tissue just above the abdomen. Qa-Hrrzl writhed in agony as Belial twisted his hand, destroying vital organs.

Belial shouted a warrior's cry of victory and hissed balefully at the assembled spectators. Marcus understood what he said. "Vermin scum!" Belial quickly programmed Qa-Hrrzl's transportal to his personal cave within the Council chambers on Tau.

"Oh my God do you see that?" Becky cried, coming out of shock. One of the huge reptiles bled dark green blood onto the sandy floor of the cave. The group at the entrance cautiously approached the dead creature. All were recording and posting to the WorldNet.

The Vatican

Pietro Adolfone sat in his private office in the Vatican, watching in horrified fascination as the two great gods fought like animals. There had been no communication from Qa-Hrrzl for the past two weeks. He had not forgotten the terrible promise of the god to suck the brains from his head. Their great Sabbatean bloodline (whose proud antecedents had come from Sumeria through Babylonia after the last ice age) had aligned themselves irrevocably with the great serpent-gods. It was shocking to think they had failed.

He had waited, trembling, for Qa-Hrrzl to come forth during his nightly incantations. A part of him wished that the serpent god would punish him for his failure. Night after night He had failed to materialize during the sacred rituals. Now, as the terrifying Belial impaled Qa-Hrrzl, he felt a profound sadness tinged with the excitement of the blood lust.

Pietro Adolfone realized that it was over. Their glorious plan to cleanse the earth and improve the human race had failed. He rose quickly from his desk and stumbled on weakened legs to the door. He must do something. He would descend to the ritual meeting place …he would call the great serpent-god Belial himself …he would receive instructions that would put their glorious plan back on track…. His hand on the doorknob, Adolfone suddenly understood with complete certainty that he would never stand before those mighty gods again. What now was to be done?

Pietro Adolphone walked slowly back to his chair and sat down. What would the great Belial do in his place? Of a certainty he would reorganize their effort. He would continue their plan for mastery of the human race. His mind cleared. Like a drunk who spots a half-empty bottle of whiskey in the dumpster, Adolfone saw his way. They had become too dependent upon the great beings, they had lost their initiative. Perhaps Conte's faction had always had the better plan. There was still time to implement it!

Pietro Adolfone leaned back in his chair and laughed. He considered the value of the Conte faction's plan. For the first time he saw its merits. It would be the most frightening event humanity had ever experienced and piggyback upon the release of the bioenhancer and the fear of the great serpent-gods. The trick was to persuade the population that all extraterrestrial life was malignant like the Tau, with designs upon humanity. He saw now that the secrecy necessary for the success of their original plan had worked against them. Conte's plan would overwhelm the population. The satellites with their sophisticated holographs had already been prepared and tested. The 'alien' craft were already manufactured and waiting for launch at the propitious moment.

Pietro Adolfone chuckled to himself. Conte thought he had the upper hand, but he would show the admiral who was really in charge. The factions within the bloodline families were constantly shifting their alliances for greater power just as the serpent-gods had recommended. He would nominally ally his faction with Conte. Soon after the admiral would discover that his position was untenable.

He saw now how the progress of events could not have been more fortuitous. Perhaps the great gods were still looking over his shoulder! This thought strengthened him. Why rule a mere half-billion when there were eight billion vermin to do their bidding? His association with the great gods had taught him the proper attitude toward his fellow human beings. He felt the power the sacred rituals had given him. He would model his conduct upon that of the great Belial: awe-inspiring, powerful, and dominant. He would rule by the mere force of his personality.

Pietro Adolfone picked up his communication device and called Admiral Conte.

Royalty Services, Chicago

As Holderness Parkinson watched the battle between the two Tau his private line rang. He tapped the button under his desk with his foot. The old-fashioned red phone on its platform rose from the floor. He had a feeling that this call was important and quickly routed it to his big screen monitor for voice and imagery.

"Holderness Parkinson." The voice was flat and understated, but Parkinson recognized its unstated power. The man behind the voice, scrunched over in a metal chair, was a giant.

"Yes."

"You don't know me. I was at Minot."

Several things suddenly clicked into place in Parkinson's labyrinthine mind. He remembered the reports sent from Minot AFB by Commander Dawson the night before his death. "I know a lot more than you think colonel, especially about Conte."

The voice on the other end swore admiringly. "That tells me everything I need to know. I'm coming in. I've had it with the Committee and their insanity."

"Then you are welcome colonel," Parkinson replied without hesitation.

The colonel gave him a short, concise report of his recent activities. The two men arranged to meet that evening in a back room at a downtown Chicago restaurant. Holderness Parkinson hung up the phone, smiling. He was getting more tired every day, but he still had enough energy to meet Colonel Zimring.

One half-hour later Holderness Parkinson received a phone call from Li Qiang in China. He was sitting in the basement at his desk, surrounded by the eight huge monitors. Beside him, at a smaller desk, sat Nils van Bergen. For the past two weeks he had been intensively training Nils in intelligence. He had no worries about van Bergen, who would succeed him as head of the White Hat network. Hopefully, if all went well, their intelligence service would no longer be needed on a united earth. Elder Li was the head of the Unification Board, a hastily assembled group of world leaders who were well aware now of the Tau presence on earth. These leaders had decided to come together to face the danger. Parkinson chuckled to himself. How else could human beings come together unless forced to by a crisis of worldwide proportions? Behind the scenes the Unfication Board had coordinated the effort to locate and irradiate the biotoxin outside North America.

"I am honored, Elder Li." Holderness bowed his head slightly to the presence on the screen before him.

"We are counting on you to use your influence and have President Sensenbaugh present at our announcement," the Elder said in Chinese.

Parkinson smiled. "That should be no problem Elder Li. Former president Foley has already briefed the acting president. Sensebaugh feels as we do."

Li Qiang permitted himself a smile. It was a pleasure working with this great hulk of a man; a man of supreme intelligence and ability. "Very well then. There is no time for pleasantries. The announcement of the worldwide press conference will be in a few hours. We have much work to do before and after that."

"*Sài ʔwēng ʔshī ʔma, yān? zhī ʔfēi ʔfú?,*"Parkinson said. The Elder smiled and his screen went blank.

Holderness leaned back in his chair. He felt the exhaustion in every cell of his body now and knew that his time was short. But he was in at the dénouement, that was what counted. To think that the Tau had unwittingly organized humanity! It was a great blessing in disguise. Li Qiang had understood his closing statement: From disaster may come hope and deliverance; and even wisdom.

Utah desert, three days later

Admiral Conte and Captain York stared at his display panels in the control ceneter under the Utah desert. "Adolfone and the Sabbateans are trying to screw the pooch," Conte said. "We have to act now." Above him were fifteen huge white tesseracts, similar to but not as sophisticated as the ones used by the Tau. They showed in rich and brilliant detail the entire collection of satellites with their sophisticated holographic imagers, and inside the underground bases with their Alien Reproduction Vehicles. All he had to do was wave his hand over a laser controlled display button. Thousands of the drone ARVs would almost instantly fill the skies over most major cities in the United States, and major population centers around the world. Another wave, and sophisticated holographic imagery from specially launched satellites in space would project incredibly lifelike "motherships" visible from every point on earth. It would appear that the earth was being invaded by extraterrestrials with overwhelming force.

"Halloran and Carlysle aren't going to like it," said Captain York, looking around at the elaborate control center for the Twelve-controlled Terrestrial Space Command. "Neither will Adolfone." York stood about ten feet to Conte's right. He gazed at his superior with contempt and not a little fear. The meaty Conte, barrel-chested with a thick bald head, blunt features and big hands, reminded him of a playground bully. The quick-tempered Conte carried a machine pistol with him at all times. The man was a paranoid genius, and mentally unstable as well.

"Fuck Halloran, Carlysle, and especially that sicko Adolfone," Conte replied, referring to the leaders of the other bloodline factions. The admiral placed his weapon on the edge of the main control panel to the left of Captain York. "They don't have the balls to grasp opportunity when it's staring them in the face." He waved his hand around the big control area. "Why the fuck did we spend all this money?" Conte regarded his aide with distaste.

York shrugged. The hardliners in the Twelve were making their play now on one roll of the dice. If it worked they would win the competition between the blood-line families and be in the driver's seat at the apex of power in the world. "The system is breaking down anyway," York replied, justifying his superior's statement. "We couldn't have maintained it more than a few more months."

"Goddam right. We've got the technology but we're still dealing within the system, and the system is run by money. We've got lots of zeros in our accounts but the goddam governments and the White Hats are wise to us now." It was now or never.

"Aren't you going to clear it with Adolphone first?" Captain York asked. Their faction had an agreement with the Sabbateans, led by the Jesuit General.

Conte snorted. "I told him a lot of bullshit about how we're all cooperating now." He waved his arm about the huge control center. "That overbred little bastard can't wait for the show. He thinks he's going to call the shots after it goes down, but he'll be out of the loop by then."

York shrugged. As usual, there was conflict at the top. Why were these guys always fighting each other? Apparently Conte had plans to double-cross the Sab-bateans. "The Sabbateans failed with their bioenhancer gambit," York remarked, trying to draw out the admiral. "That was a good idea in principle but it didn't work."

"Yeah." Conte looked at the boards and made sure that all systems were initial-izing correctly. He had wanted nothing to do with those reptiles and their human agents, who scared the living crap out of him. That, and their disgusting blood sac-rifices, made him sick to his stomach. What was wrong with a good old-fashioned takeover? "Earth for the earthlings," Conte joked. "They made their play and lost. Now it's our turn."

"We don't have enough ARVs, weaponry, or troops to win a war against the world's established armies," York said. "But we've got enough to put on a great show and scare the crap out of the sheeple."

"Yeah!" Conte agreed enthusiastically, critically inspecting his control instru-mentation. "This time nobody's going to pull back the curtain on the Wizard of Oz." The public had no idea how far advanced they were. Their satellites, armed with so-phisticated scalar weaponry, had been shooting down non-terrestrial craft for over fifty years. Reverse-engineering these craft had been extremely difficult. They only understood a fraction of the advanced technology but had put it to good use.

"I can't wait for the shit to hit the fan," the admiral said, rubbing his meaty hands together. He glanced up at his assistant. "Are you ready to start the show?"

Suddenly York heard a rumbling sound down the corridor, which was over 100 feet wide. "Somebody's coming!" York shouted. The pad of boots on the hard flooring of the base became louder and louder.

Conte worked furiously. He knew what was coming and he only needed a few more minutes ...

"Conte! CONTE, GODDAMIT, CEASE AND DESIST!"

Captain York turned, facing several hundred troops crowding the corridor and spilling out into the command and control center. At its head was a giant who moved with an easy grace. He carried an automatic weapon in one huge hand and a rocket launcher in the other. The launcher weighed at least 50 pounds but the intruder held it as easily as he would hold his own sidearm. The automatic was pointed at Conte and the rocket launcher at the sophisticated grid of control panels. Beside him was a short, balding man with a demonic grin. The small man stepped forward and Conte's head turned almost hypnotically. The admiral's eyes locked with the balding man's and Conte's jaw went slack.

The giant turned toward Pietro Adolfone. "How the hell did you do that?"

Adolfone, deep in a powerful trance state, grinned. Conte staggered forward as if punch-drunk, but regained his footing. "What are you doing here Adolfone? I thought we had a deal."

Adolfone laughed. "Certainly we did admiral. But the gods taught us never to trust; always to look out for our own gain."

"You stupid bastard! We are only a few minutes from world domination." As he spoke, he noticed that Adolfone's men had surrounded the control station.

There was something wrong with those men. They were too small ..."What have you done with our troops?" York cried.

Adolfone chuckled. "Don't try anything stupid, Conte." He pointed to the machine pistol on the control board. "These are PLFs. They are programmed to respond to my command."

Conte groaned with frustration. These Sabbateans always did things the hard way. The programmed life forms were their answer to robot soldiers but the things were so stupid they never did what they were told. "We're this close to a nice little takeover, you idiot. Don't fuck it up now."

"Don't worry admiral," Adolphone said. "We're just here to see that you follow orders."

"You mean your orders."

"That is correct." He needed Conte now, but of course he would no longer be necessary after the invasion program had launched.

Conte growled and went back to his preparations. Everyone had forgotten about Captain York, who had casually taken a slow step to his left. He grabbed the machine pistol and quickly began firing, spraying bullets everywhere. The giant anticipated his movements and fell to the floor, still holding his weapon. Pietro Adolfone crumpled to the ground. Before he hit the floor he screamed, "Attack!" Hundreds of PLFs charged Conte and York. In a frenzy of mindless artificial intelligence they began smashing the sensitive CCC's brain.

Colonel Zimring laughed. The crazy little fuckers reminded him of an old Star Trek episode when Landreau, that old mainframe, popped its cork.

"STOP!" Conte shouted. "You fools!" He turned to see that York had taken several in the head and was bleeding out on the floor. The giant rose and gestured to him.

"We'd best leave now admiral." Zimring gestured toward the door. The PLFs were now attacking each other. It was just a matter of time before they were both killed.

Conte ran with the giant toward the entrance around the L of the corridor. "You're on my side?" Conte asked, out of breath.

"I'm on the winning side," the giant answered, breathing easily.

The two men ran out of the corridor and into the hangar at the far end. PLFs milled around, firing off their weapons. Zimring flung the rocket launcher over his shoulder. "Quick!" the huge man said, striding into one of the intelligent ARVs. "Get in."

"Can you pilot this thing?' Conte asked.

The big man put on a headset and placed his hand around what looked like a rubber ball sticking out of a black panel. "It's a piece of cake. Learned from Bobo Jacoby himself."

The roof of the hangar opened and the ship shot straight up into the atmosphere. The craft made an abrupt ninety-degree turn and began to move with incredible speed to a position ten miles above the surface of the earth. Admiral Conte wondered whether any of the ARVs around the world had launched, and whether any of the motherships were visible. He had managed to activate a few of the satellites and fire off a few of the ARVs before Adolfone fucked everything up.

"Look, there's one over the Great Lakes," Conte said, awed by the magnificence of the thing.

"Are there any more of those control centers?" Colonel Zimring asked.

"No. Too many cooks spoil the broth. We all want to be the Big Kahuna."

Colonel Zimring shrugged contemptuously. These idiots wanted to take over the world but had built only one control center? Destroy that and their entire plan would fail.

"If only it were real," Conte said sadly, looking at the great mothership. "With a ship like that I could take over the world."

"I don't think so," the big man said. He reached over and grabbed Conte's neck with one of his huge hands. "You're supposed to be with us!" Conte gasped.

"I changed my mind," the giant said. He twisted sharply. The lifeless body of Admiral Conte fell to the floor of the craft.

Colonel Zimring looked out at the holographic image of the giant mothership hovering over Chicago. He moved his craft in closer. Several dozen ARVs floated motionless over the city. These drones were apparently directionless now that the command and control center had been destroyed by those mindless PLFs. The colonel moved out into earth orbit and saw that several of the holographic motherships were now over cities in China, India, and Europe. Zimring moved in and out of the atmosphere with lightning speed, effortlessly making 90 degree turns to avoid intercept. About one thousand of the ARVs were now floating over random cities. He saw several over Tokyo, Beijing, Djakarta, Moscow, Seoul, London, Paris, Bonn, Delhi, and several others. He quickly dived over to North America and saw that only Chicago had any of the 'alien' ships. The South Americans were free of flying craft.

Zimring looked at the dark gray control panel for a fuel gauge. He realized again that these vehicles were powered from the invisible energy contained within the fabric of space itself. Colonel Zimring chuckled. Right now he was the most powerful man on earth, for he had one of only five intelligent ARVs on the planet. Hopefully the PLFs destroyed the other intelligent ARVs in the Utah CCC.

Colonel Zimring took the craft effortlessly out to the orbit of the moon and gazed out of the cockpit window at the vacuum of space. He felt a sense of power and elation that was indescribable. Flying one of these things – it wasn't really flying – was like being in a dream. The craft would literally go anywhere in space close to the speed of light. He could control the thing with a few directed thoughts into the headset he wore. This was why almost all of the ARVs were drones. The training required to operate these intelligent craft was beyond the mental abilities of even the most veteran pilot. It required a certain level of consciousness to master. Zimring wondered now, looking out into the infinite vastness of the universe, why he had waited so long to come over to right side.

He moved his craft closer to earth and gazed out at the beautiful blue planet, covered in clouds. He felt uplifted, connected to a powerful but benign force that was present everywhere. Colonel Zimring smiled and understood that the plans of the Committee and the Twelve had always been doomed to failure. He thought of the Tau and how pathetic they were. Zimring understood that the earth was not in danger and had never been in danger from these degraded beings. They had been brought here by the low consciousness of the entire human race, aided by fools like Admiral Conte, who were hijacking the human race for their own purposes. Laughing, he brought the craft into the earth's atmosphere and down the east coast to Washington DC. He would land this thing right on the fucking White House lawn! Then he'd step out of the craft like a visitor from outer space and say "Klatu Borada Nikto." Or maybe "Jesus is here. Everybody look busy."

Zimring used his long-range communications device to call a number in Beijing, given to him by Holderness Parkinson.

Marcus and Darcy were sitting in their living room at Royalty Services, watching a streaming movie. The movie disappeared and an old Chinese guy appeared on the screen surrounded by two other men. Marcus saw dozens of official looking figures in the background, including acting president Sensenbaugh.

"I recognize that guy," Marcus said, pointing to the man on the older man's right. "That's Prime Minister Venkaraman, from India. I worked with him a little when we were locating those canisters of bioenhancer."

"What's going on?"

Marcus snapped his fingers in annoyance. "Sorry, I forgot to tell you. Parkinson said yesterday there'd be an important announcement coming up this afternoon."

"Holderness is looking tired Marcus."

"I agree. Maybe that bioenhancer antidote doesn't work if you're too old."

Darcy's phone rang. It was her friend Kathleen, who never failed to call if there was something unusual going on. "Darcy, what's happening?" The excitable Kathleen reminded her of a bird on a feeder, constantly flapping its little wings and looking for a perch to settle onto.

"I don't know Kathy."

"I was watching a video on the net and it just stopped. Do you see the same ugly little guy?"

Just then Holderness Parkinson walked slowly into their suite's living room, using a cane. "Mind if I join you?"

Darcy indicated a spot on the couch next to her.

"That's Elder Li Qiang, my dear. One of the most important men in the world."

"Oh hello Mr. Parkinson," Kathleen replied on her mobile, seeing the old man stroll past Darcy. "If he's so important how come I've never heard of him?" Darcy added her question to Kathleen's by glancing up at her mentor. She wanted to ask him how he was feeling. He looked a lot older now, like a faded shirt after too many washings.

Parkinson laughed. He was always amazed at the naïveté of Darcy's friends. Of course their lives were in the world, whereas he and Nils, and to a certain extent Marcus, were of the world but not in it. And now I am almost ready to leave. He could feel something settling into his essence like a blanket thrown over a fire. His only regret was that he would no longer be able to see Darcy.

"The most important persons are never seen, my dear. At least not until now."

As Holderness settled his bulk on the couch next to Darcy he thought of the latest White Hat briefing. He could only hope that Colonel Zimring and his forces had been able to neutralize the crazies in the Twelve group, and that Elder Li Qiang had been successful in his mission to gather together the world's leaders for the most important announcement in human history. He had little worries about Zimring. The colonel had a personality and a force that matched his giant stature.

"What are they waiting for?" Kathleen asked. "I want to see my movie."

Parkinson found the energy to chuckle. "All communications worldwide have been interrupted. If you pay attention I think you'll find that this presentation will be far more fascinating than your video. The leaders of the world have gathered together in a planet-wide conference call. They will be discussing a subject that has been carefully guarded for almost a century. It should be quite exciting."

Elder Li Qiang of China, Premier Vishnan Venkaraman of India, and President Reinaldo Couto of Brazil began the statement together, sitting in the conference room at Tsinghua University in Beijing. Over 100 other world leaders, including Acting President Robert Sensenbaugh (standing in for the resigned President Foley), were seen behind the three elder world figures.

They were not physically present in China but sophisticated teleconferencing software made it appear to the casual viewer that all of the world's leaders had gathered together in one place. The stream was being simultaneously translated into over 100 languages.

As they waited for things to get started Darcy glanced out the window. People were running, pointing upward. "Look Marcus!"

Parkinson was too tired to get up but Marcus hurried over to the window. "There's a gigantic spaceship hovering over the city!"

At that moment every digital device in the world went black.

CHAPTER **35**

Darcy ran over to the window and craned her neck upward. "Oh my God, look at that thing." The ship looked just like one of the gigantic spacecraft in the old Star Wars movies. Hovering in the air over the city were several small craft. "What are they doing up there?"

Marcus was excited. "That big ship is awesome."

Darcy shrieked as a beam of light exited from one of the hovering ARVs. The beam landed somewhere over the horizon. Smoke and debris filled the air. Below, people were beginning to panic.

Parkinson growled. So Conte had acted, just like he said he would. Zimring had failed!

Holderness Parkinson grabbed his phone but the screen was black and the device wouldn't connect. No, they couldn't fail now, not at the very end …

Marcus stared out the window in disbelief. All traffic came to a halt. He opened the window, looking on to a movie scene. The city was eerily quiet. The ARVs hovered silently, the great ship far up in the sky made no sound. Several fighter aircraft (from Wright-Patterson AFB in Ohio, Marcus learned later, the closest AFB to Chicago) flew up to one of the ARVs and fired a rocket. A beam of light emerged from the craft, exploding the missile. The other two fighters also shot mis-

435

siles. One was destroyed but the other went home, creating a massive hole along the side of the craft. "They hit it!" Marcus cried.

Just then the interrupted broadcast from the world leaders came back on line. "People of earth!" Li Qiang said urgently. "The ships you see in the skies are not alien ships. The earth is not being invaded; we repeat, the earth is not being invaded. Do not be frightened."

Every cell phone, mobile device, radio, and every television set all over the world was now broadcasting Elder Li Qiang's message.

"What you see in the skies are spacecraft manufactured right here on earth to simulate alien ships. This is a ruse; stay calm."

The broadcast abruptly shifted to the White House lawn. Marcus watched as one of the alien craft landed smoothly in front of the historic building. Even Parkinson held his breath as the great ship sat silent and motionless. After several moments, a door slid open in the craft's side.

Darcy couldn't believe it. "Oh my God, we're going to see another alien."

Slowly the gigantic figure of Colonel Zimring emerged from the craft. Parkinson let out his breath and all of his pent-up tension in a loud sigh of immense relief.

The man bowed and said, "Colonel Ralph Zimring, *a votre service.*"

Holderness Parkinson laughed out loud. Darcy, Marcus, and Kathleen, screaming in excitement over her phone, plied him with questions.

Chapter **36**

Iᴛ would go down as the greatest speech in human history.

Colonel Ralph Zimring, standing on the White House lawn next to one of the great 'extraterrestrial' spacecraft, gave an impromptu briefing to the people of the world.

"I am Colonel Ralph Zimring," he began, "and I was born in Ann Arbor, Michigan." Later, an entire category of one-liner jokes would be spawned from that historic opening. Now the assembled world leaders, and billions of people, listened on the World Net as the colonel gave a brief summary of his experiences at the underground base in Utah. The colonel left out the part where he had snapped the neck of Admiral Conte, who was still lying dead inside the craft.

Holderness Parkinson was able to relax for the first time in weeks. Watching with a feeling of hope for the human race for perhaps the first time in his life, he knew that his battles had all been fought now.

In Beijing Elder Li Qiang, Elder Zhou Wei, and Elder Xiang Ri sat around an ancient bamboo table at Tsinghua University in a private conference room. Chen Yi-chun sat to the right of Elder Li. Yi-chun represented China's secretive Exobiology Department, a branch of the Ministry of State Security. The Elders listened in astonishment and satisfaction.

Yi-Chun nodded his head approvingly. This imposing giant, the friend of the American agent Parkinson, looked the part of an extraterrestrial. He was dressed all in black and wore a black beret. The man seemed to dominate the tremendous craft he had landed. His perfectly chiseled face and smooth skin made him look other-worldly. Li Qiang nodded. "You see Yi-Chun, Mr. Parkinson was true to his word."

The Elder resumed his report surrounded by the world's leaders. Acting President Sensebaugh was nattily attired in a three-piece suit. President Amalonga Nubaru of Nigeria was dressed in a long ceremonial robe, holding an intricately carved wooden staff with a decorative head. President Ronaldo Cuoto of Brazil wore a white leisure suit and white leather shoes. Chief Brilliant Feather of the Hopi nation sported a beautiful ceremonial headdress. For the first time in human history all of the world's heads of state were assembled together, representing the human race in all its diversity.

Elder Li read quietly but powerfully from a teleprompter in the conference room at Tsinghua University. The report was a brief explanation of the hidden, covert programs that had developed fantastic advances in physics and space travel. It was about their origins and their relationship to off-planet technology and extraterrestrials. The people of earth learned that there were two civilizations upon their planet: a small, private one with advanced space technology and the ability to travel in space. The other, composed of billions of human beings kept in ignorance.

After the report the world's leaders made a statement, read by Acting President Sensebaugh of the United States (Li Qiang, by this time, was too tired and hoarse to continue). Marcus, Darcy, and Parkinson were still seated on the couch. Darcy noticed that the old man had dozed off.

"Ladies and gentlemen of earth!" Sensebaugh said in a powerful voice, waking Parkinson. "What you have just seen is the very briefest introduction to information that has been withheld from you for many decades. For the next six months, all media outlets over the entire planet will be exclusively broadcasting a detailed program explaining what has been going on behind the scenes on planet earth. We will be showing you the outlines of a new science and a new physics that can help us to solve some of the world's intractable problems. For those without access to computing or mobile devices, outdoor and indoor presentations will be provided. No section of earth, no matter how underpopulated, will be overlooked.

"People of earth, we can longer believe the delusion that we are alone in the universe. We have all seen the videos of the Draco Tau. These beings are not science-fiction creatures. They come from the Draco Sector of our galaxy, from the star we identify as Tau, a blue-white sun, classified as a B7III giant. There are other civilizations out there. Many of them have interacted and are interacting with us. Our isolation was a convenient fiction for thousands of years, used by those who are here to take advantage of us. Unless we stand united, sovereign, and free, the human race cannot fulfill its destiny.

"All persons on the planet are encouraged to listen to the entire program. At the end of six months the human race will have been educated enough to decide its future, and to decide how we will deal with those who have committed execrable acts against humanity. We must also decide our planetary relations with the other intelligent life that, we are assured by experts, fills the galaxy around us.

"Talk and debate this information amongst yourselves and your friends. Some with much knowledge will come forward to help you. Undoubtedly charlatans, thrill seekers, and those interested in power and control will also come forward. The rest of the galaxy is waiting to see if we will stand together and declare our sovereignty, united in peace, or whether we will continue our violent ways. It is your choice; it is our choice!

"Our technicians even now are preparing for a planet-wide referendum on the human race's future. All eight billion will have a vote. For the first time in our planet's history WE, the human race, will decide our future without outside inter-ference or influence. The earth has been a playground for far too long. But first, we must become educated to the true situation.

"It is your job, brothers and sisters, to digest this information and prepare yourselves for the planet-wide referendum. Let us now throw aside our petty dif-ferences and, as we Americans say, 'get with it.' That is all."

"Wow!" Marcus said, turning on the couch to look at Parkinson. "What do we do now?"

Holderness was gazing at Darcy with a look of sweet poignancy. He wanted to tell them that in six months they would all have to make the most important decision of their lives. He felt a strange, pleasant lethargy settle over him.

"Holderness!" Darcy cried. She could see the old man fading. "Marcus, do something!"

Marcus sent out his web of light into Parkinson but he could see it was no use. Holderness Parkinson died on Darcy's couch with a smile on his face.

CHAPTER 37

Two weeks after the sensational announcement by the world's leaders the holographic motherships disappeared from the skies. The satellites projecting them had all been identified and disabled. The ARVs were another problem because the CCC which directed them had been destroyed. The craft were not fueled and could stay hovering above the cities of earth indefinitely. But the debonair and now world-famous Ralph Zimring, the former colonel who had resigned from the military, came to the rescue. Using the world's only intelligent ARV he managed, after several months, to tow the vehicles out of the sky and into the underground storage bases. These fantastic facilities had now been opened to the governments and established militaries of the world. Ralph Zimring went on to have a successful movie career, starring in over fifty popular productions.

Six months later Darcy and Marcus were married in the Royalty Services building. Holderness Parkinson's will was read; his entire estate was left to Darcy Regier. Darcy decided to honor Parkinson's legacy and continue his sophisticated escort service. However, part of the building would be devoted to a studio for Audrey's Creations. Gradually, Darcy would eliminate the escort service but she and Marcus agreed always to live in the old brownstone.

Marcus looked forward to driving the Rolls Royces.

Darcy threw a banquet for all former Royalty customers at the swanky Chicago Convention Center. Thousands of diplomats, presidents, CEOs, entertainment and movie stars, Crims, and royalty from all over the world participated. Thom Madigan gave the keynote address: "A Tribute to Holderness Parkinson." Luca Carcelli roasted the old man, and was a hit. Darcy thought it was the least she could do for her dear friend and mentor. Every time she walked by his office she expected to see him in his gigantic easy chair. She would never believe that he was completely dead to her.

Marcus enjoyed hob-nobbing with the rich and famous.

Nils van Bergen married Barbara Napier and continued Parkinson's intelligence service, although it was now completely disassociated from the escort service and housed in a small office complex downtown.

Marcus started his own financial services company. Using Parkinson's old connections he soon had several billion dollars under management.

Shortly afterwards the people of earth voted, in a worldwide referendum, to establish a Truth and Reconciliation Commission. The Commission would hear testimony from those like Oleg Brentkowski, Bobo Jacoby, Senator Fazio, Pietro Adalfone (who had survived the battle with Conte in Utah) and others who had acted against the best interests of the human race and the planet. Their names, images, and bios, with a list of their activities, were published in a website called Revelations.

None of those who were named, even those who had killed or murdered, were themselves killed. Psychopaths and other anti-social elements were either incarcerated or sent to secure, park-like and non-threatening areas with meadows, trees, and birds, with no human contact. Their faces and their deeds were now known to everyone on earth. Their disgrace and humiliation was complete. Clemency was offered to all those who could demonstrate mental and emotional stability, as determined by psychologists expert in psychopathy.

The people of earth also agreed, by a vote of 98% to 2%, on a Sovereignty Statement, which was read by Elder Li Qiang for the people of earth. The statement said, "We, the people of earth, declare that the planet earth, the human race, and all species, subspecies, and biological resources, are hereby united and sovereign. We demand that all those who are here to exploit and to take advantage of our beautiful world leave immediately and never return."

Within hours, several hundred spacecraft, and several thousand off-planet entities, left the solar system. Finally, after eons, the earth was free.

Notes

1 Douglas McIntyre, "Citigroup: Rebuilt Against Its Will," *Time Magazine,* Jan. 16, 2009.

2 The information in this section taken from an excellent article entitled "Defeating Time Itself |Nanosecond Trades & Positions" from ZFT Logistics at http://zftfinancial.tumblr.com/

3 Ibid.

4 Ibid.

5 Ibid.

6 Ibid.

7 Ibid.

8 http://www.minyanville.com/businessmarkets/articles/wall-street-cocaine-bernie-madoff-fridays/10/27/2009/id/25132#ixzz2JlnoPfr5

9 Like the Mongols and other warrior, nomadic tribes on earth, when a chief was killed in war or was defeated in battle, a convention was held to determine the new leader. On Tau, weakness or defeat required a Hangul, or a trial by combat of the strongest warriors.

10 Source: *The Dragon's Pearl* by Julie Lawson, Oxford University Press, 1992.

11 Story taken from an interview with Jordan Maxwell. See jordanmaxwell.com

12 Heb., 9:22

13 Lev., 17:11

14 See http://www.colombiasupport.net/199608/solomon_cia.html, Media Focus on CIA's Cocaine Links Is Long Overdue, by Norman Solomon, Creators Syndicate

See also http://www.gwu.edu/~nsarchiv/NSAEBB/NSAEBB2/nsaebb2.htm, National Security Archive Electronic Briefing Book No. 2, The Contras, Cocaine, and Covert Operations.

See also http://www.idfiles.com/sltrib2.htm, SERIES ON CIA-RUN DRUG RING SPARKS CALL FOR PROBE, the *Salt Lake City Tribune*, August 30, 1996.

[15] Dr. Werner von Braun, founder of America's space program, described this fake "alien invasion" program to his assistant, Dr. Carol Rosin, just before his death in 1977.

APPENDIX **A**

Closed System vs Open System

The history of the world has essentially been a battle between the closed system concept and the open system concept. The closed system idea can be summed up in three words: centralization of control, or control from above. Closed systems favor dictatorial governments as in Communism, Nazism, and Fascism; science that utilizes scarce fossil fuels whose distribution can be controlled, religions controlled by priesthoods, and interest bearing loans and currencies that can be issued from a central source.

The open system concept can also be described in three words: sovereignty through unity, or unity with individual freedom. The open system idea favors democracy, greater decentralization, government issued currencies, religious tolerance, non-interest bearing loans, and a more open science that investigates more open, frontier physics concepts.

The two opposing viewpoints can also be described very simply: control the wealth as opposed to share the wealth. You can fit the entire political, financial, and scientific history of earth for the past 5,000 years into these two broad concepts. Paradoxically, the exotic technology in our hidden black programs must of necessity have been developed using the open system, frontier physics idea (if what I've read is true, this technology is well beyond our current scientific understanding), but those who have hidden this technology in "black" programs have used it to attempt establish a closed system, with them at the top of the pyramid.

Here there exists a massive contradiction. Either the closed system concept will prevail, and humanity will subjugate itself by giving up its freedoms for a phony "collective security" (Borg) concept, or humanity will recognize its higher potential, and choose an evolutionary path based on an open system concept of the celebration of the individual. Paradoxically, the recognition of the individual leads to an understanding of our greater potential, and a connection to a higher consciousness, which naturally leads to greater cooperation and creativity on a broad scale.

Those who desire to pollute human biology with electronics, or engage in cloning, or place human consciousness in artificial containers, are pushing humanity down a dead-end evolutionary path. It will eventually be discovered (if the human race does not take these dead-end evolutionary branches) that biology is nature's most successful path of evolution, for biology contains the highest amount of life force. Those who favor these efforts will eventually discover, after it is too late, that their labors will only lead to race sterility, atrophy, and decreased intelligence and elan vital (just like the Draco Epsilon Alephs in the novel). Let us hope that humanity is smart enough not to go down this road. We are at the crossroads right now!

Author's Note

This second edition was written to eliminate, as Elmore Leonard once said, "the stuff readers will skip." It is identical to the first edition in plot and characters. The motivation for the second edition was to comply more strictly with the basic principles of novel writing. I began my writing career as an essayist, but novel writing is much different from essay writing. I have shortened run-on sentences and eliminated verbosity, making the narrative read quicker and smoother.

About the Author

Kenneth J. M. MacLean is a freelance writer and book editor living in Ann Arbor, Michigan. He can be reached at:

kmaclean@kjmaclean.com
Website at http://www.kjmaclean.com
For book and manuscript editing:
http://www.macleanediting.com

OTHER BOOKS BY THE AUTHOR
(see complete list at
kjmaclean.com/Products/MainProductPage.php):

A Geometric Analysis of the Platonic Solids and other Semi-Regular Polyhedra –– A meticulous mathematical analysis of some important polyhedra. For teachers, researchers, and the generally curious

The Vibrational Universe –– The relationship between consciousness and the physical universe.

The End of the Universe (SF novel) –– What if the universe we see through our telescopes was merely a sophisticated holographic illusion?

Dialogues – Conversations with my Higher Self –– A look at life, the universe and everything from a broader perspective.

www.ingramcontent.com/pod-product-compliance
Lightning Source LLC
Chambersburg PA
CBHW060805030726
47503CB00002B/336